D0424592

EMILY'S SECRET

Winner of the prestigious "Maggie" Award from Georgia Romance Writers

"A magnificent novel!"

—Affaire de Coeur

"A totally unique premise that lingers in the heart long after the final page is turned."

—Rendezvous

"An outstanding debut by a highly talented new author. Snap up this delightful and visionary tale ASAP!"

—Romantic Times

"Beautifully written and compelling . . . I loved it . . . A must read!"

—Heather Graham

"Lovely! It's the book I've always wanted to write."

—Marion Zimmer Bradley

"A great debut for a talented new author."

—Jasmine Cresswell

"Wonderful!"

—Barbara Erskine

THE
ISLAND

JILL JONES

St. Martin's Paperbacks

This is a work of fiction. Any resemblance of characters to persons living or dead or events and actions of the plot to real life is entirely coincidental.

THE ISLAND

Copyright © 1999 by Jill Jones.

ISBN: 0-312-97073-0

Printed in the United States of America

St. Martin's Paperbacks edition/July 1999

St. Martin's Paperbacks are published by St. Martin's Press, 175 Fifth Avenue, New York, N.Y. 10010.

10 9 8 7 6 5 4 3 2 1

For the "Dragon Women"
in my North Carolina critique group—
Susan Alvis, Frankie Schelly,
Joanna Schulman and Lezley Suleiman
Thanks for everything!

ACKNOWLEDGMENTS

My deepest thanks to the talented and generous musician, Marita Brake, for finding the music for the ballad "Kiss of the Dragon" and recording my words to this ancient tune in her hauntingly beautiful voice.

Special thanks to Jeanne Brown and Alistair Scott for flyspecking the story and authenticating details. I also wish to thank my husband, Jerry Jones, for his steadfast and unconditional support of my work. Thanks to Morning Naughton and Jason Michaels for taking care of things in my absence. And thanks to the many friends who have encouraged me along the way.

As always, my heartfelt thanks goes out to the "team," my editor, Jennifer Enderlin, SMP publicity manager Walter Halee, my agent, Denise Marcil, and to a very special publisher, Matthew Shear.

FEAR IN HEALTHY MEASURE DOTH PROTECT,
IN EXCESS, POISONS.

ANONYMOUS

ONE

THE ISLAND OF KEINADRAIG, IN CORNWALL, JUNE, PRESENT DAY

From within a troubled dream she heard the knocking, an urgent demand she fought desperately to ignore. Sleep was precious, and dawn would arrive too soon. Grasping the quilt that covered her, Keely Cochrane pulled it over her head and held it tightly around her ears, determined to make the sound become part of the dream and not something to which she must awaken and attend.

But the knocking did not stop. Instead, it grew louder, more insistent, jarring her awake at last. She threw off the covers irritably. Her body ached with fatigue and her eyes felt gritty and she was annoyed at being denied even a moment of much-needed rest. But her irritation turned to alarm with a return to full consciousness. No one came calling at this time of night.

Snatching up her cotton robe, Keely ran on bare feet down the ancient wooden stairs to the back door. "Coming!" But before she could reach the door, a figure rushed in, slammed the heavy portal behind her, and leaned against it, breathing hard. Even in the dark, Keely instantly recognized her best friend and kinswoman, Genevieve Sloan. But her eyes were wide and her hair was in wild disarray.

"Genny! What is wrong?" Keely cried, hurrying toward her. "Whatever are ye doing here at this time o' night? Did Ninian send ye? Is someone ill?" Keely reached for the light switch, but Genny clamped her wrist tightly with a hand as cold as ice.

"Do na! Please, do na turn on th' light." Her voice was hushed, breathy, urgent. "None must know I am here."

"What is th' matter?" Keely could feel the younger woman shaking. "What on earth . . . ? Here, sweeting, sit ye down. I will make tea." Deeply troubled, she led her friend to a chair by the small table in the kitchen and groped about in the dark for the kettle, her heart pounding, for she had never seen Genevieve in such a state.

Placing the kettle on the small stove, Keely turned to her friend. The moonlight shone directly on Genny, turning her fiery untamed locks to a billow of smoky gray and revealing extreme confusion and panic in her eyes. "What has happened?" Keely asked again, forcing a calm she did not feel.

"Help me." Genny's voice was low and ragged. "Ye must help me." She reached across the table and clutched Keely's hand again. "I must leave here. *We* must leave! Now! Tonight! Come with me, Keely! Let us leave this place for good, like we have always talked about."

"Leave?" Keely's skin prickled. "Genny, that was just childish talk. We were never serious." Never in her twenty-five years had she been truly serious about leaving the tiny island they called home.

Genny set her jaw. "I am serious now," she said. "Serious as death."

The prickle on her flesh crawled along her skin, and her stomach tightened. "But . . . but why?" Keely knew Genny was unhappy that Alyn Runyon, the village Keeper, was insisting that she marry William Reedy, a man who at forty-two was twice her age. But it was the law, it was their way on the island. One married the man or woman chosen for them by the Council. As head of the Council, Keely's uncle Alyn was charged with making appropriate matches to keep the bloodlines pure in the small, isolated island community of Keinadraig. Here, for centuries, the villagers had dwelt in peace, harmony, and good health as a result of abiding by the ancient laws.

To break them was unthinkable.

Genny couldn't do this. She was making a terrible mistake. No one left the island. Not the way she seemed set on. Everyone knew that bad things happened to those who left. It was the way of the Dragon.

Genevieve dropped her head into her hands and began to sob. "I . . . I can na . . . I just can na do it, Keely."

"Marry William? But, Genny, William is a good man. And he is one of us. He will be kind t' ye and take care o' ye. 'Tis better than marrying some stranger Alyn brings t' ye."

Genny's head jerked up, and she looked at Keely with tragic eyes. " 'Tis na about William."

Keely frowned. "Then what . . . ?"

"I can na do what Ninian asks. I can na become th' Healer."

Ninian was Genevieve's mother and the village Healer. She was a skilled herbalist and a wise woman who tended to both the physical and spiritual needs of the villagers. To become the Healer was an honor. "What is she asking? What are ye talking about?" Keely asked, more than perplexed.

"I can na do it," Genny repeated. "I . . . I do na have it in me, Keely."

Keely suddenly understood why Genny was upset and let out a breath of relief. Her friend had always been squeamish at the sight of blood. Maybe she wasn't the right one to take over Ninian's role, but she needn't run away. "Surely Ninian will understand and will find another apprentice."

Genevieve jumped out of her chair. "Ninian understands nothing!" she cried. "She . . . I . . . , oh, forget it.

I'll na say more. I am leaving, and do na try t' scare me because I am breaking th' law. I do na care about th' law.''

Keely stared at her openmouthed. No one talked like this. The law was sacred. It protected everyone. It was what made the island of Keinadraig so special, a haven against the corrupting influences of the outside world. ''But ye can na leave. What about your Dragon's promise? What about . . . this?'' She reached out and touched a tiny mark just beneath Genny's left ear. The kiss of the Dragon, worn proudly by all Dragoners.

''I wish I had ne'er made such a promise. I was young and foolish. Everyone who believes that rubbish is foolish.''

Keely was appalled. She had never known Genevieve to speak such blasphemy. ''But Genny, ye've heard what happens when a Dragoner leaves . . .''

''Nothing happens. 'Tis just an old tale they tell t' keep us here doing as they bid. But I am leaving. Right now. With or without your help.''

Keely recognized the stubborn tone and knew there would be no dissuading her friend until she changed her mind on her own. Which would probably be about daybreak, when she overcame her emotions, realized her error, and came creeping back to the island. She sighed in resignation. ''What do ye need? Where are ye going?''

''I need ye t' help me launch a boat from th' harbor. I will tie it up at th' docks in Penzance and someone can come fetch it in the morning. I . . . I will take the train from there.''

''And go where?'' Keely detected a tremor in Genevieve's voice and knew her bravado was mostly pretense.

''Oh, t' London, I suppose. I can find work there. But do na tell. None must know where I am. I will be dead as far as they're concerned. Ye know that. And that sits fine by me.''

Telling herself that Genevieve's insanity was only temporary, Keely gave her some money from the cash drawer of the pub that occupied the front of the house, the business Keely had inherited. She scribbled a number on a scrap of paper. " 'Tis th' telephone at th' Council office," she explained. "Use it in case of emergency. Someone will come for ye, wherever ye are." She paused and smiled through unshed tears. "If ye change your mind, that is."

"Oh, Keely, ye are th' best friend anyone could ever have. I wish ye would come with me. There is no future for ye here."

"Nay, love. I belong here. And so do ye. Ye'll see. Ye'll be back."

Genevieve rushed into Keely's arms, sobbing her good-byes as if they truly were forever. Keely held her tightly, willing her not to go, but at last Genny broke free and made for the door. Keely turned off the stove and followed.

Keeping to the shadows, they slipped noiselessly down the narrow cobblestone lane to the harbor. The tide was receding, leaving the small fishing boats wallowing in the mud. They made for one that was moored in deeper water and was still afloat. Keely hitched up her nightclothes and waded into the shallow water, holding the boat steady while Genny clambered aboard. Then she handed her kinswoman the small bag of belongings that was all Genny owned in the world.

The outside world, that is. She had everything she needed here in Keinadraig.

She'd be back.

Keely untied the mooring line and gave the boat a shove in the direction of the mouth of the harbor. Genny picked up the oars and began to silently stroke the calm waters, edging the small craft between the fingers of the ancient quay and out past the jetty. Keely knew that when she was far enough offshore to be out of earshot,

Genny would start the small engine and be quickly on her way.

As Keely watched the boat disappear into the midnight darkness, the knot in her stomach turned to stone and a terrible premonition washed over her.

No matter how much Keely willed it, Genny would not be coming back.

LONDON

The string quartet playing unobtrusively in the elegant dining room of the five-star hotel was beginning to grate on his nerves. Jack Knight glanced around, taking in the crisp white linen, the gleaming silver, and the battalion of impeccably uniformed waiters poised along one wall. His shirt collar seemed suddenly too tight. He'd dined in fine restaurants before, but he was more comfortable in the sleazy bars and back alleyways of Los Angeles. Until his recent "retirement" he had prowled L.A. in derelict fashion, setting up drug busts, arresting pushers, and struggling against growing odds to put an end to the death dealers as an undercover narc for the LAPD.

"Wine?" Across the table, Brad's voice interrupted his thoughts. His longtime friend raised the bottle containing the remainder of an excellent sangiovese. Jack's taste ran to Kentucky bourbon, but the wine was rich and smooth, satisfying with the rack of lamb he'd just devoured.

"Sure." He slid his glass toward Brad, who topped it off, then refilled his own.

Brad Holstedt raised his glass in a gesture of a toast and gave Jack a sardonic smile. "You'll get used to it."

"What?"

"The fancy restaurants. The fine hotels. They come with the job."

Jack didn't return the smile. "Let's talk about the job, Brad."

The made-up job, Jack thought darkly, thrust on him when Brad's father, Garrison, had learned Jack was quitting the force to become a private investigator.

"Get over it, Jack. The job's for real. Dad would have hired someone to check out these people. Might as well be you."

But there was more to it than that, and they both knew it. This issue went back a long way.

"Whether it's for real or not, I didn't ask for this job, and I don't want that damned stock."

"Like I said, get over it. You know Dad. When he makes up his mind about something, that's it." Jack heard the unmistakable bitterness behind his words, and it hit him for the first time that Brad resented his well-meaning but controlling father. Did he resent Jack now as well? Jack, who had always found favor with Garrison Holstedt but who now had become a part of the family business, albeit unwillingly? If so, he'd resign immediately, no matter what Garrison wanted. No job or amount of money was worth the price of his friendship with Brad.

"This is bullshit," Jack said, throwing his napkin on the table. "I don't want you hating me because your father insisted on hiring me. I quit."

Brad leaned forward, his blue eyes blazing. "Let's get this straight, old friend. Like it or not, you're in it now, and it's too late to back out. This is one big frigging deal I'm supposed to pull off, and I'll be damned if I let you blow it for me by quitting now. I need you to do exactly what you've been hired to do, so get a grip and get on with it." He narrowed his gaze and added, "And I really don't give a rat's ass about the stock."

Jack became aware that other diners had overheard their heated discussion and were staring at them. He shifted uncomfortably in his seat. He took a sip of water, not quite sure what to make of Brad's uncharacteristic

outburst. "Then maybe you'd like to give me a few
details of my duties," he said, holding on to his temper.
"So far, it seems I'm nothing but a highly paid travel
companion."

The tension between them was explosive, Brad's expression fierce. Fierce, and also desperate. Suddenly,
Jack looked behind Brad's anger and saw the fear that
lurked just beneath. Brad Holstedt, outwardly the young,
self-possessed financial lion, walked in the shadow of
fear. What was he afraid of? His personal safety? Jack
could not imagine anyone wanting to harm Brad. No,
there was something else. His well-bred friend rarely
used raunchy language. More likely, he was afraid of
failing in this "big frigging deal."

Afraid of failing his father.

Something painful twisted inside of Jack, and he felt
sorry for the son of the rich man who seemed obsessed
with success, driven by achievement. This was not the
Brad Jack had known for over two decades, the man he
considered to be his best friend. The Brad he knew was
of a gentler nature, a Brad who took time to watch a
sunset, who taught a younger, poorer boy the nuances
of surfing, then loaned him his expensive surfboard to
let him give it a try. He felt sorry that Brad was trying
so hard to please Garrison and losing his own identity
in the process.

"I was going to wait until morning, but since you're
in such a damned snit . . ." Brad reached beneath the
table and took out his briefcase, snapping it open
sharply. He rustled through thick sheaves of paper and
drew out several manila envelopes and shoved them at
Jack. "Here. These are the dossiers on the potential British players in this deal. Dad . . . I mean, I want you to
dig up anything you can find on them . . . personal, po-
litical, religious, whatever. These guys have got to be
squeaky clean coming in, because the investment in-
volves our national government, and if there ever was
any kind of Congressional investigation into any of the

partners, one bad apple could bring down our entire company.''

With that, Brad rose to go. He glared at Jack a moment, then his expression softened. ''Get over it, Jack. It's a real job. I need you. I'll catch up with you tomorrow night.''

Late the next evening, Jack stalked into his hotel room, wondering what the hell had made him think he wanted to be a gumshoe. He was accustomed to the action of the streets, not the guileful sniffing into other people's lives that was the life of a PI.

But he'd chosen this new career precisely for the lack of street action. In his twelve years on the police force, he had seen too much death and dying. His sister's murder had been the last straw, a senseless death and one for which he blamed himself. He hadn't known his cover had been blown, that the drug dealer he had fingered was waiting outside his house, finger on the trigger, ready to exact his revenge. He hadn't known. But Melinda was just as dead.

If only he hadn't invited her over for supper that night. If only the bullet had struck its intended target . . .

Pouring three fingers of Jack Daniels into a glass he found on the bar in his hotel room, Jack forced those memories and his gut-wrenching grief into a dark corner of his mind where he didn't have to look at them. At least for the moment, until they unexpectedly surfaced again, as they so frequently did, hitting him squarely and painfully in the solar plexus.

Taking his drink in hand, Jack stacked some pillows at the head of the bed and slouched against them, kicking off his shoes and thinking about his day. He'd call Brad in a few minutes. Maybe they could meet for dinner. It was after eight o'clock and he was starved, but he wanted to unwind first.

Jack sipped the whiskey and thought with regret about the harsh words he'd exchanged with Brad the night before. He knew they'd stemmed from his own hang-ups, not Brad's. Jack hated charity, and he strongly suspected that charity was Garrison's motive in bringing him on board. Garrison, who doggedly and unnecessarily continued to honor a promise made long, long ago.

Jack's friendship with Brad was an unlikely one, but one that had lasted nearly a quarter of a century. Jack, a boy from the poorer streets of L.A., and Brad, the son of a millionaire, had been brought together by a promise made on a battlefield half a world away. Garrison and Jack's father, John Knight, had served together in Vietnam. Garrison came home. John did not. Before John died, he'd asked Garrison to keep an eye out for Jack, his younger sister, Melinda, and their mother, Suzanne.

Jack often wondered if his father had known that Garrison Holstedt was a wealthy man. Beyond wealthy. He wondered if John Knight had had any clue that when Garrison honored his dying wishes, it would mean lavish gifts for his wife and children at Christmas and birthdays, delivered in long, shiny cars to their tiny apartment. Money when his mother couldn't pay the rent. Eventually a college education for him and his sister.

In Jack's eyes, Garrison Holstedt had long ago discharged his obligation. But Garrison wouldn't let it go. It was almost as if he felt guilty that he'd survived and John had died.

His latest generosity included this job, along with a substantial percentage of stock in Odyssey Investments International, stock that Jack believed by birthright should have been Brad's. But Garrison had insisted on it as part of the incentive package for Jack to come on board the multinational company. "Consider it hazardous duty pay," he'd said.

Jack looked at his surroundings. His duty hadn't been too hazardous so far.

His stomach growled loudly, rousing him from his reverie. Jack looked at his watch. It was almost nine. Reaching for the phone, he dialed Brad's room, which was just down the hall. After six rings, he hung up. If Brad was there, he must be in the shower. More likely, he'd probably already gone to dinner. Jack decided to wait a few minutes and call again. If he didn't get an answer, he'd just order from room service. Jack hated eating alone in a restaurant. He leaned his head back against the pillows and closed his eyes.

It was then he heard the screams.

They were high-pitched screams. A woman's screams, shrieking in terror. Jack bolted for the door, where he followed the sound down the hallway. He heard a crash just as he reached an open doorway, and one of the hotel's chambermaids careened out of the room, running headlong into him, nearly knocking him over. He grasped her arm, saving her from a fall, but she twisted away, leaned her head against the wall, and vomited.

Jack glanced at the door, and his blood suddenly ran cold. Whatever had frightened the maid was in this room.

Brass numbers on the door read 716.

Brad's room.

Cautiously, he edged the door open, wishing he was carrying a gun.

The sight that met his eyes turned his own stomach. Beyond a shattered lamp the maid must have knocked over in her fright, a woman lay faceup on the floor about halfway across the room. Her eyes stared at the ceiling in lifeless surprise. Blood had seeped from the area of her heart onto her pale pink blouse, staining it like a crimson rose. He glanced to the left, where the small entrance hall opened into a larger room and saw the body of a man on the floor just inside the bathroom. Jack's heart seemed to stop beating.

This was Brad's room . . .

He dashed to the doorway of the bath, then halted, his eyes wide in horror and disbelief.

Jack had thought he was through with violence. He

never wanted to hear another gunshot. See another dead body. Yet here he was, halfway around the world from Los Angeles, staring into the face of his best friend, whose blood was splattered on the white tile wall of the bathroom.

"Oh my God."

Jack heard a noise behind him and turned to find several people who had also heard the screams peering around him, trying to see what had happened. "For God's sake, somebody call the police," he managed to say, although he himself was frozen to the spot. This couldn't be real. This was a bad dream.

He forced himself to move on feet of lead to where Brad lay, careful not to step on him or in the blood that pooled around his head. "Oh, dear God," he whispered again, looking down at the carnage, his mind reeling, not from the shock, or the blood, but from the sight of a small pistol held in Brad's right hand that lay across his chest.

Jack knelt by his friend's side, unable to register the implications of what he saw. His mind had gone numb. He couldn't think. Tenderly, he touched Brad's cheek, expecting to find it already growing cold. But it was not. Astonished, Jack pressed on a pulse point at Brad's throat and felt a faint intimation of life.

Hope suddenly galvanized him, and he ran to the telephone by the bed. Aware that 911 didn't work in this country, but unable to remember England's emergency number, he hammered at the button to reach the hotel switchboard. "Hello? Hello?"

"Front desk. May I help you?"

"I'm in room 716," he said, trying to think like a cop, not like Brad's best friend. "There's been . . . an attempted murder. Two murders. Get an ambulance here right now. At least one of the victims might still be alive. And call the police! Hurry!"

Jack's heart was pounding furiously now, and he started to turn away from the nightstand when his eye lit on a scrap of paper peeking from beneath the telephone. He pulled it out. It was just a scribbled phone number, not in Brad's handwriting. Probably something an earlier guest had forgotten. Without thinking, Jack stuck it in his pocket and turned to see if by some miracle the other victim was alive.

She was not.

Kneeling beside her, Jack stared down into her face. She couldn't have been more than twenty, maybe twenty-one. Her beauty was haunting, macabre, the pallor of death peculiarly enhanced by a mane of vibrant red hair that writhed in spiraling waves past her shoulders. He saw something just below her left earlobe and brushed the hair aside gently. It was a small red mark and looked to be a burn or scrape.

Jack stood up again, trying to absorb facts that his brain refused to comprehend. Who the hell was this woman? And what had she been doing in Brad's hotel room? Before his mind could get a grasp on these and a thousand other questions, Jack felt a hand on his shoulder.

"Pardon me, sir."

Slowly, Jack turned to see who was speaking, and he managed to focus on the face of a uniformed policeman. The officer's voice somehow penetrated the ringing in his ears and the murk in his brain. "I'm sorry, sir." His lips formed words that sounded as if they came from far away. "I'm afraid you're going to have to answer some questions."

TWO

K eely stood at the far end of the jetty that protruded into the ocean outside the harbor, straining with eyes that burned from lack of sleep, hoping without expectation to see her friend returning through the mists.

It had been three days since Genevieve's frantic flight, and the entire village was in a state of shock. She could not have run away. Not Genevieve. Not Ninian's beautiful, bright daughter. Their future Healer. Genevieve would never have betrayed the Dragon in such a way. Something must have happened to her.

Everyone was talking about it. Everyone, that is, except Keely and Ninian. And perhaps her uncle Alyn, the Keeper, although she had managed to avoid him since Genny left. Since she was a child, he'd had a way of seeing through her secrets, and she did not want him to know she had aided in Genny's escape.

The morning after Genevieve had left, Keely had gone to Ninian's house, hoping to find that her friend had returned home and was safe in her bed. Instead, she'd found Ninian, eyes swollen and red from crying, nearly hysterical that Genevieve was nowhere to be found. "I thought mayhap she'd gone t' th' grove or th' circle t' sort out her thoughts after . . . well, after what happened," Ninian said. "But she surely would have returned by now. Alyn's gone in search o' her. Mayhap she's run t' th' forbidden caves . . ."

Keely knew that her uncle would not find Genny in the forbidden realm of the caves or anywhere else on the island, but she held her tongue. She attempted to comfort Ninian, but her efforts felt awkward and hypocritical, as she was too ashamed to admit her own part in the misadventure. She found it odd that Erica, Genevieve's fourteen-year-old sister, was not there to comfort her mother, but then, the girl had never shown much compassion for anyone other than herself. Or maybe, she told herself more hopefully, Erica, too, had gone in search of her sister.

After a few gentle probes, Keely gave up on trying to learn from Ninian what had caused Genevieve to take flight. Genny's mother seemed no more disposed to talk of it than Keely was to reveal her complicity. So neither said anything, not to one another and not to the rest of the villagers.

Keely guessed they shared one hope in common— that Genevieve would come back, all would be forgiven, and life would go on in the village as it had for centuries.

For nothing ever changed in Keinadraig.

The village had existed in peace and prosperity since the laws of the Dragon had been set down some seven centuries before, just after a great plague had ravaged the island and the Black Death had nearly destroyed the isolated community. The laws were simple: As the pestilence had been brought by a stranger, no strangers were to be allowed again on Keinadraig. The Dragoners were to keep the island's very existence a secret, and no one who wore the kiss of the Dragon was to leave.

The laws had come to the first Healer in the form of a ballad that had been handed down through the ages. It was sung at sacred ceremonies, and over ale in the pub on Saturday night. Young mothers of the village even hummed it to their babes at the breast.

The laws were ingrained in all who lived on Keinadraig, and Keely had never doubted their virtue. Never in over seven hundred years had the town been beset again with pestilence. The villagers had dwelt for ages in comfort and security, most living to a very advanced age.

They had kept the laws, and the Dragon had kept his promise.

Standing her futile watch on the jetty, Keely shivered in the noonday sun. She had a bad feeling, a frightening apprehension that something was terribly wrong. She had never questioned the laws, or thought about the consequences of breaking them because she, like the rest of the villagers, had been content to live with them. She'd never really believed that something bad would happen if a Dragoner actually tried to leave for good. But then, no one had ever left before, at least not that she could remember.

But now . . .

Gazing across the bay in the direction of Penzance, Keely tried to picture Genny in her mind. Where was she? Had she made it safely to London? Did she like living in the outside world? Or was she frightened but too ashamed to come home? Keely ached with grief clear down to her fingernails. Grief, and guilt. She should have stopped Genny from running. Whatever had sent her off could have been resolved. It was a mistake Keely would likely regret for the rest of her life.

The question of what had caused Genevieve to flee continued to haunt Keely. She had wanted to press Ninian for an answer again yesterday when the older woman hinted at some discord that had transpired between her and Genevieve, but she'd decided against it just then. Ninian's distress was too great.

Keely had seen Erica around the village earlier in the day, but she had not had the chance to speak with her yet. Keely was not fond of the girl, who had always been sullen and resentful of her older sister. But their cottage was small. If Genny and Ninian had argued, Erica must have heard something. Maybe she knew what had occurred between Genny and her mother that was so terrible neither of them could speak of it.

Something that had driven Genevieve away, maybe forever.

For if Genny did not return soon, she would not be able to return at all. The thought sickened Keely, but already talk of excommunication had begun. Once the villagers performed that ritual, Genevieve could never come back. If she were excommunicated by the Dragon, the woman known as Genevieve Sloan would no longer exist. If she showed up again, she would be shunned, invisible even to her own mother.

With a heavy heart, Keely turned and slowly made her way across the gray granite stones toward the village. Behind her the island of Keinadraig rose sharply from the sheltered harbor on the northeast coast to the high ridge on the southwest, where it dropped in sheer, dark cliffs into the sea. Midway up the wide slope, beyond a thick grove of ancient oak trees, lay the mystical stone circle where the Dragon was said to have brought forth the laws.

The laws that when broken brought tragedy to Keinadraig.

Like now.

Why, Genny? she asked herself.

Why?

The three days that had passed since Jack had come upon the bloody scene in the hotel room were among the longest in his life. Brad, who had been rushed to the hospital and was immediately operated on by one of Britain's top brain surgeons, clung to life but remained in a coma. The prognosis offered little hope.

It had been Jack's unhappy duty to call Garrison in L.A. and inform him of what had happened, and twelve hours later, to pick him up at the airport and bring him to his son's bedside where Brad lay unconscious, his head swathed like a mummy, his skin whiter than the bed linens. As Jack looked on helplessly, this giant of international finance, the man who had been like a second father to him in many ways, had crumbled before his eyes. For all his faults, his need to control Brad's life—maybe even Jack's own—Garrison Holstedt was a good man. He did not deserve this.

In that instant, Jack had recanted his earlier vow to avoid violence and swore at that moment he would do whatever it took to find the sorry son of a bitch who was responsible for the tragedy.

Sometime during the course of the nightmarish events, he had endured a grueling inquiry by detectives with the Metropolitan Police from New Scotland Yard. While his friend was unconsciously fighting for his life, Jack was fighting to convince a certain Inspector Richard Sandringham and his superiors that the crime was not a murder-suicide attempt.

"For one thing, Brad was left-handed," Jack had informed them. "He would never have shot anyone with his right hand." He would never have shot anyone, period, Jack wanted to add, but held his temper.

Jack had gained some small satisfaction when he'd seen the inspector's bushy eyebrows rise slightly on his wrinkled brow. But his satisfaction was short-lived. "Perhaps. But stranger things have happened. We'll have to check the forensics report." His voice faded away, and he looked thoughtfully perplexed. Then he seemed to shift gears. "Do you know anything about the young lady?"

"Nothing. I never saw her before. Do you have an ID on her yet?"

"No. All we found in her bag were a few items of clothing, a small sum of money, and a train ticket from Penzance to London, dated that same morning, the twenty-first." He paused, then asked pointedly, "Mr. Knight, why would such a woman be with your friend?"

"I have no idea." Summoning patience, Jack had explained in detail why he and Brad had come to London, hoping to convince the inspector of Brad's innocence with his impressive credentials as a businessman. "Brad spent most of his time in meetings. I don't think he previously knew any women in London, and he wasn't a womanizer. It's not likely he picked her up in a bar.''

Jack could read the clear skepticism on the inspector's face and knew if their roles were reversed, he, too, would be doubtful. This mystery woman had ended up in Brad's company somehow. A pickup was the most logical explanation.

"She could have been a streetwalker," Sandringham speculated out loud. "I suppose the killer could have been her pimp." He continued musing aloud. "It doesn't look like a drug deal. We found no paraphernalia . . ."

"Brad didn't do hookers," Jack snapped. "Or drugs. What about robbery? It seems more likely Brad walked in on an attempted burglary . . ."

"I suppose that's a possibility. The thief could have shot the girl, turned the gun on Brad, and then planted it on him. Or, it could be just what it looks like. Your friend shot the girl, and then himself."

"He didn't shoot her!" Jack jumped up and slammed his fist on the inspector's desk. "Brad carried no weapon. He hated guns."

Sandringham sighed. "Very well. So who shot her?"

"The burglar, like you said. The burglar shot them both."

"Possible, but unlikely. Your friend's wallet was on his person, full of money. Other valuables were untouched in the room." He tapped his pencil thoughtfully on the desk blotter. "So, if it wasn't an interrupted burglary, or a crime of passion, or someone after the girl, or a murder-suicide, why were they shot? Mr. Knight, who might have wanted your friend dead?"

Jack had only stared stupidly at the inspector in reply. Who could possibly want Brad dead? Someone involved in the high-stakes investment deal Brad was putting together? Jack had read the dossiers Brad had given him, and although a couple of the investors might not be above manipulation for financial gain, none had the profile of a murderer. He immediately dismissed the possibility. "No one in his right mind," he answered.

"A madman?" Inspector Sandringham gave him a cynical look.

Jack raised his head and glared at the inspector. "It makes as much sense as anything else."

At the conclusion of their interview, Jack had managed to gain Sandringham's grudging confidence by calling his contacts at the Los Angeles Police Department, who gave him exemplary character references. He'd offered New Scotland Yard his skills and experience to help solve the mystery, but he couldn't say his offer was welcomed with open arms. It seemed professional jealousy wasn't limited to American law enforcement agencies. But Sandringham had given him off-the-record approval to investigate the crime as Garrison's hired private eye.

"The truth of the matter is that we are overworked and understaffed," Sandringham had said at last. "If you come up with something, we'd be happy to take a look at it. Just don't break any laws, and don't leave the country. You know, you are a possible suspect as well, having been found at the scene of the crime."

That said, the inspector had provided Jack with a photocopy of a police sketch of the girl and wished him luck in coming up with an ID on her.

But forty-eight hours had passed since then, and Jack was not one whit closer to solving the mystery. Brad remained unconscious, in critical condition. Garrison was barely holding himself together as he kept a vigil at his son's bedside. The investment deal had gone down the tubes. And Jack's small victory in procuring the blessing of Inspector Sandringham meant little, for there was virtually nothing for him to go on.

Pacing his hotel room in frustration, Jack thrust his hands into the pockets of his pants, where his fingers encountered a crumpled slip of paper. He drew it out and frowned at the number scribbled on it. How did this get into his pants pocket? And then he remembered. He'd been wearing these trousers the night Brad was shot. He'd found the paper by the telephone in Brad's room. He'd dismissed it then, forgotten about it even, thinking it irrelevant to the murder. Now . . .

It still might be irrelevant, but something was better than nothing.

Jack grabbed the telephone in his room and dialed the number. His heart pounded as he heard the first set of double rings. They sounded very far away. The phone rang again. Again. And again. Discouraged, Jack was about to hang up after the seventh time, when someone lifted the receiver.

"Hallo." It was a man's voice—heavy, mature, gruff.

"My name's Knight. Jackson Knight. Who is speaking, please?"

"Who d'ye say is calling?" The man sounded surprised.

"My name is Jackson Knight," he repeated. "I'm calling from London."

"What d'ye want?"

"I'm an investigator. There's been a murder, and this number was found at the scene of the crime."

Dead silence. "Must be some mistake," the man said at last. "Ye've reached the wrong number." And he hung up.

Jack sat on the bed, perplexed. He was certain he had dialed the number correctly, but when he tried again, there was no answer. Either he had misdialed, or whoever had answered the phone wanted to avoid his call. Instinct told him it was the latter.

Where had he called? He looked at the number on the paper. If it were the United States, he could determine the general location by the area code. Was it the same here?

It took only minutes and a couple of phone calls to pinpoint the location of the number. "That is in Cornwall," the phone company representative told him. "In a town called Keinadraig." She paused, then added, "I say, but that's odd. It appears to be the only number listed for that entire village. Must be one of those very remote little places."

Cornwall. Jack didn't know British geography well, but he thought Penzance might also be in Cornwall. There'd been a train ticket from Penzance among the dead woman's belongings. Jack's cop consciousness snapped to attention. He did not believe in coincidence.

Obtaining a tourist map from the hotel where he and Garrison were now registered, one close to the hospital and as far as possible from the scene of the crime, he soon verified that Penzance was indeed in Cornwall. And not far away, a few miles south along the coast, lay a tiny island and a village called Keinadraig. He studied the map, noting it was illustrated by a cartoonist. There were whimsical drawings of points of interest, caricatures of castles, lighthouses, monoliths, and ruins. Drawn in the waters just off the island of Keinadraig was a humpbacked dragon, with a notation written in an archaic style: HERE THERE BE DRAGONS. Jack allowed a tight smile as he folded the map, but it did little to cheer him.

The next morning, he was on the motorway, headed south and west in a rental car, the map open on the passenger seat to his left. He reached Penzance late in the evening and parked the red Nissan in front of the train station. He had bet on some long shots before, but this was by far the most unlikely SWAG he'd ever checked out. That's what his fellow narcs had called a lead that was little more than a hunch: a silly wild-ass guess—SWAG.

His timing could not have been better, however. The night manager was just coming on duty. Jack gave him one of the cards he'd had printed before Garrison had insisted he come to work for Odyssey. It read: "Jackson

Knight, Private Investigator.'' He showed the man the police sketch.

"Oh, indeed, I do remember 'er. Just th' other night she came in lookin' like a scared rabbit. 'Twas after midnight when she got 'ere, and she sat up all night waitin' for th' first train t' take 'er into London. I offered 'er a cup o' coffee,'' he went on, "but she said nay. Kept lookin' over 'er shoulder, like somebody might be after 'er.''

"Did you recognize her as being from around here?''

The man shook his head. "No, na that I recall. But Penzance is a big place.''

"Ever hear of a place called Keinadraig?'' Jack asked and saw the man's eyes narrow ever so slightly.

"Aye. Keinadraig's a village down th' coast a bit. Out on an island. Don't know much about it, just 'eard some rumors.''

"Rumors?''

"Oh, th' locals like t' tell tales, y'know. Some say th' Dragoners, that's what they call 'em, are still pagan and worship a dragon. Others say they're descendents of Merlin. Whatever, they're an odd lot.''

Dragoners.

Here there be dragons.

"They worship a dragon?'' Jack said, raising his eyebrows. "Well, I suppose that's why they're called Dragoners.''

The station manager laughed. "Oh, nay. 'Tis nothing that dramatic. 'Tis just because Keinadraig in Cornish means 'back o' th' dragon.' There's a 'igh ridge on th' south side o' th' island, looks kind o' like a dragon's back. I guess that's where th' name came from. At any rate, a long time ago, locals took t' callin' them Dragoners, and th' name stuck. We see little o' them actually. They come t' town t' buy what they need and t' sell their fish and 'andicrafts. But mostly they keep t' themselves and th' old ways, although I know they have electricity because my nephew 'elped bring it out there.''

Electricity. And a telephone?

The man's description of the Dragoners reminded Jack of the Amish and their benign avoidance of the twentieth century. Then his thoughts took a darker turn as he recalled a cult in Southern California he'd once had to infiltrate. The neighboring townfolk had considered them "an odd lot," too. Jack had found them downright terrifying because of the dogmatic brainwashing they had practiced. The station manager had told him the young woman had appeared afraid, like someone might be following her. Had the murdered girl been running away from a cult environment?

Jack jotted his cell phone number on the back of the card. "Thanks for the information. I'd appreciate a call if you remember anything else." He returned to the car, encouraged that his SWAG wasn't so WA after all. He was certain the victim was from Keinadraig. But he was disconcerted by what else he'd learned about the island.

The only way to find out was to go there, but it was too late in the day. Taking a room in a waterfront inn, he called Garrison to check on Brad's condition. Garrison had taken up a round-the-clock vigil by Brad's bedside, as if through the sheer power of his will he could bring his son back.

Maybe he could, Jack mused as he hung up the phone after a short conversation. Garrison had told him that although Brad's condition hadn't changed, he was still alive. It was more than the doctors had expected, and it renewed Jack's determination.

I'll find the sorry son of a bitch . . .

Keely stared out into the night. She could see the flicker of torches as the villagers gathered in the square. She did not cry, for she had no more tears left in her. She was not angry with her uncle for carrying out the excommunication ceremony, for such was part of their law, and keeping the law was Alyn's job. She knew that he'd put it off for as long as he could, hoping Genny would return.

But the time had come to uphold the law, and shortly, the woman who had grown up here, who had been beloved by everyone, would cease to exist. Her best friend, Genevieve Sloan, would be cast out of Keinadraig, unable ever to return.

Keely heard the sound of a single drum begin a slow, solemn cadence and saw the glow from the torches stretch upward along the High Street as the bearers began their processional to the circle of stones, where Alyn would speak to them words of both condolence and warning. The excommunication rite would normally be the responsibilty of the Healer, as the spiritual leader. But Ninian had collapsed, enfolded in her grief, so the duty fell to Alyn.

After the speaking, the villagers would torch the wood that had been stacked in the center, a pyre that symbolized the physical body of the missing girl. And when the flames died, Genevieve Sloan would exist no longer.

Distraught, Keely turned away and went down the stairs to sit in the darkness of the pub room. She would not participate in the ceremony. She could not bear it, for she could not bear the thought that even if Genny returned, Keely would not be allowed to speak with her. It was the law.

For the first time in her life, Keely questioned the law. What she'd once accepted as reasonable and venerable now seemed archaic and unnecessary. There had been no plague anywhere that she knew of for hundreds of years. True, their tradition had provided a safe, protected place for their people, but now, Genevieve was being made an outcast. And for what? Tradition?

Keely quaked with anger and no small amount of fear. Not fear of the Dragon, or the laws, or tradition, but rather fear of the disturbing rebellion that boiled within her. She wanted to go screaming up the hillside and put a stop to the ritual. It wasn't right that this should be happening. Not to Genevieve.

But what could she do about it? The ways of the Dragon had governed the lives of the people of Keinadraig for centuries. She had little expectation that things would ever change. She inhaled a deep breath, trying to calm her troubled soul.

Change.

Did she really want change? Change was a frightening thing. Mayhap it was better to keep to the old ways. On Keinadraig, the Dragoners remained safe, protected, untouched by the dangers of the outside world.

Yet nothing Keely had seen of that forbidden world had seemed particularly dangerous or threatening to the people or the traditions of Keinadraig. Granted, she had seen little. Just tempting glimpses of a life very different from her own when she and Genny had been entrusted to take a catch of fish now and then to market in nearby Penzance. While in town, they'd always lingered long enough to experience for a short while the wealth of unfamiliar sights and sounds of the outside world—the unbelievable array of food and other commodities at the supermarket, the temptation of frosty ice cream cones at a small cafe, the scandalous tabloids and romantic magazines sold by street vendors.

As budding young women, they were entranced by the shiny cars speeding down the streets, the provocative clothing worn by outsiders, the trains that offered to take them to far away places with names like Brighton and London. On the return trip to Keinadraig, they would swear that someday, when they grew up, they would leave the island forever and find romance and adventure in the wide world that awaited them.

Keely bit her lip. Oh, by the Saints, how wrong they had been to entertain such foolish daydreams. If Genevieve hadn't known where to run, then she would never have run.

A sound reached her ears, carried on the light breeze

through the open window. It was a thin, high, youthful voice, singing the familiar words of the ancient ballad:

Away, hide awuy, on this distant shore,
Let ne'er a stranger in thy door.
Keep your secret safe, hidden in the mist,
And let no one leave who be Dragon
    kiss'd.

Keely wanted to cry out in anger and disgust. It was Erica. How could she? How could she so eagerly join in the ritual that would damn her own sister from ever returning? The sound of her voice soured, ringing out bitterly in Keely's ears as she continued.

A sailor man from across the sea
Was found half-dead at the Dragon's feet,
They took him in, put him on a bed,
And in the morn, they did find him dead.

In her mind's eye, Keely could see Erica, always watching everything she and Genny did with a spiteful stare. Always finding fault. Always whining for what her older sister had. As she was whining at the moment, singing their island's history in a self-righteous tone.

Then one by one, they too did fall,
Struck down by his plague that did touch
    them all,
When their poor souls did at last depart,
They were cleansed by the fires in the
    Dragon's heart.

Keely rose and went to the window, wanting to shut it, to shut out the sound, and the story. For she knew where it would lead. But the air was too hot, and she did not wish to endure her pain stifling in the darkness. Erica's voice became a taunt in the night.

Then up from the flames in the sacred ring
Rose the Dragon fierce and to them did
    sing—

Always before, the tale of how the sacred Dragon had sung out the laws to the first Healer had warmed her heart and brought her a solid sense of peace and security. Now it chilled her to the marrow.

The Healer. Genny was to have become the Healer. But now . . . Erica had wished out loud many times that she would become the Healer instead of Genevieve. She was next in the familial line, so Keely guessed that when she was old enough, she would get her wish. The thought made her shudder. Erica was cold, uncaring about anyone other than herself. How could she ever take Ninian's place? Talk about change . . .

Keely dropped her head and cradled it between her hands as Erica began singing one of the verses that had been added by some bard much later than the original refrain.

'Twas a miller's son ran off to sea,
A privateer John longed to be.
He scorned the law and the Dragon's kiss,
And he died at the stroke of a cannon's
    fist.

Suddenly, the song raised the hair on Keely's arms. Hearing this part of the ballad always stirred unsettling emotions within her. From the time she was born, she had been surrounded by a village of people who loved her and cared about her, as was their way toward one another. Theirs was a gentle village, quiet, serene. Each man, woman, and child had his place in the scheme of things and no one questioned it.

Nothing bad ever happened to the villagers, except, according to the song, when someone like the miller's son, John, broke the law.

And then, if the ballad could be believed, the Dragon awoke and exacted retribution in the most mysterious and violent of ways. The deaths were always accidental, but everyone knew that somehow they were caused by the Dragon who had taken his revenge.

The violence wreaked upon lawbreakers was too great a contradiction for Keely to accept. She doubted if those terrible things had ever really happened to anyone. Rather, she believed the stories had been made up as entertainment by her more primitive ancestors, or at worst, contrived to make sure the people didn't stray from the law.

A few minutes later, Keely heard Erica launch into the last verses of the long ballad:

> To the Dragon's back a young man came,
> And Timothy Jenkyns was his name.
> A chosen one for an island bride,
> But his scorn for her he could not hide.
> He took her coin, took the Dragon's kiss,
> The wedding vow was all he missed.
> He ran away, thought he'd not be found,
> But the morning tide brought his body,
>   drowned.

Without warning, a memory surfaced from the deep recesses of her mind, and Keely drew in a sharp breath. It was a dark and frightening memory, vague and still half-hidden, but she struggled to see it. It was something she had secretly witnessed as a child, here in this very room. She recalled her father and her uncle Alyn and some other men arguing about something. Something that had to do with a young man named . . .

. . . Timothy Jenkyns.

THREE

After a restless, mostly sleepless night, Jack showered and dressed and made his way to a boat rental service at the busy docks in Penzance where he hired a boat.

"Ye familiar with these waters?" Kevin Spearman, owner of the concession, asked as he filled out the paperwork. "Or would ye be needin' a guide?"

"I'm just going to the island."

"St. Michael's Mount?"

"No. Keinadraig." Jack peered across the water, squinting in the morning sun, but the mists obscured the island in the distance.

Spearman jerked his head around and frowned. "Keinadraig? What are ye goin' there for?"

After what the stationmaster had told him, Jack wasn't too surprised at Spearman's response. He gave the man his card and showed him the dead girl's picture. "Do you know her?"

Spearman took a quick look at the drawing, then shook his head. "Never saw 'er before," he said quickly. Too quickly, Jack thought. "What d'ye want with 'er?"

"I want to know who killed her." Jack saw the man's face lose some of its robust color. He went on, curious to know if the man was lying. And why. "She was murdered in London, and I have reason to believe she comes from Keinadraig."

Spearman looked away and returned to his paperwork. His hands trembled slightly. "They'll na welcome ye out there, y'know, especially comin' with that kind o' news. If 'twas me, I'd na risk it."

"Risk it? Are they . . . militant or something?"

The man scowled. "Nay. But they don't like outsiders, and there's been rumors from time t' time about outsiders meetin' with certain . . . accidents. What difference does it make anyway whether th' girl was from there or na? She's dead, isn't she?"

Jack was shocked. "Wouldn't they want to know if one of their own had been murdered?"

Kevin Spearman gave him an enigmatic look. "From what I've 'eard tell o' them and their peculiar ways, it seems t' me they might not."

Uneasy, Jack thanked the man and paid for the boat. "If I don't come back by sunset, send a posse," he said, only half joking, as he stepped into the boat.

Spearman did not laugh.

Keely awoke with the same lump of despair around her heart that she had taken to bed with her the night before. Woodenly, she dressed, pulling on a long skirt and a knit short-sleeved jersey. Like all of her clothes, they were conservative, this a dark blue, the skirt adorned with tiny white flowers. She glanced in the mirror and sighed at the image reflected there. The skin around her eyes was puffy, her face strained. She brushed her thick black hair, grateful for the natural curls that bounced back in healthy resilience. That helped somewhat.

But Keely Cochrane didn't much care about her appearance this morning. Didn't much care about anything. With Genny's departure and subsequent excommunication, Keely's world had cracked wide open, and it threatened to split apart unless she could find a way to hold it together until her spirit, severely daunted after last night's ritual, could mend.

Not expecting her first customer in the pub until eleven, she decided to take a walk to clear her head and steady her heart. She let herself out the front door and made her way down the cobblestone lane toward the harbor. Around her, villagers went about their business as if nothing had happened. Housewives hung freshly laundered clothing on lines in their back gardens. Fishermen made ready for a day on the bay, loading their small fishing boats with gear and supplies.

Keely gazed at the activity in the small harbor and suddenly frowned. She counted the boats. They were all there. Her heart lurched. How could that be? She'd not told anyone where Genevieve had taken the boat. Alyn must have guessed and gone to fetch it from Penzance, Keely surmised. There wasn't much her uncle missed. Had he guessed Keely's complicity in the incident as well?

Sometimes Keely thought the town had eyes of its own. There was little one could hide when everyone knew everyone else's business, and gossip was the mainstay of their small society.

A man approached her with a melancholy smile. ''Good mornin', Keely.'' He paused to greet her.

''Good morning, William,'' she said, feeling sorry for him. It was William Reedy, the man Alyn had intended for Genevieve to marry. One of Keely's cousins. She knew William had wanted to marry Genny, despite the difference in their ages. William's wife had died in childbirth two years before, and he was a lonely man struggling to raise his children on his own. Now that Genevieve was gone, Keely wondered what William would do. Most likely, he'd ask Alyn to find him a bride from the mainland, for there were no other eligible women on the island.

Except herself.

And cousins couldn't marry cousins, she thought

thankfully. She had no desire to marry William Reedy, or anyone else for that matter.

They exchanged small talk for a few minutes, then Keely excused herself and made her way to the path at the edge of the village that led to the grove. The cluster of ancient oak trees was said to have been a sacred place of worship for the ancient druids. For Keely, it was a refuge where she found peace whenever she was distraught. As she was at the moment. Not only about Genevieve, but also about her own future.

Meeting William had served to remind her that it was only a matter of time until she, too, must face the subject of marriage. Alyn had already broached it with her more than once. Since there was no one on the island she could marry without breaking the law prohibiting marriage within a family, Keely faced the prospect of having to accept an outsider chosen for her by the Keeper. She'd managed to avoid the issue so far only because she'd been taking care of her invalid mother. But Sharine had died nearly half a year ago, and Keely knew she could not escape Alyn's pressure for her to wed for much longer.

Reaching the grove, she made her way to a secluded spot guarded by boulders that overlooked the ocean. She nestled into a natural seat eroded from the granite by eons of weather. The rock was already warmed by the morning sun, and it felt good against her back. She let out a long, deep sigh and looked up at the sky, wishing life were not so difficult. She missed Genevieve, whose lighthearted laughter had always cheered her when she was dispirited. Genny, who hadn't a care, or so it would have seemed. Whereas Keely had carried the responsibilities of an adult since her father died when she was only thirteen, Genevieve had been given free run of the island, asked only from time to time to perform a chore for her mother or Keely's uncle Alyn. Chores that weren't chores, like delivering a boatload of fish and other goods, then lingering in the local villages, feeding her daydreams.

Keely closed her eyes, longing for the peace of mind that continued to elude her. If only . . .

If only her mother hadn't died.

If only Genevieve hadn't run away.

If only Alyn would drop the subject of marriage.

Keely thought she would be content to live alone the rest of her life, running the pub and living independently. Better than being strapped with a man she didn't love. She might later regret not having children, but her freedom seemed worth the sacrifice.

For a fleeting moment, Keely considered the possibility of marrying an outsider. She supposed she could do it, providing the right outsider came along. But she had never particularly cared for the men and women chosen by the Keeper to wed unmarried villagers. She grimaced. She doubted her uncle's choice for her would be any more to her liking.

Keely heard the drone of a large insect somewhere nearby and sat upright, thinking to bat it away. Then she realized it wasn't a bumblebee or dragonfly, but rather the sound of a boat approaching the island. A vessel with a more powerful engine than was rigged in any of the island's fishing boats. Alarmed, she stood and went to the edge of the rock and peered out over the shimmering water.

Someone was coming to Keinadraig. But the boat was not heading toward the harbor. Instead, it was making directly for the opposite end of the island.

For an instant her heart stood still. Genny?

Keely hurriedly picked her way over the large rocks at the edge of the grove, and then ran as fast as her feet would carry her to the top of the hill.

Oh, dear God, please let it be Genny, she prayed, although if it was Genny, that would present a whole new set of problems.

And if it wasn't Genny, who then?

The morning sun was dazzling, reflecting off the water in a thousand glittering diamonds. Even though she shielded her eyes, they watered as she strained to see who dared break the law and land upon the forbidden shore.

As the boat approached the small beach that spread at the foot of the cliffs, Keely could see the lone figure on board. It was not Genevieve Sloan. It was a man, but no one she recognized. Her heart pounded harder. Should she run to fetch Alyn? No one came to the island like this. No one was allowed to come here at all, unless given special permission by the Council, as they did periodically to the education inspectors. Couldn't this intruder read? There was a large sign posted on a tree almost directly in front of him: NO TRESPASSING.

If he saw it, the man ignored it. He ran the boat up onto the sand and hopped out. Even from high above, Keely could tell he was tall, with broad shoulders and long arms beneath the dark jacket he wore. In the glare, however, she couldn't see the details of his face. As she watched, he secured the line to a large rock and tested to make sure it held fast. Satisfied, he then looked around, first surveying the cliffs and then the stretch of beach that led to the village.

Keely was nearly in a panic. What should she do? Try to warn him away? He mustn't go to the cliffs, for the caves carved within their granite were sacred. No one but the Keeper was allowed to go into the heart of the Dragon.

But the next moment, the man turned away from the cliffs and began to walk along the beach. Breathless, Keely made her way back down the long slope, staying abreast of him but just out of his line of sight above the edge of the drop-off. When she reached the circle of stones, she ducked behind one, trying to make up her mind whether to run for the village or to call out to the man and try to turn him away herself.

Before she could decide, she saw to her dismay that he had changed directions.

He was headed up the path that led from the beach, making directly for the ancient standing stones . . . and her.

Jack found nothing particularly sinister about the island of Keinadraig. Approaching the high cliffs from the water, they gleamed in the morning sun as if freshly scrubbed. The beach was pristine. Not a sign of trash or human disturbance. The only evidence that the place was hostile to visitors was the rather obvious NO TRESPASS-ING sign. Maybe it was their way of keeping the place unsoiled. Jack couldn't blame them and momentarily considered moving the boat. Having spent time on the beaches of California, he respected anyone's attempt to protect the delicate natural environment of a coastline. Hopefully, however, he wouldn't be here long enough to worry about it.

He had chosen to come to the southernmost shore of the island, hoping it was uninhabited so his arrival would go unnoticed. He wanted a chance to reconnoiter the village, which the map had marked at the northeastern end of the island, before making his entrance. If this was a cult, his intrusion could be dangerous. If it was merely an odd isolated society, he would get more cooperation if he could observe enough of their ways to show respect for them.

Although he suspected much of what Kevin Spearman and the station manager had told him about the island was hearsay, he doubted that he would be very welcome in the village, considering the news he brought. But he must find someone who could give a positive ID on the girl and hopefully, a reason why she went to London.

Beaching the boat, he stepped onto the soft sand, which immediately recorded his footprints. Until the next rain, or maybe high tide, anyone who came along would know someone had been trespassing. He lashed the boat's painter securely to a large rock and took a look around, getting his bearings. To the south, the beach turned to rocks that became sea-embedded boulders at the foot of the cliffs. Jack saw what appeared to be several caves hollowed into the face of the wall of granite. He recalled that this area had historically been a land of smugglers and wreckers, and letting his imagination momentarily out to play, he visualized one-legged pirates carting Spanish gold to hiding places in the caves.

Jack gave a short laugh, surprised he still had a sense of humor. Then he turned in the other direction and to his more serious chore. He took off his jacket and slung it over one shoulder, careful not to drop the papers and cell phone from his pockets, then began walking down the beach.

Above, the sky was a brilliant summertime blue. Seagulls and ravens wheeled high in the air, calling raucously in the freshening wind. As he proceeded along the beach, the cliffs tapered off, becoming little more than a steep slope running parallel to the sandy beach.

There was nothing to indicate danger, but, for a fleeting moment, Jack felt the hair rise on the back of his neck, and he got the unsettling sensation that someone was watching him. He stopped and glanced up the hill. Over his shoulder, he was surprised to see a circle of standing stones, not as large as the famous circle at Stonehenge he'd seen pictures of, but of a similar nature.

"Well, I'll be damned," he said under his breath. He'd never been to any of the mysterious stone formations, but before coming to England, he'd read about them and found them fascinating. Now it seemed as if he'd stumbled onto one by dumb luck. He decided to get a closer look.

Following a narrow path leading from the beach toward the circle, Jack was unable to shake his earlier feeling that he wasn't alone out here on this remote hillside. A motion caught his eye, and he saw something dark, a piece of fabric flapping in the wind from behind one of the stones. He paused, frowning. Someone *was* here, watching him.

Unaccustomed to being without his gun, Jack tensed, prepared to defend himself with his martial arts skills if necessary. Silently, he crept closer until he reached the stone. He peered around it and found himself looking into the eyes of a young woman huddled there.

Frightened eyes.

The woman caught her breath sharply and made a move as if to run, but Jack caught her by the wrist.

"Wait. Don't run. I won't hurt you."

"Let me go." She tried to wrench her arm free.

"Please. Wait a minute." Jack was torn between not wishing to frighten her further and not wanting her to alert the village of his presence. Not just yet.

She gave him an uncertain stare. "Who are ye? Do ye na know strangers are na supposed t' come here?"

Her words, laced with a heavy accent, were more frightened than unfriendly, but he felt her muscles relax slightly. He took a chance and loosened his grip on her wrist. "My name's Jack. I'm not going to hurt you."

She didn't run, but neither did she offer him a welcoming smile from her full, perfectly formed lips. Beneath dark brows, her troubled eyes were the color of a turbulent sea, both green and gray at the same time. Her hair, long and black as a raven's wing, was tossed by the wind into winsome disarray. He noted a tiny mark, an oddly shaped discoloration beneath her left ear, the only discernible blemish on her otherwise perfect, fair skin.

She was, in short, a knockout. Jack's heart skipped a beat, and he found himself appallingly dumbstruck. He held up his hands as if in surrender. "I won't hurt you," he repeated, not knowing what else to say. She looked disturbingly close to tears.

"Why are ye here?" she murmured.

Her words were barely audible in the wind, but they brought Jack back to his senses. He was here on a mission, a deadly serious errand. This island was small, and the woman before him looked to be not much older than the one who remained a Jane Doe in a London morgue. Surely, if the victim were from here, this woman would know her.

"I'm looking for answers," he said, wishing it was something happier that had brought him face-to-face with her. "There's . . . been a tragic murder in London, and I have reason to believe one of the victims might be from your island."

Her face lost all color and her eyes widened even more, but she did not speak. Jack sensed that she was ready to flee at any moment, so he hurried with what he had to say.

"I have a picture here." He took the sketch from his inside jacket pocket and held it out to her. "Do you know this person?"

The young woman reached to take it, but when she saw the picture, she jerked her hand away as if the paper had burned her fingers. She stood frozen to the spot, staring at him as if he were the devil himself, horror etched on her features. For one long moment, Jack hated himself. Her face gave him the answer—yes, she knew this person—but he needed to know more. Reluctantly, he pressed further. "Is she . . . from here?"

His words seemed to awaken her from her dazed state, and she brought her hands to her cheeks. "Nay," she uttered, shaking her head, slowly at first, and then more violently. Then she cried out loud. "Nay!"

Before he could stop her, she turned and fled down the hill, her dark skirts clinging to her legs.

Jack swallowed hard and watched her go. Then he took a deep breath.

Why had she lied?

FOUR

The dark night of denial blinded Keely as she ran tripping and stumbling over stones and through the tall grass. No! This could not be. That picture was not Genevieve. There was no murder. The stranger had brought a terrible lie to Keinadraig, a falsehood that threatened to destroy Keely's last desperately fostered shred of hope that Genny would return.

She reached the protection of the oak grove and leaned against one of the ancient trees, heaving for breath, choking back sobs. Perhaps the Dragon was right after all. Strangers should never be allowed on the island. She wished to God she'd never laid eyes on this one.

Keely had never feared outsiders before. Both she and Genny had thought the laws barring strangers were outmoded at the very least, nothing but an archaic tradition. But she feared this one now.

For in spite of her wishing it not so, she feared he did not lie.

Bad things happen to those who betray the Dragon.
Genny? Murdered?

The idea was more than Keely could cope with. Murder was unknown on the island, something she'd only read about when sneaking a glimpse at the sensational newspapers sold in Penzance.

Something that only happened . . . outside.

But then, Genny had been on the outside.

She crumpled onto the soft moss at the base of the tree and began to cry. She'd thought there could be no tears left, but behind her closed eyelids she saw the sketch of Genevieve's lovely face, and she knew the stranger told the truth. The wound in her heart caused by Genevieve's leaving was torn open again, renewing the well of bitter tears and adding to the already enormous weight of her guilt.

Moments later, when she was able to catch her breath, Keely realized she wasn't alone in the grove. She heard a soft humming and raised her head. Across the open glade in front of her, Erica sat on a bed of grass, humming the ballad of the Dragon and staring at Keely.

"What . . . what are ye doing here?" Keely asked, suddenly unnerved by the strange, cold look in Erica's eyes.

"She is dead, is she na?"

Keely blinked. "What?"

"Genevieve is dead."

"How do ye know that?"

Erica shrugged and tore off a blade of grass. "I just know. Otherwise, why would a stranger come t' th' island just at this time?"

"Ye saw him?"

Erica gave her a look filled with contempt. "I was playing on th' beach and heard his boat." She pierced Keely with her gaze. "I saw ye talking t' him."

The cheeky, challenging tone of her voice nettled Keely, who pulled herself to her feet. "So what?"

Erica shrugged. "So nothing. What was on that paper he showed ye?"

Keely had to clench her fists to keep from slapping the girl. She'd always suspected that Erica had not just disliked but hated both Genny and her. With a mousy brown mop of hair and a face that was painfully plain, Erica had been jealous of Genny's vibrant good looks. Keely understood that the fires of the girl's envy had also been fueled by Ninian's too-obvious preference for Genevieve, her firstborn. Still, she was shocked to see a certain satisfaction on that plain face at the moment, as if Erica was actually happy that Genevieve was dead.

"Go home, Erica," she said in as calm a voice as she could summon. "Your mother is going t' need ye."

Their gazes locked in an unspoken battle of wills, but after a long moment, Erica looked away. Without speaking, she rose and started back toward the village. At the edge of the grove, she paused, and the look she threw Keely over her shoulder left no doubt of the hatred she harbored against her.

Keely thought her knees would give way beneath her. What was happening to the safe, secure world she had known for a quarter of a century? With the arrival of the stranger and the terrible news he bore, the crack that had threatened to tear her world apart suddenly widened, and nothing remained either safe or secure.

The stranger.

Who could he be? How did he know what had happened to Genevieve? Where had he come by the picture of her? Deeply troubled, Keely began to walk slowly back toward her own cottage, wishing she'd stayed to question him about Genny's fate instead of losing her wits and running away. She doubted she'd have another opportunity. She was certain Erica had gone directly to alert Alyn of his presence.

Glancing at the sun that was now high in the sky, Keely quickened her pace. It was nearly opening time, and she hadn't prepared anything for the noon meal at the pub. Forcing thoughts of the stranger to the back of her mind, she dashed through her garden door, donned her apron, and busied herself in the kitchen slicing bread, cheese, and meats, and arranging things on platters that would later make it easier to fill customers' orders for sandwiches. Rote activity. Busywork to still her mind.

But it didn't work. Her head was filled with questions

and even more so, with the image of the man she'd encountered within the sacred circle of stones. She thought his face was the most handsome she'd ever seen, with strong, even features and a square jaw. His hair was blond and his skin tan, as if he spent a good deal of time in the sun. His eyes were as blue as the summer sky over Keinadraig. His speech had been odd, however. His words were English, but strangely accented.

Keely bit her lip, trying to stop these disturbing, runaway thoughts, but they kept racing ahead of her, bringing to mind the outline of his broad shoulders, the obvious strength in the arms that were bare below his short sleeves. He was, she admitted reluctantly, the kind of man she and Genevieve had always dreamed of meeting.

Someday.

In the world outside.

Returning to the beach down the same path that had led him to the standing stones, Jack considered the look on the young woman's face when she'd seen the sketch. Recognition had certainly registered there, alongside no small amount of fear. What was she afraid of? Why had she denied the dead woman was from here?

He hurried now, determined to get to the bottom of things quickly, as his presence was most likely known by now in the village. Cult or no cult, he must try to get answers to the questions that had brought him to this remote part of the world and let someone here know of the victim's death. Regardless that they did not like strangers, surely the people of the village would want to know what had happened to one of their own.

Jack reached the end of the beach and stopped to slip on his jacket again. He walked up the steps that led to the top of an old stone quay that protectively embraced one side of a tiny harbor. A twin quay faced it from the other side, leaving a narrow passageway between them, large enough for only small craft to navigate. Above the harbor was an open square, and beyond that, a typical Cornish village, so quaint it belonged on a postcard. Lining three cobblestone streets that led away from the square were sturdy stone houses, some of them whitewashed, with metal or slate roofs, narrow chimneys and tall windows to let in the fresh sea breezes. Surprisingly modern light fixtures ringed the square and the harbor. The square itself bloomed in a bright array of summer flowers.

The scene was perfect. Too perfect, in fact. Something was wrong with this picture. Then Jack realized there were no automobiles. Not a single car or truck anywhere to be seen. None needed, he supposed, in a tiny village on a remote island. The residents probably kept their cars on the mainland.

He walked along the quay until he reached the square, where he stopped to read something that was carved into the lintel of an ornamental gate:

> Away, hide away, on this distant shore,
> Let ne'er a stranger in thy door.
> Keep your secret safe, hidden in the mist,
> And let no one leave who be Dragon
>   kiss'd.

Let ne'er a stranger in thy door? There was no mistaking that message. But what about the rest of it? He'd been warned that the so-called Dragoners didn't welcome strangers, but clearly there was more to it than that. What secret did they keep hidden? And what did "Dragon kiss'd" mean?

Tearing his gaze from the ominous sign, Jack realized something else was wrong with the picture. There were no people in it. He became acutely and uncomfortably aware that he was the only person in sight, although he suspected he was being watched from behind the lace curtains of the houses on the square.

He considered what to do next. Normally, one of the

first places to look for information in any given town was the local bar. The watering hole was always the center of gossip. Except Jack didn't see any bar. He glanced up and down the streets, but there was not a single sign dangling from any of the buildings. No Cock and Bull, or The Queen's Head. In fact, he realized with a start, there did not appear to be any businesses. No bakery, no grocer, no newsstand or flower stall. Nothing.

Where did these people go for goods and supplies? He remembered Kevin Spearman telling him that the Dragoners came to Penzance to buy what they needed, but still, Jack would have expected some kind of enterprise among them.

Suddenly, he heard someone shout, "Halt there!" He looked up the hill. Coming toward him was a large, and from the look on his face, very angry man. Jack squinted in the bright sunlight, and a movement behind the man caught his eye. A figure emerged from a house further up the street, the figure of a woman with lush dark hair, wearing a familiar long dark skirt. His heart unexpectedly jumped in his chest. Then the figure disappeared again.

Jack waited at the corner for the man to reach him. He appeared to be in his late sixties. He was wearing a flat cap that covered all but a low ridge of curly white hair just above each ear. His nose was bulbous, his eyes a piercing steel gray. He wasn't smiling.

"Who goes there?"

Jack recognized the voice he had heard when he dialed the phone number he'd found in Brad's room. Bingo. The number written on the scrap of paper just became evidence. Eyeing the man steadily, he handed him a business card. "The name's Knight. Jackson Knight. I'm a private investigator."

The man's frown increased as he studied the card. Abruptly, he handed it back and glared at Jack. "What're y' here for?"

His unmistakable and unwarranted rancor suddenly

irritated Jack. "I'm here to find out who nearly killed my best friend."

From experience, Jack knew that blunt, startling statements such as this often produced surprising, telltale reactions before the questioned party had time to hide them. He was rewarded this time by a look of alarm that passed over the man's expression before being hidden behind an even more ferocious frown.

"No one's been kilt here."

"Not here. In London."

"Then why're ye here?"

Jack produced the paper bearing the phone number he had dialed. "Because this was in the hotel room where my friend was seriously wounded and another person was killed. I called this number, and it was answered by someone on this island. I think perhaps," he added slowly, "I spoke with you."

He saw the man blanch and knew he had indeed been the one who answered the phone and claimed it was a wrong number. But the man recovered quickly and growled, "Are ye with th' police?"

Jack hedged. "I'm working with Scotland Yard on the case." He stuffed the paper into his pocket again. He must get it safely back to Inspector Sandringham and hope he wasn't charged with withholding evidence.

"I still do na know why 'tis ye're here." The stocky man crossed his arms over his chest.

Jack gave him a measured stare, then took the sketch from the other pocket and handed it to him. "Because this is the other person who was shot in that room. I have reason to believe she was from your village."

The man stared at the drawing for a long time, then looked up at Jack, as if trying to decide something. His shoulders seemed to slump, and he returned the sketch. "Come along," he said at last in a heavy voice.

Wary that this might be a setup, Jack followed him up the street, where they entered a cottage that seemed as dark inside as the daylight outside was brilliant.

Jack's senses were keenly alert to possible danger, but when his eyes adjusted, there was no one in the room except the old man. Jack spotted an old-fashioned black telephone on a stand in the narrow hallway.

"That's th' phone," the man said wearily, as if admitting a crime. "'Tis th' office of th' Council. I'm Alyn Runyon, th' Keeper o' Keinadraig."

Jack wasn't certain what that meant, but he hoped that Keeper was a position like mayor of the village and not some kind of hatchetman for a cult. Either way, it appeared he'd found the man in charge. Now if he could only find out why the man had lied and claimed Jack had reached a wrong number.

The old man went into a room opposite the phone stand and turned on a lamp. "Here. Sit." He pointed to a high-backed chair, as if Jack were a trained dog. Jack clenched his jaw at the man's rude manner, but his anger was suddenly diffused when he caught a surprising look of sadness in his eyes. "Where did ye say that young girl was kilt?"

"You know her then?"

The old man sighed. "Aye. 'Tis Genevieve Sloan. She ran away na even a week ago."

"Why did you tell me I had reached a wrong number? Weren't you alarmed when I called? I mean, didn't it occur to you that she might have been the victim of the murder I referred to?"

The man raised his eyes, and Jack saw that they shone with unshed tears. "Aye. I knew 'twas her. But ye see, in Keinadraig, when one of our own chooses t' leave th' Dragon's back, as Genevieve did, she is considered dead t' th' rest of us. She betrayed her family and her village by leavin', and she'd not be welcomed here if she tried t' return. 'Tis th' law of Keinadraig. It matters not that she was murdered, for t' us, she was already as if dead."

Jack was both astounded and appalled. "It doesn't matter that she was murdered?"

"Nay, it does na."

Runyon offered no more, but Jack was far from finished with him. "Why did she run away? And who would have wanted to kill her?"

"She ran away because she was young and foolish." Runyon's voice took on a sharp edge. "She did na respect our laws. She thought she could escape, but th' Dragon's claw reaches far. No one leaves th' Dragon's back and lives t' tell about it. 'Twas th' Dragon that kilt her."

Jack wondered wildly for a moment if he had stumbled into some kind of time warp, if somehow he had been thrust back into a medieval society that practiced a particularly morbid form of dragon worship.

"What do you mean, 'the Dragon killed her?' "

"Being an outsider, I do na expect ye t' understand it," Runyon said confidentially, leaning toward him. "And ye may choose na t' believe it, but from th' time o' th' Dragon's singing, death has been th' fate o' those who tried t' leave Keinadraig. It comes in many ways—accidents, suicide, and now . . . even murder. Whatever form he chooses, th' Dragon exacts his revenge. Genevieve would have died, one way or th' other. Th' Dragon is a jealous beast, y'see, Mr. Knight, and bad things happen t' those who betray him."

Runyon's expression remained dead earnest, and he neither blinked nor looked away. Either the guy was a fearful, superstitious provincial who believed this line of bullshit or he was a very talented actor trying to cover his knowledge of the woman's death. Jack was not sure which.

"So that's why it doesn't matter that Genevieve Sloan was murdered," Jack repeated aloud, seeking to make sure he'd heard right. "She was going to die anyway, somehow."

"Aye."

"But her death wasn't really the fault of whoever shot her. Her death was caused by the will of this . . . Dragon."

Runyon hesitated, then repeated, "Aye."

"I see." Jack started to point out that Scotland Yard might have a different opinion, then gave up. He believed he'd learned all he was going to from this man. "Do you want me to ship her body here?"

The man who called himself the Keeper shook his head. "Nay. She is na of us any longer, living or dead. Do with her what ye will."

"Nay!"

Jack jumped at the sound of a woman's voice, and both men turned toward the hallway. The woman he'd encountered in the circle of stones was standing in the corridor, her face white against the profusion of her dark hair, her eyes wide with fury.

"Keely!" Alyn Runyon's tone bespoke his displeasure. "What are ye thinkin'? How long have ye been listenin' where ye should na be?"

"Ye can na do it, Uncle. Ye can na leave Genevieve out there. She belongs here, where she can be . . . where her body can be cleansed, and she can be honored as one of us."

Alyn Runyon stood and went to the woman, who was apparently his niece. Jack saw no sign that she was afraid of him. "Now, Keely, ye know th' law. 'Twas Genny's own fault for leavin'."

"Th' Dragon can keep his laws," she hissed. "Genevieve does na deserve this."

Before Jack knew what happened, Alyn Runyon backhanded the woman on the cheek. "Ye'll na speak of it again."

Jack jumped from his chair and inserted himself between Runyon and the woman. "Don't you touch her again," he ordered, his face hot and blood pounding heavily in his veins.

"Get out," Runyon growled. "Ye know nothin' of our affairs, and they are no business o' yours. Leave, before th' Dragon finds ye, too."

Jack turned to Keely and saw the astonishment in her

eyes at what had just happened. ''Are you all right, Miss? I won't leave . . .''

''Nay,'' she whispered, touching her cheek gingerly. ''He's right. Please leave.''

Runyon faced him with a scowl. '' 'Tis my job as Keeper t' make decisions for th' island. Do na return th' girl t' us. Now, I've cooperated with ye th' best I know how. Go now, and do na come back. I do na know who kilt Genevieve, and I do na want t' know. 'Tis a painful thing for us t' lose a young one. Leave us, and let us grieve in our own way.''

Jack looked at Keely, but her eyes were now unreadable.

''Go,'' she said, her voice scarcely above a whisper. ''Please, just go.''

FIVE

K eely looked at her uncle in dismay, shocked beyond words that he had struck her. Alyn Runyon had never touched anyone in violence. At least not that she knew of. Her mother's brother had always had a gentle nature.

Something was terribly wrong here.

"Why?" The single word caught in her throat.

Alyn's expression lost its fierceness as he turned from where he stood on the front steps watching the retreating figure of the stranger and went back inside the cottage. He gathered Keely into his arms and held her close. "I am sorry," he said. " 'Twas th' stranger. I did na mean t' . . ."

But Keely stiffened and pulled away, her cheek still stinging. "Alyn, what is wrong with ye? What is wrong with all of us? We are acting like we still live in th' ancient days." She saw her uncle's face harden once again.

"Ye be treadin' on dangerous sand, girl. 'Tis th' laws o' th' Dragon that have kept us safe since those ancient days, and all who wear the kiss o' th' Dragon must never forget it." He furrowed his brow and let his gaze bore into her. "All."

Her skin prickled at his admonition, and her fingers unconsciously touched the small mark on her neck. But she was filled with warring emotions. She understood

52   JILL JONES

the importance of honoring their timeless laws, but . . .
"What harm could there be in bringing Genny's body
home?" she cried, unable to stop herself.

"There is no Genny!" Alyn roared.

Keely stared at her uncle, stunned at what he was
implying. Alyn Runyon was choosing to believe not just
that Genevieve Sloan no longer existed, but rather that
she *never had* existed. This was taking the excommunication rite beyond the extreme, and she didn't understand why.

Sick at heart, Keely pushed past her uncle and dashed
into the street, making for her own cottage up the hill.
How could he? How could he hit her? And how could
he deny Genny's existence?

A cloud passed across the sun, sending a dark shadow
over the village, and the wind seemed suddenly chill.

Only a few customers were in the pub when she returned, most of whom had already helped themselves to
the sandwich supplies, drawn their own drinks, and laid
their money on the bar to pay for it. It was like that in
Keinadraig. There was no crime. No mistrust. Everyone
was like family and worked together for the common
good.

What common good came of denying one of their
own? Keely fumed to herself as she replenished the
sandwich plate and wiped furiously at the bar. What had
Genevieve ever done to deserve such ignominy?

An unwanted answer slapped her in the face as surely
as Alyn had physically done only minutes before. Genevieve had deserted these people who were like her
family, many of whom indeed were her family. In leaving, had not Genny denied her own?

Bewildered by this unwelcome thought, Keely went
into the kitchen at the back of the cottage and gazed out
the window. Genevieve would never have denied anyone, unless there had been good cause. What, she asked
herself again, had caused Genny to run?

And what had happened to her? All Keely knew was

that she had been murdered in London. How? And by whom?

Despair flooded her once again as she realized how vulnerable Genny had been. How vulnerable she would be out there. All that prating about making their way into the outside world had been the talk of foolish, unworldly girls. Neither of them had had any business daydreaming of running away to the big city. Look at what had happened to dear little Genny because they had. Choking on her grief, Keely tore off her apron and reached for her cloak from the peg by the door.

She could not stay here a minute longer. She felt frightened and suffocated, more miserable than she had ever believed possible. Somehow, someway, she had to make peace with all this if she was ever to get on with her own life.

And to make peace, she needed some answers.

At first she thought of going to Ninian's, in hopes of learning what had happened between mother and daughter that fateful night, but she guessed that Erica had already told Ninian about the stranger, and of Genevieve's fate. Keely wasn't up to facing that truth in the presence of Ninian, nor had she any wish to encounter Erica again so soon.

Her heart went out to Ninian, for the woman had suffered greatly since Genevieve's disappearance. Keely had never seen her so completely undone before. It occurred to her that Alyn, perhaps at the excommunication rite, must have insisted that all Dragoners, including Genny's own mother, disavow her very existence. No wonder Ninian had gone into virtual isolation. Didn't Alyn know that Genny's mother needed to grieve? That they all needed to grieve? But how could they grieve if they were to believe Genny had never existed?

Keely reached the gate to Ninian's garden and paused a moment, but turned away and proceeded on up the hill. Perhaps the only answers allowed to her at the moment were those she could find in her own heart. She would go to the stone circle and pray for the soul of Genevieve Sloan, whose existence Keely would never deny, no matter what. She would pray for the peace of mind she so desperately needed. Pray for clearer understanding of the ways of the Dragon and of her uncle, the Keeper of those ways. And finally, she would pray for forgiveness for having helped Genny leave instead of holding on to her for dear life and not allowing her to make such a terrible mistake.

When she reached the stones, however, Keely forgot about praying, at least for the moment, as her eyes caught sight of a lone figure walking along the beach, headed for the far end of the island.

The stranger.

She shivered and drew her cloak closer about her, recalling the old ballad verses that told of strangers who'd died for having broken the law by trespassing upon the isle of the Dragon. The sight of the man she knew only as Jack prompted Keely to again question the truth of the old stories. This stranger was leaving, and he was obviously in one piece. One solid, good-looking piece. He was not going to die for having come here, unless the Dragon were to follow him and finish him off elsewhere, as Alyn claimed had happened to Genevieve, a claim that sounded more like the perpetuation of a legend than an actual fact.

Just in case, however, Keely kept an eye on Jack from above once again, following his progress until she knew he was safely off the island. He had, after all, stepped between her and her uncle. It had been an unnecessary gesture, but he hadn't known that. He'd done it to protect her. Keely smiled wistfully.

She wished she had the nerve to speak with him. He had answers. He knew what had happened to Genny. Maybe he knew why she had run away. But Keely was afraid. It was best that he leave right away. He had stirred up more trouble in their already distraught village, and if she were honest, he'd brought with him more questions than answers. Dark questions that fermented in the depths of her heart, questions she didn't dare ask, for she feared they had answers she didn't want to hear.

Reaching the high promontory just above the place where the stranger had tied his boat, Keely peered over the edge to catch one last glimpse of him. For a moment, sunlight pierced the gathering clouds, shining upon him in golden rays, illuminating the strength of his body and stirring other, even more deeply disturbing feelings in Keely.

She saw him stop walking, place a hand on his hip, and run the fingers of the other hand through his hair, as if perplexed.

Only then did she realize his boat was not there.

Where the hell was the boat? Jack stared at the rock where he'd so securely tied it. Surely it wouldn't have come loose of its own accord. Somebody must have deliberately set it adrift. But when he checked for footprints in the sand, all he saw were his own. He must not have tied it as tightly as he thought.

His first question—how could he have been so stupid?—was quickly replaced with a second: what was he going to do now? He didn't relish going back to the village, where he was clearly unwanted, although he would have liked to have a chance to make sure the young woman was all right. But Jack had no doubt that it was his presence that had provoked the incident, and he did not want to cause her further trouble.

He scanned the horizon but saw no sign of the small boat. Overhead, clouds were beginning to gather. Maybe he'd better take his chances and seek help in the village. A squall was brewing, and he didn't want to be stuck on the beach in a storm. Besides, he was anxious to give Garrison a call soon to check on Brad.

A call.

Jack grinned, remembering what he had in his pocket. Hope returned as his fingers closed around the cool plastic of the cellular phone. He had a card from the boat rental service, and luckily, there was a surprisingly strong cell signal. He dialed the number. Kevin Spearman was not happy when he learned that Jack had misplaced his boat, but he agreed to come for him, mainly, Jack suspected, because he had assured the man he would buy him a new boat. "It'll be about three quarters of an hour," Spearman told him. "I have some other business to attend to before I can leave."

Jack ended the call, noting the battery on the phone was running low. He kicked himself for his stupidity in not sufficiently securing the boat, but he was glad that Garrison Holstedt was a rich man.

A large drop of rain splashed against his cheek, and Jack looked up at the blustery sky. Several more cold drops assaulted him. He had no wish to wait in a rainstorm for forty-five minutes. He glanced at the gaping black holes sculpted into the cliffs. He wasn't fond of caves, but shelter from the cold drops in the nearby grotto appeared to be his only option if he wished to escape the storm. He quickly covered the short distance to the largest opening and ducked inside.

The walls were cold and damp, the back of the cave obscured in the darkness that swallowed the daylight only a few feet from the entrance. The pungent, salty smell of the sea, ripe with the stench of mud at low tide, assailed his nostrils. The place gave Jack the creeps.

Suddenly from somewhere beyond the darkness came the sound of singing. The tune was faint at first, and Jack thought he must be hearing things. Then he heard it again, this time louder. The woman's voice was clear, high and thin, the song plaintive and repetitive, although he couldn't make out the words. The tune, however, reminded him of an old Joan Baez song his mother used to listen to on the record player when he was a little boy.

Curious, Jack got over his aversion to the cave and moved a few feet inside, feeling his way along the damp wall, following the sound. Still he could not make out the words, so he proceeded on, as if mesmerized by a siren.

The singing grew louder, and at last he was able to discern the words:

> *Away, hide away, on this distant shore,*
> *Let ne'er a stranger in thy door.*
> *Keep your secret safe, hidden in the mist,*
> *And let no one leave who be Dragon*
>   *kiss'd.*

He froze and felt a shudder pass over him as he recognized the words he'd read on the village gate. Other words echoed in his mind.

Bad things happen to those who betray the Dragon.

Did that include strangers who came to the island uninvited?

'Twas th' Dragon that kilt her.

Jack laughed at his misgivings. Maybe the islanders took this Dragon thing seriously, but he knew it was nonsense.

Then suddenly, Jack considered his present predicament and became even more uneasy, not because he thought a dragon was after him, but because he was such a damned fool. He'd allowed his boat to drift away, stranding him on an island with residents who were clearly hostile to strangers. He'd wandered deep into this pitch-black cave until he feared he might be lost. And he was allowing himself to be unnerved by the Dragoners' ridiculous superstitions.

"Get a grip," he said aloud and turned to feel his way back out of the cave. Suddenly, something shoved him violently from behind, slamming him against the rock wall. A sharp pain seared his head just before an even darker blackness enveloped him and he crumpled to the floor of the cave.

*   *   *

Keely stifled a cry when she saw the stranger go into the caves. She guessed he was seeking shelter from the approaching storm, but he was seriously trespassing when he entered the most forbidden of all places on the island. Only the Keeper was allowed into the heart of the Dragon, and then only to commend the bodies of the dead to the purification fires.

Her first instinct was to call out and warn him to stay away, but she doubted he could hear her from this far above. She also didn't want to take a chance that someone else would hear her, although with the change in weather, she doubted any of the villagers would be about. She could go to the caves herself and fetch him away, but she was loath to break the law and trespass herself where she had never been in her life.

So she held her vigil, ignoring the approaching storm, watching, waiting for Jack to emerge from the caves. Why was she concerning herself so with the stranger? she wondered. She owed him nothing. And he'd caused nothing but problems for her.

But Keely knew the answer. She wanted to make certain that he left the island alive and well, which would prove the old tales were just that—tales—and that strangers did not necessarily die for intruding upon the Dragon's back. In her mind, she knew the Dragon was only mythological, an ancient Celtic symbol adopted by her ancestors as a sign of protection. But she had believed the old legends and honored the laws of Keinadraig for so long, it was not easy to get past them, even with rational thinking.

Alyn wasn't helping either. Keely was disturbed that her uncle seemed to be trying to breathe life into the symbol by insisting that the Dragon had killed Genevieve, as if the Dragon were real. Mayhap, Keely thought sadly, like her, he was desperately trying to find something to blame for Genevieve's senseless death. She softened. She knew Alyn was grieving, too, in his own way.

She couldn't blame him for making up a fiction to help him deal with the horrible truth.

The storm resulted in some gusty winds and a few large, cold pellets of rain that dashed from the clouds above, but it blew over quickly, leaving a patchy sky and an unsettled sea. Keely hugged her cloak closer to her in the wind and grew more apprehensive as each moment passed and the stranger did not emerge from the cave. Just as she had decided to climb down and go to the caves after him, she heard the sound of a small craft approaching. The boat appeared to be nearly identical to the one that had brought the stranger to their shore. The figure at the helm looked vaguely familiar, but it was hard to tell from a distance if it was someone she knew. Whoever it was must have come for the stranger.

The man beached the craft, but he did not get out. Keely saw him put his hand to his mouth and heard a distant "Hallooo." But there was no sign of the stranger, and after only five minutes or so, the boatman backed away from the beach and turned the craft toward the mainland.

Now Keely became seriously worried. Something had happened in that cave. The man had become lost . . . or . . .

She wouldn't allow herself to believe the Dragon had attacked him. That was daft thinking. But even so, her apprehension turned to fear for his safety. She must go to him.

Racing down the hill, she returned to her cottage and fetched a kerosene lantern. She knew Alyn would be furious if he found out she'd helped the stranger, but she must. For daft thinking or not, at the back of her mind, the old legends screamed at her.

Pocketing some matches to light the lantern, Keely hurried back up the hill, through the grove, past the circle of stones until she reached the path that led to the beach. Her heart thundered. She'd never done anything so bold. She'd always been the good girl, never thinking to question her elders or break the rules. She had always done as she was bidden. She shook to think that now she was doing as she was expressly *for*bidden.

Keely's steps faltered as she reached the mouth of the caves. The sacred and prohibited heart of the Dragon loomed dark and menacing before her, as if the Dragon waited there to consume in a fiery breath those who dared enter his chamber.

"Jack?" Her voice sounded weak in her own ears. "Jack, are ye in there?"

The only reply was the sound of the seabirds calling in the wind. Gathering her skirts, she went to the largest opening in the cliff's face and called again.

Again, no answer.

"Dear God," she prayed, "let him be whole." With that, she knelt and lit the lantern, then stepped inside. By the flickering light, she saw that she stood in a large, open cavern with a hard floor covered with sand and a high ceiling. There was no sign of the stranger. Or the Dragon.

On the far wall, she spied two small openings that appeared almost like tunnels. Did she dare go further? Her heartbeat was erratic and her breath came in short gasps. Where was the stranger? Keely crept toward the passageway to her left, as it was closest, and followed it for a short distance, until it became alarmingly steep and narrow. From below, she could hear the crash of the waves. She surmised it must lead to the water. "Jack?" she called again tentatively, but the only reply was the sound of the sea.

Returning to the main chamber, she held the lantern high and proceeded through the right-hand tunnel. It was larger, with more level ground, and moments later Keely found herself in another open cavern, even more spacious than the one she'd first entered. She paused and looked around, noting what appeared to be smoke stains at intervals on the walls, as if huge torches had burned

there at one time. She even thought she detected the faint
odor of old smoke. Then her gaze traveled over the floor
of the cavern, and she screamed when she saw the body
of the stranger sprawled there.

"Jack! Oh, by the Saints!" She ran to him and knelt
beside him, her terror subsiding somewhat when she detected a pulse and felt the warmth of his skin. But then
another scream escaped her when she saw what lay beyond him in the shadows. Not three feet from where
he'd fallen yawned a huge hole in the cavern floor. She
scrambled on hands and knees to the edge and peered
into the black pit, but she could not see the bottom.

Quaking, she backed away. It must be, it had to be,
the abyss known as the heart of the Dragon. The pit into
which the bodies of the dead were consigned to be purified by the sacred fires.

If Jack had gone only a few feet further, he would
have fallen to his death. There were no fires there now,
but from what Keely knew of the Dragon's heart, the
chasm was deep, and there was no way out.

Why on earth had the stranger wandered this far into
the cave? He had no light to show the way. Keely
glanced nervously over her shoulder, half expecting the
Dragon to appear in the flickering lamplight.

"Jack, wake up!" Keely whispered and shook his
inert body. "We must get away from here. Jack!"

To her enormous relief, the man stirred and raised up
on one elbow. "What? Where am I?"

"Ye've wandered into th' sacred caves. We must
leave here at once. Are ye fit?"

He touched his head and moved his shoulders, emit-
ting a low groan. Then he sat up and turned to her, his
face twisted in anger.

"What the hell is going on here?"

SIX

Jack thought he must be dreaming when he heard a woman's voice calling his name. He followed the sound out of the darkness and regained consciousness, although he felt as if someone were at work with a jackhammer inside his head. He leaned on one elbow and gingerly examined the welt on his skull while trying to orient himself. He was somewhere that smelled dank and slightly smoky. Somewhere dark and chill. And then it came rushing back. He was in a cave. He'd followed the sound of someone singing, and that someone had obviously coldcocked him in the dark.

Then he became aware of the woman who knelt next to him, her eyes anxiously searching his face. "Are ye fit?" he heard her ask.

No, he wasn't exactly fit. His head hurt like the very devil. But he didn't think he was seriously injured. He glared at the woman. "What the hell is going on here?"

"We must get out o' here, Jack," she said urgently, standing and taking his hand. "Can ye walk?"

Jack got to his feet, still not sure if he could trust the woman. But he was puzzled. If she'd been his assailant, why was she now trying to save him? Or was she just leading him into more danger? He jerked his hand away.

"I heard singing," he said. "I followed the sound of singing in here. Were you the one singing?" he demanded.

"Singing?" A look of genuine surprise lit her face, followed by equally genuine alarm. "God in heaven! We must flee this place," she said. "Now! Come. Follow me."

Before he could catch her, she dashed ahead of him, and since she had the lantern, he had no choice but to follow or be left again in the dark. But Jack wasn't through with her.

He wanted some answers about this damned strange place.

Outside, the fresh air cleared his mind, and he remembered he'd been waiting for the boat rental operator to come pick him up. Glancing at his watch, he saw that it was well past the time he'd expected his ride. "Damn." Now how was he supposed to get off this godforsaken island? Looking ahead, he saw that the woman was sprinting down the beach, running away from him. "Oh, no you don't," he said. "You cost me my ride home. You'll find me another."

He followed her at a run, overtaking her a few moments later. Catching her by the shoulder, he wheeled her around to face him. "Stop!" he called roughly. "Where the hell do you think you're going?"

"Let me go."

Jack took her by both shoulders. "Not until you explain some things to me. Like who untied my boat. And who knocked me on the head in the cave."

Her face was as white as tombstone marble, and she trembled in his hands like a frightened doe. He eased his grip but didn't let her go. "Why are you so afraid? I won't hurt you."

She jerked free and glanced nervously around. "We can na talk here."

"Why not?"

"Someone . . . might see."

"Who?" Jack asked cynically. "The Dragon?"

At that, her eyes widened even further, and their stormy green depths flashed with anger. "Ye have no idea what ye've done in trespassing on Keinadraig.''

"England's a free country."

" 'Tis privately owned, this island.''

Jack hadn't considered that possibility. Sandringham had told him not to break any laws. Had he done so by coming here? "What's the deal with this place?"

She looked perplexed. "Deal?"

Since his first encounter with this woman beside the standing stones, she'd seemed innocent, peculiarly unworldly. The entire island of Keinadraig, in fact, seemed like an anachronism, a place lost in another age. The village looked like an illustration in some old fairy-tale book. The people spoke in an archaic manner. Even their clothing, like the cloak she wore, was somehow . . . unmodern. Jack realized with a start that Keely didn't understand the expression "what's the deal?"

He rephrased the question. "I mean, why all the secrecy? Why aren't strangers allowed here?"

The woman stared up at him for a long moment, the features of her fair, lovely face so distressed it nearly broke his heart. " 'Tis . . .'tis dangerous t' talk here,'' she insisted once again, beckoning him with slender fingers. "Come with me."

He followed her along the beach and up the path he'd taken earlier to reach the standing stones. But instead of leading him there, she took him down the hill until they came to the cover of a large grove of trees. Once beneath the summer-rich canopy of leaves, daylight became dusk. The woman looked furtively around her, then again indicated for him to follow her. She led him behind some large boulders that hid them from all but the sea. She extinguished the flame in the old-fashioned kerosene lantern she'd been carrying and nestled it into a safe spot. Only then did she turn to him.

Her face was ashen, and Jack could see that she quaked with fear. "What's wrong?" he asked, wanting to touch her in reassurance, but not daring. "There's no need to be afraid."

"Aye, but there is."

The wind tossed the hood of her dark cape away from
her face, releasing the fragrant abundance of her thick
black hair. It played in the breeze, caressing her face,
teasing Jack, taunting him in unexpected ways until, unable to resist, he reached out and brought a tendril under
control, tucking it behind her ear. His fingertips seemed
to burn where they touched her skin. "Don't be afraid
of me," he murmured again, thinking perhaps she ought
to be. "I won't hurt you."

" 'Tis na o' ye that I'm afraid."

"Then what?"

She avoided the question, and his eyes. "Ye do na
know our ways. Strangers are strictly forbidden here."

"You're afraid of your uncle."

" 'Tis more than that. Our legends tell o' strangers
who died for trespassing . . ." Her voice trailed off, and
Jack wondered if her words were a warning or a threat.

"What else do your legends tell you?"

"That . . . that bad things happen t' those who leave
Keinadraig."

"Like what happened to your friend Genevieve?"

At the stricken look on her face, Jack almost wished
he hadn't brought it up. But it was the reason he was
here. He wanted some answers, and this was the person
who might give them to him. Still, his heart went out to
her, for her ambivalence was clear.

The woman nodded, her eyes misting with tears.
"Mr. . . . uh . . . Jack, please. Can ye tell me what . . .
what happened t' Genny?"

Keely fought the sickening fear that threatened to overwhelm her. She fought the idea that the stranger's life
had been endangered by the Dragon. It was impossible.
Those were old legends, nothing more. He could not
have heard singing in the cave. No one went there, certainly no woman. He must have imagined it. Maybe he'd
heard the sound of the wind whistling through the rock

formations and been lured deep within the cave, where he'd nearly fallen to his death in the pit. He'd said he'd been attacked, but he could have just lost his footing and hit his head on the stone wall of the cavern.

There were reasonable explanations for what had happened to him. For everything that had happened in the past few days.

Still, Keely was afraid. She was afraid for him, and afraid for herself. She would pay dearly for these stolen moments with him if anyone found out, but once she'd spoken with him, she knew she had to ask him the one question that burned above all others. "What happened to Genny?"

She sank onto the stone seat where the sun had warmed her earlier in the day, as if its strength might protect her. Jack sat beside her. Keely was not afraid of him. He'd promised repeatedly that he wouldn't hurt her, and there was an unexpected tenderness in his touch when he tucked a strand of her hair behind her ear. She was relieved that he was no longer angry, for he was a large man, and she would be helpless against him. No, she was not afraid of the stranger even though she was afraid *for* him.

"What do you want to know?" His voice was deep, and its rich resonance sent a strange sensation racing through her. Keely had never been alone with a man like this before. She struggled to keep her focus.

"I want t' know everything that happened t' Genny."

"Why don't we start from the beginning? When she left. Did you know she was going to run away?"

Shame burned her cheeks. Did she dare reveal the truth to the stranger? Would he tell Alyn? Her uncle would likely find out sooner or later anyway. "Aye," she replied with a small squeak. "She came t' me th' night she left. I . . . I helped her leave."

"Why did she run, Keely?"

It was so odd, sitting here with a stranger, listening to him call her name as if they were old friends. But he was asking all the questions, while it was she who desperately needed answers.

"Who are ye?" she demanded suddenly. "Why are ye asking all these questions? Are ye a policeman?"

"No. I'm a private investigator, but I'm trying to help Scotland Yard find out who killed Genevieve."

"But why?"

He was quiet for a long moment before he answered her. She glanced up at his face and saw a curious sadness creep into his eyes. When he spoke, his voice was strained. "Because the man who was in the hotel room with her at the time of her murder, the man who also almost died and who is suspected of killing her, is my best friend."

Keely sat in stunned silence, digesting this. His best friend? He'd nearly lost his best friend, too? Had his best friend killed her best friend?

"Did he?" She blurted out her question, not meaning to be so blunt.

"What?"

"Kill her?"

The sadness in his face gave way to a stormy look. "Good God, no! Somebody, whoever did it, staged it to make it look like he shot her and then turned the gun on himself."

"Shot!" Of course, Keely knew about guns, but the only one she'd ever seen was the pistol Alyn kept in the Council office. She did not know why he even had it. There was no need for guns on Keinadraig. "By the Saints," she uttered, feeling light-headed.

Jack took her hand in his, and she did not pull it away. She clung to its warmth and strength, needing something to hold onto lest she fall off the world. She listened in horror as he told her briefly how Genevieve had died. Her throat tightened when he said, "I believe she was killed instantly, Keely. I don't think she suffered."

As if that could ease the obscenity of it all.

Keely's already tormented heart ripped painfully in her breast. Breath left her and would not return. The world spun, sickening her. "Genny," she moaned, leaning over and clutching her arms. "Dear God! Poor, poor Genny." Hot tears flooded her eyes, tears she had no will or wish to stem. She hurt in every inch of her being, and only tears seemed to numb the pain.

Giving in to her grief, she allowed the tears to flow. Sobs wracked her whole body, debilitating her, and she did not resist when she felt the arms of the stranger enfold her. Without thought, she leaned against him, allowing his quiet strength to comfort her.

At last the emotional storm subsided, and Keely managed to regain at least some part of her senses. Reluctantly, she drew away from Jack with a strangled sob, knowing her behavior was improper, but instantly missing his embrace. "I am sorry," she began, feeling fire in her cheeks. "I did na mean t' . . ."

Looking up, she was shocked to see tears in his eyes as well. And she realized humbly she was not the only one who had suffered a terrible loss. She searched for words and found only a simple statement of consolation. "I am glad your friend did na die." Meant to comfort, her words seemed instead to sharpen his pain. His face hardened.

"No, he didn't die. Not yet. But he's seriously injured. He's . . . not expected to live."

She did not know what else to say except, "I am sorry."

They sat very still for a long time, side by side in the protection of the boulders that shielded them from the world. Keely's mind kept returning to the scene of the killing Jack had described, trying to grasp the impossible image of Genny in a hotel room with a strange man.

At last, she spoke. "Your friend, Brad. What is he like?"

"Brad . . ." The name seemed to catch in Jack's throat. "He was . . . is . . . one hell of a great guy. Except for the outcome, Genevieve was lucky to have known him.'' Touching her chin, he gently turned her face to his. "How did she know him, Keely?"

Keely shook her head. "She did na know him. She did na know anybody on th' outside. She was na running *to* anyone. Certainly na a lover. I think she was running *from* . . ." She broke off, not knowing how to finish her sentence.

"From what? Keely, look, I know this is hard, but if we only knew why she left, maybe we could figure out why she died. And find the killer."

Keely shrugged, helpless and miserable. She was not comfortable telling an outsider that she suspected Genny and Ninian might have had cross words the night Genny left. She did not know it for certain, and besides, she did not think it mattered. For whatever reason, Genny had run away. The Dragon legend aside, the fate she'd met had nothing to do with why she'd left.

"I do na know what she was running from. Mayhap she was na running from anything other than this village. She . . . she'd always been a dreamer, y'see." Keely sniffled and wiped a stray tear with the back of her hand. She felt a faint smile tremble across her lips as she recalled the sunny, carefree girl Genevieve had been. "She and I, well, we sometimes took fish t' th' market in Penzance, and we'd dream about one day leaving Keinadraig and going t' live in th' exciting big city. Until we returned, that is. Genny's mother, Ninian, made sure those notions were banished th' moment we got home. She'd remind us o' th' kiss o' th' Dragon, and our duty t' Keinadraig."

"The kiss of the Dragon? What is that?"

Keely hesitated. She was telling this stranger far too much. "'Tis . . .'tis nothing," she faltered, unconsciously fingering the mark on her neck. "Just another of our ways." Why was she still the one doing all the talking? She changed the subject. "Where is Genny now? Her body, I mean?"

"It's in a place called a morgue, a place where they preserve . . . the dead, until they can find relatives to assume custody and give the person a proper burial."

"Genny will have naught . . ."

"Are you related to her?" Jack brushed her cheek gently, and his touch raised the soft hair on her arms.

Alarmed, she shifted away from him and replied, "I am a cousin, but . . . I can na go t' her. I can na leave th' island." A sudden thought struck her. "But maybe ye . . . could see t' it she goes t' God proper."

"It's not that simple, I'm afraid. For one thing, I'm also a suspect in her murder."

Keely stared at him. "What?"

"That night at the hotel, I heard someone screaming and went to see what was happening. The chambermaid ran out of the room where the crime took place, and I went in. I was the one the police found . . . standing over Genny's body." He slumped back against the rock and massaged the bridge of his nose with his thumb and forefinger.

Keely had never been into a hotel, so it was hard for her to visualize the scene he described, but she could not believe Jack had killed Genny. He was grieving as deeply as she was, and she felt as sorry for his loss as she did for her own. And coming upon the victims must have been a terrible shock.

"What will happen t' her body if no one comes t' claim it?" she asked, forcing her thoughts back to the problem of Genny's final rites.

"They will eventually bury her in a public cemetery, I guess."

"Oh, she mustn't be buried," Keely declared before thinking. "Her body must be burned so it will be purified, according t' . . ." Keely stopped herself in mid-sentence. What was she thinking? She had no business telling this stranger anything of the ways of the Dragoners. "Never ye mind. 'Tis . . .'tis beyond me now." But she wished with every ounce of her soul that there was some way she could insure that Genny's spirit would be released according to their custom.

She felt Jack take her hand again, and her heart began to beat like a thousand drums. His touch awakened feelings within her she had never before experienced, sensations both pleasant and frightening. She ought not to be here, alone with him. He was an outsider, and although she fought the idea, it was possible that he was in grave danger for lingering on the island.

But oddly, being with him felt strangely right in her heart. She treasured this moment, for it was the stranger, not her own people, who seemed to understand her pain. She perceived his pain as well. Sadly, theirs was a bond of mutual grief. She wished they could work through it together, but that was impossible. She must send him away . . . soon.

"Come with me to London," he said, interrupting her melancholy thoughts.

At first, Keely thought she'd misheard him, but he continued, and she knew she had not.

"I'll take you there and bring you safely home again. You can take care of arranging for Genevieve's . . . ceremony yourself."

For one moment, Keely actually considered it. For a single fraction of a second her conscience told her that it was the most loving thing she could do for the soul of her friend and kinswoman.

And then she remembered who she was. And from where.

"Nay."

"Why not? Are you afraid?"

"Nay." Her voice quavered in her not-quite-honest reply.

"Are you afraid that if you left, your uncle would not allow you to return?"

How did this man know what was in her heart? "Nay," she protested again, but suddenly her courage deserted her in the face of the truth. "I mean, aye. 'Tis the law o' th' Dragon. If I were t' leave, I . . . I could never return.''

''Do you believe in the Dragon, Keely?''

''O' course na,'' she snapped, then stopped short. She'd been telling herself ever since Genny's disappearance that she did not believe in the Dragon other than as a symbol of the fierce independence of the people of Keinadraig. Nor did she believe in the old legends. And yet Genny lay dead. Brutally murdered.

. . . *Let no one leave who be Dragon kiss'd.*

SEVEN

Garrison Holstedt sat in an uncomfortable steel chair in Inspector Sandringham's spartan office, staring at the tiny pistol the police officer displayed from its protective container. It was the size of a derringer, the dull gray metal ornately engraved.

"We had Jeremy Ryder, an expert on valuable antiques, take a look at it," Sandringham said. "He identified it as one of a set of four made in France nearly two hundred years ago for the sons of a Scottish nobleman. The other three are in museums or private collections. The fourth," he waved the evidence bag, "was stolen from the home of a member of Parliament nearly a decade ago, along with other valuable art and antiques."

Garrison peered at the gun. Such an unlikely murder weapon. So small, so old, yet so deadly. Unique in design, it had two barrels and two triggers. All the killer needed, he thought grimly.

"Any idea where your son might have come by this gun?" The inspector's voice was neutral, but Garrison wanted to reach across the desk and punch him.

"You know damn well that Brad never 'came by' that gun until the shooter put it in his hand. First, he hates guns. Secondly, even if he'd wanted to bring in a weapon from the States, it wouldn't have passed through airport security. And as Jack told you, Brad was left-handed. He couldn't have shot himself in the right temple.''

''Forensics found gunpowder on the skin of his right hand.''

Garrison's own skin turned cold. ''What? That's impossible. Brad's still in the hospital. When would forensics . . . ?''

Sandringham gave him a patient smile along with an enigmatic answer. ''We are a very efficient outfit, Mr. Holstedt.''

Garrison wished Jack were here. This was not good.

''That still does not mean he killed the girl and then shot himself,'' Garrison argued. ''I mean, where's the motive? Why would my son, who had so much going for him, become involved in some sordid . . .'' His voice faltered.

Sandringham shrugged. ''Maybe it was a crime of passion. Or maybe your son had a secret you didn't know. Maybe the woman was blackmailing him or something. We don't have all the answers. But we do know that he was shot at close range. There was gunpowder on his hand, so the wound could have been self-inflicted. Of course, his prints are on the weapon. The bullet found in the girl's body matches the one removed from your son's skull. Both entrance wounds are the same size. Now, if it wasn't murder and attempted suicide, then what other explanation could there be? Do you know of anyone who might be better off with your son dead?''

''Of course not.'' Garrison was put off by the man's implication that the murderer could be someone other than some London lowlife. Who could he be talking about?

''When I arrived on the scene, I found Mr. Jackson Knight standing over the dead woman's body,'' the inspector droned on. ''He claims to be a friend of your family. Is this true?''

Jack. A dark thought caught Garrison unaware. Jack

stood to gain if Brad met with some fatal misfortune. After Garrison's wife had died, he had decided to add Jack to his will as a secondary beneficiary, for if Brad predeceased Garrison, there would be no one to inherit the Holstedt empire. He had told Brad at the time, and his son agreed it was a sound move. But neither had told Jack, knowing his dislike for favors. Had Brad changed his mind and let Jack know? But even if he knew, Jack would never . . .

"Jack Knight is a longtime family friend," he answered Sandringham at last. "He's . . . like another son. He came here with Brad to help put a deal together."

"Mr. Knight would have no motive, then?"

Garrison hesitated a moment too long before he replied emphatically, "No." He saw the inspector make a note on the pad in front of him.

"He had the opportunity, being on the same floor in the hotel. The maid found the bodies, but Mr. Knight was on the scene in surprisingly short order." Sandringham paused, then raised a bushy brow. "Do you think he would have had the means?"

"Means?"

"Could he have had access to the murder weapon?"

Garrison's pulse began to pound heavily, and he didn't know how to reply. Jack had been a cop. Jack knew the shady side of life. Did Jack have connections here in England? Could he have obtained the gun from some underworld source? It seemed preposterous. It made no sense to think that Jack would have tried to kill Brad. The two were firm friends, closer than blood brothers.

But then, nothing about the tragedy made any sense.

Garrison sagged in the chair, wishing to God Jack hadn't taken off on that wild goose chase down to Cornwall. He suddenly wanted to grill Jack himself, to prove to himself that the doubts this policeman was planting in his mind were groundless.

"If you're asking if Jack owned this gun," Garrison

said at last, "the answer is no. At least, I don't think
so."

The rays of the sun setting in the west reflected in shades
of rose and orange and purple on the clouds piled high
in the east. Jack, still sequestered behind the boulders in
the grove, wished he could appreciate the splendor, but
his nerves were taut and his patience nearly exhausted.

Before taking her leave, Keely had insisted he remain
hidden until dark, when she would help him escape the
same way she had helped Genny, by "borrowing" a
boat from the harbor. "I'll come for ye as soon as I can
after dark."

She had assured him she was safe with her uncle, as
long as Alyn Runyon did not suspect Jack was still on
the island and that Keely had talked to him. "He's never
hit me before. He is a good man, and he suffers th' same
sorrows as I, but because he must enforce th' law, he
can na let his real feelings show."

Jack wasn't so sure, either that Runyon was the good
man his niece thought him to be, or that she was safe
from his wrath. He'd seen the enraged expression on the
Keeper's face. It was the look of a domineering father
whose child had dared contradict him. Or a cult leader
when a member questioned his authority.

Of one thing he was certain, however. If Runyon suspected Keely was helping Jack, she would catch hell.
For that reason, and the fact that his cell phone was dead
and he couldn't contact Kevin Spearman again for rescue, he'd agreed to remain in hiding until dark. He just
hadn't counted on dark taking so long to arrive. It was
mid-June, just past the longest day of the year. It was
nine-thirty and not fully dark.

While he waited, he paced and tried to create in his
mind some scenario that would explain how Genevieve
Sloan met Brad Holstedt. But there still wasn't enough
to go on. The SWAG that had brought him to Cornwall,
to this odd little island of Keinadraig, had paid off in

that he'd learned the identity of the dead girl and some of her background.

But the answers stopped there.

Keely claimed not to know why Genevieve Sloan had run away from the island, and Jack did not think she was hiding anything from him. She seemed simply too ingenuous to lie.

Jack suspected that Alyn Runyon knew why the girl had left, and that the reason was deeper than a lack of respect for their laws. But having witnessed Runyon's earlier rough treatment of Keely, Jack thought it best not to press him, at least not at the moment. He had to remind himself he was an outsider in this investigation, and a foreigner at that. He did not want to antagonize Scotland Yard. He would go through channels.

If that didn't work, he would take matters into his own hands.

One way or another, he *would* get the answers he sought.

Darkness fell at last, and Jack waited anxiously for Keely to return. Thirty minutes passed. Forty-five. An hour. It was nearing midnight. Jack grew alarmed. Something had happened to her. His mind was overrun with all kinds of dire possibilities, most of which involved some kind of punishment from her uncle, who somehow must have found out she'd spoken with him.

Just when he thought he could take the waiting no longer, he heard the crunch of a footstep on the other side of the screen of boulders. He ducked and held very still, hoping it was Keely, but half expecting some kind of vigilante posse of Dragoners come to drag him to an unknown-but-not-very-nice fate.

"Jack?" Keely's voice whispered on the night breeze.

Jack's heart leapt. "Here. I'm still here."

And then she was beside him, her eyes shining, her breathing uneven. Neither spoke. Jack could feel his heartbeat thundering in his chest and knew it was not from anxiety. She was the cause. A woman he barely knew and yet wanted desperately to take into his arms. Striving for control, he held out his hand instead, and she took it, her gaze never leaving his. What was she feeling? he wondered. Her eyes were wide but unreadable. Was she afraid? Had she decided to come with him after all? He felt her tremble, and she seemed as fragile as china, as vulnerable as a child. He was consumed by an overwhelming urge to protect her, from her uncle, from her fear, from the ugly crime that had taken place.

His control slipping a notch, he drew her toward him, slowly so as not to alarm her. She came willingly, until they were so close he could smell the lavender scent of her hair, the honey sweetness of her breath. When he dared to touch her hair, he saw her eyes close and felt her shiver slightly.

"Keely?"

She opened her eyes again. "Ye must leave."

"Come with me."

"I can na."

"I'll keep you safe. I won't harm you."

She shook her head, releasing a tear that fell across her cheek. "Nay, Jack. Do na tempt me."

But it was Jack who was tempted. He had never met a woman like Keely Cochrane, who lit within him fires of both sweet desire and fierce protection. He did not want her to remain on this island, to live in a backward world driven by superstition and fear.

He knew she was afraid to leave, however; afraid she would meet the same fate as Genny. Her fear was unwarranted, but he didn't know how to convince her that Genny's death had nothing to do with the so-called Dragon. That it had not been punishment for running away from the island. Genevieve Sloan, Jack fully believed, was simply at the wrong place at the wrong time.

But until he found out what had really happened, who had wanted Brad dead, he had nothing with which to assure her.

"Will you be all right, Keely? I mean, your uncle . . ."

"I can handle my uncle. But ye must go, and do na come again. *Ye* do na believe in th' Dragon lore, but . . ."

Jack heard the fear in her voice. She was afraid that if he came back, something bad might happen to him.

Our legends tell of strangers who died for trespassing . . .

He could not promise her he would not return. It was highly likely that he would, and that he'd bring the police with him. Unless Inspector Sandringham had come up with the killer, he would want to interrogate both Runyon and Genny's mother. He'd probably want to talk to Keely as well.

Jack wished he could protect her from all that. But now that he knew Genny's identity, he would have to report it, and that would set the rest in motion.

"I'm not afraid, Keely. Except for you. Here . . ." He dropped her hand and reached for a business card and a ballpoint pen. On the back of the card, he hastily scribbled the number to his cellular phone. "You should be able to reach me anytime, day or night. Just dial this number." Then he remembered that the only phone in town was in Alyn Runyon's office. "Just be careful . . ."

Before he knew what he was doing, he put his arms around her, drawing her close against him, willing her to change her mind and come with him. Feeling the softness of her body as she leaned into him, Jack realized suddenly that he *was* afraid. Afraid for her, and afraid to leave her. He knew it made no sense. He had just met her, spoken with her only briefly. But there it was. He tried to blame his protective feelings on his background as a cop, but deep inside he knew there was more to it than that. And he knew, regretfully, that there was little he could do about those feelings unless she chose to come with him. Which she didn't. He kissed her hair lightly.

"Please, please be careful, Keely."

*   *   *

Keely pointed Jack in the direction of the lights of Penzance but did not remain on the quay to watch him row out into the night. Hurrying along the deserted lanes, she returned to her cottage, creeping through the midnight shadows the same as she'd done the night she'd helped Genevieve leave the island. That night, she'd been filled with fear for her friend. Tonight, it was Jack's safety she worried about.

Although he had not died in the cave, he'd had a brush with death, and she was not sure what forces might have lured him toward the heart of the Dragon. Had the incident been a mere accident, or was someone trying to frighten him, perhaps even kill him?

If so, who? And why?

To prove the truth of the legend?

Or was the legend true? Had it been the force of the Dragon's will that had nearly taken Jack's life?

With every step, Keely told herself that her fears were nothing more than a lifetime lived among superstition, that nothing would happen to Jack. She worked to convince herself that nothing bad would happen to her either, for she knew that she had now committed a serious crime against the Dragon. She had allowed herself to have feelings for a stranger, the outsider who said he came from a land called America.

Feelings.

Strange, wonderful feelings that set her on fire.

Feelings like she had never experienced. Standing close to him in the grove, she'd thought she might die from the sensations that had coursed through her. She shivered involuntarily at the memory of his arms around her, the brush of his kiss against her hair. Oddly, she had not been afraid, except of being caught. She had wanted to linger there, to explore those feelings further.

But she could not allow herself such feelings. They were dangerous. Mayhap even deadly. To Jack. And to her own heart. For she was a Dragoner. And he was forbidden.

Keely slowed her pace, considering the fate that had befallen Genevieve. Objectively, it seemed preposterous to think that her death was in any way a punishment for having broken the law, and yet she'd heard Alyn tell Jack that it came as no surprise to him, that Genny's death was one of the Dragon's mysterious accidents that happened in retribution for betrayal.

She fought that idea with her very soul. Alyn might take the Dragon literally, but she could not. She knew that no Dragon lived on Keinadraig. The only Dragon existed in the minds of the people. And yet when Jack had asked her if she believed in the Dragon, she had lied when she'd said no, because a part of her could not seem to shake the superstitious notions that she had been taught since childhood.

Saints in heaven, how she wished it would all go away. She wished time could go backward, and that Genny was home, and that she'd never met Jack Knight. But she fingered his card, which she'd slipped into the pocket of her cloak, and knew that somehow he had changed her life forever.

Now she had to hide that fact from everyone. Even from herself.

By the time she reached her back door, she had managed to suppress the fires of the unfamiliar desire that Jack had ignited within her. Jack Knight was gone, she told herself. He would not be back. She would hide her feelings, and over time, they would vanish, and life would go on as if he'd never held her . . .

She switched on the kitchen light and turned to get a drink of water when she saw the man sitting at her table. She stifled a scream.

"Alyn!"

"Where've ye been, lass?" His voice was cold and heavy.

Keely's legs felt as if they would give way beneath

her, and she covered her pounding heart with her hand. "Ye gave me a fright," she said, steadying herself on the back of a chair. "What in th' name o' th' Saints are ye doing here this time o' night?" Did he know she'd been with the stranger?

"What have ye been doin' roamin' out this time o' night?"

Suddenly Keely's fear was replaced with anger. What business was it of his where she had been? And why was he bothering to ask? She sensed he already knew the answer. Glaring at him, she moved to the sink and took a glass from the windowsill. Willing her hands not to shake, she poured it full of sweet spring water she kept in a pitcher on the shelf and took a deep drink. "I've been in th' grove," she replied sharply when she finished, "praying for th' soul o' Genevieve, since no one else in this village seems t' give a care about her." She saw her uncle's face darken.

"Keely," he said sternly, "ye must let her go. No good will come of it if ye keep this up."

"Let her go? Uncle, do ye na understand that I can na do that, na without th' proper grieving? Nor can Ninian. Ye can na insist Genevieve never lived. 'Tis na right!"

Alyn did not reply, but gazed at Keely with a long, level look. She felt her face grow warm, but she was determined he would not see inside of her, so she returned his stare until at last he spoke.

" 'Tis time ye were wed."

"Wed?" Now her knees gave way, and she sank into the chair opposite him. It was the last thing she expected him to say. She struggled for words. "But, Uncle, I have no wish t' wed."

" 'Tis na your choice, lass. Ye know that. 'Tis your duty t' th' Dragon and th' village t' wed and breed th' strong, healthy children that will come from your line. Ye know 'tis true, our family has th' most favored bloodline on Keinadraig. 'Tis your honor t' continue it.

And your duty. I was na blessed with children before Lilias died. 'Tis ye who must breed th' next Keeper.''

Her blood chilled at the thought of what he was saying, but it did not cool her anger. "Ye talk about 'breeding' like I was a prize goat," she snapped. "I will na hear such crude talk."

Surprise etched his face, followed by disbelief that she would dare talk back to him. "Ye'll na cross me on this, Keely. 'Twould grieve your father and beloved mother, rest their souls. Besides, ye made a vow t' th' Dragon when ye received th' kiss . . ." He touched the mark just below his left ear, the kiss of the Dragon impressed there when he, too, had taken the oath as a youth. "Ye made a vow t' obey th' laws o' th' Dragon. Touch it, Keely," he ordered. "Touch your own kiss. Remember your promise and your duty."

Keely began to tremble again, and she raised her fingers to the mark of the Dragon. Yes, she had pledged to live by the sacred laws. When she was only thirteen. As all Dragoners pledged when they reached that age. That day, she had received the kiss of the Dragon, a tiny burn just below her left ear, in the same place the first Healer had received it from the Dragon himself, when he sang the laws to her ancestors. It was a ceremony that called for great celebration and joy, for it brought the young person into adulthood and insured continuation of the Dragon's protection of Keinadraig.

No one ever dreamed of not taking the pledge.

" 'Tis na that I scorn my pledge or my duty, Uncle," Keely said, dropping her hand and looking directly at him. " 'Tis that I . . . I do na wish t' wed a stranger, and ye know that is my only choice. There is no other here on Keinadraig."

Her uncle's face softened. "Can ye na trust me?" he said, laying his hands flat on the tabletop. "I am th' Keeper, but I am also your kin. If ye will tell me th' kind o' man that would make ye happy, I promise I will search th' moors and th' woodlands and all th' villages about until I find th' right match for ye.''

Keely hadn't expected him to allow her to remain single, but she'd hoped he would give her more time. She had been able to avoid the issue of marriage for longer than most, since she'd been responsible for taking care of her invalid mother. Now that Sharine was gone, Keely had no excuse.

Marriage. To some strange bumpkin from the mainland she did not love. Bearing his children. She could not stand the thought. There was only one stranger to whom she might give her heart, perhaps already had, and she knew he was not an option.

''Please, Uncle, leave me in peace. I am not yet ready t' wed. I beg ye give me more time. Losing first Ma, and now Genny, I . . . I need . . . time.''

Suddenly the burdens she had carried almost from the time she'd received the Dragon's kiss weighed upon her like a stone cloak, and she was unable to stem a new flood of tears. She had been barely thirteen when her father had died, and as her mother's health was frail, Keely had had to take over most of the work at the pub. She'd managed to keep up with her schooling only by studying late at night, after closing time. Then, when Sharine had lost the use of her legs, Keely had become her nurse as well. Many nights she'd fallen exhausted into bed at some wee hour, after long days spent dragging from chore to chore. She was tired, and she felt old beyond her years.

Keely looked across at her uncle and resented his insistence that she take on yet another burden . . . motherhood.

''Do na do this t' me, Uncle. Na now.''

EIGHT

It was past one A.M. when Jack finally made it to his room at the inn in Penzance, weary to his bones from the stress of the day. Nonetheless, he picked up the phone and dialed Garrison's cellular number.

"Garrison here." The voice sounded thick.

"Garrison, it's Jack. Did I wake you?"

There was a long pause, and Jack thought he heard the sound of a lamp switch. "Yeah, but that's okay. Where are you?"

"I'm in Penzance. There's lots to brief you on, but first, how's Brad?" Jack held his breath, dreading the expected answer that Brad was gone.

Garrison exhaled heavily. "He's still alive, Jack. But there's been no change. He's still in a coma."

Jack allowed himself to hope. "What do the doctors say?"

"He might never come out of it. Or if he does, he might be a vegetable. They're not optimistic, but they say he has a slim chance of recovering. It's . . . that's . . . what's keeping me going."

It was enough to keep Jack going, too. "How are you? Where are you right now?"

"I'm okay, just tired. I'm at the hospital. They've put a bed in the private room so I don't have to go back and forth to the hotel." It was late and Jack was exhausted, so he was probably imagining it, but there seemed to be an unnatural restraint in Garrison's voice.

"Have you talked to Sandringham?"

Another long pause. "Yes. We spoke at length today."

Jack waited, but Garrison offered nothing further. Something was wrong. "Have they come up with anything?" he probed.

"Nothing substantial. They're still scratching their heads."

Something was not being said. Something important. "What is it, Garrison? What's wrong?"

"It's . . . nothing. Nothing of any consequence. We have a few things to talk about when you get back, that's all. What about on your end? Have you found out anything?"

Jack told Garrison what he'd learned about the murdered woman. "Give Sandringham a call in the morning and fill him in, will you? I'll be back soon, but he'll want to know the woman's ID right away." He paused, then said, "Good night, Garrison. Get some rest." Then he hung up the phone, deeply disturbed. Something was wrong, he could feel it in his gut. Sitting on the bed and removing his shoes, he wondered what it could be. Well, he thought, leaning back against the pillows, he'd find out soon enough. He'd leave for London tomorrow morning, make his own report to Sandringham, and turn the investigation of the people in Keinadraig over to Scotland Yard. Let them deal with Alyn Runyon and the Dragoners.

And Keely?

Jack regretted what he would have to do, for in addition to bringing the police, it could bring another very scary kind of outsider to the island. If Scotland Yard came to Keinadraig, could the media be far behind? If nothing else, it would rock the little world in which she existed.

Jack undressed and took a shower before dropping wearily into bed. He turned out the light and slipped between the cool sheets, hoping to escape his troubled thoughts in the respite of sleep. But behind closed eyes, Keely Cochrane loomed, cloak-clad and provincial, artless and hauntingly beautiful, seemingly from another age and yet more alluring than any nineties woman he'd ever met.

What was she really like? he wondered. What had it been like to grow up in that isolated, cloistered society? How vastly different her life had been from his own childhood spent in the city of Los Angeles. How vastly different their lives were now. While his world embraced a global economy and high technology, her world apparently consisted only of a tiny island and a small village of superstitious folk whose lives were ordered by old legends and, unfortunately, fear perpetuated by tradition. Yet she was not ignorant, nor uneducated. She was just . . . sheltered. And naive.

Like Sleeping Beauty, unfamiliar with the ways of the world that existed outside her tiny kingdom.

Jack wasn't sure whether to feel sorry for her, trapped in such an archaic society, or envy her for the simplicity of her life. He suspected that Genevieve, the dreamer, had left in search of the reality of the modern world. Would Keely ever escape? Did she even want to? Jack wished that if and when Keely Cochrane chose to leave the island, he could be there to protect her while she learned the ways of the world. She would be like a time traveler, thrust from a medieval world into the fast pace of modern society. A dangerous world where she, like Genevieve, would be acutely vulnerable.

Maybe it was better she didn't want to make that leap, he decided, tossing fitfully and becoming entangled in the bedclothes. Maybe her world was preferable to his after all.

Keely sat in a chair in the dark, hugging her pillow for comfort. From the tall, sashed window on the second floor of her cottage she could see the glow of lights from

Penzance. Staring across the black expanse of water in between, she felt for the first time in her life like a prisoner of the island.

Her uncle had forbidden her to leave, even to make a market delivery. He had withdrawn permission for her to take an excursion in one of the fishing boats, something she'd always enjoyed on a Sunday afternoon. She never went to any specific destination, usually just around the island to enjoy the sun and fresh air. But that was to be denied to her, at least for a time, as a reminder of her duty. She resented that he was treating her like a child.

Soon, Alyn himself would leave the island, but only for as long as it took to find a suitable husband for her. Keely could guess his thinking—if she were married and "settled," she would forget any notion of disobedience. For Keely knew that was what upset Alyn the most, that twice in one day she'd dared to challenge his authority.

Keely loved her uncle, and she did not mean to be willful. She was not asking anything beyond reason. Only that Genny's existence be acknowledged, and that she not be forced to marry. Not just yet.

Alyn had other ideas on both subjects. And Alyn was the Keeper. And the Keeper was obeyed.

It was the law.

And suddenly, Keely hated the law.

She threw her pillow across the room onto the bed. She hated not being trusted by her own uncle. She hated the notion of being forced to marry and "breed." She hated being confined on the island. Most of all, she hated what had happened to Genny.

And she hated that fear of a similar fate would always keep her on Keinadraig.

Gazing toward the mainland, Keely thought it as far away as the moon in the sky above. Was the outside world really the evil place her people had always been told? Certainly the stranger named Jack had not seemed evil. He had, in fact, shown great kindness and compassion for her sorrow.

But the outside had been evil to Genny. Keely shivered and pulled a light shawl around her shoulders. Never had she been so torn and confused. She lay across the bed, unable to sleep, feeling numbed at the dismal prospects life held for her. She recalled what Genny had said that night. *I wish ye would come with me. There is no future for ye here.*

Poor Genevieve. There had been no future for her out there either.

Other words echoed in Keely's mind. *Come with me to London. I'll take you there and bring you safely home again.*

If only that were possible. If only she could go with Jack, just for as long as it took to see to Genny's proper ceremony. If she had that, then maybe the rest of what she faced in life would be easier to accept.

Picking up Jack's card from where it lay on the small table that stood by her bed, Keely held it to her cheeks and closed her eyes, allowing herself the briefest memory of their embrace.

Memories. And this card. They were all she had of him. All she would ever have.

She'd best get Jack Knight out of her head once and for all, she told herself firmly, replacing the card on the table. Forbidden thoughts like these would only lead to trouble.

But sometime later, when she fell asleep, she dreamt of sunshine and freedom, and a man named Jack.

The next morning dawned bright but hazy, and Jack took breakfast in the small dining room of the inn overlooking the bay, directly across from the docks. To the southeast rose the historical landmark of St. Michael's Mount, for many years a holy place, now a private residence as well as a tourist attraction. Due south, scarcely discernable through the haze, was the mysterious island of Keinadraig.

The waitress, who introduced herself as Maggie Evans, poured him a second cup of coffee. "From America?" she asked, engaging in friendly conversation.

He nodded, and she smiled. "Guessed by th' accent. What part of America?"

"Los Angeles."

"My, my, Los Angeles. That's a ways off from 'ere. What brings ye t' Penzance?" She spoke with much the same quaint Cornish accent he'd heard on Keinadraig.

"Business." Jack decided to take this opportunity to get yet another local opinion about the Dragoners. "What do you know about the island out there, Keinadraig?" he asked, nodding toward the windows.

He saw a shadow of a frown cross her otherwise pleasant, round face. "Ah, na much, sir. Folks 'round 'ere have few dealings with that place."

"Why?"

She gave an uncomfortable little grimace. "They's na like th' rest of us," she said, resting the coffee pot against a chair back. "Keep t' themselves, they do."

"I've heard they believe they're protected by some sort of dragon."

Maggie Evans shrugged. "Word 'round 'ere is they do believe in some old laws 'anded down from ancient times, supposedly from a dragon, although most folks think th' Dragon must 'ave been th' symbol for their king. Whatever, th' laws forbid strangers t' go there and Dragoners aren't supposed t' leave."

Jack laughed grimly. "I learned that when I went there yesterday."

She gave him a disbelieving look. "Ye went there? Whatever for?"

Jack took out the police sketch of Genevieve Sloan. "I'm a private investigator. I was looking for information about this woman. Do you recognize her?"

The waitress studied the picture for only a moment.

"Oh, aye. She's a Dragoner, all right. She comes 'ere from time t' time deliverin' their fish t' th' market. She and 'er friend sometimes stop in for a bite, y'see. What're ye needin' 'er for?"

Jack had her undivided attention now. "She was killed in London a few days ago. I was just trying to get some information on her."

"Killed? In London? Oh, my! What was she doin' way up in London?"

"I was hoping to learn that myself," Jack said, folding the picture and replacing it in his pocket. "Seems she just ran away."

Maggie shook her head and took a swipe at the far end of the table with her rag. "And she's dead now? Maybe th' tales are true, then."

"What tales?"

She came a little closer to him and lowered her voice. " 'Tis only a rumor that I heard from my cousin who heard it from a boy in 'er village who narrowly escaped being recruited t' wed a Dragoner."

"Recruited? What are you talking about?"

"From time t' time, it 'as been necessary for th' village t' bring in new blood, t' keep from inbreedin', y'know. When that 'appens, th' old man they call th' Keeper comes t' th' mainland and finds a 'usband or wife for th' person out there needin' a mate. Well, 'e came t' my cousin's village up on th' moor yonder, and 'e made arrangements for this boy t' wed a Dragoner. Gave 'is family quite a sum of money, 'e did, before takin' th' boy off t' th' island. 'Is family feared they wouldn't see 'im again, because that's what's 'appened in th' past. Once wed into th' Dragon society, an outsider becomes a Dragoner and doesn't come again into th' outside world."

Maggie leaned a little closer, warming to her tale, and Jack listened in astounded silence.

"But th' boy let it spill that cancer was prevalent in 'is family's bloodline. Th' Dragoners are only after what they consider 'pure,' y'know. When they found 'e wasn't good enough for them, they returned 'im t' 'is parents, but 'e claims they threatened 'im that th' Dragon would seek 'is death if 'e revealed any o' what 'e'd seen or 'eard.''

"Death?"

" 'Twas what 'e said. 'E was afraid for 'is life, because they'd sung 'im a song while 'e was in Keinadraig, an old ballad of some kind, telling o' tragic deaths that had come t' those who broke the laws o' th' Dragon and warnin' 'im 'e might meet th' same fate.''

Jack's heart stopped beating for a moment. A ballad. The song he'd heard in the cave? He'd read the words above the gate, but wondered now if there was more to the song than he'd heard or read.

"Where can I find this boy?" Jack laid money on the table, but Maggie did not touch it. She glanced around nervously. " 'E doesn't live 'round 'ere anymore. Moved away shortly afterwards, didn't want no one t' know where 'e went." She topped off his coffee. "Look, I've . . . I've probably said too much. I must get on with my duties," she said and hurried off toward the kitchen.

Jack stared out at the water, contemplating what he'd just learned. The woman's story confirmed much of what Keely had told him yesterday about the ways of the Dragoners. Only Keely had left out the part about the arranged marriages.

Why?

Had she not wanted him to know about the cultlike method of finding new blood for their closed community? Was she ashamed of it? She'd said she didn't know why Genevieve had run away, only that she thought she had been running from something.

From what? An enforced marriage?

Had Keely known that all along, and lied?

Suddenly, Jack had a whole new set of burning ques-

tions, and there was only one place to go for answers.
Keinadraig.

Keely's dreams faded and reality set in when she saw
Alyn leave in the morning in one of the larger boats
with another villager. She put her hand to her throat.
She knew where he was going. And she dreaded his
return.

Soon she would be trapped forever.

"Nay!" She breathed it as an oath. She would not
marry now, no matter if Alyn brought her the most handsome, clever man on earth. It was not her will to marry
now. It was her will, and her desperate need, to heal
from the recent tragedy, to put Genevieve's terrible
death behind her. Then, perhaps, she could bear to do
what Alyn asked. Why in the name of the Saints
couldn't he understand that?

Bathing and changing into fresh clothing, Keely
headed up the lane to Ninian's house. She respected the
Healer's need for privacy in this time of mourning, but
there was no one else she could talk to, and Keely was
in urgent need herself of an ear for her troubles. Maybe
the wise woman could give her some guidance.

She entered the small house without knocking, as was
her custom. She and Genny had come and gone freely
between their two houses all their lives. The cottage
seemed eerily quiet. Keely tiptoed past the small, tidy
sitting room and into the tiny, familiar kitchen. Herbs
hung in fragrant bouquets from the rafters, their leaves
drying for later use in Ninian's many healing concoc-
tions. Although Keinadraig supported a small clinic with
some modern medicines, most Dragoners trusted the old
ways and turned to the Healer, who knew the magic of
nature's remedies.

"Ninian?" Keely called softly, but there was no reply. She saw that the door to Ninian's room was closed,
and she hesitated to knock. Still, she had not seen
Genny's mother in several days, and Erica was nowhere

in sight, so she decided to make sure the Healer was all right. She knocked, but there was no response. She turned the doorknob quietly and went into the room. The curtains were drawn and an extra blanket had been hung at the window to further close out the light. The air was warm, stale, and close, scented with a faint herbal odor.

Ninian lay on her bed, fully clothed. Her face was to the ceiling, and she lay very still. Alarmed, Keely rushed to her bedside, but she was reassured when she saw the even rise and fall of her shallow breathing. She appeared to be in a deep sleep, and Keely was not about to disturb what peace she might find in slumber. Ninian's pain must surely be greater even than her own, Keely thought, closing the door behind her, wondering what it must be like to lose a child.

Suddenly, Keely was aware of the sound of someone humming. She went to the back door and spied Erica at play beneath a tree in the back garden. She opened the door and caught the familiar tune of the ballad, and as she watched, the girl, who had celebrated her own Dragon ceremony only a year ago, performed the same ritual with a doll. She had set up a circle of rocks and built a small fire in the center. She was speaking to the doll. Keely was startled to recognize the words of the ritual, which the law allowed only to be spoken by the Healer. She saw Erica take a small object from her pocket, grasp it with tongs used only for the sacred rite, and hold it over the flames. Shocked and unable to move, Keely witnessed the girl administer the kiss of the Dragon to the neck of the toy. The acrid aroma of scorched cotton brought her to her senses.

"What are ye doing?" Keely charged at the girl, furious that she should make a mockery of the ritual.

Erica turned and her face blanched before she managed to hide her surprise behind her usual sullen demeanor. "Nothing."

"Give me Ninian's ring," Keely demanded.

But the girl only stared at her defiantly and slipped

the ring, now cooled, into her pocket. " 'Tis na your ring. It belongs t' my mother.''

"It belongs t' th' Healer o' this village. No one else is allowed t' touch it. Ye know that.''

"My mother is na well. I am t' be th' next Healer. I was . . . practicing.'' Her claim to the inherited honor rang with defiance, which Keely tried to ignore. She was more concerned about the first part of her statement.

"What's wrong with your mother?''

"She's asleep. She took a draft after Alyn told us what happened t' Genevieve.'' The girl looked up at Keely through slitted eyelids. "She has been sleeping a lot since her dear Genevieve left. 'Tis like she does na wish t' awaken again.''

Discomfited by the girl's pronouncement, Keely wished she'd checked in on Ninian sooner. She held out her hand. "Give me th' ring, Erica,'' she said. "Then put out that fire and come with me. We must help your mother.''

The girl hesitated, glaring at Keely, then gave over the ring. "Ye may take th' ring now, but soon *I* will be th' Healer,'' she hissed. "I, na ye.''

Her words caught Keely completely off guard. "What makes ye say a thing such as that? I am na going t' be th' Healer. I am na o' your line. Besides, I would never wish t' be th' Healer.''

At that, Erica gave her a strange, mocking look. "Neither did Genevieve.''

NINE

After breakfast and his intriguing encounter with Maggie Evans, Jack left the hotel and headed toward the docks where he found Kevin Spearman bent over, mending a fishing net.

"Thanks for waiting for me, pal," Jack said dryly.

Spearman looked up at him, and his face darkened. "Waited as long as I could. Where were ye?"

"Got turned around in those caves. Couldn't find my way out." By the light of day, his mishap in the caves seemed no longer sinister. Maybe he'd taken a misstep, had imagined the shove against the wall. At any rate, Jack decided to drop his complaint. "Sorry about your boat. What's it going to cost me?"

"Nothing."

"What do you mean, nothing? I told you my client would replace it."

" 'Twas found this morning, just up th' coast a bit. I sent my son t' fetch it." He bit off a piece of twine.

"That's good news," Jack said, glad he wasn't going to have to spend some of Garrison's money after all. "It was fortunate it didn't drift on out to sea."

"Mayhap."

"Why do you say that?"

"A dead raven was found in 't. A bad omen, for sure."

A raven. The Dragon. Were all Cornish people this superstitious?

"What'd ye find out there?" Spearman wanted to know. "Were th' Dragoners friendly?"

"I wouldn't say that, although I got the man who calls himself the Keeper to admit the dead woman was from Keinadraig."

Spearman pierced him with a long and, Jack thought, contemptuous look, but before he could figure out why, he heard a boat approaching. Both he and Spearman looked up to see Alyn Runyon and another man headed their way.

"They're na carryin' a load o' fish," Spearman commented in a worried voice. "Wonder what they want?"

"Their boat, I imagine," Jack replied grimly, wondering if Runyon had learned that Keely had helped him steal the boat.

"What?" The Cornishman dropped his nets and stood up. "Ye stole a Dragoner boat?"

Jack pointed to the boat he'd used the night before to return from Keinadraig. "How'd you think I got here? Walked?"

"I figured one o' them brought ye." Looking distressed, he ducked into his small shack and disappeared. Jack turned to confront Alyn Runyon, who came huffing toward him, his face livid.

"Ye're ne'er t' step foot on Keinadraig again," the old man said when he reached Jack. " 'Twas bad enough trespassin' as ye did, bringin' trouble as ye did. But stealin' from th' Dragon . . ." He shook his head, and Jack noticed a small red mark just beneath his left ear. Something about it seemed familiar, yet he couldn't recall what tugged at his memory.

"I did not steal your boat," Jack countered, bringing himself to his full height, standing solidly on both feet and placing his hands on his hips. "I borrowed it. After mine somehow mysteriously came . . . untied." His tone was deliberately accusatory.

Runyon was unintimidated, however, and he brought his face even closer. "Ye have no idea th' powers ye be dealin' with, Mr. Knight. Ye have placed my niece in grave danger. Yourself as well. Begone from here before th' Dragon's wrath finds ye as it did Genevieve."

Although he scorned the man's use of the Dragon as a threat, Jack's heart lurched at his mention of Keely. He forced himself to remain impassive, however. Any show of emotion toward Runyon's niece would likely place her in danger, not from the Dragon but rather from this old man.

"It wasn't a Dragon that killed Genevieve, Runyon. It was a bullet. She was murdered, and it wasn't my friend who pulled the trigger. You can threaten me all you want, but I'm not going to stop my investigation until I find out who killed her."

He saw the stain of red deepen in the Keeper's face. "Ye'll be sorry, then, for sure." With that, he turned, spoke a few words to the other man in the boat, and hobbled away down the dock. His companion turned the small craft back toward the island, and Jack expected Runyon to follow in the boat he'd borrowed. Instead, the old man left the docks and headed up the street at a brisk pace.

Jack would have been lying to himself if he'd claimed Runyon's threats had not shaken him. Not because he believed he was in any danger from some kind of supernatural recrimination by a dragon, but because of the man's obscure but ominous threat against Keely. His eyes followed Runyon until he turned a corner and disappeared.

Unsettled, Jack returned to the inn, where he found Maggie Evans peering out the back windows of the dining room, looking up the street where Runyon had just passed. "That's th' Keeper I was tellin' ye about," she said, dropping the curtain.

"Where's he going?"

She coughed nervously and darted a knowing glance

at Jack. "Th' only time 'e comes t' town and takes off like that, 'e's in search of a mate for someone on th' island, like I was tellin' ye about with my cousin's story. They don't drive, th' Dragoners, so 'e goes on foot t' th' villages around here, till 'e finds someone either foolish enough or greedy enough t' accept 'is offer."

"He buys a bride?"

"Or a groom . . ."

An alarm went off in Jack's head. Keely had told him she was unwed. Was Runyon off to find a groom . . . for her? The thought turned his stomach, but he knew that in the States, cults often used such methods for perpetuating their populations. Was she a willing participant? Or was some stranger about to be forced on her?

He returned to the docks and Kevin Spearman. "I need to rent your boat again."

"What do ye know o' Genevieve's wishes toward becoming th' Healer?" Keely was enraged at Erica's smirk and wanted to slap it off her face. But she wanted even more to know what had happened between Genny and Ninian the night she left.

"Genevieve betrayed her sacred oath," Erica replied, avoiding the question. "She did na deserve t' be Healer. She deserved exactly what she got."

"Ye little snip," Keely cried, clenching her fists to control her rage. "I'd almost believe 'twas ye who killed her." Erica's cunning smile sent a chill through her. "Do ye know who killed her?"

But Erica didn't answer. She just turned away and went toward the cottage, the doll tucked beneath her arm. When she reached the door, she looked back at Keely. " 'Twas th' Dragon that killed Genevieve. Ye know that."

Keely followed her inside, where she grabbed the girl by the arm and whirled her around to face her. She did not wish to disturb Ninian, but she needed to set Erica

straight right now. "There *is* no Dragon, Erica. Th'
Dragon is a myth."

Erica raised one eyebrow, all pretense of a smile van-
ishing from her too-small face. "Ye stand in th' house
o' th' Healer and dare profane th' Dragon?"

"Ye are too young, or too stupid, t' understand that
th' Dragon is a symbol. Nothing more. There is no
Dragon on Keinadraig, only th' legend and th' laws we
live by. 'Twas a human that killed Genevieve. Na a
Dragon."

"Genny scorned th' laws. She scorned her duty. And
th' Dragon killed her," Erica insisted, jerking her arm
away from Keely's grasp. "And if ye do na stop breaking th' laws, th' Dragon will kill ye, too."

Her tone alarmed Keely. "What do ye mean, breaking th' laws? I have broken no law."

"I know ye aided th' stranger last night. I know ye
met him in th' grove. I know ye talked with him, and
that . . . ye let him touch ye."

Keely wanted to shriek out a denial, but she could
not. She was furious that Erica had obviously spied on
her all along. "Why ye . . . who do ye think ye are,
snooping around in things that are none o' your business?"

"I am th' Healer. Or will be when Ninian passes.
Things such as your treacherous actions will be my business." She moved to where a large book lay open on
the kitchen table and very slowly closed the cover. "I
know th' laws, Keely, because I have been studying
them. It says in this book that no Dragoner other than
th' Keeper is t' speak t' strangers." She paused for effect, then added, "But then, surely ye know that."

Keely stared at the book, then raised her eyes to lock
her gaze on Erica's. She'd be damned by the Saints if
she'd let this girl intimidate her. "I also know that book
is only t' be read by th' Healer. Did Ninian give ye
permission t' . . . study?"

Erica's expression changed from defiant to uneasy.

She looked away and shrugged. "Ninian is sleeping. She may never awaken. I am o' th' bloodline o' th' Healer. I must prepare myself."

It was the second time Erica had mentioned that her mother might not awaken. "Why do ye think your mother will na awaken?"

"She told me she wanted t' die," Erica said simply. "It broke her heart when Genevieve refused t' become Healer." This last was spoken with bitter resentment.

"Why did Genny refuse?" Keely softened her voice, hoping to use Erica's jealousy of her sister to find out what had happened.

Erica's defiance returned. "Because Genevieve did na have it in her t' perform certain . . . duties o' th' Healer. Genevieve was soft and lazy. She did na have th' inborn qualities of a true Healer."

"And ye do?" Keely could not keep the sarcasm from her voice.

"More than ye will ever know," Erica replied with a curl of the lip.

Keely recalled the girl's earlier curious comment about the succession of the Healer going to Keely instead of Erica, and she decided to find out what that had been about. "Are ye na pressing this too quickly? Mayhap the new apprentice should be chosen by Ninian." She paused, poised to thrust her barb. "Mayhap I should reconsider what I said earlier. Mayhap 'tis I Ninian will choose, when she awakens." Again she locked her eyes on Erica's. "And she will awaken, Erica. Her grief will pass."

"Get out," the girl cried, and threw her doll at Keely.

But Keely was undaunted. "Ye will na threaten me again," she replied, picking the doll off the floor and regarding the mark burned into its neck. "Ye are overstepping yourself, Erica. I know Uncle Alyn would find it interesting that ye've taken th' apprenticeship upon yourself." She tucked the doll under her arm as Erica had done earlier and turned to leave. She paused at the door and said, "Let us call a truce, shall we? I will na speak o' this t' him, and ye will na mention that I spoke with th' stranger."

Keely was shaking as she shut the door behind her. She found it difficult to believe that Genevieve and Erica had been spawned by the same parents. Genevieve had been filled with goodness and light, while Erica seemed dark, evil almost. She recalled the acid smile on Erica's face when she'd asked if the girl knew who had killed Genevieve. Of course she didn't know, but that smile left no doubt that Erica was glad somebody had done the deed.

Deeply disturbed, Keely returned to her cottage. The day had started off badly when she'd seen Alyn leave on his despicable errand, and it had gone further downhill with her encounter with Erica. What else could happen?

How Keely longed for someone to talk to. Her best friend was gone. Ninian was lost in her grief. She could not talk to Alyn, for he was no longer on her side. She had no one . . .

No one but the stranger.

The thought popped unbidden into her head, dangerous and tempting at the same time. Jack Knight would listen. Jack, the stranger, cared when none of her own seemed to.

Jack had said to call him anytime, day or night. Did she dare? Alyn was gone. The Council office would be empty.

What would she say? That Erica was a monster and Alyn not much better?

No. She would not waste precious words complaining about those two. If she called Jack, all she wanted was to hear the sound of his voice. To know he was safe. Of course, Alyn would find out later that she had made the call, when the charges came, but that did not matter to her at the moment.

She didn't need to fetch the card that lay on her bedside table. The number was etched in her mind. Heart pounding, Keely went out the back door and through the garden gate, walking as if she had not a care in the world, as if she did not know Alyn was gone, as if she were paying her uncle a visit.

Only after she had picked up the receiver and dialed the number did she lose her nerve. Only when she heard the ring on the other end did she come to her senses. She must not do this! She must not create more trouble than she already had. Trouble for her. Trouble for Jack.

She slammed the phone down and dashed out the door, where she ran headlong into Mrs. Parsons, an odious woman with a sharp tongue and a delight in gossip.

"My dear, are ye all right? Ye look a fright."

"Thank ye, Mrs. Parsons," Keely croaked. "I was just looking for Uncle Alyn. I don't suppose ye have seen him?"

The old woman's eyes gleamed, and Keely guessed the gossip had already spread about Alyn's errand. "Never mind. I'll talk t' him later." And before Mrs. Parsons could corner her for further torture, Keely ran back to the safety of her cottage.

Jack waited impatiently while Kevin Spearman filled the boat's fuel tank. Spearman had not wanted to rent to Jack again, saying he needed to use the boat himself. But Jack suspected the real reason was because Spearman was just a little afraid of the old Dragoner and thought he might put the dragon hoodoo on him if he learned he'd provided the stranger with transportation to the island.

As he waited, Jack reminded himself that he was returning to Keinadraig to learn if Genevieve's motive for running away might have been a pending but undesired arranged marriage. It would be easier to make his inquiries with Runyon gone.

But he knew the real reason he was anxious to return was to find out if Keely herself was in any kind of sim-

ilar situation. He wanted to make certain she was safe
and that it was her choice to wed the man Runyon might
be bringing back. He didn't know exactly what he would
do about it if it wasn't, but at the least, he could offer
her another chance to escape.

He was startled at the sound of his cell phone ringing.
Taking it from where it hung on his belt, he instantly
recognized the number of the incoming call that was
identified on the digital screen.

It was the number at the Council office.

Keely!

He pressed the button. "Hello?" He heard a click,
and the line went dead. He started to redial the number,
then hesitated. If Keely had tried to call him, she would
have done so in secret. Suppose someone had come into
the office just as the call went through, and she'd hung
up to avoid getting caught? He did not want to jeopard-
ize her by calling back and exposing her.

"Hurry it up, would you?" He paid Spearman the
exorbitant amount the man required this time, jumped
into the boat, and revved the engine unmercifully.

This time, he did not head for the cliffs, but steered
the boat directly toward the small harbor, his mind fixed
on the phone call. Why had Keely called him? Either
she had learned something relevant to the mystery of
Genevieve's murder, or she was in danger. He desperately hoped it was the former.

He did not attempt to hide his approach by beaching
the boat outside the quay. He'd had enough of the se-
cretive ways of the islanders and refused to buy into
their superstitious fears. He motored straight through the
narrow passageway between the two stone quays and
pulled up to the dock. He tied the boat securely to a
piling, double-knotting the line, then bringing it back
into the boat and wrapping it around a seat and tying
another knot. Spearman's boat would not drift off of its
own accord again.

Stepping onto the dock, Jack glanced around to check

out his situation. This time, he'd caught the town out in the open, for he saw more than a dozen people in the square. They were not exactly busily going about their daily routine, however. They all seemed frozen to the spot, gaping at him. The only person who didn't seem surprised to see a stranger in the Dragon's lair was a girl in her early teens who was jumping a rope by the sea wall. Jack approached her.

"Excuse me, miss. Can you direct me to Keely Cochrane?" he asked.

The girl stopped jumping and gave him an insolent glare, as if angry that he'd interrupted her play. "Strangers are na t' come here," she informed him.

"I am here on business," Jack replied. "Police business." Thinking he was wasting his time, he started on down the quay.

"Wait," called the girl. "I will take ye t' her."

He followed her, ignoring the open stares of the townspeople. She led him up the same street he'd traversed yesterday, past the Council office, to a cottage on the corner of a cross lane. She did not knock, but walked right in and nodded for him to follow. Inside, he saw that the cottage did not contain living quarters as he'd expected, but rather was set up like a pub, with small, lace-covered tables and a dark wooden bar along the back wall. Conversation among the handful of customers ceased when they saw Jack.

"This *stranger* has come t' see Keely," the girl announced, loudly and pointedly.

Jack stiffened. Why hadn't he told the girl he needed to see Keely in private? But he quickly surmised that the girl was a mischief-maker and was undoubtedly taking great delight in stirring up trouble. Was she like this with everyone, he wondered, or did she have some kind of personal vendetta against Keely?

Before she could speak further, however, the door at the back of the room swished open and Keely entered, carrying two plates of steaming food. She did not see

Jack at first, as she set the meals in front of customers at the bar. "Fresh made pasties, hot from th' oven," she announced.

It must have been the astonished look on their faces or their dumbfounded silence that told her something was wrong, for she immediately skimmed her gaze around the room. Her mouth dropped open when she saw the stranger.

"Jack! Whatever are ye doing here?" she cried, then covered her mouth with her apron.

Well, that secret was out of the bag, Jack thought darkly. No one could doubt Keely Cochrane had somehow become acquainted with the stranger who had paid her uncle a visit yesterday. What hell she would catch from Runyon for this indiscretion Jack could only imagine.

Concerned, he did his best to make his visit look official. He took out a card and handed it to her, aware that all eyes were on them. "I understand your uncle is away, Miss Cochrane," he said in a voice loud enough that all could hear. "I am here on official police business, and I thought that in his absence, perhaps you could answer some questions."

Keely stared at him blankly a moment, and then she understood and attempted to play along. "Oh, aye, th' Keeper, my uncle, told me ye might return with more questions. Wait . . . wait just a minute." She disappeared through the door again, and Jack wondered if she would take the opportunity to run away from him out the back door. But she reappeared momentarily, her apron having been left in the kitchen. She smoothed her hair in a nervous gesture.

"Come outside," she said to Jack, then turned to those in the room who continued to gawk. "Free refills in th' kitchen. Please, serve yourselves. I will return shortly."

Jack saw her gaze bore into the girl's for a moment,

and he heard the sarcasm in her voice when she said,
"Thank ye, Erica. Thank ye ever so much."

Then she turned her anxious face to him and said,
"Come along."

TEN

W hat on earth are ye doing here?'' Keely lashed
out once they had reached a place along the
street where she thought they would be out of earshot.
"Uncle Alyn will be furious.''

"I thought you weren't afraid of your uncle.'' Jack
stood several feet away from her, a respectable, professional distance, but Keely heard a more personal note in
his voice.

"I . . . I'm na,'' she protested. "Na truly. But your
coming here is going t' put me in a pretty pickle.''

"But you called me, didn't you?''

Keely's head jerked up in astonishment. "Aye,'' she
said. "But how did ye know?''

Jack showed her the cell phone. "When a call comes
in, the number of the caller shows up here. It's a little
device that comes in handy from time to time. Like today.'' He replaced the phone on his belt. "Why did you
call, Keely? And why did you hang up? Is something
wrong?''

Was something wrong? Only every single thing in
her life, she thought, her heart leaden with despair. And
with Jack's unexpected appearance, it had all gotten
worse. It had been a terrible mistake to make that call.
What had she been thinking?

"Ye should na have come here, Jack. Now we're
both in that pickle.''

"I was coming anyway, before you called."

"Why? What has happened? Did ye learn who killed Genny?"

"No, but I heard something about your traditions here on the island I didn't much like. I heard that even though outsiders are not welcome, sometimes a person is forced to marry a particular outsider, someone picked by your uncle, whether she wants to or not." He paused, and Keely averted her gaze. The way he described their tradition, it indeed sounded . . . heathen. When she didn't speak, he continued. "I was wondering . . . is that why Genevieve ran away? Was she being forced into a marriage she didn't want?"

Keely felt the blood drain from her face. Now that she was in those shoes, she could understand that maybe it *was* at least part of the reason for Genny's flight. But should she tell the stranger? "Where . . . where did ye hear this?" she asked, raising her chin.

"About your . . . ah, tradition? From some of the locals on the mainland. Seems some of your secrets aren't so secret after all. Then I saw your uncle this morning in Penzance, and those locals seemed to think he was on just such an errand, that he was off to search the nearby villages for a mate for someone here on Keinadraig." His statement was posed as a question, and his eyes searched hers, probing to know if she was that someone.

This time she could not look away. She saw in his eyes something that touched her heart. This stranger, this man from a place far away, seemed truly to care about her. His questioning was not the nosing about of a police investigator. It was not about Genevieve. It was about her. She did not know why he cared, but it was clear he wanted to know if she was being forced into a marriage she did not want.

Keely's already fragile world cracked further as Jack's questioning forced her to face the reality she had been trying to ignore. That was exactly what was about to happen to her. At any time now. Uncle Alyn would soon be on his way with a man he'd bribed to become her husband. It could be that in a matter of days, her fate would be sealed for the rest of her life. If she obeyed the laws, followed tradition, she would soon wed the man chosen for her, bear his children, and grow old in the village without ever having any choice over her own life.

She looked into Jack's handsome face, etched now with concern, and knew what she truly wanted. She wanted to have a choice. In a mate. In her life. Before she had met Jack, before Genny had run away, perhaps she would not have questioned her uncle's decision and choice for her life. Now . . .

"My uncle has, shall we say, gone shopping," she replied bitterly, "for a husband for me."

She saw the concern in Jack's face turn to anguish. "Is that what you want, Keely?" he asked.

Keely felt as if she were standing on the edge of the precipice of her deeply cracked world, staring dizzily down into a dark unknown. Fear clutched her. No, marriage to some man Alyn dragged to her doorstep was not what she wanted. But what could she do about it? She realized she was trembling.

"Nay," she murmured. "'Tis na what I want. But . . ."

"I will take you away from here, before your uncle returns."

There it was. The choice she'd just claimed she wanted. And she was paralyzed with fear at the very idea. Fear. The Dragon in the darkness. Beads of sweat broke out on her brow. What if she left with Jack? She could never return to Keinadraig, of that she was certain. She would leave behind forever everything and everybody she'd ever known, all sense of security and belonging. She would go into a land she had been taught was evil, into a world she was little prepared to face. Could she survive?

But the raw fear that clawed at her heart was more than the fear of leaving the island or of making it in the outside world. It was fear of the old legend. Fear that she, too, would meet a fate as terrible as Genevieve's. That she would die for breaking the laws of the Dragon, and that she would cause Jack's death as well.

She caught a movement out of the corner of her eye and spied Erica, innocently skipping rope but getting just a little too near, close enough to hear their conversation. She gave Keely a meaningful look and began to skip in time to the song she sang:

> Away, hide away, on this distant shore,
> Let ne'er a stranger in thy door.
> Keep your secret safe, hidden in the mist,
> And let no one leave who be Dragon
>   kiss'd.

Suddenly, Erica Sloan and the ancient ballad and her uncle Alyn and the prying eyes of the Dragoners she felt even now watching her from behind curtained windows represented all that Keely had begun to dislike about Keinadraig. She resented being controlled by her uncle, the Keeper, a well-meaning but uncompromising leader whose weapon was fear. She had no freedom of choice, whether it be of a husband, a livelihood, or a home. All were decided by the Keeper.

Erica's singing grew louder, more insistent as she rolled into another verse.

> "Oh, mother mine," cried the sweet
>   Diane,
> "Marry me not to that old, old man."
> "But daughter dear, 'tis the Dragon's way,
> 'Tis the Dragon's choice, and you must
>   obey."

"Walk with me," Keely said to Jack and started down the cobblestones toward the harbor. Blood thundered in her temples, and her mouth had gone dry. But her feet were decisive, and they took her directly to where Jack's boat was tethered. She stared at it bobbing on the gentle tide, seeing not a boat, but the abyss.

She looked behind her at the handful of villagers peering at them hungrily, as if they expected the Dragon himself to come forth at any moment and inflict punishment on them. She looked at Erica and saw a smirk of contempt on the girl's plain face.

And then she looked at Jack, and she saw hope.

"Take me away from this place," she said, breathing the words over the painful constriction of her throat.

With that, Keely Cochrane stepped from the dock into the boat, going over the edge as the crack in her world at last gave way.

Do it! Erica's gaze followed Keely as she walked beside the tall stranger, heading in the direction of the harbor. *Go with him. Betray th' Dragon and go t' th' fate ye deserve.*

With every ounce of her will, Erica urged Keely to make the same mistake her sister had made. They both deserved to die, for neither respected the Dragon's laws. And if she left, Keely *would* die, as would the stranger, for it was written in the ancient book she'd found on Ninian's top shelf.

A gratified smile crept onto her lips when she saw Keely step off the dock into the boat. Her heartbeat picked up as she watched the man untie the line and start the engine. She scarcely dared to breathe as the entire town witnessed Keely leaving with the stranger.

The boat disappeared between the quays, and Erica wiped her sweaty palms on her skirt. There could be no turning back now. Keely had cast her fate, and Erica was not sorry to see her go. Now she would be the favored one in her mother's eyes. She would receive the looks of love and words of praise Ninian had reserved for Genevieve and Keely. Now her mother could no longer withhold her permission for Erica to become her apprentice, as she had after Genevieve had left. Bitterness burned at the back of Erica's throat that Ninian had dared consider that Keely should become the Healer instead of her. How could she? Keely was not of their line. Did no one respect the laws anymore?

Erica saw that the villagers who had watched Keely leave were now walking in small groups up the hill, heads bent in gossip and speculation. Although it was midday and most should be about their chores, she guessed that instead they were going to the pub to discuss this shocking turn of events. The only pub in town belonged to Keely. Or *had* belonged to Keely, Erica realized with grim satisfaction. Now that Keely had left, she owned nothing.

But who would run the pub? Who would inherit the business? Keely had been only thirteen when she'd taken over. Erica was already fourteen. A plan began to take shape in her mind, and she turned and hurried up the hill in order to reach the pub before the others. She dashed into the kitchen and donned the apron Keely had taken off only a short time ago. She quickly took stock of the food that Keely had left in various states of preparation and pulled together a tray of sandwiches which she carried into the main salon as the villagers began to pour in, hot and thirsty, and not just for ale.

Mrs. Parsons approached Erica and patted her head. "Poor babe," she murmured in consolation. "First your sister, and now our dear Keely. 'Tis madness that must have claimed 'em. Does your mother know?"

Erica stiffened. She was happy that Keely had run away, but she dreaded telling Ninian. Her mother had been almost as fond of Keely as she had been of Genevieve. "Nay, Mrs. Parsons. Mum is na feeling well, and I daren't disturb her sleep. She'll learn o' th' betrayal soon enough."

The older woman's eyes were solemn. "Aye, for sure. Poor Ninian. 'Tis tragic indeed." Then a glitter came into those eyes. "We heard that Keely knew th' stranger when she saw him. How d'ye suppose she knew him?"

Erica placed the sandwich tray on the bar. "Help yourselves," she announced as if she already owned the place. "There's plenty." Then she turned to Mrs. Parsons and leaned close to her.

"I saw her in th' grove with him yesterday," she whispered, watching her words go to work in the old gossip's mind.

"Th' grove! Ye do na say! Oh, dear, dear." Mrs. Parsons paused, then asked, "Did ye see what they did in th' grove?"

Erica allowed a knowing grin to cross her lips. "Oh, aye. But I should na carry tales. 'Tis na nice."

Others had overheard and gathered around, eager to hear. "Tell," said one old man. "We must know th' truth. Did she betray th' Dragon, right here on th' island?"

Erica's pulse began to race. Never had any of these people paid her much heed. She had always been Genny's little sister, Ninian's secondborn. A late-in-life child. An accident.

She straightened her back. Well, no more. She was Ninian's *only* child now. Soon she would be the Healer. From this day forward, Erica Sloan would be respected by the Dragoners. Sought out for her wisdom and secret knowledge. She would begin at once to prove to them her worthiness.

"Aye," she answered with a sad shake of her head. "'Tis true. I saw it with my own eyes. She did na just happen upon him in th' grove either. She took him there, after they trysted in th' sacred caves."

Erica heard a communal intake of breath and gathered courage to continue. Filled with a new sense of power, she toyed with the eager villagers, stretching out her tale. She told of how she'd seen the stranger first arrive, and how she'd followed him and watched him climb deliberately to the stone circle, where Keely awaited him. She reported seeing a raven release the boat's line and set it adrift, and saw heads nod in grave understanding. Everyone knew that the raven was the Dragon's lieutenant. The Dragon had known of the stranger's presence from the start and had begun seeking its revenge for his trespass.

"He pretended t' be from th' police," Erica continued, warming to the attention that was now solidly riveted upon her. "But 'twas Keely he came for."

Silence. Then Mrs. Parsons spoke up. "But how did he know Keely?"

Erica fixed her with a sardonic stare and decided to share her own speculation on the matter. "Th' same way Genevieve knew th' man she ran away with. They met in Penzance when they went t' deliver fish t' th' market." She saw the old lady's eyes widen and realized with a start that no one other than Alyn, Keely, Ninian, and herself knew what had actually happened to Genny. All they knew was that she had run away and later been excommunicated for leaving.

But Erica had overheard the whole story when Jack told Keely the circumstances surrounding Genevieve's murder. What harm would there be in letting everyone know the truth? They deserved to know, and to know that in his own mysterious way, the Dragon had taken his revenge.

"That's right," she continued with determination. "Genevieve was in London with a man when she died. She was murdered, in a hotel room, by a man." She spit out every short piece of the despicable story as if it rotted in her mouth, and she reveled in the astonishment on their faces. It was high time everyone in this village knew what Genevieve was really like.

Later, after the villagers had dispersed, their heads filled with new and scandalous gossip, Erica roamed Keely's cottage at will. She would petition Alyn Runyon to make it hers as soon as he returned. Whoever he brought to be Keely's husband would be returned to wherever he had come from. All others were already assigned to communal tasks. There would be no one to run the pub. Erica could do it. She had proven it solidly this very afternoon. She had taken care of everyone, and everyone had shown a new respect for her.

She climbed the stairs to Keely's bedroom, thinking of it now as her own. She took in the lace curtains fluttering at the open window, the bed covered with a lovely print spread, quilted by Sharine before she became too ill to hold a needle. Keely had even placed Erica's doll on the chair as if in welcome. The room was light and airy, far more pleasant than her small, cramped quarters at home. She went to the bed and sat on it, testing it for comfort, and she noticed Ninian's ring on the table beside the bed. Next to it lay a small white rectangle of paper.

She picked up the card. "Jackson Knight. Private Investigator." Beneath those words was printed an address and some numbers she did not understand. Turning it over, however, she saw a number that resembled the one on the Council telephone.

Erica stared at the card, her heart racing. This was not just an omen. This was a clear message from the Dragon.

She was the new Healer, and she had been chosen to punish Keely and the stranger.

The enormity of Keely's decision to leave Keinadraig was not lost on Jack. She sat in the bow of the boat, face to the wind, her back rigid, unmindful of her hair whipping in the brisk sea air. He suspected she was crying.

A thousand doubts suddenly assailed him. Had he been wrong to return to the island, to offer to take her away? He had known her for only one day. What right did he have to interfere with her life?

Although Jack's experience with cults was limited,

he knew that when a cult member chose to leave, he or she usually faced a substantial crisis of ambivalence and self-doubt, sometimes for years. He would not exactly describe the isolated society that dwelt on the "Dragon's back" as a cult, but there were many similarities, and he did not doubt that Keely would suffer some form of mental anguish because he had encouraged her to leave.

Even more troubling was the possibility that he placed her in physical danger. Sometimes cult members would come after deserters and try to convince them to return, using all kinds of brainwashing tactics to instill guilt and fear. Jack worried that somehow Alyn Runyon would find his niece and prey upon her already-substantial fear of the Dragon's revenge to get her to come home.

Then he remembered what Keely had told him about Genevieve being excommunicated. If that were their custom, he doubted anyone would try to get Keely to return. Still he could not discount a move by the cult to bring her back.

But what if Keely did not like life in the outside world and wished to return, but could not? Jack wondered gloomily if Keely would have been happier in the long run if he had stayed out of her life. Although he tried to convince himself his motives were altruistic, that he simply had rescued her from an unwanted fate, he suspected other, more selfish motives were behind his actions. Still, it was a crime, he argued with himself, for such a bright and attractive young woman to be trapped in a life of fear and domination. But those were *his* perceptions of life on the island. Were they hers?

Beleaguered by doubts, Jack knew only one thing for certain. Although she had made the decision to leave, he was responsible for making it happen. Now he must protect her as she began her new life. He must keep her from harm and help her make the difficult adjustments he knew lay ahead of her.

But could he keep his selfish motives out of it? For

among those motives was an undeniable and intense physical attraction to Keely Cochrane.

When they reached the dock at Penzance, Kevin Spearman took the line of the boat with an air of amazement that turned to a deep scowl.

"Ye should na be meddlin' with th' Dragoners," he scolded Jack.

"Just keep your mouth shut," Jack said, and handed him a hefty tip. "You didn't see us."

He led Keely to the inn where he quickly gathered his belongings and made sure Maggie Evans's lips were sealed. She promised to say nothing, and this time took his money.

Jack helped Keely, who was clearly dazed, into the passenger seat of the rental car and fastened the seatbelt around her. He caught the scent of lavender in her hair, which sent a disconcerting message straight to those selfish motives he worried about. He longed to lose himself in those black cascades, to kiss those full lips in reassurance, but he reminded himself that his was the role of protector, not seducer.

"You okay?" he asked gently.

Her face was pale, her eyes large and worried, but he couldn't tell what thoughts lay behind their turbulent beauty.

"What's 'okay'?" she asked.

Her naive reply tugged at his heartstrings. Jack grinned and tousled her hair, explaining what the expression "okay" meant. "You've got a lot to learn, Keely," he said, "but please don't be afraid. And don't worry. I'll help you."

His playful gesture with her hair bared her neck briefly, revealing the curious, tiny red mark similar to the one he'd seen on Alyn Runyon's neck. He recalled now noticing it yesterday when he first met Keely. A birthmark shared by uncle and niece? He closed the door and locked it. He'd ask her about it sometime, but right now his only concern was to get her out of the area unseen by anyone who might recognize her.

ELEVEN

Keely remained silent as he drove, and Jack guessed she was in a mild state of shock. He had to remind himself that everything she saw and experienced right now, everything he took for granted, even something as common as riding in a car, was unfamiliar to her, and he must be careful not to overwhelm her. She was frightened enough as it was.

He kept to the main highway, speculating that Alyn Runyon was stalking his prey in more rural areas. Reaching the A30, he headed northeast, automatically returning to London, when it occurred to him that if he didn't want to overwhelm her, he probably ought to give her a few days to adjust to the outside world in a more familiar locale. A check of the map showed several towns on the Cornish coast far enough to the north of Keinadraig that her uncle would not likely come searching for her there.

"How about starting your new life on vacation?" he suggested, taking her hand and giving it a gentle squeeze.

She furrowed her brows. "On vacation?"

"On holiday," he explained, using the British expression. It had never occurred to him that her vocabulary would be so limited.

"Would that be . . . okay?" Her voice was soft, child-like, trusting, and it wrenched Jack's heart.

"To take a break? Of course it's okay. You're tired and have been through a lot. You could use a few days rest, some good food, and some peace and quiet to think things through before we head into London. Everyone takes a vacation every once in a while."

"Except Dragoners," Keely replied without humor.

"You're no longer a Dragoner," he ventured. "What do you say?"

She considered that for a long moment, then nodded slowly, but there were tears in her eyes.

It was midafternoon when Jack and Keely arrived in Fowey, a village carved into a coastal hillside, with narrow winding streets and houses perched on steep slopes that commanded a view of the protected harbor. Jack found an inn and booked two rooms, both with an ocean view. It was only then, when there was but one suitcase to carry in, that it hit him that all Keely owned in the world were the clothes on her back.

After they were settled, he suggested they explore the quaint village on foot. "First stop, somewhere to eat," he said, affecting an ease he didn't quite feel. "Then we'll find a store or two and get what you need, at least for now."

Although it was faint, she rewarded him with the first smile he'd seen on her face that day. But it faded as quickly as it came.

"What's the matter?" Jack asked.

"Jack . . ." she said, seeming to search for words. "I . . . I do na wish t' be a burden t' ye, but I have no money." She looked miserable as she added, "I fear I am bringing ye nothing but trouble."

Jack tipped her chin up, forcing her to look at him, his emotions tightening his throat. "I told you not to worry, didn't I? You don't need money, not for now. I have money. Let me help you get on your feet."

She shook her head. "I do na like favors, Jack."

As much as he wanted her to accept his help, he could relate to her hesitation. He'd always resisted the gifts from Garrison, considering them little more than charity. But now he was on the giving end, and it felt good that he could help someone else. It occurred to him for the first time that maybe that was one reason Garrison had helped him: because it felt good.

"I do na either," he replied with a grin, imitating her speech. "So don't consider this a favor. Look, Keely, we all need help at some time in our lives. People have helped me. Now let me help you."

"It's just that I do na . . . do not," she mimicked his speech in return, "know when . . . or how . . . I can re-pay ye."

Jack guessed she was afraid of the kind of payment he might be looking for. He placed both hands on her shoulders and looked directly into her eyes. "You are safe with me," he told her solemnly. "I will not hurt you, and I won't ask anything . . . untoward."

Her expression said she wanted to believe him, but he wasn't sure she did.

Keely hoped she was in a dream and that soon she would awaken and find that she had not done the unthinkable. That she had not betrayed the Dragon and the laws and her uncle.

That she had not run away with a total stranger.

It appeared, however, as if she had done all that. This was no dream. The sky above was blue, the trees green. The sun was warm on her face. Scents from the garden tweaked her nose. Jack Knight, solid as a mountain, stood in front of her, his hands resting on her shoulders.

No. This was real. But how did she get here? Everything that had happened in the past few hours seemed like a blur. She vaguely remembered getting into the boat with Jack, recalled traveling in the car at an alarming rate of speed down a ribbon of serpentine road. But there seemed to be no thoughts attached to those actions or any others since she'd left Keinadraig. It was as if her mind had clouded over and was only now beginning to clear again.

Keely shivered in spite of the warmth of the sun's rays. What had she done? By the Saints, she was a fool! She did not know anything about the man who stood disconcertingly close to her. Although he had promised to help her, he could be Genny's murderer for all she knew.

She closed her eyes and bit her lower lip to keep her emotions in check. She must not come apart now. She must think clearly, decide what to do. She could not stay with a stranger, no matter how kind he had been to her. She should not remain here at all. Perhaps if she went back now, before Alyn had time to return, she would be allowed to stay.

Behind her eyelids, however, she saw Alyn's face as she'd seen it the day before, reddened, contorted with anger . . . just before he'd hit her. And again last night, when he'd sentenced her to confinement on the island, and to a marriage she did not want. It was not a face she wanted to confront again. And as far as staying with the stranger, would she not be forced to stay—for the rest of her life—with the stranger Alyn was bringing for her to wed?

Her heart palpitated furiously, making her lightheaded and a little nauseous. She turned away from Jack and went to a nearby bench, sinking onto it, holding her head in her hands until the wave passed.

"Keely! What's wrong?" Jack covered the distance between them in one long stride.

"I . . . I'm feeling a little strange, 'tis all."

He knelt beside her and took her hand again. He touched her face lightly and smoothed her hair. "You've a right to feel strange, Keely. It wasn't easy what you did. You are a very brave woman."

How comforting his words sounded. Supportive. Encouraging. Not threatening or fearful. She let them float down into her heart, hoping they would soothe her troubled spirit. They helped, but they didn't remove her fear and confusion. "Oh, Jack, I'm so addled," she admitted.

He moved to sit beside her, and she felt his arm encircle her protectively. She allowed herself to lean into him, to take courage from him, if only for a moment. He held her tenderly, as a father would a frightened child, and yet not like that at all. He calmed her with quiet reassurances uttered somewhere near her ear.

"Shhh, it'll be okay," he told her, and his attempt to comfort her brought new tears to her eyes. How she wished she could believe him.

But Keely knew her life was not okay. Would not be okay for a long time, maybe never. It was tempting to huddle in Jack's arms and trust him. To let him take care of her. But she must not do that, or she would just be trading one kind of prison for another. She had run from Keinadraig because she desperately wanted the freedom to make choices in her life. Now she must sort things out for herself and not depend on this stranger, no matter how appealing both he and his reassurances were.

"You must be hungry." Jack's voice filtered into her thoughts, and she realized that she was hungry indeed.

"I . . . I've had nothing all day," she murmured, distressed that she had left in such a hurry, she'd brought no money with her. She could not even buy a meal. She did not wish this man's charity, but at the moment, it was her only choice. But she would keep an accounting, and as soon as she could, she would repay every pence he spent on her.

They found a cozy pub along a side street near the quay, and Keely was relieved to discover the food listed on the menu was much the same as she'd served in her own tiny pub—Cornish pasties, meat-and-cheese sandwiches, fish and chips. Something familiar in this all-new world. But there were other items as well, with names like pizza and cappuccino, things she and Genny had seen on their forays, but never tried.

"What sounds good to you?" Jack asked, gazing at her over the top of his menu. Why did she find those sea-blue depths so . . . captivating? She felt her heart flutter again, but this time not from distress.

She started to select something familiar, then hesitated and grinned. She had wanted choices. Now, even in small matters, she had choices of things she'd never dreamed about.

"What's pizza?"

Keely thought she'd never tasted anything so divine when she sank her teeth into a cheese-drenched piece of the steaming hot pizza they shared a short while later. She felt a little guilty at the pleasure. It seemed so . . . decadent. Yet Jack assured her it was common fare all over the world.

The world! How big it must be. Keely shut out that thought before she could frighten herself. She must take one step at a time. Her world at the moment was already almost more than she could handle. There was so much to think about. So many new experiences. So many choices and decisions to make.

But her new world seemed a friendly place. There did not appear to be evil lurking in every corner, as she and Genny had been led to believe. Jack certainly was not evil, and the innkeeper and pub servant had both been amiable and helpful. She finished one of the pie-shaped pieces and leaned back against the wooden booth with a sigh, relaxing for the first time since Genevieve had left.

She heard a ringing sound and watched as Jack took his portable telephone from its carrier on his belt. It was another of the miracles of the outside world. A tiny black box with no wires leading to it. Yet he claimed it carried the voices of callers as clearly as the old-fashioned phone in Alyn's office. Keely had little experience with phones, but she had answered the one in the Council office for her uncle a time or two. Maybe sometime Jack would show her how to use this one.

Jack looked at the phone, and his face darkened before he even answered it. Keely's nerves tensed immediately. Something was wrong. Jack jammed his finger at a button and put the phone to his ear.

"Hello. Who is this?" His voice was harsh, angry almost. "Hello? Hello?" He listened a moment, then took the phone from his ear and pressed another button.

"Who was it?" Keely asked, deeply apprehensive.

Jack glanced at her, and she saw him work to replace his own worried look with a smile. He shrugged and returned the telephone to its holder.

"Nobody. Wrong number, I suppose."

Jack had not lied to Keely. Not exactly. There had been nobody on the line. Or at least, nobody who said anything. But he knew it wasn't a wrong number. The digital screen had shown the number of the incoming call to be from the phone in the Council office in Keinadraig.

Somebody was trying to locate them. The thought turned his blood cold. Was there any way his phone could be traced to a particular location? He did not think so, especially without technical help. Surely no one on Keinadraig knew the technology; Jack doubted that any of the Dragoners knew the technology even existed.

Still, someone, probably Alyn Runyon, had placed a call. He frowned, trying to remember if he'd given Runyon his cellular number. He didn't think so. But if not Runyon, then who? How had some other Dragoner learned the number? And why had they hung up?

With regret, Jack saw the haunted, frightened expression had returned to Keely's face when only moments before she had shown signs of relaxing. He hated himself for revealing his concern about the call. "Don't worry," he tried to assure her, slipping a fork beneath another piece of pizza and scooping it onto her plate. "Wrong numbers happen all the time. People misdial, then hang up when they don't recognize who answered.

Here. Have another piece. I didn't know they made pizza this good in England.''

Keely ate, but she did not relax again.

After lunch, they walked the cobblestone streets of the small town in search of stores where Keely could pick out some clothing and personal toiletry items, enough to tide her over until they reached London. In a boutique, with help from a friendly clerk, she selected two dresses, a cardigan, a nightgown, a robe, and undergarments, the last of which brought some more of those selfish motives to Jack's mind.

They picked up toiletries from a chemist's shop that stocked a wealth of bath and body products alongside pharmaceuticals. Jack had grown up with a sister, so he knew some things a woman needed, but he found it embarrassing trying to guide Keely in the selection of things of an intimate nature. Finally, he cornered a saleswoman and explained that his friend was not familiar with British products and asked if she could help Keely. Obviously thinking Keely was unfamiliar because she was an American tourist on holiday, probably with a lot of money, the woman took on the assignment with gusto. But when she returned Keely to Jack, laden with a large plastic bag of items, both women looked aggravated and distressed.

While Jack paid the bill, the saleswoman told him with scarcely veiled contempt that she'd never had a customer who did not know what toothpaste was. He didn't want to think about what other items in that bag Keely might never have heard of, or know what to do with. Oh God, what had he done in urging her to leave the protection of the island?

With a glare at the rude saleswoman, Jack took the bag in one hand and Keely's elbow in the other. ''Come on,'' he said brusquely, unable to hide the embarrassment he felt for Keely at what had happened.

They walked several blocks in silence, when suddenly Keely stopped. She turned to Jack, her eyes flashing. "I did na mean t' embarrass ye." Her voice quavered with anger. "I just did na know about . . . such things." She held up the bag from the chemist's.

Jack felt like a schmuck when he realized he *had* been embarrassed, and not just for Keely. Because of the personal nature of the purchases, he'd let the woman's comments nettle him, when he should have shot back some kind of smart reply in Keely's defense. Some kind of protector he was.

"I'm sorry, Keely. I should have told the old bat off. She had no right to talk to you like that. You did just fine. I was the one who screwed up."

"Screwed up?"

Jack laughed and touched her cheek lightly with the knuckles of one hand. "Botched it. Blew it. Made a mistake." He paused, the desire to kiss her almost overwhelming his good sense. He swallowed. He didn't want to botch-it-blow-it-make-another-mistake with her now. Or ever. "Forgive me?"

Her face softened. "There is nothing t' forgive. I do have much t' learn." She laughed nervously, revealing her own embarrassment. "And there are some things a man just can na teach a woman."

Jack's mind immediately conjured up some things a man could teach a woman like her, and his mouth went dry. He must quit thinking like that.

"I know you're tired. I'll take you back to the inn and you can take a hot bath, catch a nap. I need to make some calls. Then we'll meet up again for dinner." He knew his plans sounded military, dictatorial even, but it was the only way to discipline his thoughts and bring them back into line.

He saw her to her room, which was next door to his, and showed her how to latch the door securely from the inside. "This world is safe enough, but you must be careful," he warned. "Always lock your doors." He waited outside her room until he heard the dead bolt turn. What if somehow her uncle found her? Would a dead bolt be enough to protect her from that old dragon?

In the quiet of his own room, he fell into an armchair and tried to gather his thoughts before he called Garrison. He'd gone to Cornwall to find answers to a murder, and he'd come away with a woman. A woman he did not know quite what to do with. He thought about her next door, soaking in a hot bath, slipping into the silken robe, stretching out on the bed . . .

It had been a long time since Jack had ached at the thought of a woman.

He wished he had some whiskey.

That not being an option, he picked up the phone and dialed Garrison's number, feeling suddenly abashed that with all that had happened today, he had not once thought about Brad.

"Garrison Holstedt." His old friend's voice was a welcome sound in Jack's ear.

"Garrison, it's Jack. I'm sorry I didn't call earlier, but something's come up. How's Brad?"

He heard a heavy sigh on the other end and prepared himself for the worst. "He's just the same," Garrison told him. "No better. No worse. Look, Jack, can you get back soon? There are some things we need to go over, and I'd like to do it in person."

There it was again, that intimation of trouble. "What's up, Garrison? What's wrong?"

There was a long silence. Then Garrison spoke again, his words measured. "The police think you might be the killer."

Jack let out the breath he had been holding. "That's old news, Garrison. Inspector Sandringham told me that the day he also gave me his okay to investigate this thing."

"Yes, but there are things he doesn't know . . . yet. Things that . . . well, if he finds out, could turn the case against you."

Jack was too astounded to reply. What on earth could Garrison be talking about? He found his tongue at last.

"I don't suppose you want to tell me what those things might be . . . ?"

"Not on the phone. No," he added. "We need to have a talk, face-to-face, in private."

A knot of foreboding hardened in Jack's belly. He had hoped to allow Keely more time to adjust before taking on London, but whatever was on Garrison's mind sounded serious. He also thought about the phone call from Keinadraig. Maybe it would be better after all to put more distance between her and those who might wish her harm. In London, she could put Genevieve's affairs in order. And there were others more qualified than Jack who could help her get started on a new life.

"I'll be there tomorrow," he said at last and hung up before he realized he had not mentioned Keely.

He slipped off his shoes. He guessed it would be a day of surprises for both of them.

TWELVE

Keely locked the door behind Jack as he'd instructed and leaned back against the old wood. She had never been so humiliated in her entire life. The woman at that last store had treated her like she was unclean when she did not know what to make of certain "products," as she'd called the various items.

Cleanliness was important to the way of life on Keinadraig, for everyone knew cleanliness promoted health. Of course Keely took baths and saw to her personal well-being. She was outraged when that woman had intimated perhaps she did not. It was just that Keely, like all Dragoners, used Ninian's herbals instead of cakes of deodorant soap wrapped in bright paper. They used salt and water for cleansing teeth, not a paste that tasted like mint candy. And as for the other, Keely had never heard of a tampon. It sounded strange and unnatural, and she was not at all sure she wished to learn how to use what modern women used for the moon flow.

In spite of the woman's rude inferences, however, Keely was grateful it had not been Jack who helped her find what she needed. At the moment, she was merely humiliated. If Jack had tried to explain women's products to her, she thought she might have died right on the spot.

Keely went to the bed and emptied the bags. She was very pleased with the clothing, which Jack had insisted

she buy, for she had never had such fine things. The
dresses were modern, stylish, and brightly colored, making her own clothing look drab in comparison. And the
undergarments! They were so soft and sensuous, surely
they must be sinful to wear. She held the shimmery
green robe up to her and looked at herself in the mirror.
The color accented the green in her eyes and comple-
mented her skin and dark hair. It, too, was sinfully soft
to the touch. She laughed quietly. It reminded her of the
pizza—so decadent she felt almost guilty.

Keely sank onto the bed and found that it, too, was
plush and luxurious. There were fine hangings at the
windows, elegant light fixtures, carpeting beneath her
feet. She had never considered her home shabby, but in
comparison, it was . . . plain at best.

And suddenly, she was struck by a twinge of longing
to be back among that plainness.

It was, at least, familiar. It was clean, it served her
needs. Why in the name of the Saints had she left it?
All this . . . decadence . . . was nice, but it was not better,
she decided. What was better was the closeness of
friends and family, people who cared about her.

And ordered her to obey them with unquestioning
loyalty? People who gave her no choice in matters that
concerned her life? Who were willing to excommunicate
Genny and claim that she had never existed . . . ?

Was that better?

Keely hugged her knees to her chest, feeling lost and
alone, like a small child who has strayed off the path in
a dark forest. The only friends and family she had would
no longer want her. She had no one, except Jack, who
could ease the loneliness that wrapped like a serpent
around her heart, who could calm the quiet desperation
she felt gnawing at her nerves. Jack, who had been so
kind, but who also seemed to have become a reluctant
hero.

She knew she had embarrassed him today. She'd felt
his awkwardness and guessed that he would be glad to

rid himself of her as soon as possible. He was just too honorable to say so. She must depend on him for the moment, but as soon as she was able, she would repay his money and release him from his self-imposed obligation. She would talk to him later about cutting this "vacation" short. He'd mentioned that in London there were people who could help her get a new start in life, and she was anxious to get on with it.

In the meantime, the hot bath he had also mentioned beckoned her. She sorted through the various packages from the chemist's until she came to the foil-wrapped container of scented bath salts. "House of Rutledge," the label read. The lavender crystals inside smelled divine.

She went into the adjoining chamber wherein stood a huge, claw-footed tub with golden fixtures. Thick, white towels rested on gold rods, and long lace curtains draped gracefully from ceiling to floor. Keely had to catch her breath again at this elegance in a room she had always considered to be merely functional.

She ran a small amount of water into the tub, for she was used to the frugal use of that precious commodity on the semiarid island. And then she remembered she was no longer on that island. Was water scarce here as well? Or did she dare enjoy the decadence of deeper water?

She dared. She ran the water as hot and deep as her conscience would allow, added a generous amount of the fragrant bath salts, and eased her tired body and soul into the most sublime bathing experience of her life.

She soaked until her fingers looked like wrinkled fruit and the water grew tepid. She warmed the tub by adding more hot water, then she lathered her body with the strangely scented soap bar the woman had recommended. Keely preferred Ninian's herbal soap, but this would have to do for now.

Scrunching down into the water, she flooded her black hair, then emerged again and massaged a palm full of hair soap—''shampoo'' was written on the bottle—into the thick, dark mass. This product smelled like the peaches that were sometimes brought to the island as a special treat.

After her bath, Keely stroked her hair with the new brush, working out the tangles and fluffing it to help it dry. She wished she could stand in the breeze, as she did at home, to hurry the process.

At home.

Keely gulped. She had no home. Right now, this lovely but unfamiliar room was her only home.

That she had no home was too depressing to consider, so she draped her new clothing over a chair, donned the sleeping gown, turned back the covers and slipped between the cool sheets, her bath-limp body crying out for rest.

She closed her eyes and immediately drifted off, but soon began to toss fitfully. Instead of a peaceful rest, hers was an uneasy, dream-filled sleep. Something lurked in the midnight of her slumber, a dark, unnameable terror, a creature that knew her every move and stalked her like a predator. She tried to run, but she could not escape. Her body seemed to be floating helplessly in a black void. There was nothing to hold on to, no foothold to ground her, nothing, except the terror coming closer and closer.

A flash of red lit the darkness, and flames lashed into the abyss, turning it into an inferno. The unseen threat took shape and form. It reared, terrible and fierce, before her eyes, ready to tear out her heart with its wicked dragon's claw.

Keely screamed, desperately crying out for someone to save her. But the Dragon only roared with wicked laughter as he came nearer and nearer . . .

Jack was struck with a sickening sense of déjà vu when he heard Keely scream. The last time he'd heard screaming, he'd found the bloodbath in Brad's room. He raced for her door and pounded on it, cursing himself for not getting a second key when he checked in. "Keely! Keely! It's Jack. Are you all right? Let me in!"

He was ready to break down the door when Keely finally opened it. Her face was pale and drawn, her eyes wide, and she clutched the green silk robe tightly across her breasts. Jack pushed past her, searching the room for an intruder. "What's wrong? What happened?"

" 'Twas . . .'twas only a nightmare," Keely murmured weakly, closing the door, fingering the silk collar of her robe nervously. "I . . . I did na mean t' cause alarm."

Jack wheeled around, his heart still thundering, but relief flooding through him. "A nightmare?"

Keely nodded. "I dreamt th' Dragon had come for me." Her voice was barely more than a whisper, and her lower lip trembled.

"My God," Jack swore, outraged at the fear that had been so instilled in Keely that it spilled over into her dreams. She crouched against the door like a frightened animal, and the terror had not left her eyes. He took a step toward her and saw her flinch. "I won't hurt you, Keely," he told her as he had before. If he hadn't thought it would frighten her more, he would have reached out for her and taken her into his arms, to reassure himself as much as her that she was all right.

Jack had had more experience than he ever wanted in consoling victims of violent crimes. He had comforted widows, orphans, even men who had lost someone they loved through senseless violence. But he had never felt as helpless as he did at the moment, for Keely was a victim of another kind of crime that made no sense— manipulation through fear—and he was at a loss as to how to help her get past it.

"It was only a dream, Keely," he offered, trying not to notice the soft curves visible beneath the green silk. "There is no Dragon."

"I know in my head 'twas only a dream, but Alyn

insists 'twas th' Dragon that killed Genevieve.'' Her voice cracked. "He says that somehow th' Dragon finds a way t' take his revenge against people like Genny. And me.''

Jack could stand it no longer. He went to her. "Come here," he said softly and drew her into his arms, silently cursing Alyn Runyon and all the rest on the island of Keinadraig who were responsible for this woman's needless terror.

"There is no Dragon, Keely," he repeated patiently, searching for the right thing to say that would comfort her. But his anger got in the way. "Your uncle is either a fool or a criminal for filling your head with that trash."

Keely tensed and moved away from him. "I know there is no Dragon, na in th' flesh. But t' th' people on my island, th' Dragon is as real as day," she replied, and he heard her defensive tone. She twisted her fingers in distress. "Ye do na understand, Jack."

"Then help me understand," he said, unable to hide his impatience. "Help me understand how an entire village can be controlled by an old legend. This is the twentieth century, for God's sake. There are no dragons in this day and age. What is everyone so afraid of?"

She lifted her chin. "If ye will pardon me, I am na dressed proper t' be in a room alone with a man."

But Jack was not going to let her out of this so easily. "I'll wait while you change." He gestured toward the bathroom.

She glared at him but reached for pieces of the clothing that she had laid across the chair and headed for the bathroom. Moments later, she emerged in a soft, flowing dress the color of ripe melon that reached to her ankles. A multicolored sash was tied at her waist. Her hair shone, obviously freshly brushed. She wore no makeup, for not only was she unfamiliar with it, she needed none. Her skin glowed with natural vitality, and her lips invited him with their own deep pink hue.

She was just as distracting fully clothed as she had

been in her robe. Jack groaned to himself. She was not making this easy on him either.

"You look really pretty," he said fatuously, feeling like a schoolboy.

Keely's cheeks deepened in color. "Thank ye, but we must na stay here. 'Tis na proper for a man and a woman t' be alone together like this."

Jack let out a long sigh and rubbed the back of his neck with one hand. "This is a different world than you are accustomed to, Keely. Men and women are often alone . . . together. I have told you I won't hurt you. Can you not trust me?"

She hesitated. "Did Genevieve trust your friend?"

Jack saw her point, but refuted her implication. "Brad did not kill her, Keely."

"If 'twas na Brad, and na th' Dragon, then who killed Genny?"

Jack shook his head. "Your guess is as good as mine," he said, then in deference to her obvious discomfort at their being alone together, he went to the door. "Come on. Let's get out of here."

The day had rolled into early evening, and the birds were well into their final chorus for the day. The lazily retiring sun turned the tree trunks golden, and a light breeze caught Keely's hair. She paused, turned her face to the wind, and took a deep breath.

"The scent o' th' ocean always makes me feel better," she said, smiling up at him.

Her skin seemed to glow in the golden sunlight, and highlights gleamed in her rich, dark hair. The sleeveless dress revealed soft shoulders that offered a dangerous invitation to a man's touch, and Jack wished he'd helped her select something less tempting. "Are you chilly? Would you like to take along a wrap?"

She looked at him as if he were nuts. " 'Tis th' middle o' summer."

He shrugged. "The breeze can be cool at night." Well, you tried, old boy, he thought wryly, and wondered how he would keep his hands off those shoulders for the rest of the evening.

They meandered along the stone sidewalk, admiring the profusion of flowers at riot in the lush garden outside the inn. "Look, there's a fish!" Keely cried in delight, discovering a lurking koi in the pond that was carefully designed into the landscape. She clapped her hands, as excited as a child. Jack's heart swelled to see her earlier fear vanish and her innocence return. He wanted to give her that, a renewed innocence, but he knew it was not possible. But he could give her this, a brief time in between yesterday and tomorrow, where, free from the fears of the past, she could begin to discover the exciting new world that soon would be hers.

The frightful images from her dream began to fade as Keely walked beside Jack along the sunlit lane that took them back down the steep hill and into the village. So, too, did her apprehension about being with him. She had been surprised and troubled when he'd become so angry a short while ago. It was hard for her to understand how a stranger could possibly care about what her people thought or how they lived their lives. But it was obvious he felt strongly that their ways were wrong. Although she had felt the need to defend them, he'd struck a chord somewhere deep inside when he'd asked what everyone was so afraid of.

What *was* she so afraid of? Her dreams? Retribution from a Dragon Jack said did not exist? A Dragon that even she knew did not exist except as a monster of the mind? Drawing in another deep breath of the fresh, tangy sea air, Keely tossed her hair back and raised her face to the sky. She smiled as she saw the twinkle of a single star poke its face into the summer night. It was the same sky, the same star, she'd seen on summer nights all her life, but suddenly, seeing it from the outside, here with Jack, it seemed more precious, more enchanting.

In fact, everything felt differently delicious to her, even her clothing. She became aware of the caress of the soft fabric of the luscious pink dress against her calves as she walked. Her shoulders were brazenly bare against the soft night air, arousing some distinctly sensual but not unpleasant sensations. The skin of her left arm tingled where it mingled with Jack's body heat as they walked close together.

He had not touched her since their words back at the inn. Suddenly, Keely wanted him to touch her. She realized that his little outburst against her people and their ways had been protective, not accusatory. Protective in the same manner as when he'd stepped between her and Alyn to protect her from her uncle's wrath. She did not know why he cared, but she was glad he did. Boldly, she slipped her hand into his, and a charge like electricity shot through her when he tightened his fingers around hers.

"Beautiful evening," he said, giving her one of his rare smiles. Keely's insides turned to melted butter.

She searched for words in reply, but all she could muster was a weak, "Aye."

As they reached the center of the village, Keely noticed a crowd was gathering down by the quay. "What's happening?" she asked.

"Let's find out." Jack grasped her hand even more tightly and wove them through the crowd until they came upon a scene unlike anything she'd ever laid eyes on. To one side of the town square, a yellow tent was set up, inside of which four men were tuning musical instruments. Along the waterfront, strings of gaily colored lights cast merry reflections in the water of the quiet harbor. At quayside, a man with a little cart was selling some kind of sausage in a bun, and Keely's mouth watered at the smell of the cooking meat. Nearby, another vendor offered "The World's Best Ice Cream."

"What is this?" she asked, turning to Jack.

"Hot dogs, ice cream, and a band. Looks like a party to me." He grinned. Then he glanced toward the musicians and gave a hearty laugh. "Well, I'll be damned."

"What?"

"The group. They call themselves the Joe Boudreaux and his Louisiana Cajun Swamp Water Zydeco Band." He continued to laugh until tears came to his eyes.

"What's so funny?" She had no idea what the name meant, or why it should be comical.

"It's just strange to see a band like that here, in Cornwall of all places," Jack said, wiping a tear from the edge of one eye. "Louisiana is a state in the southern part of America," he explained. "They like hot food called 'Cajun' and a certain style of music called 'zydeco.' You don't see zydeco bands that often even in the States. I never dreamed I'd see one here."

As if on cue, the band struck up a lively number, and with a whoop several of the bystanders partnered up and began to dance in the plaza. Keely stared in amazement at the uninhibited swaying and swinging of the men and women who laughed and made strange gestures into the air in time to the music. A bubble of laughter formed in her belly, and it rose with a tickle upward until it spilled from her lips, and she joined Jack in the pure joy of the moment.

Then to her surprise, he took her other hand and led her into the dancing. "But . . . I do na know how . . ." she protested.

"Look around. There's nothing to know," he shouted over the din.

He began to move in time to the music, and she felt her own body take over and give way to the zesty rhythm. He guided her with both hands, shifting weight from right to left and back again, then turning her in circles until she was dizzy. The musicians were merciless, rolling from one song into the next until the dancers were flushed and breathless. Just as Keely thought she might pass out, they finally took a break.

"Oh, Jack," she gasped, holding her side and laughing. "I have never done such dancing."

"Did you like it?" he asked, drawing her away from the throng to where it was cooler on the grassy bank.

Keely's face hurt from smiling. Her side hurt from the frenetic exercise and from laughing so hard. But everything else had ceased to hurt. The night, the music, the man by her side had all worked magic to ease the dark fears of her dream. "Aye," she said, catching her breath at last. "I liked it all right, Jack."

"Wait here. I'll be right back."

Before she could say a word, Jack slipped away into the crowd, leaving Keely slightly panicked at being alone. Her heart began to beat heavily again, and worry trickled back under her skin. What if he didn't come back? Keely knew he would, but his absence reminded her of how very alone she was in this unfamiliar world.

Her worry faded moments later when Jack reappeared, carrying two objects, rounded on top and pointed on the bottom. He handed her one. "Hope you like Cherry Garcia."

Keely had seen ice cream cones in pictures, but she had never tried one. "Cherry Garcia?"

"Cherry ice cream with chocolate chips." He bit into his with relish, surfacing with a dab on his nose. Keely giggled and reached to rub it away.

" 'Tis heavenly sounding," she said, not wanting him to know she'd never tasted such a thing. He might be embarrassed at her ignorance, as he had been at the chemist's shop. She licked her way around the cone. " 'Tis heavenly tasting."

"My favorite," he told her, taking her hand easily and beginning to stroll along a side street. "I asked around. Seems this is some kind of special American festival they're having tonight. That explains the Louisiana music and the hot dogs. They've even got Ben & Jerry's ice cream."

Keely had no idea who Ben and Jerry were, but they made very good ice cream. As for Americans, Keely thought she liked them even more than Cherry Garcia.

THIRTEEN

The only thing wrong with most zydeco music, Jack decided, was that it did not allow a man to take a woman into his arms for a slow dance. And he had a keen desire to do exactly that with Keely Cochrane. Watching her move as she danced to the fast numbers, he'd felt those selfish motives begin to get his attention again, and he had to work to quench the appetite of his desire.

His own motivations aside, however, he had overcome his earlier doubts about the wisdom of encouraging Keely to leave Keinadraig. He was glad he'd helped her to escape her island prison. He thought it would have been a crime unto itself for this vivacious, spirited woman to have languished the rest of her life in that throwback medieval society. She belonged to this time and this place, to hot music and cherry ice cream.

And to him?

Jack knew better than to let those kinds of thoughts wreck his objectivity, but he found the idea as appealing as the ice cream.

They finished their cones as they wandered along a narrow street and peered into several shop windows, where Keely exclaimed about the abundance and luxury of what she saw displayed there. "We do na have shops on Keinadraig," she explained. "Only I with th' pub; Mistress Olthorpe, who bakes bread; and John Lange, who organizes th' distribution o' food and other goods brought onto th' island, had small stores, but they are na like this. They're in th' front rooms of our houses.''

So that's why he had seen no signs of commerce on the streets of the village. ''You had no choice of clothing?'' Jack continued to be amazed by the limitations of the world she had come from.

''Not much,'' she replied wistfully. ''Once a month, we prepared a list o' what we needed, including clothing, and my uncle took it t' th' mainland and did his best t' find what we wanted.''

''He shopped for the whole village?''

Keely shrugged. ''Aye. 'Tis part o' his job as th' Keeper. Few are allowed t' meet with people on th' outside.''

''I see.'' Jack thought that was one of the most bizarre things he'd ever heard, but he brushed it off. He didn't want to talk about the strange habits of the Dragoners. He wanted Keely to look forward, not backward. He heard the music begin again one street over.

This time, instead of breaking into another frenzied tune, the band leader began singing a slow love song, one Jack had requested when he'd gone for their ice cream and secured with a considerable contribution to the charity the band supported. Jack grinned. ''Come on. Let's dance.''

Oblivious to the other dancers, Jack took Keely into his arms as they reached the town square, and with an effort, managed not to hold her too tightly against him. She was relaxed and happy, and he wanted her to enjoy this first glimpse of her new life without apprehension of any kind.

''Girl, ye look wonderful tonight,'' the singer crooned in a very non-American accent.

''He sounds like a Cornishman,'' Keely said, leaning away slightly and raising her face to look up at Jack, who was more than half a foot taller than she. ''I thought ye said th' band was from America.''

"Nope. Just the music. I talked to the lead singer when I went for ice cream. The band's from a town up the road about five miles." He grinned again at the thought. "They just like the zydeco sound and put together a group that plays at local gigs for charity."

"Gigs?"

"Engagements. Like this. They play for tips to raise money to help underprivileged children."

Keely looked thoughtful. "Do they know these children?"

Jack shrugged. "I doubt it. Why?"

"It . . . it just seems odd they do this kindness . . . for strangers."

Jack didn't know how to reply to that, so he just swung her around and gathered her into his arms, humming the tune to the song in his head, glad he'd requested it. This girl certainly looked wonderful tonight.

Too soon, the number was over, and Joe Boudreaux and his Louisiana Cajun Swamp Water Zydeco Band reeled into another spicy round that drew throngs onto the small patch of concrete in the square.

"Want another go, or would you rather sit this one out?" he shouted to Keely.

She tossed her head back and fluffed her thick hair away from her neck. "I think I have had all o' th' Louisiana dancing I can take for this night," she said, laughing gaily. "Unless ye wish t' stay?"

Jack slipped his arm around her waist and led her away from the lights and the music. When they reached the quiet of the lane that led to the inn, he asked, "What's your pleasure? We can walk some more, or if you'd like, I'll take you back to your room."

At that, he felt her stiffen. "I . . . I'd rather walk."

Jack got it clearly that she was afraid to go back to her room. Why? Was she afraid of another nightmare? Or was she afraid that he might try to come on to her? Maybe he'd overstepped himself in indulging in that slow dance. "Okay," he said, trying to sound reassuring. "Anyplace in particular?"

" 'Tis such a lovely evening. Would there be a high place where we could look out over th' water?"

Jack was unfamiliar with Fowey, but up was up, and he knew where the harbor lay. "Let's see what we can find." They started up the steep cobblestone road.

They were both breathless when at last the tree-darkened lane spilled them out onto an open grassy hillside park that overlooked the ocean. Far below they could see the lights of the festival, although the distance drowned the sound of the music and laughter. A park bench beckoned, and they collapsed in mutual fatigue. Keely tilted her head back and looked up into the darkening night sky.

"I love th' stars," she said. "Ever since I was a little girl, I have gone out on moonless nights like this and gazed up at them, wondering what they are and what lies out there in th' vast darkness."

"There are worlds upon worlds we know nothing about," Jack said.

"Do ye suppose there are others like us?"

"I suppose there are."

"What would ye do if they came here, t' our shore?"

Jack wondered where she was leading. "Me personally? Or us as a society?"

"This world. What would th' people o' this world do if strangers came here from a faraway star? And what if," she continued without waiting for his answer, "what if those strangers brought a terrible plague that killed many people? What would we do t' protect ourselves?"

Jack frowned. "Why do you ask something like that?"

But she just stared out at the stars and did not reply.

Keely had often wondered if there might be others who lived out beyond the stars, but the thoughts she'd just uttered to Jack had only occurred to her as she spoke them aloud. It was startling to make such an analogy, and refreshing to think in such ways. There was something about Jack that stirred her imagination and made her think more clearly than she had at any time in her life. Or mayhap it wasn't him at all. Mayhap the air was different here in the outside world.

"My mother once told me that th' stars were little windows t' Heaven," she remarked. "I wonder if Genny is up there, looking down on us right this very minute." Keely's throat tightened, and she felt moisture sting her eyes.

"Do you want to talk about Genny?" Jack asked quietly.

Keely sighed. Genny wasn't in Heaven. Not yet. For she had not received the purification ceremony to prepare her for that journey. It was up to Keely to make sure her beloved kinswoman reached the stars.

"I . . . I suppose 'tis time t' think about what t' do for Genny," she said, clearing her throat. She shifted on the bench to face Jack, stretching her arm toward him along the top slat of wood. " 'Twas one thing that made me leave Keinadraig. I must make arrangements for her ceremony when we get t' London. Will ye help me, Jack?"

Jack crooked an elbow over the back of the bench and took her fingers in his. "Of course," he said, stroking them lightly and sending goose prickles along Keely's arm. "But I need your help as well."

With all Jack had done for her, Keely was happy to have some way to return his kindness. But she was dumbfounded. "Help? How can I help?"

"I was hired by my friend's father to find out what happened to him, and to Genny. She . . . was not exactly the kind of girl one would expect Brad to become acquainted with," he said, not unkindly. "If I could figure out how he met her and why she was with him that night, it might lead to other answers. You can help me, Keely, by telling me more about Genevieve."

Keely studied him for a long moment. In the gloaming, his features were unreadable. Was this the reason for his kindness to her, to use her to try to solve the crime? Was this why he'd enabled her to run away? Because he needed her to answer his questions? It was possible.

But then she thought about the way he had stepped in to protect her from her uncle's wrath. She recalled his generous offer to help her as she started her new life. She remembered the feel of his arms around her as they danced, how gently and tenderly he had guided her across the floor. These were not the actions of one who had deliberately manipulated her life for his own gain. He simply needed her help. Did she not wish to find Genny's killer, too?

Still, a chill of fear crept over her. She had taken a sacred vow not to disclose the secrets of the Dragon to anyone. A whisper of a warning brushed through her mind.

Bad things happen to those who betray the Dragon.

Keely fought to banish the notion, but she withdrew her hand and folded it with the other into her lap, where together they worried the cloth of the brightly colored sash.

"I will do what I can. What do ye wish t' know?"

"For starters, I'd like to know why she left Keinadraig. What made her run away? Alyn fed me a line about her not respecting the laws. But she was your friend, Keely, and you respect the laws. Didn't Genevieve share your views?"

Round and round her finger Keely twisted the tie. "Aye," she answered after giving it long consideration, "she did." Although Genny had been a dreamer, she was a Dragoner at heart. Keely forced herself to think back over that night. " 'Twas something t' do with Ninian. Genny was t' become th' next Healer. When she reached her twenty-first birthday, Ninian required her t' go into apprenticeship, for Ninian is growing older. I did na know Genevieve did na wish t' become Healer. She never spoke t' me of it. Na until that night.''

"What did she say?"

Keely recalled the words clearly. "That she did na have it in her t' become th' Healer.''

"Why not?"

But Keely was at a dead end. "I do na know. Th' Healer takes care o' th' sick and binds up wounds and performs ceremonies. Genny never liked th' sight o' blood, and she hated t' go on sick rounds with her mother. Maybe that was it.''

"I assume it's an honor to be the Healer?"

"Aye. 'Twas t' th' first Healer th' Dragon in th' flames gave th' laws. She heard them in th' Dragon's song.''

"Dragon's song?"

Keely chewed on her bottom lip. " 'Tis th' song inscribed on th' gate t' Keinadraig. 'Tis said th' Dragon rose up from th' flames in th' sacred circle o' stones and sang those words t' th' Healer, and as long as th' Dragoners abide by his law, he will protect them from a return o' th' pestilence that nearly destroyed them in th' old days.''

"The pestilence? Are you talking about the Black Plague?"

"Aye. 'Tis referred t' as that.''

Jack leaned forward, balancing his arms across his knees. "So that's what you were talking about a while ago, about aliens landing on earth and bringing a plague. That explains what happened to your people, doesn't it? A stranger brought the plague. That explains the law forbidding strangers. But there hasn't been any plague for centuries,'' he pointed out. "Why must you keep 'hiding away on your distant shore,' as I believe the song goes?''

"Because . . . because th' Dragon's laws have always kept us safe and protected," Keely stammered, feeling

compelled to defend what she had believed for twenty-
five years.

"Protected? Or under control? Seven hundred years
is a long time to abide by any set of laws without some
changes. But no one on Keinadraig questions them because they're all too damned scared of the Dragon's so-
called revenge. That sounds more like brainwashing than
protection."

Jack's voice had changed. His earlier caring compassion had vanished, replaced now by a harsh anger. His
attitude and curt questions made her very nervous and
uncomfortable. Renewed anxiety washed over Keely.
Mayhap she'd made a terrible mistake to trust him. She
should not have told him the Dragon's tale. She could
tell he scorned it. She had risked much to share it with
him, for Genny's sake, and now he'd ridiculed it. It was
easy for an outsider to make light of the Dragon's revenge, but she could not.

She glanced around, half expecting to see the Dragon
waiting to get even for what she'd just done. At that
moment she heard a rustle overhead and looked up to
see a large raven flap out of the sky and settle on a rock
not far away. The bird blinked at her with a malignant
eye and emitted a rough caw.

"Holy Saints!" she cried in pure terror. The raven,
by tradition a messenger of the Dragon, glared at her
malevolently and gave another harsh caw. Certain of her
imminent demise, Keely turned and fled down the hill
into the protection of darkness.

Lost in his thoughts, Jack had not seen the raven until
he heard Keely's cry. He looked up just in time to see
it take flight as she turned on her heel and dashed down
the lane. Jack took off at a run to catch up with Keely,
remembering Kevin Spearman's claim that a raven was
a bad omen. He knew Keely was afraid of the mythical
Dragon. Was she afraid of a raven as well?

Or was it him she was running from?

He caught up with her just as she reached the twin globes of the lights that illumined the steps to the inn. "Keely, what's the matter?" He took her firmly by the shoulders. "What frightened you? Look, I'm sorry if . . ."

He could feel her body twitching with tension. " 'Twas na ye, Jack," Keely said in a small voice. She crumpled into his embrace. "Oh, Jack. I am so frightened. 'Tis childish, I know, but I have never been frightened like this."

The fear in her voice pierced Jack's heart all over again, and he held her tightly, rocking her back and forth and brushing kisses into her hair, murmuring soft reassurances. Jack wished like hell that he'd taken training in the techniques of exit counseling when it had been offered to him while on the force. Psychologists and social workers used exit counseling to help people who were leaving a cult environment adjust to the real world. And from what Keely had told him so far, Jack believed that the isolated society from which she had just escaped was undeniably a type of cult. It fit the mold. The lives of the Dragoners were driven by a strict set of rules, enforced by a leader with no tolerance for betrayal. Lawbreakers were punished—by death, it would seem in this case—and fear was the primary motivator. Often, people who were victimized by a cult continued to defend its practices even after escaping, as Keely had done just a short time ago.

"Shhh. Don't be afraid," he crooned, wishing he knew how to dissolve her fears. She was bright and beautiful, strong and self-determined enough to change her destiny, yet she was a woman-child, driven by senseless fears imbedded in her psyche since childhood. Jack damned the Dragon cult all to hell and vowed he would do whatever it took to help her heal from her nightmares. "I told you I would help you, Keely," he murmured, kissing her on the forehead. "I promise I will be here for you, for as long as you need me."

Keely's eyes met his, but she did not respond to his promise. "Let's go inside."

A few moments later, Jack took a seat next to Keely on the small sofa in his room, as she'd been too frightened to return to her own. "It was just a bird," Jack tried to reason with her after she told him what had caused her to run away. He put his arm around her, and she did not resist.

"I . . . I know that," she sniffed miserably. "But on Keinadraig, th' raven is th' herald o' th' Dragon . . ."

"That's a crock, Keely," Jack growled. "Besides, you are no longer on Keinadraig," he reminded her, "and you no longer have to believe all that."

She shook out her hair and raised her face to his. "I know that, too. In fact, tonight was so . . . magical, I thought I could put it all behind me. Then we started talking about Genny, and I told ye things I should na have, and then th' raven came, and then. . . ." She broke off, looking so distraught Jack thought she might be ill. "I don't understand it, Jack. I'm na a stupid woman. I know this fear is all in my head, but I just can't seem t' make it go away."

Jack thought his heart was going to break. Tenderly, he placed his hand on her upper arms and looked into her face. "Have you ever heard of brainwashing?"

Her bewildered look answered his question. He stroked the downy skin of her cheek.

"In my country, there are people who try to control the lives of other people," he began, attempting to describe a cult, but realizing with a grin that he'd just defined politicians. He ignored the irony and went on. "They live away from the rest of us, usually on a farm or ranch in the countryside. They form communities called 'cults.' Usually in a cult, there is a strong, charismatic leader who demands unquestioned loyalty from the rest, and uses fear of punishment to insure that loyalty. The fear is instilled in the people by a process called 'brainwashing.' "

Jack did not see the need to go into the grim details of life inside a cult, for from Keely's silent nod, she had obviously already caught on.

"Are ye saying I come from a cult?"

Jack grimaced. "Not exactly, because your society lacks the kind of power-hungry leader usually found in a cult. But in a way, the legends of the Dragon have brainwashed the people into following certain laws that have long since been unnecessary, like arranged marriages, for example. They keep your people living in fear, when, to my mind, there is nothing to be fearful of."

"Brainwashed." Keely turned the word over in her mouth. "That sounds more like clearing away thoughts than putting them into your head."

This was one intelligent woman, Jack thought, not for the first time. That sharp mind would help her adjust quickly to her new environment. But brainwashing often reached past the intellect and poisoned the heart, making it difficult if not impossible for some victims to ever completely shake the effects of the exploitative manipulation.

"You are exactly right," Jack answered her. "When a person is brainwashed by a cult, they are coerced into giving up old attitudes and behavior, to 'wash' them away, so to speak, so the leader can replace them with thoughts and actions he deems to be in his best interest."

"But on Keinadraig, there is no brainwashing," Keely insisted. "We grow up with our legends."

Jack sighed and took one of her hands in both of his. "That's true," he said. "But the minds of children are clean slates, so there is no need to wash them before instilling the fear that will later control them. Don't you see, you have been manipulated ever since you were a little girl into believing something that might not be real at all."

Keely shifted in her chair and withdrew her hand. "I

understand that. But th' fear . . ." she said hesitantly, "th' fear is very real, Jack."

Jack could almost feel her distress. "Yes," he replied, "fear that is planted so early and so deeply can become part of your psyche, your soul. It is not an easy thing to get rid of."

Her eyes were bright with unshed tears. "Jack," she whispered after a long moment, "have ye ever been afraid?"

FOURTEEN

182   HELIONE

Had he ever been afraid? Jack drew in a deep breath. If she only knew. "Of course. I've been afraid many times."

"When was th' first time ye remember being afraid?"

It was Jack's turn to be unsettled. That was a difficult question. There had been so many moments of fear during his career as a cop. But he had to go back many years before that to reach his first memory of having been afraid. "When I was five," he said at last, struggling with the emotions that had launched a surprise attack on him. "When two men came to my house and told my mother that my father had been killed in Vietnam."

"Vietnam?"

Jack forgot that Keely would never have heard of a country called Vietnam, much less that a nasty little war had been fought there. He explained it to her briefly.

"I am so sorry," she said.

Jack shrugged. "It was a long time ago, and I barely remember him."

"Did ye grow up without a father?"

"Yes . . ." he started to reply, but was hit with another sudden realization. ". . . And no."

Keely frowned. "I do na understand."

For years, Jack had considered Garrison's financial support to be an excessive gesture of battlefield loyalty.

But Keely's questions sparked a memory . . .

"The man who I told you hired me to find Brad's killer, Garrison Holstedt, was in the war with my father. When Dad died, he promised to take care of us." A painful knot constricted his throat as the memory grew clearer, and Jack was ashamed that he'd forgotten how much more Garrison had done for him than provide for him financially.

How could he have forgotten the day when Garrison had intervened on behalf of a reckless teenager about to take some wrong turns in life? The day he'd taken on the role of the father Jack had so desperately needed?

Jack took a deep breath and told Keely something he'd never shared with anyone in his life, not even his sister.

"When I was a teenager, I got into a lot of trouble for fighting in school," he said. "I was unhappy, angry all the time, and I didn't know why. So I became sullen and rebellious." It was odd to hear himself talk objectively about those days. He'd tried hard to forget them, for he was not proud of the way he'd been. He cleared his throat and went on.

"One day I was catching hell in the principal's office when Garrison unexpectedly showed up. I never knew it, but he had kept a close eye on Melinda and me as we grew up. My mother couldn't handle me, and I was about to get kicked out of school, so the principal called him. I guess," Jack said, the picture continuing to unfold, "he decided to step in where my own father could not."

Jack could not continue until he could process that idea. When he spoke again, it was barely above a whisper. "Garrison changed my life that day. The principal left us alone, and Garrison began to talk about my father. He told me that John Knight had been an honorable man, and that I would have been proud of him. He said Dad would have wanted to be proud of me, too, but that he didn't think my fighting and poor grades would make him very proud.''

Keely remained silent, listening intently. Jack bit his lip and fought to control his emotions. ''It was the first time anyone had talked to me about my father like that, like he was somehow looking down from heaven and not liking what he was seeing in his son.

''My father had always been just a shadowy childhood memory to me until Garrison said that. At first, I resented the mention of the father who had never been there for me, but then I realized that was why I was so angry. I was angry because my father had left me.''

The finale of the long-buried memory finally surfaced, and he shared it with Keely. Alone with Garrison in the principal's office, Jack had begun to shake. He didn't want to admit how desperately he wanted a father. But Garrison knew. And he'd been there for him. ''It's okay to cry, son,'' he'd said quietly. And Jack had cried. And Garrison had held him.

And neither had mentioned it since.

Keely sat in stunned silence and watched Jack work through pain and grief he must have been carrying with him for most of his life, and her heart opened to him. No one, it seemed, escaped fear.

Jack's fear had led him to destructive behavior, until Garrison had rescued him. ''He was there for me,'' Jack had just told her.

He'd promised her the same thing only a short while ago, that he would be there for her as long as she needed him, but she had found it difficult to believe that a stranger could honestly make such a pledge. But now, knowing he had once been frightened and alone, knowing someone had been there for him, Keely could allow herself to trust that he meant what he had said. And trust that he would offer help, not harm.

She also understood clearly why he was so determined to prove his friend's innocence. Garrison Holstedt was the only father Jack had ever known. She suspected Garrison's son, Brad, had been more a brother than a friend.

Unsure exactly how to return his kindness and support, Keely offered the only thing she could: time for him to get on with his investigation.

"Jack." She spoke softly, interrupting his thoughts, which seemed to be miles away. "I do na need t' stay on this vacation any longer. Could we go on t' London tomorrow?"

He looked at her, the worry on his face melting into relief. "I really do need to get back."

"Let us leave early then."

Jack's stomach chose that moment to loudly protest the late hour and its empty state, and Keely laughed, glad to lighten the atmosphere. "Ye sound as if ye have a dragon in your belly."

His grin lit up his handsome face, and Keely felt her heart skip a beat or two. She'd never met a man like this. Somehow, the men on Keinadraig lacked the depth, the soul, that Jack Knight had revealed to her. He was, in fact, the most fascinating person, man or woman, she had ever encountered.

"Ever hear of takeout?" he asked, picking up a menu that lay by the telephone.

Half an hour later, with paper cartons strewn around them, Keely dug into the second delicious experience of the day. Chinese food. Strange vegetables. Succulent spicing that warmed her inside and out.

The panic engendered by her encounter with the raven had vanished in Jack's presence and was replaced by a kind of calm inner glow. She relaxed as they shared the meal, and she listened to him describe life in the new world she was about to explore. In spite of some of the frightening things he told her about his life as a "cop," and regardless of what had happened to Genny and Brad, Jack seemed to believe that his world was worth living in, and by the time they finished the last of the Chinese food, Keely was confident that she, too, would find it everything she hoped for and more.

"Fortune cookie?" he asked, offering her a strange-looking dainty.

"What's this?"

Jack broke his open with a snap and pulled out a small piece of paper. "Good luck awaits you." He laughed. "We could use some of that. Open yours."

Keely opened her cookie, enjoying the playfulness of the game. But her heart lurched when she read her fortune: "The dragon watches over you."

"Good grief," Jack exclaimed and held out his hand. "Give that to me." He threw both fortunes away, cookies and all. "Don't let it worry you. To the Chinese, the dragon is a symbol of great good fortune."

Keely was amazed. It had never occurred to her that a dragon might exist anywhere other than on Keinadraig. "I did na know there were dragons elsewhere," she told him, wishing she was not so unschooled and vowing to better her education as soon as she could.

"There are dragons the world over," he told her, "but like yours, they are mythical. They don't really exist except as symbols for other things, like power, or good fortune."

The dragon watches over you. Keely shivered despite Jack's cheery reassurances. Why would she get such a message, unless . . .

"It's late," Jack said. "If we want to be on the road early, we'd better get some sleep. Come on, I'll walk you to your room."

The glow of the evening dissolved into gray uncertainty once again. Keely opened the door to her room and was greeted by darkness. Jack flipped on the switch, flooding the room with light, but Keely faltered. She did not want to be alone. She turned to Jack.

"Stay with me."

He touched her cheek and gave her a wry grin. "You don't know what you are asking, lady. Whatever happened to 'a man and a woman should na be together alone?' '' he teased.

She did not laugh. "I am trying t' learn na t' be afraid. When I am with ye, I am na." She turned to the empty room. "But when I am alone . . ."

She felt Jack's hands on her shoulders, and she leaned against him, her back to his chest, glad of his protection.

He whispered a kiss into her hair. "Oh God, Keely, you have so much to learn."

His arms slipped around her, crossing in front. She was completely enclosed in his embrace, and she had never felt so good or so safe. "Aye," she whispered. "That I do. Will ye teach me, Jack?"

He turned her to face him, and she saw a curious expression in his eyes, as if he were fighting with himself. "Yes," he answered. "But you don't need to learn it all in one day."

Jack held her gaze for a long moment, then lowered his head. Before she knew what was happening, his lips touched hers, and suddenly the unfamiliar territory of her new world shifted once again.

Keely feared her knees would give way. She had never been kissed by a man before, not like this. Her father, her uncle, well-wishers on birthdays had brushed kisses on her cheeks. But Jack's kiss jolted her to the core, sending strange but delicious sensations shooting through every nerve in her body. His touch aroused all those disturbing feelings she had struggled with earlier and tried to bury deep inside.

Yet she chose not to fight them now.

Jack's kiss felt right and good, and Keely melted against him as naturally as if she'd done it all her life. Encircling him with her arms, she relished the feel of the muscles of his back against the palms of her hands. Unexpectedly, he parted her lips with his tongue, heightening the already almost-unbearable sensations of desire that now raged through her. Her heart pounded so heavily she could hear it in her ears, but she was not afraid.

She opened her mouth to his tender explorations, thinking she might die at any moment from the sweet pleasure of it.

Abruptly, he drew away. "Keely," he said in a hoarse whisper. "We can't do this."

His words hit her like ice water, and she drew away, trying to recover her breath. He was right. They should not be doing this. He was a stranger. Forbidden. Not of her world. She did not know him, or his ways. He might even be dangerous.

But she did not care. Her body, trembling from the effect of his embrace, wanted more of him in ways she did not understand but was willing, no, *eager* to learn.

Her heart sank when she saw the dark and troubled look on his face. She wanted more of him, but obviously, he did not want more of her. Why, then, had he kissed her like that?

Confused, hurt and more than a little angry, Keely moved out of his arms and crossed the room. "I was wrong," she stammered, working hard to regain control. "I do na need ye t' stay with me. I must wash my brain and learn na t' be afraid when I am alone."

Much later, Jack tossed on his bed, wishing to God he had not succumbed to the temptation of Keely's lips. He was supposed to be her guardian. Her protector. Not her lover. Yet that's what it had felt like to be in her arms. Who knew where it might have led if he hadn't managed to stop?

It was obvious that, as in other aspects of her life, Keely Cochrane was incredibly sexually naive. From her response, Jack knew she had not objected to his kiss. She had, in fact, opened to him with an innocent sensuality that stirred him just to recall. But she seemed to have no idea what it did to him, or where that kiss, those caresses, might lead. God in heaven, what would happen to her if . . . when . . . she met another man who found her lips as irresistible as he had? What if that man was unable to control his urges and took advantage of her? The very thought made Jack ill.

When he'd offered Keely a way out of her predicament, Jack had obviously not considered some of the possible consequences. He'd thought merely to rescue her from an unwanted fate, deliver her to some social service agency in London that could help her get back on her feet, and then he could be on his way. He hadn't counted on becoming involved with her, not like this. He stared into the darkness, seeing Keely's beautiful face, her alluring eyes. And he knew he was involved whether he meant to be or not.

How, in less than two days, could he have become so completely captivated by this woman?

And what in hell was he going to do about it?

Jack was almost asleep when he heard a familiar ringing. He blinked, focusing on the sound, and realized it was coming from the cellular phone that he'd laid on the desk across the room. Turning on the bedside lamp, he went to answer it.

His blood chilled when he saw the digital screen. Someone was calling again from Keinadraig. At two o'clock in the morning.

"Hello?"

At first there was no response. Then he heard a guttural voice. "She has betrayed th' Dragon," the caller hissed. Jack couldn't tell whether it was a man or a woman.

"Who the hell is this?"

"Soon she will die."

Before he could think of anything to say that would keep the caller on the line, it went dead.

Jack sat on the edge of the bed, vacillating between anger and frustration. Never had he felt so . . . ill-equipped. He was a stranger in a foreign country with no weapon to rely on, yet he'd assumed responsibility for a woman whose life he may have inadvertently put in danger. He'd vowed to protect her, but from what?

In the beginning, he'd thought it was nothing more than her own superstitious fears and naivete. But after this second call, he knew something more human, and more deadly, stalked Keely.

He resisted the urge to go to her room to make sure she was all right. After what had transpired earlier, the last thing he needed was to have another close encounter with Keely, especially dressed as she would be now in her nightgown.

The call had come from Keinadraig. The threat lay there, not in the next room, Jack reasoned. Still, he opened his door and peered down the darkened hallway. Keely's door was shut, and he heard no sound of distress.

Reassured, but restless and unable to sleep, he went to his briefcase and took out his small notebook. Sitting at the desk, he filled pages with notations on all that had transpired since he'd left London. He was usually not so negligent. Usually he made notes on an investigation right away in case memory did not serve him accurately. But he'd been sloppy this time.

Sloppy. Or distracted.

An hour passed before he made his final note, jotting down the words that had been spoken on the phone. Jack turned out his light and at last fell asleep, exhaustion overcoming restlessness. But it was a troubled sleep. It was not a dragon that stalked his dreams, but rather a beautiful, dark-haired woman in a pink dress, her face one moment flushed with joy, the next pale with fear.

His own words sifted through the dreamscape. "I will be there for you." She turned and smiled at him, then vanished into the mists.

FIFTEEN

Alyn Runyon had never before failed to recruit a husband or wife for someone on Keinadraig. As a rule, the generous settlement made with the families of the young men and women, along with the promise of a home and secure income for the imported bride or groom, was enough to lure them away from the small moorland villages where life was hard and wages low.

On this trip, however, he had not been so fortunate. Mayhap he had been overselective, for he wanted badly to please his niece, but none of the lads from the nearby towns had the quality one looked for in a prospective Dragoner. Lazy, they'd seemed. Or ill-bred. None could have been considered handsome.

Runyon was in a foul mood by the time he returned to Penzance to claim the boat the damnable stranger had so boldly stolen from the Dragon's harbor. He chose not to think about what Erica had told him before he set out on his journey, that Keely had trysted with the man named Jack Knight in the forbidden caves and had spoken at length with him, the two of them hidden away in the grove. That it was Keely, in fact, who had enabled the stranger to leave the island by taking a boat.

The same way Erica had told him she'd aided Genevieve.

His mood turned even darker. He must find a husband for Keely. In her present state of mind, she was dangerous. She needed a man to settle her and control her flights of fancy, children to teach her responsibility. He must find a mate for her, and soon, before she did something foolish, like question the laws of the Dragon.

As Genevieve had done.

A sharp pain of remorse cut through him, and Alyn Runyon stopped by the side of the street to catch his breath. He still could not believe what had happened. How had it run so out of control? Genevieve had always been a good girl, if a little flighty. Neither he nor Ninian had suspected she would have a problem with training to become the next Healer.

He resumed his trek, wondering how Ninian was faring. She was one reason he had returned home instead of expanding his search. He was seriously worried about the Healer. Ninian had always been strong, able to face whatever came her way with courage and tenacity, but when she'd heard the news about Genevieve, she had come completely undone.

Runyon himself was still in shock over it. He had never meant for things to get so out of hand. But it was the work of the Dragon, he told himself, heading toward the docks. It was not his fault, but Genevieve's. She defied her mother and betrayed the Dragon, and for that, she died.

The boat was where the stranger had left it, still tied securely to the dock. He was almost ready to step into it when he saw Kevin Spearman running toward him. Runyon frowned. He was not supposed to speak with this man in public. But Spearman called to him before he could get away.

"Ye'd better know before ye get t' th' island," he said, heaving for breath. "Your niece is gone. Ran away yesterday with that stranger."

A wave of cold despair washed over the Keeper, and he sagged against a piling. He'd failed again. What a fool he was for thinking the strong-headed girl would obey him. He was glad his sister, Keely's mother, was no longer alive to witness this shame.

"Any idea where she went?" he asked, struggling to hide his distress. That she had run away was bad enough, but to have left in the company of a man of the law . . .

Outside law.

"No. But I wrote down th' number o' th' license tag on his car. D'ye want it?"

Despair turned to trepidation. Should he go after Keely? He wanted no part of it, but he would talk it over with Ninian before deciding. "Nay. Ye keep it for now. I will let ye know."

Runyon settled heavily into the boat, his heart like a stone in his chest. Where would all this end?

Ninian's house was dark when he entered. Erica was nowhere to be seen, for which Runyon was grateful. The girl was a snake of a child, not to be trusted. He didn't blame Ninian for not wanting her to become Healer after Genevieve's betrayal. He thought she was wise in her plan for going outside the traditional bloodline and naming Keely instead. He released a heavy sigh. Obviously, that was not to be. God in Heaven, he prayed the odious girl would not become Healer in his own time, for that meant he would have to do her bidding in certain matters. Alyn Runyon would rather die first.

"Ninian?" he called into the silence. "Ninian? Are ye here?"

At first he heard nothing in reply, but then thought he detected a shuffling noise from behind the door to the Healer's bedroom. He opened the door and peered through the gloom. The sight that met his eyes shocked him even more than the news of Keely's flight. Ninian Sloan had once been a handsome woman, tall and proud, with strong Celtic features and clear green eyes. The old woman who struggled to sit up on the bed was bent and cronelike, with vacant eyes and unkempt white hair that stuck out at odd angles from her head. She looked a lifetime older than her true age. He hurried to her bed-side.

"Ninian, what is wrong? Why are ye . . . like this?"
But he knew. The tragedy that had befallen Genevieve
had come as a terrible blow to Ninian. And now losing
Keely . . .

"They have left us, Alyn," she croaked. "Both
Genny and Keely have gone. They no longer believed,
they no longer loved th' Dragon."

Scarcely able to stem his own grief, he took one of
her hands in his. It felt small and brittle, aged. Once
he'd hoped to court this distant cousin, but as she was
destined to become Healer and he the Keeper, their
union was forbidden by the elders of the Council, who
insisted upon a separation between family and duty to
the Dragon. They had been young, like Keely and Genevieve, but unlike them, they had obeyed the laws and
found others with which to mate. Theirs had not been
unhappy lives, but he had never stopped loving her.

It broke his heart to see her like this and to know it
was because of his own terrible misjudgment. In a moment of fury, he'd made a mistake that had destroyed
her spirit, and in truth might lead to the downfall of them
all. Ninian had forgiven him, or so she had said, but she
had not recovered. She had instead taken to her bed,
seeking escape from her pain and grief in potion-induced
sleep.

"What shall we do?" he asked.

Slowly, she turned her eyes on him, and he could tell
from the size of her pupils she was under the influence
of a powerful physic. She was in such a weakened condition, he wondered that she had the energy to concoct
her own medicine.

"Water," she murmured. "Please get me water."

He brought her a glass and waited while she sipped.
She handed it back to him with shaking hands, then said,
"We must na let it happen again. Find her, Alyn. Bring

her back t' Keinadraig. Our ways are na for th' world
t' know."

Keely's heart began to pound with excitement as Jack
steered the car into the city of London.

London!

She'd seen pictures of London on a sign at the train
station in Penzance, but nothing prepared her for the size
and speed of the city that ebbed and flowed around her
as Jack maneuvered the red vehicle through traffic.
Where could all these people be going in such a hurry?
What did they do with their lives?

Keely had difficulty catching her breath as a new kind
of fear crept over her. Not fear of the Dragon—somehow by daylight, here in this new and modern world,
superstitions from Keinadraig seemed not so imminently
menacing. The fear that clutched at her had more to do
with the reality of her situation, and the fact that she was
so ill-prepared to fit into this world. Would she be able
to adjust to this place? Would she be able to learn, and
quickly, what she needed to know in order to be a part
of it?

One thing was certain. She could never do it alone.
Thank the Saints she had Jack.

Or did she?

After what had happened last night, Keely was unsure
of how Jack felt about her.

Ever since she'd chosen to leave Keinadraig with
him, Jack had seemed to be her friend. He had helped
her in every way, showing great patience with her ignorance of the outside world and helping her to feel
more comfortable among alien surroundings. He had
even shared a secret and painful part of his life with her.
That could only happen between friends. She had begun
to take heart and shed the shell of fear she had carried
with her off the island, trusting in him to be her friend.
And he had been. Until he had kissed her. And then,
he'd pushed her away, his face stormy, and minutes

later, he'd left her alone in the silence of her room.

Keely did not know what to make of that kiss. Even though she had been taught that a woman should not kiss a man who was not her husband, she was not ashamed that she had kissed Jack. It had been the most pleasurable thing she had ever experienced, and she had decided that the old prohibition was just another Dragoner rule she could live without.

Yet Keely knew little about kissing, and Jack's caress had stirred a passion in her that troubled as well as delighted her. His touch had sparked a fierce desire somewhere deep within, an unquenched need that had made it nearly impossible to fall asleep after he left. She suspected it had to do with that mysterious process called breeding that her mother and Ninian had explained to her. But although they had described the physical contact it took between a man and a woman to make a child, they had failed to mention the exquisite sensations that came from being held and kissed by a man. Was it like this to kiss any man? Or was it just Jack?

A horrifying thought occurred to her. Had Jack thought she wanted him to breed with her? Was that why he had broken off the kiss and changed his attitude toward her so abruptly?

That thought was followed by an even more appalling notion. Is that what would have happened if he had not broken off their kiss?

Sitting next to Jack in the car, Keely was glad he could not hear her thoughts. Even so, she was so embarrassed, she wished she could become invisible. How could she be so ignorant of the ways of men and women?

She had made a terrible mistake in returning Jack's kiss so eagerly. In her ignorance, she had led him to believe the wrong thing about her. She scrunched down in the seat, humiliated, trying furiously to think of a way to set this misunderstanding aright. Keely desperately needed Jack to still be her friend. What would she do if he brought her to London and then just dropped her, leaving her alone in this huge and terrifying city?

With an effort, she stopped her runaway thoughts. There she went again, letting fear get the better of her. She did not *need* Jack to be her friend. Keely was strong, and she would survive. No, she *wanted* Jack to be her friend. In the short time she had known the handsome stranger, she had developed tender feelings for him, feelings that were somehow linked to breeding and all that, but more so, feelings that made her heart swell when she thought of him. He was kind and caring. He had nurtured her and eased her fears. Jack Knight made a very good friend, and Keely was determined not to let last night's misunderstanding get in the way.

She would explain things. And she would not kiss him again. But at that, her outlook turned even more bleak.

Jack pulled the car into a smaller lane that led beneath a covered entryway to a tall building. "We're here," he said. He gave the car keys to a man in oddly decorated attire and came to her side and opened the door.

"Where are we?" she asked, looking at the wall of glass that rose as high as the sky.

Although Jack had driven most of the way in silence, his expression remaining impassive and his attitude toward her distant, he softened when he looked at her and gave her a reassuring smile. "London's version of an inn. It's our hotel."

Genny had been found dead in a hotel room in London.

This hotel?

She did not ask, but the notion shook her. Straightening to prepare herself for whatever lay ahead, she allowed Jack to take her elbow and escort her through a strange doorway that turned in a circle. Inside the building, the air was crisp and cool, and people wearing the same odd clothing as the man outside bustled about moving large carrying cases. A huge vase of the most unusual flowers she had ever seen stood on a table in the center of the highly polished floor.

"Wait here," Jack said, posting her on a large plush seat nearby. "Don't go anywhere. I'll be right back."

Keely was suddenly so terrified she could not have gone anywhere if she had wanted to. Her feet were frozen to the shiny stone floor and her limbs seemed to be made of clay. She had known the outside world would be different, but she'd had no idea how different. She huddled on the chair, trying to catch the breath that seemed to elude her, hoping she would not cry. She felt again like a lost, frightened child.

Within moments Jack reappeared, and Keely wanted to jump up and throw her arms around him. Instead, she managed to come demurely to her feet. He handed her a small, white, oblong object. "This is your room key."

It was the strangest-looking key she'd ever seen. "How does it work?"

"I'll show you when we get upstairs. By the way," he added, "they don't have any extra rooms right now." He looked none too happy about it. "You'll be staying with me until something opens up."

At his obvious disappointment at this turn of events, Keely's spirits fell. It was not proper, she knew, for her to stay with him, but all things considered, it was for the best. She wished he did not look so dismayed about it.

Before she could suggest that he take her straight to the people he'd said could help her start her new life, he guided her toward a niche in far wall, which to her amazement slid open, revealing a small room. They stepped inside, and Jack touched a circle that magically lit up beneath his finger, illuminating the number six. The door shut behind them, and Jack took her hand, giving her a small smile.

"Don't worry," he said, giving her fingers a squeeze. "You'll like this. We're going up."

Before she could ask him to explain further, the entire

room began to move upward, and Keely cried out and held onto Jack's hand for dear life.

"It's called an elevator," he told her. "I should have warned you beforehand what was going to happen. It's like a car, only it takes us up and down in the hotel, rather than across roads and streets."

The elevator rose slowly. It emerged from behind some kind of barrier and seemed to continue on its journey floating only on thin air. Keely caught her breath, afraid she might fall, but then she realized the outside wall of the elevator was made of glass. Looking out of it, she saw what looked like an indoor park, with trees and a waterfall, and the people seemed to shrink to the size of ants as they rose.

The last of her waning courage deserted her. Already light-headed from the strange breathing attack, Keely saw bright sparks of light dance in her vision, just before she passed out.

Jack carried Keely off the elevator, ignoring the open stares of the people who were waiting for the lift. He cursed himself for not having warned her about the function of an elevator. He'd obviously scared the bejesus out of her. He'd have to be more careful. About a lot of things . . .

Halfway to their room, Keely stirred in his arms. "Jack?" she uttered, looking up at him, bemused.

He set her gently on her feet again. "Are you okay? Can you walk?"

She swayed against him, then seemed to recover her balance. "Yes, I . . . I think so. What happened?"

Jack put his arm around her and supported her as they continued down the corridor. "You fainted. I'm sorry I didn't tell you about elevators before we got in that one. I never thought . . ."

Keely didn't reply, but she looked distinctly distraught. When they reached their room, he showed her how to insert the plastic door key into the slot. When he heard the lock click, he pointed out the little green light and opened the door, allowing her to precede him into the elegant suite of rooms.

When he'd checked into this hotel a few days ago, Jack had not paid much attention to the room. It was not much different from most of the upscale places where he'd stayed from time to time. But now, he looked at it through Keely's eyes. On the right was a small sitting area with a sofa, two chairs, and a television. On the left was an octagonal table and chairs with curved chrome legs. Behind that was a small kitchenette with a microwave and coffeemaker. Across the hall was the bath which he knew contained a Jacuzzi tub and a built-in hair dryer. At the far end of the suite lay a large, luxurious bedroom with a king-sized bed.

Televisions. Chrome chairs. Microwaves. Coffeemakers. Jacuzzis. Hair dryers. Conveniences of the modern world. Luxuries Jack took for granted. But after the elevator incident, he became acutely aware that Keely knew nothing of these things. He must take better care in introducing her to life in the twentieth century, or she might flee back into the arms of the Dragon.

"You can have the bedroom," he said, taking her small bag into the far room, trying to ignore the lecherous thoughts that snuck into his mind when he glanced at the silken-covered bed. "I'll sleep on the couch."

Keely walked through the apartment as if in a daze, running her fingers lightly over the furniture. When she reached the kitchenette, she turned, doubt marring her lovely features. "Jack, if ye do na wish me t' stay with ye . . ."

Had his misgivings about sharing intimate space with her been so obvious? For a fleeting moment, he thought perhaps she shared those misgivings, but he heard the fear that trembled behind her words and understood that she simply did not want to be left alone.

"Of course I want you to stay," he said, feeling like a chump. But it would not be easy, being close to her in the same hotel suite. He considered what had taken place the night before. That simply could not happen again. "Keely, about last night . . ."

"I fear I made ye angry with me," she broke in, her words rushed. "I did na understand some things that happen between . . . uh . . . between men and women, but I have thought o' them today. 'Tis na o' breeding with ye that I want."

Jack stared at her and saw two spots of red burning high on her fair cheeks. "Breeding?" Her quaint way of stating the very problem that concerned him brought a grin to his lips.

"Aye." She lowered her lashes and looked away. " 'Tis another o' th' things o' life I know too little about. I did na mean t' lead ye t' th' wrong impression last night."

Jack touched her lightly beneath the chin and brought her gaze back to his. "You do have a lot to learn," he said, struggling not to repeat the kiss that had brought them to this awkward moment. "Especially about the effect a beautiful woman has on a man. But what happened was not your fault. It was mine. Can you trust me not to try that again?"

Could he trust himself was more to the point.

Her eyes were large and liquid, and he feared he might drown in those green depths at any moment. When she spoke, her words were like a caress. "I trust ye, Jack. And I thank ye more than I can ever say. Ye said ye would be here for me, until . . . I can find myself a bit, and I . . . I could use a friend." This last was spoken with a bottom lip that quivered ever so slightly.

Jack's defenses threatened to disintegrate. He longed to reach out and touch her, to reassure her of his promise, but he did not dare. "You know I will always be your friend, Keely," he managed, wondering how on earth he could remain only a friend. He must, however, for despite last night's kiss, it was obvious friendship was all she wanted from him. But he must help her "find herself'' soon, before his body betrayed his honorable intentions toward her. "Stay here," he said. "Stay, until you are ready to be on your own."

"I do na wish t' be a burden t' ye, Jack. Mayhap ye can introduce me right away t' th' people ye told me about, and then I will be about my own way."

"There's no hurry. You are not a burden, Keely. You mustn't think that. I want to help you." But a gloomy thought crossed his mind. He wanted to help, but he did not want Keely to "be about her own way." Not without him. She did not know about the phone calls from Keinadraig, or that someone from her island might try to harm her. Who would protect her if she were on her own. But he had to admit his hesitation to let go of her stemmed from something deeper than that. Yes, he had vowed to protect her, but now his feelings toward her included something more complex than mere protection.

Did he love her? Or just desire her? Jack had never been in love before, and he doubted he had fallen in love with Keely in this short time. If he had, he was a fool. Their worlds were just too far apart for there to be any future between them. He was her rescuer, nothing more.

"We'll take things as they come," Jack added gruffly, more disturbed than he wanted to admit. He changed the subject. "For now, why don't you order up some lunch? I need to make a phone call."

She gave him a long, studied look, then a brief, almost apologetic smile. "How do we 'order up'?"

Jack explained room service, and they perused the leather-bound menu. Then he insisted that she place the order. The sooner she learned her way around her new world, the sooner she could be on her way, leaving her friend Jack cheering from the sidelines.

Jack found the notion anything but cheering.

Anxious to call Garrison and yet uneasy about it, too, Jack turned on the television while they waited for lunch to be delivered and explained to Keely as best he could how it delivered pictures from thin air to the black box sitting in the corner. Keely showed no sign of fear, just spontaneous curiosity that revealed her innate intelligence. It would not take her long to adjust, Jack thought with mixed emotions. Soon she would not need him.

They watched a news broadcast while they ate. The newscaster reported a story about the Queen, another about an issue being debated in Parliament, and finally, one about an unsolved murder case.

"The Metropolitan Police remain mystified in the case of the death of an unidentified woman whose body was found last week in a room at one of London's finest hotels. In what appeared at first to be a murder followed by a suicide attempt, Mr. Brad Holstedt, an American businessman, was also shot and clings to life in a London hospital. Investigators say that although forensics showed gunpowder on Mr. Holstedt's arms, in test firing, the gun found at the scene of the crime produced a pattern of gunpowder residue that is inconsistent with that found on Mr. Holstedt."

As the announcer issued a plea from the police for help in identifying the murder victim, the police sketch of Genevieve Sloan filled the screen. "Saints in heaven!" Keely cried in astonishment, covering her mouth with her hand.

Jack, too, gaped at the monitor. Why hadn't Garrison given Inspector Sandringham the information concerning the identity of the dead woman? He drew in a deep breath. He'd put off the call as long as he could. With an inexplicable sense of foreboding, he went at last to the phone and dialed Garrison.

"Garrison, it's Jack. I'm back in London." Before he could ask any questions, Garrison's voice boomed in his ear.

"It's about damned time. Get over here right away. I've stalled Sandringham as long as I can."

SIXTEEN

I have to go to the hospital," Jack said brusquely, re-placing the receiver with a heavy thud.

From the very brevity of the phone call and the dark expression on his face, Keely knew something was wrong, terribly wrong. A ribbon of fear snaked along her spine. "Is it your friend, Brad? Has he taken a bad turn?"

Jack glanced at her and frowned, as if her question surprised him. "No," he said in a distracted manner. "It's . . . something else."

Something he was not going to share with her. Something that had to do with the news report about Gene-vieve they had just seen on the thing called a television. Although Keely felt as if she might fall apart from fa-tigue and the strain of everything that had happened in the past few days, she stood and went to him. Jack had promised to be there for her, but she sensed that now it was he who needed someone to be there for him. It warmed her that in some small way, she might repay his kindness.

"I am going with ye."

"No. You stay and get some rest."

"I am going with ye," she repeated in a tone she hoped brooked no further argument.

Jack's troubled eyes met hers, and she thought he was going to insist that she stay behind, then he touched her shoulder lightly. "If you're afraid of being here alone . . ."

"I'm na afraid!" Keely protested, wondering if it were true. "I . . . I just want t' go with ye . . ."

She knew he didn't believe her, and that he agreed to her coming along only because he thought she was afraid to be by herself, but it didn't matter. Whatever kind of trouble awaited him, if he needed her, she would be there.

They left the hotel and hurried across several streets teeming with late afternoon traffic. Keely found this outside world more fearful by far than the hotel room. She clung to Jack's hand and let him guide her through the throngs of people and vehicles. Her heart was pounding, but she vowed to conquer this new world as quickly as she could. She must. But there was so much to learn.

Keely had been amazed when Jack had turned on the television, and even more so to see Genny's picture flashed on the screen. Jack had told her that people all over Britain were watching the same program. Would people in Penzance or Newlyn or even Mousehole see it? Would anyone recognize Genny? she wondered in dismay. The news program about the murder had made Genevieve's presence in that hotel room seem so . . . illicit. Keely was glad no one on Keinadraig could see it.

A disconcerting thought suddenly struck her. Jack knew Genny's identity. Had known for two days. Why hadn't he told the police? A hint of anger stirred within her. If he had, Genevieve's character would not have received that unkind exposure on the television. But before she could allow the anger to surface, she considered what Jack had been doing for the past two days.

Rescuing her.

Still, how could he have forgotten to call and let this Scotland Yard place know he'd learned who had been murdered?

Before she had time to consider this further, Jack whisked her into the hospital. Again the air was cooler than outside, chilled by what he'd described as "air conditioning." But it was heavy with strange, foreboding odors, and the atmosphere was hushed. A wash of anxiety crept over her.

"This way," Jack said after checking a sign giving directions to the various wings of the building. They got on another elevator, this one entirely enclosed, and got off on the fifth floor. Keely waited while Jack checked with a woman wearing all white who spoke to him in a voice too quiet for her to hear. The nurse directed them down the hallway.

"You'd better wait outside," he said as they reached the door to Brad's room.

"I will come with ye," she replied stubbornly, not wanting to admit to him how ill at ease this place made her.

She saw she had displeased him, but his only argument was a warning. "What you see in there might frighten you. Brad's in . . . pretty bad shape."

Suddenly, Keely wanted to see Brad, bad shape or not. He, too, had suffered at the hands of the murderer and she felt an urgency to go to him and to pray for him to get well, for his own sake, and because Brad Holstedt was the only one who knew the truth of what had happened.

Keely's heart pounded as Jack escorted her into the quiet of the private room. An older man rose from a chair, not bothering to conceal his surprise at seeing her with Jack.

"Who's she?"

"Garrison, meet Keely Cochrane. She is . . . was . . . a friend of Genevieve Sloan."

The man's surprise turned to astonishment. "You knew her?" he asked Keely.

"She was a kinswoman and a dear friend," Keely told him, the words catching in her throat. In spite of the man's surprise, grief had etched lines of sorrow on

his face, an expression of such sadness that it reawake-
ned her own mourning for Genevieve.

Garrison turned to Jack. "Why didn't you tell me she
was with you?"

"It's a long story. I'll tell you later," Jack replied
stiffly. "How's Brad?"

"Much the same, although his vital signs appear to
be strengthening."

Keely summoned her courage. "May I . . . see him?"

Garrison exchanged glances with Jack, who nodded
with a reluctant shrug. Brad's father motioned to the
other side of the room where his son lay behind a cloth
partition.

Keely was not prepared for what met her eyes. She
had never seen anything like this in any sick room on
Keinadraig. On the bed, the figure of a person lay still
as death, the head swathed in white bandages that con-
cealed most of the face. The body was covered with a
white blanket, with only the arms exposed. Into those
arms were stuck what horrifyingly appeared to be nee-
dles. These in turn were attached to some sort of tubing
that hung from bags suspended from hooks overhead.
Other wires were attached to his body, sending some
kind of signal to machines of equally strange nature that
pulsed at the head of the bed. Keely grimaced at the
grotesque sight, but she did not look away.

Instead, she stepped timidly up to the bedside and
reached between the bars of the railing that protected the
patient from falling. With shaking hands, she lightly
touched the man's fingers. They were white. They felt
cold. She closed her eyes and swallowed over the lump
that ached in her throat.

Who was this man, and why did he have to suffer
so? How had he come to know Genevieve? And who
had done this terrible thing to the two of them?

Keely looked across at Jack and Garrison Holstedt.
Both faces reflected anguish as deep as her own. How
she longed for some way to right this wrong. For them

all. But she knew of only one thing that was within her power at the moment.

"May I be alone with him for a few moments?" she asked. "I wish t' pray for him."

Her request took Jack by surprise. Until that moment, Keely had not mentioned anything even remotely religious. He had assumed her religious faith stopped at the Dragon's door. Did she hold another more traditional belief? Or was she reverting to the Dragon worship, attempting to make some kind of plea bargain on Brad's behalf?

The notion concerned Jack. Surely she would not do something as crazy as offer to return to Keinadraig if the Dragon would spare Brad's life. He hoped she was beyond that, but he decided to keep a close eye on her.

He turned to Garrison. "Let's go outside."

Jack could tell Garrison was not entirely comfortable leaving Brad alone with Keely, but he touched the older man's arm and said, "It'll be all right. Keely's on our side."

The two men stepped into the hall, but neither spoke until they reached the lounge area several doors away. They were alone there, and Jack finally broke the silence.

"What's going on, Garrison? Why didn't you give Sandringham an ID on the girl after I called you?"

Garrison looked away. "Because I've been trying to avoid him until we had a chance to talk," he replied after a moment.

"Why?" Jack did not like the look on Garrison's face.

"Sit down," Garrison growled, indicating a chair while folding himself into one opposite. He cleared his throat before continuing. "Jack, did Brad tell you anything before . . . the shooting?"

"What kind of anything?" Irritation tinged his curiosity. Why didn't the man just come out and say what was on his mind? "He told me about the deal he was putting together, if that's what you mean."

"Anything about my will."

"Your will? Why would he tell me anything about your will?"

"Because last year, after Betty died, I changed it."

"Why would Brad tell me that? It's none of my business."

Garrison eyed him evenly. "Yes, it is your business, Jack. You see, I added you as a secondary beneficiary when it occurred to me that if for some reason Brad died before I did, there would be no one to inherit all that I've worked for my entire life. You've been like a second son to me, Jack. It was only natural . . ."

Jack was out of his seat like a rocket. "You did what? How could you? Why didn't you tell me?"

Garrison shook his head. "Because I know you, Jack. I know what you think of my having helped you over the years. You don't much like it, because you're too damned proud to recognize the difference between caring and charity." His voice went flat. "I just didn't feel like arguing with you about it. I was hoping you might never know, because I fully expected to die and leave everything to Brad. It would be up to him to decide what to do about you."

Jack vacillated between horror and disbelief. He wanted no part of Odyssey Investments International. He wouldn't know what to do with it if he had it. But this explained why Garrison had been so adamant about Jack joining the company.

"Garrison, how could you . . . ? I mean, how could you do such a thing without asking me?"

Brad's father gave a short, bitter laugh. "Brad asked me the same thing, not long ago. Not about the will, but about my appointing him to take over the company. Seems he doesn't much like my line of work."

Jack stared at Garrison. "You mean you never asked Brad if he wanted to become president of Odyssey?"

Regret showed in every line in Garrison's weary face. "I wish to God I hadn't insisted. He wouldn't be lying in there right now. I just assumed he would want to take over when I retired."

Jack was torn between righteous anger at Garrison's imperious manipulation of both his and Brad's lives and a deep sense of sorrow at what it had cost Garrison.

"Why are you telling me this now?" Jack asked.

Garrison stood up and went to the window overlooking a busy London street. He wiped the back of his neck with his hand in a nervous gesture. "Because," he replied slowly, "the other day when I was interviewed by Sandringham, he asked me if I knew of anyone who stood to gain by Brad's death. Of course I told him no. But if he were to find out about the will . . ." He turned and looked at Jack in somber apology.

"He would find I have a motive," Jack finished for him. "Thanks, Garrison. Thanks a lot." He couldn't hide the bitterness. That was all he needed. For Scotland Yard to have a real reason to suspect him, other than finding him standing over the murder victim at the crime scene. They knew he was an ex-cop and probably thought he had connections in Britain to secure a gun.

Motive. Means. Opportunity. He had them all.

"Christ, why didn't you just turn me in?" he snarled.

"Calm down," Garrison said, recovering some of his grit. "And shut up. I know you didn't kill that young woman. Neither did Brad. But we must find the real killer before Sandringham finds out about the will." Garrison paced to the window and back. "So what else did you learn while you were away? And what the hell is that girl doing here anyway?" he added in afterthought.

They turned simultaneously to look in the direction of Brad's room, and Jack cursed silently when he saw Keely standing at the doorway to the lounge, watching them with wide eyes. How much had she overheard?

"This girl," she said curtly, "has come a long way

t' find out th' truth about th' murder o' her best friend.''
The glare she shot in Jack's direction told him she'd
learned too much. Then she looked at Garrison. ''I am
truly sorry about your son, Mr. Holstedt. But at least he
has a chance t' live. Genny will never see another sun-
rise, and I want t' know why. Can ye tell me?''

Jack saw Garrison's face turn crimson. ''No. I cannot.
The only one who knows the truth of what happened is
lying in that room in a coma.''

''Th' killer knows th' truth.'' Keely approached
them, keeping a wary eye on Jack. ''Why aren't ye trying t' find him?''

Garrison raised his eyebrows and gave Jack a rather
pointed look. ''Why indeed?''

''What do you think I've been doing?'' Jack snapped
irritably, but Garrison interrupted him.

''Just a minute.'' He left Jack and Keely standing in
awkward silence as he hurried down the corridor to
Brad's room. He returned momentarily with something
in his hands. He thrust it at Jack. ''It's a photo of Brad.
Check around the area of the hotel where he was staying.
You might come across somebody who saw him earlier
that night who could shed some light on this thing. I'm
paying you to solve this crime. Now get on with it.''

Jack's face burned. This was the Garrison he did not
much like. The Garrison who seemed compelled always
to run the show. He had hired Jack to investigate the
crime, now he was telling him how to do it. It rankled,
because what he was suggesting was exactly what Jack
already had in mind.

Keely did not fully understand everything she had overheard between Jack and Garrison, something about a
will, whatever that was, but from Jack's angry words,
she concluded Garrison had accused Jack of the murder.
Why didn't you just turn me in?
The echo of those words sent chills up her spine.
Surely Mr. Holstedt could not believe Jack had tried to

kill his own best friend. And yet, had she not considered it a possibility more than once? Keely's newly formed trust in Jack faltered, leaving her more vulnerable and confused than ever. Jack, her friend and protector. Or Jack, the murderer? Should she stay with him, or should she flee at the first possible moment and try to find help on her own?

Jack gave her no time to decide. "Let's get out of here." Roughly, he took her elbow and led her to the elevator without so much as a backward glance at Garrison Holstedt.

"Wait! Where are we going?" Keely was not at all certain she wanted to go with Jack, whose mood had turned black.

"To find a killer."

Every nerve on alert, Keely hesitated as the door to the elevator opened. She could jerk loose from Jack's grip and beg safety from Mr. Holstedt. But she knew even less about him than she knew about Jack. On top of that, Jack had said he was going to find the killer. Was that not what she had demanded only moments before? Jack had interrupted his search to help her. The least she could do in return was cooperate. Mayhap she would even find a way to help. A buzzer sounded on the elevator, and Jack impatiently motioned her inside. With only a quick glance over her shoulder at Garrison, Keely followed Jack, hoping she would not die as a result.

Outside the hospital, Jack waved his hand at a large black automobile, signaling it to the curb. He helped Keely into the backseat, then got in and gave the driver some directions. Keely tried to stop the pounding of her runaway heartbeat. Where was he taking her? Fear began to seep into its familiar dark places as she watched the city go by in a blur, but she remained silent.

They arrived at last at another hotel, and Jack paid the driver.

"Where are we?" Keely asked.

"This is the hotel where Genevieve Sloan was murdered." His words were cold, clipped, official. She sensed he was burying his anger beneath the manners of his former police work, but she knew he was seething. His attitude frightened her, but at least his anger was vented in the right direction. Mayhap soon he would find out who killed Genny.

Jack nodded toward a crowded pub across the street from the hotel. "We'll start there."

The moment they entered, Keely noticed an acrid, smoky, almost nauseating smell and saw a blue haze hanging just above the heads of the patrons, many of whom held small smoking white sticks between their fingers. "They're on fire!" she exclaimed to Jack.

"They're supposed to be," he replied curtly. "They're cigarettes." He explained briefly that people smoked cigarettes for pleasure, but Keely could not imagine anyone inhaling smoke on purpose.

Ignoring her dislike for the odd practice, Keely shut her mouth and watched Jack approach the barkeeper. Gone was any sign of the gentleness he had shown her. With this man, he was all business. He handed him a card, then showed him the sketch of Genny and the photo of Brad. The barkeeper shook his head.

Moments later, they left the pub and walked briskly down the street without speaking a single word to each other. Keely was torn between wanting to apologize to Jack for giving Garrison an opening to criticize Jack's efforts and thinking it wiser to hold her tongue.

As it turned out, she held her tongue, for he set such a vigorous pace, it was all she could do to keep up with him.

They stopped in several more crowded eating and drinking establishments where Jack interviewed numerous people, all with the same results. She sensed his disappointment and thought he might be about to give up, when they turned onto a side street and came across a smaller, out-of-the-way pub tucked into the corner of an old building.

Jack surveyed it critically. "Looks more like Brad's kind of place. Let's go."

There were fewer people in this pub, some seated at small tables reading newspapers, others playing some sort of game or just chatting with one another. There was no smoke in here. He caught the barkeeper's eye.

"I wasn't on duty that night, guv," the barman responded to Jack's questioning. "But Roger was. He's in the back alley, taking a smoke." They found him near the doorway that led from the kitchen.

This time it was quiet enough for Keely to hear Jack, and it seemed to her his tone was less angry. Maybe he was getting tired. "Sorry to bother you," he said. "I'm a private investigator looking into a murder that happened last week. Have you ever seen either of these people?" Again he brought out the sketch and the photograph.

The man looked at them, inhaled deeply of the cigarette, flicked the still-burning ember to the street, and exhaled as he handed the items back to Jack.

"I wondered when th' police would get 'round t' this." He headed back inside, and they followed, Keely trailing Jack.

"I'm not with the police," Jack reminded him. "You recognize them?"

"It's that bloody bloke all right. And th' girl. They was in 'ere th' night 'e killed 'er."

"He didn't kill her," Jack said in a menacing tone, and the man straightened and raised an eyebrow.

" 'E didn't? That's wot they've been sayin' on th' telly."

"He did not kill her," Jack repeated, his jaw tense. "I am trying to find out who did. Do you remember what happened that night?"

The man glanced at Keely, and she smiled, reassuringly, she hoped. She wanted desperately to hear what he had to say.

" 'E came in 'round half past five, must've been. Sat by th' window over there, makin' notes on some papers. Th' girl came in about 'alf an hour later and sat by 'erself over there.'' He indicated a small table in the corner, clearly visible from where he'd said Brad had been seated.

"What happened then?" Jack prodded impatiently.

"Th' girl looked frightened," he said. "Kept glancing at th' door, like she was waitin' for someone, or afraid that someone would find 'er."

Moisture stung Keely's eyes at the picture he brought to her mind. Of course Genny would have been frightened. By the Saints! She'd been all alone in this terrifying big city.

"She bought a 'alf-pint," he went on. "It was just a shandy, but I guess she wasn't used t' drinkin', because it seemed t' go t' 'er 'ead right on, y'know? She started cryin' then. I was about t' go over t' see if I could 'elp 'er, when th' bloke by th' window picked up 'is drink and went t' 'er table. 'E bought 'er a soft drink, and a bite t' eat, if me mind serves right, and they talked for a bit. Then they left. Must've been around seven. I didn't think much of it at th' time. Men pick up good-lookin' women in 'ere all th' time. That's why they come 'ere, y'know?"

"When you learned that she was murdered, why didn't you go to the police?" Jack wanted to know.

The man shrugged. "Didn't know what good it'd do. I didn't see 'im kill 'er, y'know. Besides, I try t' stay away from th' police."

Keely knew little of policemen or their work, but she found it strange that Scotland Yard had not made the simple investigation Jack had just made. It had not answered the question of who had committed the murder, but at least now they knew how Brad and Genny had come to know one another.

Jack took the man's name and thanked him with a twenty-pound note. "Let's get out of here," he said to Keely.

When they reached the street, Keely looked up at Jack, wondering what he would do next. She was heartened by what she'd just heard, for now Keely believed that Jack's friend, Brad, had indeed tried to help Genevieve. But when she saw Jack's face, it was clear that instead of being pleased to learn the truth, he was shaken by the man's story.

"Jack. What's wrong?"

SEVENTEEN

What was wrong was that apparently Brad had done exactly what Jack had adamantly denied he would do to Inspector Sandringham. The Scotland Yard investigator figured that Brad had picked up a girl, probably a streetwalker, in a bar, and took her back to the hotel with him. It was so unlike Brad to do such a thing that Jack had vehemently denied it as a possibility. He wondered how the truth would affect his credibility with Sandringham.

He wondered, too, what Sandringham thought Brad's motive to be in killing a strange girl he had only just met? There had been no evidence of sexual contact. Did he believe Genevieve had tried to rob Brad, who had shot her in self-defense, then in a fit of recrimination turned the gun on himself? It was too ludicrous to even consider.

"Nothing," he growled a response to Keely's question. "Let's go back to the hotel." Seeing the exhaustion on her face, Jack repented of the foul mood that had driven him on this relentless trek into the bars and back streets of central London. He wasn't angry with her. He was angry with Garrison for his unnecessary directive. Jack sighed. Let it go, he thought. Garrison didn't have the full story on why he'd stayed away longer than he'd planned, and Jack knew he was anxious to find the criminal, not only to bring him to justice, but to prevent any suspicion of Jack.

At least the outcome was worth the aggravation. They'd discovered how Brad met Genevieve. Not that it brought them one whit closer to understanding the mystery. But one piece of the puzzle usually led to another . . .

Keely did not speak as they rode in the taxi, and Jack wished he had not been so hard on her. He should have taken her back to the hotel instead of dragging her along on this rather sordid mission. Then he recalled her determination to go with him to the hospital and knew she would have wanted to go on this afternoon's quest as well. She would have insisted on coming along, because the bottom line was, she didn't want to be left alone.

But her silence bothered him. Jack knew she'd heard Garrison all but accuse him of the crime. Could she possibly believe he might be the killer?

He cursed Garrison all over again for making him an unwilling heir. It was crucial that he find the killer before Sandringham learned he had a motive. Jack wouldn't be much use to Garrison or Brad, or Keely for that matter, if they threw his ass in the slammer. But he needed more information to work with. He turned to Keely.

"You knew Genevieve better than anybody. Do you think that guy's telling the truth? Would she have gone with Brad that easily?"

Keely looked at him and chewed on her lower lip. "I think 'tis possible," she told him. "All this," she gestured out of the window of the vehicle, "was as new t' her as 'tis t' me, Jack, and ye know how it has affrightened me. But she was all alone. Genny did na have someone like ye t' lean on." She furrowed her brow slightly. "Was Brad . . . a good man? I mean, could Genevieve have trusted him t' help her that night? Or did he . . . ?"

"Have other things on his mind?" Jack snapped, his earlier irritation returning. He was sick of people thinking the wrong thing about Brad. ''He wasn't the type to hang out in bars looking for a one-night stand, if that's what you mean.''

He saw that she did not understand the expression ''one-night stand,'' and it brought home again the extent of her naivete, an innocence Genevieve Sloan must have had in common with her friend. ''Keely, Brad would never have taken advantage of Genevieve.'' He spoke more gently now. ''More likely, he brought her back to the hotel with him to protect her from men who might prey on her inexperience. Brad was . . . is like that.''

He must stop thinking of him in the past tense.

''But he did na protect her.''

Her stubborn continuing doubts about Brad annoyed Jack. How could she possibly believe Brad had done such a monstrous thing?

''What do you mean by that?'' He did not try to hide his contempt. But she seemed not to notice.

''I mean . . .'' She faltered, struggling for words. ''He could na protect her, if it truly was th' work o' th' Dragon.''

''Cripes!'' Jack nearly shouted in exasperation. ''It wasn't the work of your damnable Dragon. For God's sake, Keely. There is no Dragon! Get real!'' But he could see renewed doubt in her eyes.

Brad did not protect her because he *could not* protect her, he knew she was thinking. The Dragon had found Genny regardless.

Jack did not know how to argue against such superstition.

''If Brad had known there was any danger, he would never have taken Genny back to his room. I think there must have been someone, likely an employee of the hotel, who knew Brad was a wealthy guest and who was in the process of burglarizing the room when they came in. It's my guess he shot the first person who entered the room, which would have been Genevieve, and then attacked Brad, pushed him into the bathroom, and put the gun to his head. But he was sloppy, probably pan-icked, and his bullet missed the mark. It was a burglar, Keely, not the Dragon.''

Keely thought this over for a long moment, then asked, ''Then why haven't th' police gone looking for this . . . this burglar person?''

''Maybe they have,'' Jack said, giving up an argu-ment he knew he could not win at the moment. ''I'll call Scotland Yard tomorrow and see what they're up to.'' The taxi pulled up to the front of the hotel just as the clock chimed seven.

He was tired and irritated and suddenly wanted to be alone with his thoughts to try to sort out the events of that fateful night. He'd get Keely settled in and then go to the bar for a while. But when they reached the suite overlooking the atrium, Keely looked up at him, her own frustration clouding those enormous gray-green eyes.

''I did na mean t' cause ye t' be vexed,'' she said, raising her chin slightly. ''Like ye, I am trying t' un-derstand what Genevieve did. Why she went t' a hotel room with a total stranger. 'Tis so unlike a Dragoner's ways.''

''It was unlike Brad to bring a strange woman home,'' he shot back.

They stood outside the door, their gazes locked, each searching for answers neither could find and blaming one another in their frustration.

Jack blinked first. ''Oh, hell, Keely. Why are we do-ing this?''

Her shoulders relaxed, and her expression softened. ''I do na know, Jack. 'Tis part o' th' grief mayhap.''

Jack knew he should leave her, escape to the bar, but he could not. This was something they had to sort out together.

He handed her his plastic key card. ''You do it,'' he said, indicating for her to unlock the door.

*   *   *

Keely felt as if her body had been twisted like laundry on the line. Her muscles were tense, her neck stiff and sore. Another soak in a hot bath sounded inviting, but she found it awkward to bathe with Jack in the very next room.

She preceded him into their set of rooms, thinking about what she'd just said, that it was not like a Dragoner to go to a hotel room with a strange man, and yet, wasn't that exactly what she was doing? She knew she should be wary of Jack, especially in light of what she'd overheard that afternoon. But standing outside the door just now, something in Jack's expression tugged at her heartstrings. Something that reassured her that no matter what she had overheard, Jack Knight was not a killer. He was as frustrated as she, mayhap more so, for it was his job to solve the crime, and so far he had failed.

He followed her into the suite and went to a small box sitting on the counter in the kitchen area. Opening it, he took out two bottles, a small one filled with honey-colored liquid, a large one with orange juice. As she watched, he took two drinking glasses from the cupboard, opened the bottles, mixed the liquids in the glasses, and handed her one.

"One of the bennies of staying in a high-priced joint like this is the private bar." He raised his glass in salute.

Keely did not understand "bennies" or "joint," but she knew what a bar was, and she raised her own glass in salute. Mayhap they were calling a truce.

Jack downed his drink in a few swallows and poured himself another. Keely wondered what was in the little bottles, but decided not to ask. Her own juice was delicious and in a few moments it fortified her flagging spirits.

Jack removed the small phone from his belt and laid it on the table. He ran his hands through his hair and sat down on the sofa, exhaling a heavy sigh.

"Who did it, Keely? Who the hell shot them?"

Keely wished with all her heart she knew the answer,

not only for her own sake, but to end Jack's torment. But she was no longer sure there was an answer. At least not a logical one. She'd been troubled ever since she had realized that Brad had tried to protect Genny, yet she had died nonetheless. Keely took a seat next to Jack and reached for his hand.

"I know ye do na believe in th' Dragon lore," she began, hoping he would hold his temper until she finished what she had to say. She needed desperately to talk to someone who could dislodge her renewed fear, and Jack was the only candidate for the job. "But what if 'tis true, that somehow death comes, accidentally maybe, t' those who betray th' Dragon? If 'twas a burglar who shot Genny, 'twas an accident o' sorts, wasn't it, I mean, that she would be in such a situation?"

Jack leaned back against the sofa and took her with him, draping his arm around her shoulder. "Yes, I suppose you could consider it an accident. But you're listening to the part of you that's been brainwashed, Keely," he said patiently.

"*Let no one leave who be Dragon kiss'd,*" she sang in a low voice. " 'Tis . . .'tis like a curse, Jack."

" 'Dragon kiss'd.' What does that mean?"

Keely had already told Jack so many of the Dragon's secrets, what harm could there be in telling him more? she thought grimly. Mayhap if he understood the depth of what he called their brainwashing, he could find some way to reassure her that she was not in danger of meeting with one of the Dragon's tragic "accidents."

She drew away from him and turned her head slightly to one side, lifting her hair from her neck and revealing the mark beneath her left ear.

" 'Tis th' kiss o' th' Dragon," she said in a low voice. " 'Tis a mark o' protection Dragoners receive when they pledge their loyalty t' th' Dragon upon passing from childhood. 'Tis said th' Dragon himself placed such a kiss on th' first Healer."

*   *   *

Jack was distraught that Keely seemed to have relapsed into the fears she'd brought with her from that godforsaken island, but he knew the importance of helping her to work through them. He was curious as well, for he remembered seeing the small, raised mark on both her neck and Alyn Runyon's. He leaned closer and saw that it was in the shape of a tiny triad of flames. It was not a tattoo. It looked uncomfortably like a brand.

"How do they make the mark?" he asked, knowing it was not a kiss from any Dragon.

" 'Tis made with th' ring o' th' Healer, heated in th' sacred fire and touched t' th' skin but briefly."

"They do that to cattle in my country." Jack didn't want to offend her again, but he couldn't help murmuring the sarcastic comment under his breath. The thought of people laying a brand on their children struck him as barbaric. "Does it hurt?"

"Na now. It did when Ninian marked me, but 'twas long ago. 'Tis na a torture, as ye might think. 'Tis a mark anxiously awaited by young Dragoners, as 'tis evidence that they are no longer children."

Jack recalled seeing a red mark on Genevieve's neck as well, but it seemed there had been something different about it.

Gently, he touched his finger to Keely's neck. "What does the Dragon require in return for this . . . kiss?" Her skin was cool and silken to his touch, and he longed to caress the entire length of her throat. He saw her swallow, but she did not move away.

"Loyalty," she said. "T' th' Dragon and t' th' laws o' Keinadraig."

"What about to oneself?" he asked solemnly, lowering his head until his lips were mere inches from hers.

"One . . . thinks na o' oneself." Her words were just above a whisper. "One lives for th' good of all."

With his face so close to hers, Jack could see even more clearly the strain on her face, the dark shadows beneath her eyes. She seemed burdened, older than the years she claimed. What had she already been called upon to do "for the good of all?" And had she done those things willingly?

He took her face in both hands, and he could see the ambivalence in her eyes. He sensed she was glad to be away from Keinadraig, but in making that break, she had also run away from responsibility, and from a lifetime promise. He did not think that came easily to her.

"It's time you thought of yourself, Keely," he told her. "Time to get past all the fear and the brainwashing and look out for your own best interests, not the good of all."

He heard a small sigh escape her lips. "I . . . know that, and yet . . . Oh, Jack . . . I'm . . . so confused . . ."

Jack drew her closer, wanting to kill every Dragoner responsible for her superstitious fear with his bare hands, wanting to shield her from every danger, real and imagined. "Let it go, Keely. Let go of the past. Let me help you get rid of your dragons."

Her entire body began to shake. He pressed her head against his chest and felt the wetness of tears through his shirt. He did not speak, for he had no words that could adequately convey the feelings that suddenly erupted in his heart. The intensity of his emotions surprised him, but he knew at that moment he would hold her forever, if that's what it took, to restore her spirit and keep her safe.

Jack thought about his sister, streetwise and tough at twenty-five, a teacher in the ghetto. How different she was from Keely. Yet even all her savvy had not protected her from the violence of his world. Jack had made a mistake, and Melinda had died because of it. He would not let it happen to Keely. He would do whatever it took, he would be there for her until she no longer needed him. Until he was certain she was safe and that no dragons stalked her dreams.

*   *   *

Keely clung to Jack, hungry for his reassurance and the protection he promised, yet hating that she was so weak that she continued to fall prey to old fears and superstitions. She had always been strong, independent, had in fact been virtually on her own since her father died. She had never needed a man's protection. Until Genny ran away, the protection of the Dragon had been sufficient.

Now it was that very Dragon, or at least her superstitious fear of it, that threatened her. She knew it was irrational, but at the moment, that fear was as real in her heart as was the mark on her neck.

She must pull herself together. She must find a way to take control of her life, as Jack had encouraged her to do. She was grateful for his offer to help her get rid of her "dragons," but she could not cower in his arms forever.

Protection. Of a Dragon. Of a man. What was the difference? She must be strong, and find protection in her own heart. Only then would she be truly free.

Keely squeezed what she hoped were the last of her tears from between her lashes and fought to compose herself. Her fears were foolish. Groundless. Jack was right. There was no Dragon. There was only legend and her own ignorant beliefs that had held her prisoner for a lifetime.

She had made her choice. She had made her break with the past. Now she must learn to live with it.

She straightened and cleared her throat. "Thank ye, Jack." She smiled at him. "I'll find my way soon."

"So where do we go from here, Keely?" His voice was solemn, his eyes probing.

For a moment, she was unsure of what he meant. If his question concerned the murder investigation, she could not answer. He was the policeman, or investigator, or whatever. She knew nothing of all that. But his question sounded like he meant something more personal, something she did not want to think about at the moment. A rumble in her stomach gave her an excuse to change the subject.

"For pizza?"

Jack raised his head sharply, gazed at her in momentary confusion, then warmed her with a slow grin. By the Saints, but he was a handsome man. She wished he would smile more often.

"You suppose they make pizza in this joint?" he said.

Keely grinned in return and shrugged, glad for a release of the terrible tension that had stretched between them all afternoon. "Shall I call room service?"

She did, only to learn that apparently this high-priced hotel did not do pizza. But the man on the phone had been very helpful and had directed her to call a nearby pizzeria. Jack showed her how to make the call, instructed her on what to order, and gave her an unexpected hug when she hung up the phone, triumphant, proud of another small victory in her bout with the modern world.

She wished the hug had lasted longer.

Fifteen minutes later, he left to pick up the pizza, as the pizzeria did not deliver to the hotel.

Keely kicked off her shoes, wondering how long he would be gone and if she'd have time for that soak in the tub. She went in search of her small bag of belongings and stopped in the doorway to the bedroom, stunned by the elegance of her surroundings. It made last night's inn look shabby in comparison. A four-poster bed commanded the far wall, its overhead frame draped with gauzy material that looked as if it might be made from fairy wings. A white satin spread covered the bed, which was piled high with pillows.

A long, low chair stretched near the window, and a cabinet of rich, dark red wood stood sentinel on another wall. Jack had called this a "high-priced joint." He must have meant a palace, for indeed this room looked like pictures of royal residences she had seen in the books brought to the islanders by the Education Ministry.

Gingerly, Keely knelt next to her bag on the floor near the long chair, not wanting perchance to soil the elegant fabric by placing the bag there. From the depths she withdrew the bath salts. It would feel good to relax and wash away the dirt of the city. She was still wearing the melon-colored dress she'd worn yesterday. A change of clothing would be refreshing as well.

After a short but refreshing soak, Keely dressed and exited the bathroom, headed for the bedroom, but stopped when she heard a faint ringing sound. She frowned and listened intently. She heard it again. She followed the sound toward the front of the suite and realized Jack's little phone was ringing.

Should she answer it? Keely was not sure if he would want her to or not. But she had conquered the telephone. After all, she'd just ordered out for pizza, and before that she had used the house phone here in the hotel. With a mischievous grin, she reached for the object and pressed the button that read SEND/RECEIVE.

"Hello?"

EIGHTEEN

Keely expected a man's voice. Mayhap Mr. Holstedt was calling. Or the inspector from Scotland Yard.

Instead, she heard a female voice. A terrifyingly familiar voice that after an initial hesitation, began to sing a terrifyingly familiar tune. But the words, unfamiliar, terrified her most:

> " 'Twas a fair maid who was called to
>   serve,
> But the Dragon's law she would not
>   observe,
> A midnight flight to another shore,
> Sweet Genevieve shall return no more."

"Who is this?" Keely demanded, already knowing the answer. The singer did not reply, but continued her torment:

> "For the Dragon's reach is far and wide,
> By the Dragon's claw sweet Genny
>   died . . ."

The singer paused, then hissed, "Genny died by th' Dragon's claw, Keely, and so will ye."

Panic-stricken, Keely pressed the button to disconnect the call and crumpled into a nearby chair. Undeniably, the caller had been Erica. How on earth had Erica Sloan managed to find her here?

Keely's heartbeat pulsed like that of a frightened rabbit. Moisture broke out on her skin, turning it clammy in the air-conditioned room. A dark thought crossed her mind. If Erica had found her, had she also found Genevieve? Was Erica somehow responsible for Genny's murder?

Was Erica about to murder her as well?

These were impossible notions, but nonetheless Keely went to the door and locked it as Jack had shown her.

She paced the small room. There had to be some reasonable explanation for this. And then she remembered. She had left Jack's card beside her bed. That little sneak must have found it and decided to play a prank. No telling what other of her possessions she'd gotten into.

And then Keely remembered. It didn't matter.

She would never be going back to her cottage or her things. Nonetheless, she did not want Erica Sloan touching anything that had been hers.

The phone rang again.

"Hello?" This time Keely's voice was sharp.

"Ye have betrayed th' Dragon, like th' whore that ye are. Beware th' Dragon's claw." Although the voice on the phone was now both disguised and muffled, Keely was not fooled.

"Go home, Erica. Do na call me again."

She pressed the button that cut off further threats, but her pulse continued to thrum. What was she to do if Erica kept this up? What if that bold snippet called Jack?

Or had she already called him? Keely thought about the wrong number he had received at the pizza restaurant in Fowey. Had that been Erica? What had she said? Had she threatened him as well?

The phone rang again. Keely looked at the tiny screen at the top of the little black box. Numbers appeared like magic. Numbers she recognized. Erica was trespassing in the Council office. If she had not been so distraught, Keely would have laughed at the girl's stupidity. Did she not know it cost money to make telephone calls? Wait until Uncle Alyn found out . . .

It rang again.

"Stop it!" Keely screamed into the phone.

"Ye will die," the voice promised in a dire, harsh whisper. "Th' Dragon's claw is long. It reached Genevieve, and 'twill reach ye."

This time, the caller disconnected, leaving Keely staring speechless at the contraption.

There was a sharp knock at the door, scaring her nearly out of her wits.

"Who's there?"

"Pizza man."

She let out her breath and ran to open the door, knowing full well it was Jack, but half expecting to find the Dragon there instead.

Jack barely had time to toss the box containing the hot pizza onto the table before Keely, appealingly damp and scented from a bath and wearing the other dress they had bought in the boutique, careened into his arms, nearly knocking him to the floor.

"What's the matter?" he asked, holding her tightly against him, trying to still her violent trembling.

"They've found me." She choked on a sob.

"Who? Who's found you?"

"Th' . . . th' Dragoners. Erica Sloan must have found your card in my room, and she called and . . . and . . ."

"Threatened you." Jack groaned. Dear God, this was all he needed. He cursed himself for leaving the cell phone in the room. "Don't worry, Keely. It's just harassment, nothing more. They don't know where you are. They just know where you aren't. Who's Erica Sloan?"

"Genny's little sister. She's a sly, nasty girl. Th' one

who brought ye t' th' pub, then made sure everyone knew a stranger had come t' see me.''

"Oh. That one." Jack remembered the sour expression on the girl's face as they'd left the dock in Keinadraig. "But she's just a child, Keely. She can't hurt you."

He felt her take a deep, calming breath, and her quaking eased.

"I know that," she said. "In my head, I know she's just making a prank. But after what happened t' Genny . . ."

"What happened to Genny had nothing to do with the Dragon legend. There is no Dragon." It was beginning to sound like a mantra.

"I know that, too. I . . . I just wish she would stop."

"I'll get a different phone number tomorrow," Jack promised, but he hoped he would get just one more phone call from the brat who had unnerved Keely all over again. He'd like to tell her a few things that might put Dragons in her dreams for a change. "Try to forget it, okay? Want some pizza?"

Keely released him from her death grip and raised her head. "I feel terrible," she murmured. "I do na think I can eat."

"Why don't you lie down for a little while?" he suggested, going to the sofa and piling some pillows at one end before indicating for her to plop down. Then he had another idea. As she slipped onto the couch, he went into the kitchen and opened the bar. He found several splits of wine and chose a hearty red. Jack doubted that Keely was much of a drinker, in spite of having run the only pub on Keinadraig. But perhaps a small glass of wine might soothe her nerves, and then they could enjoy the pizza.

"Here, drink this. Slowly." He handed her the glass, and as she put it to her mouth, he found it disturbingly erotic to see the deep ruby liquid touch her full red lips.

" 'Tis delicious," she said, savoring the cabernet. "What is it?"

"Wine."

"I have heard o' wine, but we do na have it on th' island. Just ale, brewed by th' villagers." She gave him a sad little smile that wrenched his heart, and he knew she was still torn about leaving.

Jack poured himself another whiskey, wondering what on earth he was going do with this beautiful, innocent woman. She seemed so eager to learn the ways of the world that had escaped her for so long, but she was still haunted by the fears she had lived with all her life. He sat opposite her. "Feeling better?"

She took another sip of the wine. "Aye. Thank ye. I am sorry I became so distraught. I did na mean . . ."

"Quit apologizing. That was a terrible thing for that kid to do."

"She's a terrible . . . what did ye call her, a 'kid'?" Jack grinned. "A young boy or girl is a kid."

"Like a goat?" Keely laughed, then added, "Erica *is* kind o' like a goat." Her expression grew serious. "She can na find me, can she, Jack?"

He shook his head. "No. You know yourself the islanders don't go into the outside world, not for long anyway."

Keely's gaze grew distant. " 'Tis true. Na even Uncle Alyn stays away for long." He saw a shudder creep over her.

They sat nursing their drinks in silence, and Jack considered again the fate that would have awaited her if she hadn't come with him. Somehow, in spite of everything, he believed she was going to fare better in his world than she would have in hers.

When she finished her wine, he brought the box of pizza to the coffee table. She nibbled at it, but her appetite had obviously flown with the phone calls. She lay back against the pillows, and in a few moments, he saw that she was dozing. Jack stood up. His own fatigue was deadening. He didn't want to awaken her, so he opted for a shower while she slept. He gathered clean clothing from his suitcase and made sure the cell phone stayed with him, even in the bathroom.

Jack stood beneath the shower far longer than he usually did, letting the warm water ease the tense muscles of his neck. He thought of Keely, so close and yet so out of reach.

Keely.

The woman-child. So sensuous it set his teeth on edge, yet so vulnerable . . .

He would have to watch himself while they cohabited this place. Everything about her called out to him—her smile, her hauntingly beautiful face, the rich dark hair that framed it and the quick wit behind it. He vowed to keep his distance, but he was only human, with healthy male appetites, and she was a tempting morsel, slumbering innocently only a few feet on the other side of the bathroom wall.

He toweled dry and donned a pair of fresh shorts, then stepped from the steaming room just as Keely came down the hall toward him.

"Oh!" she cried out. "Ye startled me."

The top two buttons on the pale yellow dress had come undone as she slept, revealing a tempting glimpse of the roundness of her breasts, and Jack felt himself harden in spite of his good intentions.

He should have gone to the bar.

Keely had awakened alone in the room, and for a moment she thought Jack had left her. Panic struck her as she considered again how very alone she would be in this strange and frightening world without Jack.

And with that panic had come renewed fear when she remembered Erica's threatening telephone calls.

Only when she heard the sound of water running in the bathroom did she realize that she was not alone, after all.

She ought to feel reassured, she knew, but the idea of Jack bathing naked in the next room filled her with a different kind of apprehension, a concern that grew as a tremor of that mysterious attraction made its way from her heart to a place somewhere in the core of her very soul. Someplace hot, and dark, and hungry. She did not exactly understand these feelings, but she suspected they could get her in serious trouble.

Keely jumped from the couch, thinking to make her escape into the bedroom before he finished his shower, but just as she stepped down the hallway, he opened the door. The sight of him, shirtless, in pants that did not reach below his knees, his feet bare, made her mouth go dry.

"Hi," he said, toweling his blond hair that shimmered even in the dim light. "Have a good nap?"

Knowing that Jack was nearby had assuaged her fear, which had been rekindled by the phone calls, but at the moment, this man posed more of a real threat than any mythical Dragon. She took a step backward. She was not afraid of him because she thought he was a killer. She knew better than that. It was not him, in fact, she was afraid of at all. She was afraid of herself and the inexplicable yearnings that rocked through her.

She swallowed hard as she watched his eyes roam the length of her, and her cheeks burned when she realized his gaze had come to rest where two tiny buttons had betrayed her just above her breasts. She felt suddenly naked and vulnerable before him. When his gaze returned to hers, she saw that he, too, was under the spell of those same kinds of mysterious feelings. He had the look of a man who wanted a woman, in the same way that the woman wanted him.

Jack took her hand and drew her to him with gentle pressure. She did not resist but went into his arms eagerly and with open curiosity. Her inner hunger blazed as she felt her breasts crushed against the hardness of his chest. His lips met hers and parted them, stirring an even deeper fire, and in spite of her fear, she prayed that this time he would not end the kiss.

But he did, although he did not release her from his arms. "Keely."

He said her name in a voice that was something between a whisper and a groan, and it sent another shiver through her, making her bold when she should be alarmed. She touched his lips with her forefinger. "Do na kiss me like that and then leave me, Jack."

His eyes searched hers. "I won't leave you," he replied at last, his words full of promise. "I won't. But I don't want to hurt you."

"Your kiss did na hurt me."

A thrill shuddered through her as he pulled her close to him again. "Oh, God, how I want you, Keely. I shouldn't, but I do. You are the most beautiful, incredible woman I have ever known."

Keely felt exactly the same. "Ye said ye would teach me things, Jack," she murmured. "Teach me o' this wanting."

Before she knew what he was doing, Jack swept her into his arms, and she locked her own around his neck. She nestled her cheek against the golden hair that curled on his chest as he carried her into the bedroom. He turned down the bed and laid her gently back against the soft pillows.

"You're sure?" he asked again, easing onto the bed beside her.

Allowing all her natural feelings to guide her, Keely moved to give him more room on the bed while raising her lips to his. "Teach me," she said, more urgently.

She heard Jack emit a small groan before he claimed her lips again in a kiss even more passionate than before. He kissed her along the delicate line of her cheekbone, beneath her ear, down her throat, his kisses scorching her wherever his lips touched her skin. Keely caught her breath when he began to unfasten the rest of the long line of buttons that marched down the front of the dress, and she was certain she might faint the moment Jack's hands pulled the soft yellow material away from her breasts. He caressed them gently through the silken fabric of her underclothes, first one, then the other, his touch causing each nipple to rise and harden, silently begging for more. They got more when he freed them from the lacy underwear he had bought for her, baring both breasts to his appetite, and he suckled there, inflaming her with his sensual indulgence.

She could take her breath only in shallow gasps from the pleasure of it. Surely it could not get any sweeter, she thought, just as she felt him remove her dress completely. She found no breath at all when he began to explore places on her body that only she had touched since becoming a woman. He eased her panties downwards until she lay naked next to him. He ran his hand slowly upward along one leg until it came to rest against the dark curls at the place she considered most private.

He kissed her mouth again and shifted his weight to encircle her with one arm, enabling that hand to caress her exposed breast. The other remained where it was, touching her, exploring her in tantalizing intimacy, enticing hot moisture from the depths of her being with each stroke that penetrated ever more deeply. Keely could not have escaped if she wanted to. Her body was on fire and had taken control, and she was helpless, only able to follow its demands.

Just when she thought she could bear his touch no longer, he withdrew it and eased himself onto one elbow. His gaze raked her body, caressing her as he took in every inch.

"My God, but you're beautiful," he whispered, worshipping her skin from neck to thigh and back again with the lightest of touches, raising goose bumps along the way.

By the low lamplight, his own skin appeared a burnished gold. His chest was wide, his shoulders broad, his arms well-muscled. He could protect her against the world, Keely thought. And suddenly she wanted to gaze upon all of him, as he was doing to her. "Jack?" She ran her hand along the waist of the short pants he was wearing.

He got the message. Pausing in his ministrations for only a moment, he stood by the bedside and shed the clothing, and with a short intake of breath, Keely lowered her gaze and looked for the first time upon a man.

He did not move, but allowed her to see him even as his own eyes feasted upon her. He was naked and unashamed. As was she. It felt natural, as it should between a man and a woman who wanted one another in this manner, Keely thought.

She did not know what lay ahead for her or Jack, but she knew in her heart that she would always cherish these moments of tender exploration. It was nothing like what she had been told. Nothing like anything she had ever imagined. It was not a frightening experience to be dreaded, as her mother had claimed. As she gazed upon Jack, she was filled instead with a love that surged through her so strongly she almost wept.

He knelt above her on the bed, and instinctively she opened to him. He entered her slowly, respecting that she had known no man before him. She winced at the prick of pain when he pierced her maidenhead, but instantly afterward, her body cried out for the fullness of him. It craved some unknown satisfaction and would not be silenced until it found release. Keely encircled him with her legs and drove him into her with a fierceness that in turn dissolved his own restraint.

The sweet pleasures of their earlier intimacy became insignificant in the wave of passion that swept Keely into near unconsciousness. She heard herself cry out as at last Jack touched a place deep within where surely her soul must reside, for she felt as if she were shattered into a thousand stars and flung to the nether reaches of heaven.

NINETEEN

Jack had known this would happen. When he had discovered the hotel had no available rooms and come to grips with the fact they would be sharing close quarters, he'd promised himself that he would keep his hands off, no matter what. But he'd known at that moment he was lying. His intentions had been good, but they were worthless.

He lay quietly next to her, listening to her even breathing, guessing she had fallen asleep after what had been for him the most incredible sex in his life. No. It was more than incredible sex. This was like nothing he'd ever experienced with a woman.

Perhaps it was because she was such an innocent, although Jack had never considered himself to be a virgin-hunter. But he couldn't deny that her guileless curiosity had been arousing.

Or perhaps it had been her surprisingly erotic response. He knew she was sexually inexperienced, but she had reacted to his touch with such a natural, raw passion that Jack had found it hard to hold back his own release.

But there was more to it even than that. Jack thought back to his earlier suspicions that he had fallen just a little bit in love with Keely Cochrane.

It wasn't a little bit, he feared. It was head-over-heels

crazy in love. With a woman who only yesterday learned what a pizza was.

Swell.

How could he be such a damned fool? It wasn't possible to fall in love so quickly. Was it? Surely it was just his celibate libido in need of exercise. That did not strike him as a particularly noble excuse for what he'd just done. Nor did he think it was true.

He raised himself again on one elbow and looked down at the woman beside him. She looked like some fairy-tale princess with her hair spread in profusion on the pillow, stark black curls against creamy white satin. She was, indeed, Sleeping Beauty.

Jack tried to remember what had happened to Sleeping Beauty after the prince had awakened her with a kiss, but he couldn't recall the story. It had been a long time since he'd heard his last fairy tale. But he guessed that when she awoke, this princess might regret his kiss.

He regretted it, in spite of his feelings for her and the incredible intensity of the experience. He regretted it because it complicated everything. Before, he had been merely Keely's protector. Her friend. Someone who was going to deliver her into the hands of others who would help her make a new life, and then be on his way.

Now . . .

Damn it all.

Now, Jack could no more envision taking Keely to the doorstep of some social service agency and just leaving her there than he could fly to the moon.

But what the hell would he do with her? Ask her to go with him back to California? Talk about another world . . .

What an egotistical bastard I am, he thought, rolling away from her and sitting up on the bed. Just because he'd let his sexual appetites get out of hand, and in spite of her open desire to learn about sexuality, what made him think she would want anything other than what they had already discussed? She needed more help than he could give her. She needed some education, job skills. She needed a place to call home.

Right now, he could give her none of the above.

The only home he had to offer her at the moment was this hotel room, and unless he got on the ball and solved Genevieve's murder, he might not even have that. He doubted that Keely would want to cohabit in a jail cell.

And all he could teach her were things like how to order out for pizza, and . . .

His mind stumbled over her earlier soft supplication, "Teach me, Jack," and what it had led to. He gave a quiet, unhappy laugh. He hadn't taught her a thing. She was a natural, passionate woman who knew instinctively what to do when it came to making love. The very thought stirred him again.

Keely shifted on the bed, and Jack realized she might be cold. Gently so as not to awaken her, he lifted the satin comforter over her, and when he smoothed her hair away from her face, he caught sight of the small red mark on her neck.

The kiss of the Dragon.

A permanent scar that would never let her forget where she came from. Would she ever be able to conquer the fear that had been ingrained in her on Keinadraig?

Jack wondered how the Dragoners had gotten away with such primitive practices for so long. They'd obviously done a good job of hiding away in the mists of faraway Cornwall.

But not for much longer, Jack thought with grim satisfaction. Tomorrow, he and Keely would visit Sandringham, and hopefully Scotland Yard would investigate for themselves and discover the truth of what went on in Keinadraig. Jack intended to fill the inspector in on what he'd uncovered there, including the islanders' bizarre little practice of branding children. Perhaps if nothing else came of all this, some of the uncouth medieval practices and superstitions could be done away with, and future generations would no longer be brought up in fear.

Keely's eyes fluttered open, and she looked at him anxiously. "Jack? Ye are na leaving, are ye?"

It had been Jack's intention to pick up his clothes, turn off the light, and return to his self-assigned bed on the sofa before Keely woke up. It was a little like closing the proverbial barn door, but tonight they had both succumbed to a passion that by the light of day they would probably both regret. It had seemed like a way to put some needed distance between them.

But from the look on her face, Keely neither needed nor wanted distance. Feeling his body harden in anticipation, he gave up trying to pretend his intentions were altruistic.

"I won't leave if you don't want me to."

Her face relaxed into a wide, gentle smile. "I do na want ye to."

To assuage his guilt, Jack felt compelled to offer some sort of apology for taking advantage of her innocence. "Look, Keely, I'm sorry . . ." he began,

Her face fell immediately, and Jack knew an apology was the last thing she wanted. And damn it all, he was not sorry. He had wanted that to happen. And from all bodily indications, he wanted it to happen again. Before he could argue himself out of it, he turned out the light and slipped beneath the covers and drew her close to him. "I take that back," he whispered. "I'm not sorry at all."

The feel of her naked skin next to his was nearly enough to send him over the edge again. She snuggled against him, nuzzling his neck.

"Jack?"

"Yes?"

"Thank ye."

"For what?"

He heard a girlish giggle in the darkness.

"For teaching me so well."

The following morning, Keely awoke to find herself alone amidst a tumble of bedclothes in a palatial room . . . somewhere. It took a moment for her to remember where she was. And what had happened in this room, on this bed, the night before.

She raised up from the pillows like a shot. Where was Jack?

With a sigh of despair, she saw the door to the bedroom was closed. Had he left her after all? Had he not really wanted that to happen and only shared those intimate moments with her because she had begged him? As those fears clutched her heart, humiliation burned her cheeks. If that was the case, then she was nothing but a wanton. And she had no one to blame but herself. She had wanted to discover the mysteries of that physical yearning for him, and he had complied. What man would not?

Sometime during their interlude, her feelings for the handsome stranger had crept across the boundary from intimate exploration for its own sake to a deeper level that she could not quite describe, and Keely did not deny that she cared for him deeply. Mayhap she even loved him. But he did not care for her in the same way, or he would not have left.

Keely wrapped her arms around her knees and frowned. What a stupid girl I am, she thought. Seducing this man, taking him into her bed, and expecting him to . . . what? Make some kind of commitment to her? She barely knew him! He had come to her rescue, had been a good friend. Was she so needy that she had thrown herself at him, hoping for more than that? She might as well have bedded the stranger Alyn had brought for her mate. At least she would not feel the shame she felt at the moment.

Shame. And yet . . . She shivered at the memory of

Jack's caresses and knew if he walked through the door, she would do it all again. Her body tingled, her skin felt feverish, and that mysterious need deep within called out to her again.

Dragging herself from the bed, she pulled the top covering along with her and draped it around her body. She opened the door between the bedroom and the other part of the suite, expecting to find the rooms empty, when the rich smell of coffee assailed her nose. Keely frowned, and for a moment her heart seemed to stop beating.

"Good morning." Jack's voice was deep, as rich as the scent of the brew. He stepped out of the small kitchen and stood in front of her, his hair wet again and combed away from his face. The clothing he wore was dressier than any she'd seen him in, the dark blue trousers outlining his magnificent legs and the crisp white shirt possessively spanning the width of his chest. He was more handsome than ever. Devastatingly handsome. But it wasn't his beauty that caused her heart to leap as it started to beat again.

He had not left her after all.

"Want some coffee?" he asked.

Keely looked down at her non-attire, feeling those troubling sensations growing more intense as she gazed at him. "I . . . I thought ye had gone," she stammered. "I had better put on something."

Jack grinned. "Yes. Unless you want a repeat of last night."

Saints in heaven, did she want that! Craved it. But she would never admit it to him. For although she suspected she had fallen in love with him, she had no reason to believe he felt the same toward her. She had acted irresponsibly in virtually demanding that he satisfy her curiosity and physical longings last night, and she could blame no one but herself for the outcome. He had reacted like her mother had described any man would. Rise to the opportunity.

Keely bit her lip. She could not, would not allow her wanton notions to put her in another such shameful situation. Today was a new day. She must try to forget what she had done and not let it happen again.

"I'll only be a moment," she muttered, turning back to the bedroom.

"Take your time. We have an appointment later this morning, but not until eleven-thirty."

Keely glanced over her shoulder. "Appointment?"

Jack's face grew somber. "I thought you would want to take care of Genevieve's . . . arrangements."

Cold hard reality slammed into place. Genevieve's arrangements. Her purification ceremony. How could she have forgotten? Her cheeks burned with another kind of shame. In the past two days, she had scarcely thought of Genny's spiritual needs.

"O' course," she murmured, guilt washing through her. It was one of the things that had caused her to flee Keinadraig in the first place. Forcing thoughts of Jack and the intimacy they'd shared to the back of her mind, Keely hurried to get ready.

Jack had told her he would meet her in the lobby, and she was thankful that he was giving her time alone to prepare herself for the sad mission of the morning. As she bathed, she attempted to convince herself that her feelings toward him were merely due to her physical inexperience, and that with an effort, she could control them.

Both the melon-colored dress and her own clothing from Keinadraig were soiled from the journey, leaving Keely no choice but the yellow dress whose tiny pearl buttons had created such havoc the night before. She wished she had some other option, because as she buttoned it, she couldn't avoid thinking about the way Jack's fingers had felt as they toyed with the buttons. Her nipples grew tight at the memory and to her distress, pressed visibly against the thin fabric. Oh, Saints, what made them do that?

She worked at clearing away any arousing thoughts and managed to appear unperturbed when she joined Jack in the hotel lobby. She strained to keep her distance, both physically and emotionally, from him . . . until they entered the building where she was to identify the body of her best friend. The place called the morgue was cold, and the man called a coroner was polite but distant. A chill crept over her, and without thinking, Keely slipped her hand into Jack's, taking instant comfort from its warmth and strength.

"You sure you're okay with this?" he whispered while they waited to be called into the next room. "They can let you see her on the video screen if you would rather."

The idea of seeing Genny lying dead on the small television screen mounted in one corner was revolting to Keely. Genny had been her kinswoman, her dear friend. She wanted to go to her, to touch her face and to tell her she would be cared for.

No. This was one time the conveniences of the modern world would not suffice.

Keely had seen death many times. She had helped Ninian prepare bodies, including those of her own parents, for the purification ceremony. But never had she seen the body of someone who had been dead for more than a short time, who had been packed away like a fish on ice. When she saw Genevieve's face, she could not prevent the small whimper that escaped her throat. She clung more tightly to Jack's hand.

The corpse was that of Genevieve Sloan, she heard herself tell the coroner, but her voice sounded far away, as if someone else spoke the words. She recognized the profusion of red hair, the shape of the face. But Genny had been vivacious, full of life. It seemed impossible that this could be her, lying so still, her skin white and cold as marble.

"Can you describe any particular identifying marks?" the coroner asked.

Holding back the tears that threatened to spill at any moment, Keely reached out and swept the hair away from her friend's neck. " 'Tis a mark made by our people." She searched for a way to explain the kiss of the Dragon without going into detail, but when she looked at that mark, all words deserted her and her blood turn to ice.

Jack recalled seeing a red mark on Genevieve's neck the night of the murder, and after learning about the kiss of the Dragon from Keely, thought that must have been what he'd seen.

But the mark revealed beneath Genny's bright hair was nothing like the one Keely wore or that he'd seen on Alyn Runyon.

This red mark was a scrape about the size of a quarter but rectangular in shape.

"What on earth?" Keely exclaimed.

"Looks like someone cut her around the time of death," the coroner told her, "but we can't tell exactly if it happened before or after she was shot."

Jack stared at it, revolted at the idea that someone had deliberately removed the Dragon's kiss from Genevieve's neck.

Keely turned away from the sickening sight and buried herself in Jack's embrace. "Oh, by th' Saints, Jack," she sobbed. " *'Twas* the Dragon."

. . . *Before or after she was shot*. Jack's mind raced, trying to come up with an explanation for this small cruelty. Unless in wanting so desperately to get away from the cult Genevieve had done it to herself, a possibility that made Jack's own flesh crawl, it must be the work of someone who wanted to punish Genevieve for running away.

Someone from the island of Keinadraig.

Someone who might at this very moment be stalking Keely.

He did not verbalize his suspicions to the coroner. He

wanted to take them straight to the top. "Let's go," he said, guiding her away from the macabre atmosphere of the frigid morgue. "We can make her arrangements in Sandringham's office."

Inspector Richard Sandringham's office was typical of law enforcement agencies—utilitarian, cluttered, and efficient only to the man who worked there. "Come in," he said genially, standing to greet Jack and Keely. He indicated for them to take the two seats across the desk from his own. "So, Mr. Knight, what have you found that might interest Scotland Yard?"

Jack felt Keely slip her hand into his again, and he closed his over hers to quell her trembling. She had not said a word since viewing the body of her friend, but he knew she was horrified. He turned to the inspector. "We have an ID on the murder victim," he told him. "This is Keely Cochrane, a cousin of the woman who was killed. Her name was Genevieve Sloan."

Sandringham's bushy eyebrows rose like two pads of steel wool over his wrinkled brow. "I say. Good work. Mind telling me how you pulled off this miracle? I've had her face on every television set in the country and had my men on it since the murder, and have come up empty-handed."

Jack squirmed slightly in his chair, then produced the scrap of paper bearing the phone number of the Council office on Keinadraig. "I found this under the telephone in Brad's hotel room the night of the murder." He handed it to the inspector. "I didn't relate it to the crime at the time I found it. In fact, I was so shocked by the shootings, I stuffed it in my pocket without thinking and forgot about it."

Now Sandringham's brows furrowed. "Go on."

"At the time, I had no reason to think it was evidence," Jack said defensively, knowing it was a lame excuse for not having told the police about the find. "That's why I forgot all about it until I came across it later, quite by accident, just after our last visit. You had told me the victim had a train ticket from Penzance to London in her possession. Penzance is in Cornwall. When I learned that this number reached a phone in Cornwall, in a village not far from Penzance, I decided to make a quick trip there to check it out.''

The inspector steepled his fingers and gave Jack a wry look. ''You do know the consequences of withholding evidence, Mr. Knight?''

Jack grimaced and gave him his best apologetic look. ''Like I said, I'd forgotten all about it. But to continue.'' He quickly related the story of his visit to Keinadraig, hoping the end justified the means. When he had finished, Sandringham was silent for a long moment.

''You're telling me there is a cult on that island?'' he asked. ''I thought we had a handle on all cult activity in the U.K. I've never heard of this one.''

''I wouldn't exactly call it a cult,'' Jack said. ''It's more like a remnant of a medieval culture. But they are ruled by some pretty strict laws that forbid strangers from coming to the island and, more cogent to this case, forbid islanders to leave. Genevieve Sloan ran away, Inspector. We don't know exactly why, but she broke the laws of the, uh, society, and . . .''

''Are you suggesting that someone from the island killed her?'' Sandringham frowned his skepticism.

Jack started to deny it, for it was such a remote possibility, and he did not want Keely to fear retribution any more than she already did. But Keely jerked her hand away.

'' 'Twas th' Dragon killed her,'' she said sharply, her eyes wide, her face white.

''I beg your pardon?'' The policeman leaned toward her.

Jack's heart bled for Keely as she tried to explain to the staid inspector her rustic belief that somehow, the Dragon that reigned in the hearts of her people was responsible for Genevieve's murder. '' 'Twas th' Dragon who took this from Genny's neck.'' Keely pulled her hair back and exposed the kiss of the Dragon, which she then had to explain to Sandringham. "No one but th' Dragon would do such a thing." Her fear and horror seemingly eased somewhat by her outburst, she collapsed against the chair in tears.

Jack went to her and put his arms around her, wishing he'd never brought her here. He should have handled this himself, at least until she had had time to recover from the shock of seeing Genevieve's body. "I think we'd better go, Inspector. She's just come from the morgue . . ."

"I understand her distress," the man replied, "but I'm afraid I must pursue this with her. If the killer was someone from her island, her own life could be in danger. Here." He handed her a tissue. "I'll be back in a moment." He stepped outside, and Jack bent to one knee at Keely's side.

"It couldn't have been someone from the island," he tried to reassure her, wishing he could believe it. "You know as well as I no one leaves Keinadraig. You told me that no one, not even your uncle, has ever been farther than the local villages. And besides, how could anyone have found her in all of London?"

Keely blew into the tissue. "Ye heard Alyn. The Dragon works in mysterious ways."

Jack started to protest, but Inspector Sandringham returned, carrying a small object encased in plastic. He leaned against his desk in front of Keely. When he spoke, his voice was quiet but firm. "Miss Cochrane, I do not wish to upset you further, but I must assure you that your friend was not killed by some kind of mythical dragon. She was killed by someone who shot her with this." He handed the parcel to her, and Jack saw that it was the murder weapon, the strange little gun he'd last seen held in Brad's hand.

He started to object, thinking Keely had seen enough

evidence of that violence for one day, but the inspector spoke first.

"This is what killed your friend, Miss Cochrane," he said gently. "A person, not a dragon, used it to murder your friend. Now, tell me, do you recognize this gun?"

TWENTY

Keely took the parcel in her hand, confused at first, not fully understanding what it was or why he was showing it to her. But when she gazed at the tiny pistol, saw the unique design and the engravings on the handle, her blood began to thunder in her ears and her skin felt like it was on fire. She thought she might be sick.

She'd seen this gun before, in Alyn's desk in the Council office.

Her instinct was to recoil from it as if it were a snake, but somehow she managed to retain it in her grasp.

Her breath came in short gasps as her new world crashed down around her. Alyn, or someone using his gun, had murdered Genevieve in the name of the Dragon. If it happened to Genny, it would happen to her. And possibly Jack.

Her mind reeled. This could not be. There must be some explanation. Hadn't Jack just told her it was impossible that someone from the island . . .

With shaking hands, she gave the gun back to the inspector. She must not let them know, not until she could discover the truth for herself. What was being suggested was too horrible to imagine. If it were true, then everything she'd believed in her whole life had been a lie. If it were not, and the police invaded Keinadraig with false suspicions, it might do irreparable harm to the ways of her people. Even though she wanted a new life in the outside world, she did not wish to destroy the lives of those for whom the ways of the Dragon were still sacred.

But most of all, she must move quickly to protect Jack. If she had been followed, and if the killer was poised to strike again, he very well could end up like his friend, Brad. Or worse.

"No," she managed to lie over the tightness in her throat. "No, I do na recognize it."

Jack stood up again, and she felt the reassuring pressure of his hand on her shoulder. "Are you finished, Inspector?" he asked. "Can't you see she's very upset?"

"Yes, yes, I can," the British officer replied, sounding thoughtful. "Very well, that's enough for today, I suppose. But I will be wanting to talk with you both again soon, so don't get any notions of leaving town again. You're still on the list, Mr. Knight. Don't forget that."

Jack growled something in reply, but Keely wasn't listening to the men. She was frantically searching her mind, trying to remember what Alyn's gun actually looked like. She rose and murmured a polite good-bye to the officer, but before she turned to go, she paused to gaze at the malignant little pistol that now lay on his desk. She studied it, memorizing the features, so that when she saw the other gun, the one that did not kill Genevieve, the one that surely was still hidden away in Alyn's care, she would see the dissimilarities and know she had been mistaken in thinking this gun and that were the same.

It took every ounce of will Keely could muster not to fall apart as Jack escorted her down the austere gray hallway and out the front door of the government building. So intent was she on controlling her emotions, she didn't realize Jack had spoken to her until he tugged on her arm.

"Are you okay?" he wanted to know. They were

stopped on a busy street corner, waiting for the traffic light to change.

Keely looked up at him, but she could find no words to answer him. She tried to nod her head, wanting to make him think she was fine, but it worked no better than her mouth. All she could do was stare at him with eyes that were not focused on the moment, but rather were seeing something terrible she did not want to think about.

"I shouldn't have taken you there . . ." Jack said.

At last she found her voice. "Jack, I do na feel well. Could ye please take me back t' th' hotel?"

The light changed, and they crossed the street. Keely felt Jack's arm around her, but she no longer believed he could protect her. She believed, in fact, that he was in great danger.

Because of her.

If that was Alyn's gun, then someone from her own island had killed Genevieve and shot Brad. That someone would kill again. But it was her the killer wanted. She must not put Jack's life at risk as well.

She must protect him. And to protect him, she must leave.

"I . . . I need t' be alone for a while," she told him when at last they reached the refuge of their hotel room. "I'll na be afraid. My head feels like someone is beating a drum in there."

When he took her in his arms, she did not resist or deny her body's physical need for him. Instead, she allowed him to hold her close against him and kiss her deeply. She slid her arms around his back, wanting to impress this moment, this memory, into her mind, her body, and her heart forever. For in truth, she believed this would be the last time she would ever hold this compassionate stranger who had tried so hard to set her free from dragons he could not comprehend.

She must go now and face those dragons.

She doubted she would ever come back.

Jack's little telephone rang, bringing the embrace to an abrupt end. He spoke for only a moment, then hung up and turned to Keely, his voice sounding hopeful. "It was Garrison. He thinks Brad might be coming out of the coma." He touched her hair. "You've had a rough morning. Why don't you lie down for a while? Garrison asked me to come to the hospital. I'll go see what's up, then bring you something to eat. In the meantime, lock your door, and . . . don't answer the phone."

Keely nodded and forced a smile, but her heart was breaking. After he left, she went into the bathroom and looked at her face in the mirror. It was strained, pale, as if she'd seen a ghost. Mayhap she had. The specter of the gun rose up to greet her again, and she turned from the mirror, summoning courage for what she must do.

Wasting no time, Keely went into the bedroom and changed into her old clothes. With regret, for they had been a treasured gift from Jack, she folded and tucked her new ones into the bag and zipped it closed, leaving it behind. Knowing she couldn't walk back to Keinadraig, she searched Jack's suitcase and found an envelope containing two hundred dollars in American money. She took only half, and tried to think of it as a loan.

In the small sitting room, she found a pen and some writing paper. She had to make him understand that he must not come again to Keinadraig. It could mean the death of them both.

"Dear Jack, . . ."

When she finished, she laid her room key on the table next to the note, glanced around one last time, and left, shutting the door firmly behind her.

Outside, afternoon traffic teemed in the streets, and Keely felt the rise of panic within her. Could she do this? Could she manage to find her way back to Keinadraig alone? Beneath the covered entryway of the hotel, taxis stood in a line. Keely knew a taxi could take her to the train station. She wished she'd borrowed more money from Jack. Would she have enough?

"Keely?" She heard a deep voice from behind her and whirled around in surprise.

A man dressed almost entirely in black, with black hair, a beaked nose, and dark glasses beneath a high-crowned hat, approached her. She did not recognize him, but he looked like a human version of a raven. Keely froze.

"Do I know ye?" she asked.

Before she knew what happened or could cry out for help, the man took her by the arm and forced her into the backseat of a waiting automobile. She struggled against him, but a strange odor assailed her nostrils and her world turned black.

Jack hated like hell to leave Keely alone. She was in a terrible state, shocked, he was certain, at seeing Genevieve's body, and in particular at the gruesome scrape on her neck. He wished again he had not taken her to see Sandringham so soon after. She'd nearly fallen apart when he'd forced her to look at the murder weapon.

But she'd wanted some time alone, and he could understand that. And he needed to be there for Garrison, and Brad, if indeed he was regaining consciousness. Garrison had claimed he'd seen Brad's fingers twitch. Jack hoped it was true, but he feared it was just a father's desperate wish for his son to come back from the virtual dead.

Fifteen minutes later, Jack leaned over Brad's bed, watching his friend closely. He saw no sign of consciousness. "Did you tell the doctors?" he asked.

"No." Garrison's voice was heavy. "I could have been imagining things," he admitted. "His vital signs are monitored at the nurse's station. If there had been any significant change, I'm sure they would have come running."

"Maybe." Jack had been around too many hospitals to believe the staff of any of them was above making mistakes. But he didn't say anything, because he believed in truth that Garrison had been imagining things. Looking at him, Jack saw a man who had aged years in just a few days. His eyes were streaked with red, and his face was gaunt. Jack wondered why, if he'd really seen some sign of Brad's recovery, he had called him instead of the nurse's station, but understood suddenly that Garrison needed Jack in the same way Jack had once needed him. As family.

"When was the last time you ate?" Jack asked.

Garrison turned away. "I don't know. I haven't felt much like eating."

Jack would rather have waited and shared lunch with Keely, but he could not leave Garrison like this. How long, he wondered, would the man be able to keep up this passive, hopeless bedside vigil? Knowing Garrison Holstedt was a man who preferred action, Jack was surprised he hadn't picked a fight or two with Brad's doctors when they failed to bring him promptly out of the coma.

"Let me buy you lunch. How bad is the cafeteria food?"

Jack and Garrison slid their trays along the chrome bars of the cafeteria line, selected their food, and found a place to sit in the crowded hospital dining room. Garrison picked at his food. "So, did you learn anything after you left yesterday?"

Jack's face grew warm. He should have called Garrison and let him know what he and Keely had found out about Brad's encounter with Genevieve Sloan. But then, he and Keely had become . . . distracted. Avoiding that aspect of yesterday's activities, he explained to Garrison how it was that Brad Holstedt became acquainted with Genevieve Sloan.

Garrison looked troubled. "You don't think he picked her up to . . ."

Jack gave him a dark look. "You know Brad. What do you think?"

Garrison looked down at his meal. "I don't think so."

"Knowing Brad, he was helping a damsel in distress. She was a runaway, Garrison. Scared to death, according to the bartender. Ripe pickings for the wrong sort. She was lucky Brad got her out of there before some sleazeball came on to her."

"I'd rather it was a sleazeball lying in that bed upstairs instead of Brad," Garrison replied grimly. Then he looked up at Jack, scrutinizing him for a moment. "What about that other girl? The one you brought to the hospital yesterday? How come she was with you?"

That girl.

How was Jack going to explain that after last night, Keely Cochrane was no longer just "that girl"?

He did his best to remain objective as he filled Garrison in on Keely's background and the plight she was in when he came to her rescue.

"Another damsel in distress?" Garrison remarked caustically.

"I suppose you might say that. But also someone who might shed some light on the crime. She identified the body, then I took her to see Sandringham earlier."

"Does she have any idea who the killer might be?"

"She . . . uh . . . thinks a 'dragon' did it." Jack wasn't surprised at the skeptical look on Garrison's face.

"Uh-huh. A dragon. Do you mind if I ask, what dragon?"

Jack enlarged on what he'd told Garrison earlier, describing what he knew about the strange cultlike customs on the island of Keinadraig, about the kiss of the Dragon, and the superstitious beliefs that bad things happened to those who broke the Dragon's rules.

"And the girl believes that nonsense?"

Jack felt his blood heat a few degrees. "First of all, don't call her 'the girl.' Her name is Keely. Keely Cochrane."

Garrison eyed him shrewdly. "What's going on between you and Miss Keely Cochrane?"

Jack heard the fatherly concern in his voice. "I rescued her," he stated. "Offered her a way out of that . . . lifestyle."

"And now you've fallen for her." Garrison cut to the heart of the matter with an air of incredulity. "Good God, boy, you've only known the woman a few days."

Jack started to protest that he hadn't fallen for her, but he knew it would be a lie. He *had* fallen for her. But he didn't like Garrison's tone. "I just want to protect her, that's all."

"Humph. That's what you told me Brad was doing when he picked up that girl."

"Genevieve."

Garrison glared at him. "Yeah. Her. The dead one. If Brad hadn't been such a damned idealistic fool, he wouldn't be near death himself."

Jack was aware of the stares of other diners who couldn't help but hear Garrison's raised voice.

"Get a grip, Garrison," he said, stabbing at the roast beef on his plate. "If Genevieve was running away from a cult, whoever killed her might be after Keely as well."

"That would be the Dragon, I presume."

Jack couldn't be angry at Garrison. His loss had been great, and he'd had no one to talk to since the tragedy, nowhere to vent his anger and frustration. "Look, Garrison," he said more gently, "I know this is hard. But for God's sake, don't make it any harder. The Dragon is simply a metaphor for the cult. I don't know if someone from the island is responsible for Genevieve's death. I wouldn't have believed it before this morning. But after seeing that someone had scraped the 'kiss of the Dragon' off her neck, I think we can't dismiss it as a possibility."

"Do you think Keely is in danger?"

"I don't know."

"Are you?"

Jack heard the apprehension in his voice. Garrison Holstedt did not want to lose his other son. "I don't know. I don't think so," he added, hoping he sounded more sure of it than he felt. He thought about Keely alone in the hotel room and looked at his watch. He'd been gone much longer than he'd planned. "I'd better get back to her. Even if she's not in any real danger, she is incredibly innocent about life in the twentieth century, and she could land in trouble inadvertently. It's like she's come from another time."

"She's not your responsibility, Jack."

Jack stood and touched the older man on his shoulder. "Nor was I yours."

Keely awoke to the steady drone of a car's engine and the sound of the highway sizzling beneath the wheels. She was bound and gagged, lying on the backseat. Terror seized her when she remembered what had happened. Who was the raven-man, and how had he known her name? Where was he taking her? Keely swallowed and shut her eyes against the tears that stung there.

The Dragon had found her.

In her mind, she heard Erica's threatening words, spoken over the telephone. *Soon ye will die.*

She had thought it just a mean prank then. Now she was certain the girl had told the truth.

But how did she know? Was she part of this, or was it truly the Dragon at work?

"Mind yer speed." A man's voice filtered from the front seat. "Don't want th' police stoppin' us t' inspect our cargo." He laughed.

The car slowed. "Guess there's no need t' hurry," another voice said. "The Reave gave us three days. We was lucky t' 'ave snagged 'er th' first try. 'E'll be pleased."

"We was lucky she came out alone. Wonder where th' bloke was?"

"Don't know, but 'e was easy enough t' find, eh?"

"Just a few phone calls t' th' 'otels around, and bam, we 'ad him. Wonder if 'im and 'er . . ."

A sniggering laugh. "Wot d'ye think? Wouldn't ye? She's a real nice piece, that. Too bad we can't taste it."

Keely's heart beat so hard she thought the two men might hear it. What were they talking about? Who was the Reave? It sounded to her like someone had hired these two evil men to steal her away. Or perhaps even kill her. Bile ate at the back of her throat. Were these Genevieve's killers?

"Suppose we should've tried for 'im as well? Maybe 'e'd a been worth a few more quid in our pockets."

"Too risky. Besides, it wasn't 'im they wanted. Just th' girl. If 'e's smart, 'e'll keep 'is nose out o' this."

Another laugh, derisive this time. " 'E probably won't. Not if 'e's doin' 'er. 'E'll probably come after 'er like some lovesick whelp."

A long silence, then, "I wouldn't want t' be 'im if 'e walks onto that island again."

Jack. They were talking about Jack. Oh, God, what was going on here? *That island*. They must be talking about Keinadraig. Were these men Dragoners? But their voices were unfamiliar, and their speech not that of her people. They spoke of "that island" as if it were a dreaded place to them. No, these men were not from Keinadraig. These men were strangers, sent by someone to return her to the island.

Strangers in service to the Dragon?

That could not be.

Keely felt as if she were adrift in that void again, the black abyss of her nightmares. She was falling, falling toward some fiery unknown terror. She was defenseless, unable to stop the forces that drew her back into a world once familiar but now more evil than anything she had ever known. And she was alone. She could not call out for the one person who might save her, for in so doing, she would destroy him as well.

Fear, confusion, and despair assailed her, but she

struggled to remain calm. She was defenseless, but not witless. She fought to keep those wits, for they were all she had that might save her life. Those wits warned her to pretend she was still unconscious, but to remain awake and alert to whatever came next.

Her captors turned on the radio. ''Think we'll wake 'er?'' she heard one of them say.

''Wot difference does it make? She's na going anywhere.''

Keely was glad for the music. It gave her mind something to hold on to for what seemed an eternity of a ride. At last, she felt the car slow and then make a sharp turn.

''Ye remember where 'e said t' take 'er?''

''Same place we always make our pickups. 'E's t' 'ave th' money ready.''

Moments later, the car came to a stop, and the driver turned off the engine. The raven-man opened the back door and dragged her to a sitting position. ''C'mon,'' he said, taking her arm roughly. ''Let's go.''

Keely's arms and legs were numb, and she stumbled, nearly falling. ''Jeez,'' the man uttered, then lifted her over his shoulder like a sack of potatoes and carried her into what appeared to be the back of an old warehouse. He put her feet on the floor again, leering at her suggestively, but he did not touch her.

Keely tried to clear her mind, which had gone as numb as her limbs. Through high windows, she could tell it was almost dusk. She smelled the scent of salt air and heard sea birds in the distance. Around her, crates and boxes of all sizes and shapes littered the area which was dimly lit by a weak bulb that dangled from a line overhead.

The raven-man approached a door at the far side of the room and knocked in an irregular pattern. Keely saw a small partition at the top of the door slide open, and a pair of eyes peered out at them.

''We've brought your goods,'' he said in a low voice. She couldn't hear a reply from behind the door, but moments later it swung open. A tall, plain woman with unkempt carrot-colored hair gave Keely a nervous glance, then nodded to the men. "Bring 'er in."

They led her through the door into the back of an old cottage. On one side was a small bedroom, on the other, a kitchen. Ahead of them, down a short hall, Keely could see two other rooms opening one on either side. The home was modest but not in the least sinister, except for what was taking place here. "Place 'er there," the woman said, indicating a chair in the kitchen. "I'll ring th' Reave."

The Reave. There was that word again. Keely's senses were on full alert now. Who was this stranger, this Reave who had apparently ordered her abduction?

The woman returned in moments. " 'E'll be 'ere shortly." She gave Keely an unmistakable look of regret, as if she were sorry she had to do this to her. That look froze Keely's blood all over again.

She heard the front door open, then close shut again. Footsteps sounded heavily in the hall. A man entered the kitchen. He wore the clothes of a fisherman and smelled of the sea. His hair was windblown, and his blue eyes were lined at the edges from years of squinting in the sun.

Keely's first reaction was one of immense relief. It was the man to whom she and Genny had delivered their loads of fish many times over the years.

Mr. Spearman.

But Mr. Spearman did not smile. Indeed, he avoided looking at her at all. He handed a brown envelope to the raven-man. "Count it. Don't want any misunderstandin' 'ere."

The man counted a thick stack of bills. "It's all 'ere."

"Need I remind ye o' th' penalty for talkin'?"

The raven-man gave the fisherman a cynical grin. "We've been doin' business for years, Spearman. Good business. D'ye think we'd bugger it up now?"

TWENTY-ONE

J ack rode the elevator up to the fifth floor with Garrison, and as the two turned down the hall toward Brad's room, a nurse suddenly bustled through the door. Her face lit up when she saw them.

"Mr. Holstedt!" She hurried toward them on white squeaky shoes. "Thank the Lord you're here. The doctor sent me to find you."

"What's wrong? What's happened?" Garrison rushed in her direction and Jack followed only a step behind.

"Oh, it's a miracle. He's coming back to us."

Jack could scarcely believe his ears. Garrison pushed past both of them and raced to Brad's door.

"You mustn't get him excited," the nurse called a warning from behind him, but Jack was sure Garrison never heard it.

Jack entered Brad's room only seconds later. Garrison was already at the bedside, but the doctor signaled Jack not to come nearer.

"He's in and out," he told Jack. "His condition is still very grave. He must not be disturbed. He must come out of this in his own time." He glanced in Garrison's direction, smiled slightly, and shook his head. "I wouldn't have believed he would come out of it at all. In a way, I think it's because he knows on some level his father has been here pulling for him. Funny how sometimes families who really care can make all the difference.''

Families who really care.

As the doctor left the room, a knot tied itself in Jack's throat. Despite Garrison's controlling nature, he had always been family that cared. For Brad. For Jack. And he'd pulled them both through. His was a love Jack was only now just beginning to understand.

Jack thought of Keely, and his heart went out to her. She had left behind all the family she had ever known. Jack had promised to be there for her, and like Garrison had for him and Brad, he would see Keely through her time of crisis as well. Not out of loyalty, or duty. But out of love.

He would be her family who cared.

Lost in his reverie, he didn't hear Garrison approach, and he jumped when he touched his arm.

''He wants you.''

Jack furrowed his brows but gave a nod in answer. He moved to Brad's bedside. At first, he could discern no difference in his friend who lay inert on the bed, as he had now for nearly a week. The room was darkened, quiet except for the steady blip of one of the monitors. Jack leaned against the guardrail on the bed. ''Hey, buddy,'' he whispered.

He heard no reply, but thought he saw Brad's lips move ever so slightly. He bent to where his face was within inches of Brad's.

''Knew him.'' Brad's words were barely audible.

''Say again.''

But there was no reply. Jack waited, holding his breath, but Brad seemed to have slipped over the edge again into the twilight world of coma. Garrison came to the other side of the bed.

''What did he say?''

Jack shook his head. ''I'm not sure. It sounded like 'knew him.' But it could have been anything.''

''He said your name. I heard it clearly.''

Jack gave him a smile. "He's going to make it, Garrison. We'll just have to give him some time."

"Can you stay awhile? He might come to again. If he asked for you once . . ."

"I'll be here for him," Jack broke in. Keely was safe in the hotel room and needed rest. He was needed more here at the moment. "I think I'd better let Sandringham know Brad might be able to talk soon, though. If he can just tell us what happened that night, Scotland Yard can go after the killer, and I can rest easier for Keely's safety."

Jack left Garrison and went to a pay telephone in the lobby. Before dialing Sandringham's number, he called the hotel. The phone rang and rang, but when Keely did not answer, Jack wasn't too concerned. He had told her, half in jest, not to answer the phone. After the harassing phone calls from that creepy kid on Keinadraig, Jack wondered if Keely would ever answer another telephone.

Sandringham was more prompt. "I'll be right there," he said. "Your friend holds the key to the whole thing. We'll move on it as soon as we know who to go after."

An hour later, the inspector entered Brad's room, where Jack and Garrison both motioned with finger to lip for him not to speak. The three kept a tense vigil, the will among them for Brad to wake up so strong Jack could almost feel it.

The hands of the clock on the wall opposite the bed moved steadily through the afternoon, but Brad's early signs of consciousness did not repeat themselves. At last, Jack motioned for Sandringham to accompany him for a break.

In the lounge, they bought cold drinks from a vending machine. Then Jack spoke. "I didn't have a chance this morning to tell you, but Keely and I found out last night how Brad became acquainted with Genevieve Sloan." He described their foray into the pubs in the area of the hotel. "I know it looks at first glance like he picked up a hooker. But according to Keely, and the date on the train ticket, Genevieve had only run away earlier the same day. Not much time to set up business. I sincerely believe he was with her because he befriended her.''

The inspector looked thoughtful. ''That phone number you found in the room rang in her village. Do you think she might have tried to call for someone to come get her?''

Jack let out a sigh. ''Could be. Too bad it was too late.'' Then a sudden thought struck him. ''Unless . . . that was how someone from Keinadraig managed to find her. Good God, do you suppose . . . ?''

''The timing doesn't work, like you just said. Good try, Mr. Knight, but Cornwall is hours from here. Unless this cult flies a jet, there's no way someone could have received her phone call and come here so quickly to do the deed. Unless the Dragon has a hit man,'' he added wryly.

Their conjecture was interrupted as Garrison came toward them, gesturing urgently. ''Come quickly, both of you. He's trying to talk again.''

With Garrison on one side of the bed, and Jack and the inspector on the other, they watched Brad struggle to rejoin the world of the living. He opened his eyes, blinked, then focused on his father.

''Hi, Dad,'' he said weakly.

Garrison took his hand, his eyes filling with tears. ''Welcome back, son.'' Jack had to fight tears of his own.

Brad stared blankly for a few seconds. ''Where am I?''

''In the hospital. In London. You . . . you were shot, son.''

Brad made no effort to respond, but he did not close his eyes. His focus shifted to somewhere far away, as if he were groping for memory. Jack held his breath. The doctors had warned that even if he were to regain consciousness, Brad could suffer severe memory loss, or worse, loss of virtually all mental function. The effects of head injuries were difficult to predict.

Brad stirred at last. "Someone else." He cast his glance in Jack's direction. "A girl."

Jack nodded. "She was killed, Brad."

Now Brad closed his eyes, and Jack saw Garrison give him a warning wag of the head. Jack remembered what the doctor had said. He must come out of this in his own time. He noted Sandringham was showing remarkable restraint for a police investigator. As eager as he was, Jack had to wait until Brad was ready. They had waited a week. They could wait longer. Brad was coming back, and in time he would be able to tell them everything that happened.

Jack just hoped Keely had time.

But without prompting from any of them, Brad spoke again. "She knew him," he murmured, this time clearly enough that they all heard. "She knew the man who killed her."

Jack wasn't eager to tell Keely that Brad had all but confirmed that the killer was someone from Keinadraig. He had been unable to give a description, as he had fallen again into unconciousness, but his claim that Genevieve Sloan had known her assailant was enough for Scotland Yard to turn its search in that direction. Sandringham had reasonably asked Jack to bring Keely back to his office for questioning. It wasn't going to be easy on her, but she would have to come to grips with the truth sooner or later. The sooner the better, Jack thought, for she, too, might make the same fatal mistake he believed Genny had made. She might open her door to someone she recognized, never dreaming a friend or kinsman might be a killer.

Hurrying through the traffic on his way back to the hotel, Jack's anxiety grew. He shouldn't have left Keely alone for so long. He hoped she had ordered something from room service by now. He did not knock, but used his key and opened the door to their suite, and he knew in an instant something was wrong. It was too quiet. The room felt empty, devoid of life and breath. "Keely!" He ran to the bedroom. "Keely!"

He tried not to panic. There was a logical reason why she was not here. Maybe she'd gone downstairs to the restaurant for the lunch he'd promised and never brought her. He turned to go search for her in the hotel when his eye fell on the small tote bag standing next to his suitcase. It looked full, as if she'd packed it to leave. Unzipping it, he confirmed that it indeed held everything she owned—both dresses, the nightclothes, cosmetics—everything he'd bought for her in Fowey. The only thing missing was the clothing she'd been wearing when he had taken her away from Keinadraig.

Panic mounting, Jack stood and ran his hands through his hair. If she'd just gone downstairs for a late lunch, why would she have changed into those old clothes? A terrible premonition swept over him, and he knew that Keely had not gone for lunch. She had left for good. Dear God, he thought, breaking out in an icy sweat, had she returned to the cult? Had seeing Genevieve's body this morning renewed her fear of the Dragon's retribution and caused her to run back to the island, thinking to escape a similar fate? Jack felt sick to his stomach. If she had, she was running right into the arms of the killer.

Tormented, Jack returned to the sitting area at the front of the suite, where he spied a small white piece of paper on the coffee table, next to the spare room key.

"Dear Jack, . . ."

The writing was square, printed and childlike. "Please forgive me for leaving, but I must. My heart is torn. Thank you for your many kindnesses. You have been a good friend. Keely Cochrane."

Beneath was added a postscript: "Could I beg of you yet one more kindness? Please see to . . ." Jack turned the page over. ". . . Genevieve? I will find a way to repay you. K.C."

Jack crushed the note in his fist and dropped into a chair, awash in alarm and nearly unbearable pain. What did she mean, "my heart is torn?" Torn between her old life and her new? Or torn because of what had happened between them last night? Or both? He damned himself for letting things get so out of hand. She had been a virgin, an innocent, and even though she'd acted like their lovemaking gave her pleasure in the night, by the light of day, their interlude in bed—and all its implications—had probably frightened her. She had told him she wanted him as a friend, but he'd let his own desires take him way beyond those limits. That and the shock of seeing Genevieve, not only dead, but with her Dragon symbol cut away, must have been enough to send Keely flying back to that dreadful place.

Jack felt as if his heart had been cut away as well. Damn it, he'd known better than to become involved with her. He'd known the risk, the many risks, of losing his heart to someone like Keely Cochrane. And yet, his heart had given him no choice. It had demanded that he love her, it seemed, from the very first time he'd encountered her high on that windy hill amidst the mysterious circle of stones. But he'd pushed her too hard, taken things too fast. And now he'd lost her. His selfish desires might even cost her her life.

He must go after her, even though she would not welcome him. He'd vowed to protect her, but now her life was in danger because of him. He glanced at his watch. Five-thirty. How long had she been gone? In the three hours he'd spent at the hospital, she could have caught a train and be halfway to Cornwall. But Keely had no money. What would she use for train fare? A flicker of hope lit within him. Maybe she hadn't gone back to Keinadraig after all. But then he recalled the two bags lined up neatly in the bedroom and remembered that his had been sitting open on the chaise when he'd left. A quick check confirmed that half of his emergency money was missing. Enough to buy a ticket to Penzance.

If she was on the train, he would never be able to catch her, even if he drove like a madman. But he must prevent her from going to the island. He doubted the cult would accept her back, especially if she let them know what she'd seen on Genevieve's neck. Jack doubted that Alyn Runyon or whoever had killed Genny would want to share that dark little secret, and he suspected that if Keely returned to Keinadraig, she would meet with one of those nasty little "accidents" the Dragoners celebrated in their ballad.

Taking the telephone from his belt, Jack dialed Inspector Sandringham. "She's gone."

Thirty minutes later, he was in Sandringham's office, waiting impatiently while the inspector spoke with the Penzance police. Hanging up, he looked across at Jack. "They'll cover the train station and try to intercept her when she arrives. Guess all we can do now is wait."

"Wait?" Jack exploded. "There's a killer loose down there. Don't you people have a helicopter or something?"

Sandringham gave him a patient smile. "This isn't California," he said. "We *think* the killer might be from there. But we don't know for certain. All we have to go on is a whisper from a man just coming out of a coma. We don't go rushing off until we have some idea of who we are looking for."

Jack knew the inspector was technically correct in his procedures, but he didn't like it one bit. "I'm going back to the hospital," he snarled.

When he got there, he found a guard posted by Brad's door who challenged his entry until Garrison gave him the okay. "Scotland Yard thought it wise, in case the gunman learned that Brad might pull through and try to strike again," he explained.

Inside Brad's room, another investigator sat by Brad's bed. "In case he comes to again and can give us more information."

Jack begrudgingly had to admit that Sandringham

was more on top of things than he'd given him credit for. Still, he could not just stand by and wait. Taking Garrison out into the hall, he explained what had happened, and what he feared might happen to Keely.

"Sandringham told me the Penzance police could detain her, but only for a while. She is returning of her own will, and she's committed no crime, so if she still wants to go back to Keinadraig after being warned that the killer could be one of her own people, they'll have no way to stop her."

"Surely she wouldn't do that?" Garrison said.

"I think she suspected when she left here that it could have been one of her own who killed Genevieve, because of the removal of the kiss of the Dragon," Jack said gloomily. "I think part of why she went back was because she was afraid they would do the same to her."

He didn't mention the other reason why.

"Will they let her return?"

"I think they'll let her onto the island, where they can kill her, too, but in the privacy of their little Dragon's lair."

Garrison frowned. "Will she listen to you?"

It was a question Jack couldn't answer. "I don't know. All I know is that I've got to go to her before it gets that far. I have to try to stop her." He'd never asked anything of Garrison before, because he'd never had to. Now, he needed his help more than anything he'd needed in a long while. "Do you still know how to fly helicopters?"

Heavy clouds obscured the night sky when Kevin Spearman led Keely to his small car and drove through the shadowy streets of Penzance to a boat docked privately far from the bright lights of the marina. Her hands were still tied behind her, and the gag remained in her mouth, although the man's wife had had the mercy to release her for a time and give her food and water and let her use the loo.

Neither man nor wife had spoken to her during the course of the evening, even when she'd questioned them. It was as if she were being shunned. But these were not Dragoners. Why would they shun her? She supposed they had been instructed to do so by whoever had paid Mr. Spearman to hire those dreadful men to kidnap her.

Keely never doubted that she was being taken back to Keinadraig, and if she weren't so terrified, she would have laughed at the irony of someone spending money to drag her home when she'd been on the way on her own. She had planned to sneak onto the island unseen, make her way to Alyn's office, and hopefully, find the gun nestled at the back of his drawer where it always was, thus proving once and for all that the murderer was not one of her own people. With that knowledge, she could have breathed easier, at least for Jack. She'd believed that as long as she stayed away from him, Jack would come to no harm, although for herself, she would not have been surprised if she'd been run over by a bus. For even if the murderer was not someone from Keinadraig, Genny was just as dead. A bad thing *had* happened to her, and Keely believed something bad could happen to her as well, even if quite by accident. It could be her fate, but she would take no chances with Jack's life.

But when she was kidnapped, she could no longer deny the truth of what Jack and Inspector Sandringham had been trying to tell her. Genny's death was not some mysterious accident brought about by the Dragon. Someone very human had pulled those triggers.

Jack had told her once that he thought Genevieve was killed because she was in the wrong place at the wrong time, but after seeing the murder weapon, Keely believed it was Jack's friend, Brad, who had the misfortune of being in that position. With the kidnapping and subsequent travel back to Penzance, Keely no longer expected to find Alyn's gun in the drawer, even if she got the chance to search for it. She would not have believed it possible that her own people were responsible for Genny's death, until somehow the kidnappers had found her. In that respect, the Dragon's claw was indeed long. She prayed that Ninian would never know.

Keely was unsure of what lay ahead as they motored into the bay. Her most hopeful thought was that her uncle, maybe urged by Ninian, had found her and brought her home, either to protect her, or more likely, to bend her to his will. She would not allow herself to consider a darker fate. Alyn, or the Council, might have hired a killer to take revenge far away, but surely they wouldn't commit cold-blooded murder on the island. It was unthinkable.

Whatever her fate, she would soon learn it, for the black shadow of Keinadraig loomed dead ahead.

Keely was surprised when the boatman bypassed the entrance to the harbor and continued around the circumference of the island, beaching the boat at last in almost the identical spot where Jack had first landed, near the caves at the far end of the island. Keely swallowed the lump of fear that formed in her throat. This was not good.

The beach appeared deserted, but a strange, faint glow emitted from the mouth of one of the caves. Suddenly a figure stepped from the shadows and helped heave the boat higher onto the sand. A stout figure, wearing a flat hat.

"Your contacts are very . . . efficient, Reave Spearman," said her uncle. "I thank ye for your help in returning what was lost."

"Aye, they're good men t' know."

"Did they take th' shipment?"

"Aye. Safely away. Do ye need me further tonight?" Kevin Spearman sounded nervous. Keely wondered what "shipment" he was talking about. And why had Alyn addressed him as "Reave Spearman?"

"Nay. Th' rest is between us. Ye understand th' oath o' silence . . ."

Even in the darkness, Keely saw the grim look on Spearman's face. "I do." He glanced in her direction. "And I've no doubt o' th' consequences."

She was lifted bodily out of the boat, passed like a trussed turkey from one man to the other. Then Alyn set her feet upon the soft sand and held her by one arm as he shoved the boat back in the water. Neither man spoke to the other again.

Then he turned to her. In his face, she read anger, and fear, and undisguised sorrow. "Ye've no idea what tragedy ye've brought among us, lass."

Keely was surprised he spoke to her, for she expected to be shunned, but his words infuriated her. As if this whole thing were her fault! She tried to speak back, but the words caught in the gag.

He tightened his grip on her arm. "Come."

Instead of leading her down the beach toward the village, he took her in the direction of the caves. The sacred place where only the Keeper could go. As they approached, she saw firelight coming from the mouth of the largest one.

He paused outside the cave, and she saw his shoulders slump as he released a heavy sigh. He turned to her, and his eyes were glassy with tears. "Ah, Keely, why'd ye do it?" Gently, he reached out and removed the material that had begun to eat into the edges of her mouth. Her tongue was dry, and she swallowed several times before saliva enabled her to speak at last.

" 'Tis th' very question I would ask o' ye, Uncle," she said. "What in th' name o' th' Saints is going on here? Where's Ninian?"

But Alyn Runyon did not answer. He simply shook his head, took her arm again, and together they entered the forbidden caves.

TWENTY-TWO

Inspector Sandringham thought he'd seen it all in his twenty-two years at Scotland Yard. There'd been the female impersonator who thought he was the Queen. And the Jack the Ripper copycat who created havoc for a short while over in the East End. He'd even been called in on a bizarre case recently involving an attack on a man supposedly by black magic.

But he was more unsettled than he'd been in a while over the still-unsolved murder of a young woman from a distant island in Cornwall, not because the killing of a runaway was so unusual in London, but because of Jack Knight's insistence that it was the work of a cult. And because Knight believed the life of the other woman, Keely Cochrane, was in danger as well.

It was one of those fine lines he had to walk as a police inspector. Whether to go by the book, as he had done earlier today, and wait for the proper evidence before investigating a situation that in all likelihood was perfectly innocent, or to listen to the gut-level feelings of an experienced police officer and possibly prevent another tragedy.

Sandringham sat in his quiet study and drew on his pipe. His Brittany spaniel snored at his side. A tot of fine single malt whiskey glimmered from a crystal glass on the table next to his overstuffed chair. The clock in the hall chimed eleven. This was his time of day, the only time he found peace in the hectic, demanding life he lived. But that peace was not forthcoming this night. He picked up the glass and swirled the amber liquid, staring into it absently.

What if Knight was right? What if the cult had indeed murdered one of their own, and Keely Cochrane, who according to Knight had also violated the law of the cult by leaving, was headed back to her own death? Sandringham's stomach tightened. If that happened, how could he live with himself?

Yet there was no proof of any of it. None. Not even the existence of the cult. He wished he'd asked the constable in Penzance about possible cult activity on Keinadraig when he'd spoken to him earlier, but they'd both been distracted at the time. Sandringham sipped at the whiskey, wondering if they'd intercepted Miss Cochrane at the train station. Surely they would have called if they had. Perhaps she hadn't taken a train. There were other means of transport, including hitching a ride. The idea of Keely Cochrane, alone and vulnerable on the roadways, made his skin crawl, heightening his unease.

Richard Sandringham considered the relationship between the young California ex-cop and the woman from the strange, isolated Cornish island. What an odd match. But then, love did that, he supposed. From the way the two had looked at one another and the protective gestures Jack Knight had made toward her, he had no doubt they were in love.

He had been in love once. Still was, for that matter. But he had never married. Eleanor was too practical for that. Said she wouldn't be married to his police work. He laughed. Eleanor was one to talk. She was, in her own way, married to her work as well. People came to her at all hours of the day and night, and she helped them sort out their lives that had gone askew. She talked people out of suicide. Sheltered battered women. Guided the lost and lonely to those who could help. The life of a public social worker was no easier than the life of a cop.

But Eleanor was right. They had no business being married. Still, Sandringham regretted just a little that she wasn't here to share these quiet hours with him.

At quarter past eleven, he jumped when the ringing of his telephone shattered the silence of his apartment. "Sandringham here."

"Holstedt is awake," said the officer assigned to Brad's bedside. "I've just taken a complete deposition."

"What did he have to say?" Richard Sandringham listened in growing dismay and knew he'd made the wrong call in not listening to Jack Knight earlier.

"Let me speak to Knight," he said.

"He's not here. The senior Holstedt either. They left a couple of hours ago, but they gave me a phone number to call in case of emergency."

"Well, give it to me, damn it!"

The inspector dialed the numbers but got no answer. Where in the hell could they be? Garrison Holstedt had scarcely left his son's bedside for a week, and now that Brad was regaining consciousness, his father wasn't there? It made no sense. He dialed again, in case he had pressed a wrong number. Still no answer.

Sandringham paced the study, his hands shoved deep into his pockets. Then he made a decision. His superiors might have his hide for it, because it was a costly decision, and it could prove dangerous. But he knew instinctively it was the right one. He could not risk allowing that young woman to meet the same fate as her friend.

He picked up the phone and made several other calls. Then he went to his bedroom, took out a small valise, and packed a few articles of clothing. Changing into street clothes again, he picked up his cell phone on the way out and dialed his office. Reaching the voice mail at his extension, he left a message for his secretary. "I won't be in tomorrow . . ."

Then he turned out the lights and left his small flat. This was why Eleanor would not marry him.

Hiring a helicopter had not been as easy as Jack and Garrison had thought, for even though Garrison had flying credentials, he was not licensed in the U.K. Finding a qualified pilot in the middle of the night had proven to be a problem.

It was after midnight, and Jack thought he might explode from anxiety and frustration when he turned and saw Inspector Sandringham press through the door of the small heliport. The two men stared at one another in astonishment. "What are you doing here?" they asked simultaneously.

"I'm trying to find a way to get to Cornwall in a hurry, but I could have walked faster than this," Jack growled.

Sandringham grinned. "Want a ride?"

Thirty minutes later, the three of them, along with two other officers from Scotland Yard, took off in a helicopter that rose into the city-lit skies over London, banked, and headed southwest. Jack was so afraid now for Keely that his heart was in his throat, for Sandringham had filled them in on Brad's complete account of what had happened the night of the murder.

The inspector had mustered the might of Scotland Yard to try to prevent anything from happening to Keely, operating more from police instinct than procedures, increasing Jack's professional respect.

If only they weren't too late.

Keely saw the flicker of flame and smelled the stench of smoke as her uncle led her into the cave. They crossed the large cavern where Keely had looked for Jack and went through the passageway that led to the chamber wherein gaped the hideous pit. Torches mounted at intervals on the walls lit the cave, revealing something stretched out on a low, flat table at the edge of the abyss.

Keely's eyes widened in disbelief. It was a body. Her heart thundered as she approached, and her mouth turned dry as dust. She crumpled into a heap beside the form. "Nay!"

It was Ninian.

She turned to her uncle. "When?" she sobbed. "How?"

Alyn stared down at the body, no longer able to restrain his own tears. "She died this morning," he managed hoarsely. "She grieved for Genny so deeply it nearly kilt her, but when ye left, she lost all will t' live."

Saints in heaven, Keely thought, appalled. It *was* her fault. She had helped Genny run away in the first place, and then she, too, had broken the laws that she knew Ninian, maybe more than all others, had held sacred. Still, after what she'd discovered in the outside world, Keely was not sorry she had run away. She had discovered that the outside world was filled with wonderful things and people who cared, even about strangers. She had come to understand that the old legends served only to keep the Dragoners in bondage. Her only regret was that now she could not share those wonders with this woman who had been like a second mother to her.

"Is this why ye brought me back?" she asked quietly. "T' say farewell t' her?" She stood up again, her eyes never leaving Ninian's lifeless face.

Alyn's face hardened. "I brought ye back because ye must face your punishment. But here, on th' Dragon's back, na in some yon land."

"Punishment? For what, Uncle?" Keely rose to face him, the flames from the torches that lit the room paling in heat compared to the fire of her sudden anger. Her best friend was dead, and now Ninian, too. And for what? The perpetuation of a seven-hundred-year-old legend?

"Am I t' die for wanting t' learn th' truth? For wanting a chance t' make choices in my own life?" She stepped toward him, emboldened by rage. "This is th' twentieth century, Alyn. There is no plague. The laws that once protected our people now only enslave them.''

Alyn glared at her. ''Ye have no idea how those laws ye defame protect ye. Protect us all.''

''Enough t' protect ye from being charged with Genny's murder, Uncle? I saw it, Alyn. I saw your gun. Ye killed her, didn't ye?''

He did not reply, but he looked away, and she knew she'd learned the sick truth about her friend's murder. She shivered in revulsion. ''Alyn,'' she whispered. ''How could ye? Even in th' name o' the Dragon . . .''

He turned his gaze on her again, fierce and unrepentant. ''She na only betrayed th' Dragon, she turned whore.''

''What?''

''I saw it with my own eyes. Oh, ye think ye are sly, Keely, but I have known all along how ye helped Genevieve slip away that night. Erica saw th' two o' ye down in th' harbor and fetched me. I followed Genevieve, guessing she would be going t' Penzance. I wanted only t' bring her back, before 'twas too late. I got there just as dawn broke and saw her board th' London train. There were too many people for me t' make a scene, so I rode that train, too, in another car. Her mind was so addled by meetin' up with her lover that she never noticed me.''

''Genevieve had no lover!''

''Aye, but she did. I followed her through th' streets o' that obscene city, watched her traipse like a common whore into that public house.'' Alyn's eyes took on a feral sheen as he spoke. ''Watched her come out with him, weavin' on her feet in drunkenness. I followed them t' th' fancy hotel where he took her. When I knocked on th' door t' th' room, she opened it . . . and . . .''

Alyn's face suddenly fell, his fury overwritten by despair.

''And what?'' Keely prompted quietly, confounded

that her uncle could possibly have done what he was claiming.

"She called my name." He said it as if in disbelief. "She called my name," he repeated, crumbling visibly before her eyes, "and then . . . I shot her." He went to where Ninian's body listened with the patience of the dead. "I did na mean to," he said to her. "I did na mean t' kill her. I went off my head when I saw her with th' man."

Keely suddenly understood why Ninian's grief had been so intense. She had hoped Alyn would return with Genny. Instead, he'd killed her.

"Did Ninian know ye did it?"

"No one knew anything about it, until th' stranger came. I told Ninian I could na find her, and then we had th' excommunication." His eyes became fierce again. " 'Twas th' stranger who brought th' trouble."

" 'Twas th' stranger who brought th' truth, Uncle. Did ye really believe ye could murder someone and get away with it?"

Alyn gave her a look of contempt. "Was it I, Keely, or was it th' Dragon? Was I na merely th' instrument o' th' Dragon, who would have reached out and found Genevieve sooner or later?"

Even as recently as a week before, Keely might have believed her uncle's claim. Superstition ran deep among the people of Keinadraig. But now, she knew it was simply an excuse for an old man to refuse to accept responsibility for an unspeakable act.

"Nay," she said. "Ye killed her. Na th' Dragon. And ye will be found out."

"Th' Dragon has protected me. I kilt th' man she was with. I left th' gun on him t' make it look as if he kilt Genny. There is no one but ye and me who know what happened."

"And soon ye will kill me, too?"

He looked sad as he nodded his head. " 'Tis th' law, Keely."

"Law?" she almost screamed. "Since when is murder acceptable in th' eyes o' God? Or have ye forgotten your Christian beliefs?"

Another voice pierced the tension. " 'Twas na th' Christian God who brought protection t' Keinadraig."

Keely whirled around, astounded to find herself facing Erica Sloan. Incredibly, the girl wore the blue robe of the Healer, the one Keely had seen often on Ninian. Where had she come from, and what was she doing here, in this forbidden place? "Erica?"

The girl smirked and raised an eyebrow. "Why do ye act so surprised? Did ye na think I would become Healer when Ninian died?"

The girl's eyes glittered harshly in the firelight, and Keely shuddered, for those eyes held the look of madness. She recalled Ninian's deep slumber the last time she'd looked upon her lying in her bed and wondered suddenly if Erica had not given her mother some kind of potion to help her into the next world. It was a dark thought, but after what she'd just learned, not impossible.

Keely looked to Alyn for explanation. As Keeper, he should banish Erica from this chamber, but instead, he seemed to have been expecting her. And on his face was an inexplicable mixture of dismay and contempt.

"She is Healer," he confirmed in a heavy voice. "Ninian died without naming another t' become th' Healer's apprentice. Erica is o' her line. There is no other t' serve."

Keely could not imagine Erica ever serving anyone other than herself. That she claimed to be a Healer was laughable. But Erica was not laughing. And neither was Alyn. "Do ye know th' ceremony?" he asked the girl.

"What ceremony?" Keely broke in before she could reply. Erica turned to her with a sneer.

"Why, th' purification ceremony, o' course."

"I thought 'twas th' duty o' th' Keeper," Keely said, her confusion mounting. "Just as I thought no one but th' Keeper was allowed into th' heart o' th' Dragon.''

Erica laughed bitterly. ''And ye thought ye knew it all. Why would na th' Healer perform this ceremony? 'Tis th' Healer who tends t' all rituals.''

''Then why is it kept secret?''

''There are many secrets in Keinadraig,'' she replied cryptically.

Keely thought that might be an understatement. ''Secrets that caused Genevieve t' run away?''

At the sound of her sister's name, Erica's face flushed with anger. ''Genevieve was a fool, like ye are a fool. She did na respect th' Dragon's law. She was weak and did na have it in her t' become th' Healer.''

''Why?'' Keely pressed. ''What did she na have it in her t' do?''

Erica's face turned crimson, but she did not answer directly. ''Take her away,'' she ordered Alyn Runyon, and Keely thought she must not have heard right. Erica Sloan giving orders to Alyn Runyon, the Keeper? But the girl continued. ''Ye have followed Ninian's wishes t' have her brought back here for punishment. Now ye must follow mine. Let us waste no more time. Lock her behind th' sea door. Th' tide is rising.''

Ninian's wishes? Sea door?

''What is she saying, Alyn?'' Keely demanded, alarmed that her uncle seemed suddenly impotent in the face of the girl's bold disrespect. ''Why are ye listening t' this snippet?''

''He's listening,'' Erica interrupted, speaking slowly, ''and he will obey, because th' true keeper o' th' laws o' th' Dragon is na th' Keeper o' Keinadraig, but th' Healer.''

It took a moment for this to penetrate Keely's already overtaxed mind. Although Alyn was obviously distraught, he did not in any way refute the girl's statement when she claimed the Healer to be the ultimate power on the island.

" 'Tis true?" Keely asked, her voice quavering slightly.

He looked at her in resignation and nodded. "Aye."

"Was it Ninian's wish that I be brought back t' Kei-nadraig?"

"Aye."

"For punishment?"

He exhaled, and his eyes watered. "Aye."

The full force of the implication stunned Keely. Ninian, her second mother, beloved since childhood, had ordered her death. "Did she . . . did she order ye t' kill Genevieve, too?" she asked.

This time Alyn shook his head. "Nay. I was t' bring her home."

"For punishment?"

Another nod. "Unless she could be convinced t' remain loyal t' th' Dragon and become th' Healer."

"Ninian called for th' death o' her own daughter?" Already aghast at what she had just learned, Keely felt light-headed when she realized that was exactly what Ninian had been prepared to do.

Erica's voice intruded into her thoughts. "Genevieve could never become Healer . . ."

". . . Because she did na have it in her t' call for th' murder o' someone who broke th' laws o' th' Dragon," Keely finished for her, feeling her blood turn cold. She understood now why Genny had run, and why she had been unable to speak of her reasons. And why she had been so afraid.

" 'Tis na murder," Erica insisted. " 'Tis punishment under th' law. And she needn't have made such a thing of it. A Healer has na had t' call down punishment anytime in recent memory. If she had na run away and broken th' law herself, none o' this would have happened."

A ghost of a memory stirred at the back of Keely's mind. She was a child, hiding in the pub, listening to Alyn and others discussing what to do about a young man who had broken the laws.

It had happened in her lifetime, to someone named
... Timothy Jenkyns. Shards of words from the ballad
crashed through her mind:

> *To the Dragon's back a young man came,*
> *And Timothy Jenkyns was his name ...*
> *... He ran away, thought he'd not be*
>   *found,*
> *But the morning tide brought his body,*
>   *drowned.*

"Timothy Jenkyns," she murmured, looking at Alyn.
"Ninian was Healer then, too, wasn't she?"

Erica frowned, not knowing what Keely was talking
about. She was too young to remember. But Alyn knew.
He looked away, but Keely lashed out.

"Ninian ordered his death, did she na, Uncle?"

Alyn Runyon looked perfectly miserable. "Aye," he
answered reluctantly.

She turned on Erica. "It *has* happened, Erica, in recent memory. And Genny knew it could happen again.
Murder may mean nothing t' ye," she fumed, "but your
sister was a decent woman. Ye are right, she could na
order someone's death, na because she was weak, but
because she refused t' believe that death was a justifiable
punishment for breaking laws that are archaic and senseless. Murder, in case ye do na know, is against th' laws
o' both England and God. She was right t' flee."

Erica raised her head and jutted her chin out defiantly.
"She knew th' secrets o' Keinadraig," she said with
silent menace. "She would tell. She promised she would
na, but in time, something would have slipped out."

"She did na tell me," Keely reminded her.

"Genevieve was a traitor. In time she would have
betrayed us all. As ye would have done if left on th'
outside. 'Tis why Ninian ordered ye be brought back
here. T' keep safe our sacred secrets."

"Sacred! Profane secrets they are! And they'll na be

safe much longer, for Alyn made a bad mistake. He thinks he closed forever the mouth o' th' one who witnessed Genny's slaying. But he did na. That man is alive, and 'tis only a matter o' time until th' police catch up with ye. Kill me, and ye will only make matters worse for yourselves.'' Keely hoped she hadn't just issued a death warrant for Brad. It was possible Alyn might try to finish the job. With these two, anything was possible. But she hoped that instead they would see the cruel insanity of what they had done and would spare her life.

Erica raised one lip in a snarl. ''I've heard enough, Alyn. Lock her behind th' sea door. We must get on with th' purification.''

With a look that bespoke deep regret and confusion, Alyn Runyon reached for a torch with one hand and took Keely again by the arm with his other and led her out of the chamber. He virtually dragged her to the other passageway, the one she had not explored when looking for Jack. She did not know what the sea door was. Nor did she wish to be locked behind it.

''Alyn, please, don't. Let me go, I beg ye.''

But he did not reply. Finding a niche, he secured the torch to light the way for his foul deed. Then with arms far stronger than hers, he shoved her down the narrow tunnel. In the dim light, she saw a door secured across the passageway, fashioned of wide wooden planks held together with two rusted iron crossbars. The wood was wet and encrusted with sea salt. Beyond, she could hear the hungry appetite of the sea.

''Uncle, no!'' she begged, but he would not hear. Instead, he lifted a heavy latch, shoved the door open, and thrust her through it. She landed with a splash in shallow water, surrounded by darkness. Behind her, she heard the squeak of rusty hinges and the sound of the latch falling back into place. She righted herself and, following the sound, groped her way toward it until she reached the soggy planks of the sea door. She pressed her cheek against it and called out until she was hoarse.

"Alyn! Please! Let me go!"

She turned and faced the darkness. The water ebbed and flowed slightly, but with each incoming current, it seemed to edge higher around her ankles. To her horror, Keely realized the tide was rising. The ballad spoke of a number of traitors who had met with tragic accidental drownings, and with sudden understanding, she knew none of them had been accidents.

TWENTY-THREE

A lyn Runyon had been a loyal servant to the Dragon since assuming the responsibility of Keeper upon the death of his father more than three decades before. He had sworn his oath to defend the laws he'd held sacred since he was old enough to understand them. He believed in Keinadraig, and he believed in the Dragon, at least as a symbol of the unique power that protected the island and its people. The Dragon no longer rose from the fire and sang out to the people as it had to the first Healer, but his laws were sound.

With Ninian as Healer, Alyn had found the strength to do many things an ordinary man would not have had the courage to do. He was her servant, as well as the Dragon's, and he'd loved her always. For Ninian, for the Dragon, he had lied, stolen, and murdered. He had never considered it wrong. He had not thought it murder when he'd locked the Jenkyns boy away behind the sea door, just as he'd now locked his own niece there. It had been the rightful punishment of the Dragon. It was the Dragon, working through him, who had thrown the latch, leaving the traitor to drown at high tide, thereby keeping the secrets of Keinadraig safe from outside eyes.

Alyn paused, listening to Keely's terrified pleas, her frantic screams from the far side of the door. He thought about the startled look in Genevieve's eyes when he'd shot her, and the blood that had spurted from her heart.

He thought about the kiss of the Dragon he'd removed from her neck in his rage.

Were these the acts of a Dragon or a man?

Genevieve had betrayed the Dragon by fleeing the island, but she'd shamed her mother by becoming a whore. Had he killed her for the Dragon, or for Ninian?

Alyn could no longer think clearly. Within the heart of the Dragon, Erica awaited him to assist with her mother's purification ceremony, a sad but important duty if he wished to cleanse Ninian's soul and free her of earthly bonds. Erica was the new Healer, and he must obey, although he was repulsed at the thought. Erica should not be the Healer. It was she, not Genevieve, who did not have the qualities of the Healer, although she had no qualms about ordering an execution.

Only Alyn knew the truth of Erica's birth, that she was not the child of Ninian's husband, but the offspring of a rape that took place here in this very chamber, by a stranger who had come, he said, at the request of the Reave, to move a shipment of goods from the caves to the mainland. He had attacked Ninian when she came to investigate, for she had discovered that he was not sent by Kevin Spearman at all, but was a local thief who had learned of their illicit traffic and had planned to pirate some of their goods. Alyn had come upon them, but not in time.

The intruder had already raped Ninian, although she had fought him fiercely. Alyn had killed him, stabbing him repeatedly until his blood spilled freely upon the cavern floor. Together, they'd thrown him into the pit. He'd opened the sea door to allow the flood tide to wash away the man's blood. To protect the traffic that kept Keinadraig economically alive, they'd agreed between them not to mention what had happened, but Erica had been the unfortunate outcome.

Alyn thought about that illicit traffic. It had started centuries ago as a means of protecting the Dragoners not from plague but from famine. He had never considered it a crime either.

But hearing the terrified screams of his niece, Alyn Runyon for the first time allowed doubts to enter his mind. He was the instrument of her death, and Genny's, and that of Timothy Jenkyns, because they broke the laws. But had not the Keepers of old broken the laws when they began the trade? Had they not entered into commerce with strangers, the very thing most forbidden by the Dragon in the first place?

Let ne'er a stranger in thy door.

Many a stranger had passed through that sea door, when the tide was out and small boats filled with contraband could safely maneuver into the hidden cove just beyond where Keely was trapped. Yet none of them had been punished by the Dragon. Even Ninian's rapist had died from Alyn's fury, not because his death was called for by the Dragon.

And now Erica was Healer. Erica, who was not of the pure blood of Ninian's line. Erica, who had virtually commandeered the title even knowing it was not her mother's wish and who had been caught many times with her nose between the pages of the Healer's book of secret wisdom.

Everything was all wrong.

With despair in his heart, Alyn retrieved his torch and forced himself to return to the heart of the Dragon, where he listened absently while Erica chanted the ancient invocation for the dead, words that had been used since the time of the Black Death to purify the souls of the dead in preparation for them to be received into heaven.

He heard instead his niece's cries for help. And suddenly, he heard something else. From outside the caves came a thundering clatter, an unholy commotion unlike anything he'd ever heard, drowning Erica's incantations.

"What's that?" Erica yelled at him. "What's that noise?"

It sounded as if the Dragon himself were flying above Keinadraig. Ignoring Erica, Alyn ran from the inner chamber, through the outer cavern and onto the beach, his heart pounding painfully in his chest. Looking up, he nearly passed out from fright.

It wasn't the Dragon. It was a white helicopter flying low over his head, close enough for him to see the figures of the men inside in the gray light of dawn. On the side of the aircraft, painted in white on a large red stripe, was the word "Police."

His mistakes had come back to visit him. Ninian had warned him not to punish Genevieve on the outside, but to bring her back to the mists of Keinadraig. Keely had told him that he had not killed the man who had been with Genny. Two mistakes that had now brought strangers to their shores who would surely discover the rest of the island's secrets.

Alyn dropped his head. It was over. After seven hundred years, it was over. And it was his fault.

He turned back toward the caves. Mayhap it was just as well. Suddenly everything he had believed in all his life and worked so hard to protect seemed like a lie. Keely was right. The laws that once protected the people had now destroyed them.

Keely. Her name shot through his befuddled mind like a lightning bolt.

He had been wrong to kill, even in the name of the Dragon, and he would not do it again. He headed toward the sea door.

"Where are ye going?" Erica stood at the entrance to the Dragon's heart, her hands invisible beneath the draped sleeves of the Healer's gown.

"I'm going t' free my niece," he told her flatly. He saw her eyes widen as her face became contorted with fury.

"Ye will na!" Erica ordered. "I am th' Healer, and I forbid it."

Alyn could not hold back the words that he'd wanted to say to this loathsome girl for years. "Ye are a bastard child and do na even know it, Erica. Here in this very chamber, a thief, a common thief, committed an abominable sin against your mother. He raped her, and ye were th' progeny. Ye have tainted blood, Erica. Ye deserve na th' honor o' th' ancient line o' Healers. Ye are an obscenity in th' eyes o' God and th' Dragon.''

With that, he continued toward the sea door.

'' 'Tis a lie! Ye are th' obscenity!'' Erica shrieked. "Halt now!'' Her enraged voice echoed in the chamber behind him, but he did not slow his pace. "Die, then, traitor,'' she screamed.

Alyn Runyon heard the sound of an explosion, felt something hot rip through his spine, saw blood gush from a hole in his chest, but felt strangely peaceful as he crumpled to the floor, enshrouded in a gathering cold darkness.

When it became apparent that her uncle would show no mercy, Keely had stopped screaming and leaned her head against the dank rock of the subterranean prison, sobbing. She wished with all her heart she had never left Jack, that by some miracle he would find her and save her, take her away from this horrible place.

Keinadraig.

Her home. A haven. A place of protection.

Ha! she thought bitterly. The cold water lapping ever higher up her legs told of another Keinadraig.

Keinadraig. A refuge for murderers.

And Jack would not come. She'd worded her note to imply that she cared more for Keinadraig than she did for him. She had hurt him, and she didn't expect him to follow her.

She had hurt him because she loved him, and her only consolation was that by leaving him, she believed she had saved him from death, not at the claws of the Dragon, but at the hands of people she had once trusted.

"Oh, Jack,'' she whispered into the darkness. Only yesterday she had discovered her true womanhood in his arms. Today she knew she would never see him again. Hot tears spilled down her cheeks unchecked, for her hands were bound, and she could not wipe them away.

"Jack." She repeated his name like a prayer. "Please know that I loved you."

Lost in her litany, she did not hear the sound until it was already loud in her ears. A strange rhythmical roar overhead shattered the quiet of her underground prison. A mechanical sound, a sound from the outside world. Her heart began to beat with hope. Had her prayers been answered? Had Jack forgiven her and come anyway?

She listened as the thunder of engines passed overhead, then faded away again. Come back! Please come back! she prayed silently from her watery tomb. As if in answer, the sound grew louder again.

Suddenly above the din, she heard the voices of Alyn and Erica, although at first she could not discern their words. They sounded harsh, argumentative.

"I'm going t' free my niece," she heard Alyn say, followed by something muffled from Erica. And then she heard the most astounding tale issue from her uncle's mouth, and she understood at last why Erica was so unlike Genevieve.

"My God," she croaked. Another dark and horrible secret brought to light.

Keely heard more sharp words between them, but Alyn seemed to have found the courage to disregard Erica's commands. She could hear his footsteps approaching, and her heart beat faster. He was going to free her!

And then she heard an explosion.

And then silence.

She started to call out for her uncle, but if that explosion was what she suspected, then Alyn lay dead on the floor outside the sea door, and Erica Sloan was out there with a gun. Where the girl had come by a gun, Keely could not imagine. But there was much of late her imagination could not encompass, and she was taking no chances.

The chamber echoed again with the sound of the mechanical beast that flew over head, and a new fear suffused Keely. If by some miracle it was Jack coming to her rescue, he must not come to the caves, not while Erica was still here. Erica had just shot Alyn Runyon, the Keeper of Keinadraig. She would not hesitate to shoot a stranger. As much as she wanted to cry out to warn him, Keely bit her lip instead and willed Jack away with all her might. He must not come here. She must not cry out or do anything to attract Jack's attention to the caves. For if he did, he would die.

"Nay, Jack," she whispered. "Do na come for me. If ye love me as I love ye, do na come."

"That's him." Jack had seen the figure emerge on the beach before it retreated again into the mouth of the cavern. "That's Runyon, her uncle. They must have her in the caves."

"Where can we land this thing?" Sandringham asked.

"There's no flat area, but there, just above the standing stones, I think the pilot can get us close enough that we can jump out."

The inspector instructed the pilot, who maneuvered the helicopter close enough to the ground for them to bail onto the island, then took off into the skies overhead and hovered on standby.

"This way," Jack shouted over the din, and headed toward the path to the beach. But before they reached it, a throng of angry villagers emerged from the oak grove, bearing torches and headed directly for them. "Welcome party," he said grimly.

"And I thought Vietnamese guerrillas used primitive weapons," Garrison remarked, looking at the ragtag mob armed only with fire, the weapon of days long past.

Sandringham radioed the chopper. "Dive at them," he ordered. "See if you can frighten them at least long enough to get us onto the beach, but hold them off as long as you can.'' The ploy worked, and Jack, Garrison, and Sandringham dashed to the edge of the incline and scrambled down to the beach.

Out of the corner of his eye, Jack glimpsed what appeared to be an armada of boats approaching the island, emergency lights flashing. He shot a quick glance at the inspector, who grinned and said, ''I think in the movies you Yanks call that the cavalry.''

''The cavalry! Looks like half the damned British Navy to me.'' Jack returned his grin, giving the inspector an enthusiastic thumbs-up. The landing team would be more than a match for a handful of frightened, superstitious Dragoners. Sandringham's cool control of what could have been a crisis situation again impressed Jack beyond measure.

''Let's find Keely,'' he shouted, and the three tore off down the beach toward the southernmost end of Keinadraig.

Their arrival at the mouth of the caves was greeted with a gunshot, and they dived for cover behind nearby boulders. ''Must be the old man,'' Jack said. ''Cover me.''

Before Sandringham could object, Jack darted out from behind the rocks and into the shadows of the cave, just before another shot was fired. He'd been issued a gun by the inspector, and he held it tightly in sweaty palms. Where was Keely? He didn't want to take a chance of shooting her. What if the old man was using her as a shield?

The cavern was lit by the glow of firelight coming from the second chamber where Keely had found him knocked unconscious. As his eyes adjusted, he could see there was no one in the outer cave, so he dashed to the far wall. His heart was pounding with fear, not for himself, but for Keely. These people were killers. Was he too late?

Jack edged through the passageway, expecting another shot in his direction. The inner chamber was lit by the flare of torches set into holders in the rock wall. They smoked and flickered, creating sinister shadows in the cave. He became aware of the sound of heavy breathing. Peering around the edge of the passageway, instead of coming face to face with Alyn Runyon, he saw the sour-faced girl he'd met on the docks, struggling to reload a large, old-fashioned pistol.

"I'll take that," he said, leaping to disarm her before she could finish the task.

Erica struggled, but was no match for Jack's superior strength. He twisted the gun from her grasp and threw it to the other side of the cave. That was when he saw the body at the edge of the pit. "What the hell?" But the girl struggled in his arms like a lioness trying to free herself, regaining his full attention. He tightened his grip.

"Where is Keely?"

She gave him a wicked sneer. "Your whore has gone t' her fate," she spat.

Her words twisted like a knife in his gut. "You're lying. Where is she?" He bent her arm higher behind her, knowing it was hurting her, wanting to hurt her more.

"Jack!" He heard Garrison shout from the outer cave.

"In here. Hurry!"

Garrison and Sandringham followed one another single file through the narrow passage into the room and stopped in their tracks, gaping at the macabre scene before them.

"What the hell?" Garrison echoed Jack's earlier words.

"Welcome to the Dragon's lair," Jack said. "Be careful. The old man's bound to be around here somewhere."

Erica gave a hideous laugh. "Ye've nothing t' worry about from th' likes o' him," she raved, clearly now out of control. "He betrayed th' Dragon same as your whore, and th' Dragon took swift revenge.''

"Quick, grab a torch," Jack said to the other two men. He forced Erica to look at him and glared into her ugly little face. "Where is he?" he demanded. "And where is Keely?"

But the girl just glared back defiantly and jutted her jaw forward, clenching her teeth and refusing to speak. Jack swore beneath his breath, then snarled, "Let's go."

Garrison preceded them back to the main cave, where the light from the torch revealed the body of Alyn Runyon, his life's blood seeping into the stony cavern floor. "Good God," he said, kneeling to examine the large entry wound. "What the hell kind of gun caused that?"

Sandringham looked down on the corpse of the large old man. "From the description Brad gave our man, I'd say we have our killer." One arm was flung over his head, as if pointing down another tunnellike passageway. "Wonder where that leads?"

"Nay!" Erica shouted.

Jack looked at her and saw venom in her eyes. He knew she did not want them to go down that path, and he knew why. "Yes!" he returned with a vengeance. Turning his prisoner over to Inspector Sandringham, Jack headed toward the opening.

"Keely!" His voice reverberated on the walls of the cave. "Keely! Answer me!" Faintly but clearly, he heard the voice he loved above all others.

"Jack! Help me!"

"Garrison, give me some light," Jack said, heading toward the sound of Keely's voice.

The passage was dark and forbidding, but no demon in hell could stop him now. Behind him Garrison managed to shed enough flickering light to show him the way. He came upon a curious wooden door, its boards swollen and wet. It hung on large, rusted hinges, and it was latched with a heavy bolt.

Behind it, he heard Keely sob, "Jack, hurry! Th' water's rising."

He pressed his full weight against the wood, which eased the latch in its holder, and with a quick shove, he released the barrier. The door flung painfully against him as cold sea water flooded past him and up the passageway. With it, the water washed a wet but alive Keely into his arms. He had no time to enjoy the surprise, however, for the water was hurrying to seek its level, and they could be caught in the passageway.

"C'mon!" He took her by the shoulders and pushed her in front of him. Together they followed the incoming flow of water up the steep, narrow tunnel until the tide no longer threatened to drown them as it leveled out when it reached the cavern floor.

Keely whimpered when she saw the body of her uncle at her feet, his blood mingling with the muddy sea water. Jack turned her away from the grisly sight and into his arms. Behind her back, he untied her bonds.

"It's okay, sweetheart," he whispered. "It's okay."

Then he looked past her and saw a wall of villagers at the mouth of the cave, brandishing torches and staring openmouthed at the appalling scene. Behind them, men in uniforms formed a human barrier to their escape.

TWENTY-FOUR

Keely shivered from the cold and wet. She was weak from terror and exhaustion. But she had never been so overjoyed in all her life. She was in Jack's arms again.

A miracle had happened. She did not know how he'd found her, but she thanked God and all the Saints for her deliverance . . . and the man who had done the delivering. She huddled in the cradle of his arms and allowed his warmth and strength to surround her and infuse her with new hope. She knew the truth at last, as horrible as it was. But with Jack's help, Keely knew she could now get on with her life, free from fear.

Taking comfort from that thought, she melted even further into Jack's embrace. But suddenly, to her confusion, he eased her away from him. Why? What was wrong? She looked up at him, perplexed, then turned to see what he was looking at.

There, at the mouth of the forbidden caves, was every man, woman, and child who lived on Keinadraig. Shock registered on their faces. And horror. And fear. Keely's heart began to thunder all over again. Did any of them know the horrendous truths that she'd just learned? Were any of them killers, too?

As far as she knew, they were good, hardworking people who, like her, had been kept ignorant of the dark side of the Dragon's laws. They believed their safe, secure, and prosperous island remained that way because of the Dragon's promise and their own willing obedience to the Dragon's laws. They'd never questioned either the promise or the laws.

As far as she knew.

She was, however, no longer certain of anything concerning Keinadraig. There could be others among them who knew of the Healer's dominion and the Keeper's grim duties. Others who had killed, as surely as Alyn and Ninian.

But she could not be the only innocent. The others who were unaware of these things deserved to know the truth, and Keely intended to fully enlighten them. Right here. Right now. She took a step toward them.

"Seven hundred years ago, our people suffered th' terrible destruction of a plague that was brought by a stranger t' Keinadraig," she said, emboldened by a righteous anger. "A woman who had lost many loved ones, in her fear and grief, was said t' have seen th' figure of a dragon rise up from th' flames in th' circle o' stones, and was said t' have heard th' mythical beast sing forth th' laws that would protect them from it ever happening again."

Keely took another step in their direction and felt Jack touch her elbow. She darted a reassuring smile in his direction but shook her head for him not to interfere. She must face them all now. They must know. She looked back at the faces of her neighbors and kinsmen. Most were frowning. Some looked fearful. All were silent.

"That first Healer, Maram, was a wise woman, for whether she actually heard th' Dragon speak or na, she created laws that kept th' people o' Keinadraig safe for hundreds o' years. Because for hundreds o' years, th' Dragoners have dwelt in isolation, and people who dwell in isolation cannot contract deadly diseases from th' outside world. 'Tis that simple."

" 'Twas na Maram who made th' laws," objected one old woman. " 'Twas th' Dragon."

Keely had never been so sure of herself, or the truth, in her life, although her heart pounded at defending what the rest would deem heresy. She stood her ground and reached for Jack's hand. "There is no Dragon," she told them boldly. " 'Tis nothing but a symbol for our people and our beliefs."

"God save ye, child," said another fearfully.

"Tell me, who among ye has ever seen th' Dragon?" she challenged.

A murmur rustled through the crowd, but no one claimed to have seen the beast. " 'Tis na for us t' see," said William Reedy. " 'Tis seen only by th' Keeper, and th' Healer."

"Aye, and those who betray him and feel th' heat o' his breath and th' needle o' his claw," chimed in Mrs. Parsons.

"Do ye believe th' Dragon went t' London and shot Genevieve?" Keely asked the woman directly.

Mrs. Parsons fidgeted uncomfortably. "I do na like such talk. 'Tis likely t' draw th' wrath o' th' Dragon down upon us all."

But Keely would not let her out of it. " 'Twas na th' Dragon who shot Genevieve, Mrs. Parsons. 'Twas my own uncle, Alyn Runyon." She heard a gasp of universal denial.

"That could not be. Alyn was here . . ."

"Was he?" Keely asked. "Think back. When Genny first ran away, I was so distressed I did na notice much, but na once until he called for her excommunication three days later did I lay eyes on my uncle."

A buzz passed among them, but Keely interrupted their conjecture. "I know my uncle did it, because he told me exactly how he managed t' follow her, and how . . . he murdered her. He used th' gun he kept in his desk, at th' Council office. Some o' ye have seen it. 'Tis now in th' hands o' th' police," she said, indicating Inspector

Sandringham, who stood on guard over a handcuffed Erica Sloan, who sat on the floor, hate almost seeping from her pores. Keely shuddered upon seeing the girl, but returned to her story, determined to follow it to the end.

"Not only did Alyn murder Genny, he attempted t' murder another person as well and blame th' killings on him, as if he'd turned th' gun on himself. His second victim was someone who had never broken any law o' th' Dragon, but who had befriended Genny when she was frightened and alone."

She paused and let her gaze wander from face to face. "Is this th' way o' th' Dragoners? That we would kill our own because o' laws that are so outdated they no longer have meaning in our lives? There has been no plague for centuries. Th' outside world is filled with wondrous things that would help us, na harm us."

"But 'twas a stranger who killed th' Keeper," William Reedy said, pointing at Jack.

Keely shook her head. "Nay," she said sadly. "He, too, was killed by one of our own." She turned to Erica who sat glowering on the damp floor. "Erica, our new Healer, shot Alyn in th' back."

" 'Twas my right." The girl spoke loudly enough for them all to hear and stood up. She looked bedraggled and ridiculous in Ninian's robe, like a child playing at being a grown-up. But her face was ripe with fury. " 'Tis th' duty o' th' Healer, na th' Keeper, t' decide th' fate o' those who betray th' Dragon. He was t' leave this brazen whore t' die behind th' sea door, but he weakened and was going t' set her free. He, too, betrayed th' Dragon. He deserved t' die."

Her words, and the passionate defiance behind them, sickened Keely. Did Erica really believe, as Ninian had, that traitors must die, or was she just hungry for power?

"What Erica speaks is th' truth, according t' th' Dragon's laws," she told the shocked villagers. "Because o' these tragedies, I have learned a dark secret o'

th' Dragoners, known until now only by th' Keeper and
th' Healer. Although we have all believed 'tis th'
Keeper, th' head o' th' Council, who rules Keinadraig,
in truth, th' Keeper answers t' th' Healer.'' She paused
to give them time to let this fact sink in, then continued.
''This was why Genevieve ran away. She learned that
as th' new Healer, she would have t' call for th' death
o' someone who broke th' laws. She did na have it in
her t' commit murder.''

One of the brighter young men spoke up, his eyes
registering horror as a new understanding hit him. ''If
'tis th' Healer who gives th' orders, are ye saying Ninian
called for th' death o' her own daughter?''

Keely felt her throat tighten at Ninian's ultimate betrayal of Genevieve. She looked down at her hands, let
out a long sigh, and then returned her gaze to the young
man's face. ''Aye,'' she said quietly, ignoring the single
tear that ran down her cheek.

The raid on Keinadraig took place at dawn. By nine
o'clock, the bodies of both Ninian Sloan and Alyn Runyon had been transported to the morgue for autopsy, and
Sandringham had the entire village under house arrest
until he could question each person about their possible
involvement in the murders. Guards were posted around
the perimeter of the island. No one other than people on
official business was allowed off or onto the island, although media helicopters and boats hovered nearby.

Erica Sloan had been taken kicking and screaming
from the floor of the caves and carried bodily to a waiting launch, her captors careful to avoid the bite of her
sharp little teeth. She shouted curses against Keely and
Jack, against the weak will of Alyn and Genevieve,
against her own mother for all the slights and injustices
she had endured over the years. She was incarcerated as
a juvenile in Penzance and held for psychological ob-
servation.

Garrison returned to London and Brad's bedside, and

Keely was released into Jack's custody after answering hundreds of questions and giving the police a description of Kevin Spearman and her two kidnappers. She sat beside him in stunned silence aboard the cutter that transported them to Penzance, where Jack booked them a room at the inn where he'd stayed before.

He made arrangements with an astonished Maggie Evans to bring breakfast to their room, then led Keely up the stairway to refuge behind locked doors. Only then did he take her into his arms.

"Oh, Keely," he whispered into her hair, his heart going out to her. She had been through such pain and horror. "I am so sorry."

In the past week, she had lost her best friend, her home, her family, and her community.

This morning, she had lost her innocence.

Even Jack was shocked at the depth of the deception of Keely's uncle and her best friend's mother. But he knew the inbred teachings of seven hundred years were not easily overcome by isolated and superstitious people. In a deluded way, they had believed they were doing the right thing, he supposed. He'd seen it before among cult leaders.

The real victims were Keely and the people of Keinadraig who never knew about the deliberate executions. Their lives, their faith, had been shattered. How would they pick up the pieces? They were no longer protected by a social structure that although debased, had worked nonetheless. They, too, were innocents. He felt for them at the thought of the media finally getting to the island, as they eventually would. The press would have a heyday with this story.

But it was not the people of Keinadraig that concerned him at the moment. It was the woman in his arms, the woman he'd vowed to protect and whom he'd almost lost. She had been vulnerable before. She was downright fragile now.

He must take things very, very slowly. Jack wished

again he'd had some training in the exit process for people in her situation. The only thing he had to draw upon was his love for her. It would have to suffice.

"Go ahead and cry," he murmured, knowing she must have tears in her heart.

But she did not cry. Instead, she began to rock gently back and forth in his arms, and she began humming a mindless tune. "Nay, Jack," she said quietly after a moment. "I can na cry. The sorrow is too great t' bear."

Shock stemmed tears, Jack knew. She must cry, for she needed to grieve if she was to heal from this nightmare, but tears would come in time. For now, he would be there for her, in any way he could. A knock on the door interrupted his quandary as to what would be best for her.

"Breakfast." Maggie Evans's chipper voice sounded from the other side.

Jack released Keely and guided her to a wicker chair next to a small, round, chintz-covered table, where she sat staring into space with huge, unseeing eyes. Going to the door, he took the tray from Maggie, but did not respond to the open curiosity in her face. She'd get the story soon enough. "Thanks," was all he said, then shut the door again.

He placed the tray on the table and uncovered the plates. "Let's eat," he invited her. "You'll feel better." The sight of a full English breakfast made his own stomach growl, and he realized he had not eaten since he'd had lunch with Garrison the day before. No telling the last time Keely had food. But she showed no enthusiasm.

He poured some hot tea and sat the cup in front of her, but she did not reach for it. He buttered a slice of toast and placed it on a plate within her reach, but she seemed not to notice. Her eyes remained vacant, unfocused. She held herself and rocked ever so slightly.

Maybe he should call a doctor, Jack thought, alarmed. Her face was ashen, and there were dark smudges beneath her eyes. "Drink some tea," he urged quietly. "Please."

He went to her and raised the cup to her lips, and his touch seemed to awaken her from a faraway place.

"I understand now," she murmured after sipping the tea. "I understand Maram in her grief reaching for anything she could t' take away th' pain."

Jack wasn't sure exactly what Keely was talking about, but at least she was talking. "Go on." He knelt beside her chair and placed the teacup in her hands, where it shook slightly, but she sipped again.

"Maram. Th' first Healer o' Keinadraig. She must have lost her family, too. They say th' plague took nearly everyone." She raised her eyes and met his gaze. "There are many kinds o' plague, aren't there, Jack?" At last he saw tears shining in her eyes.

"Yes," he replied softly.

"Disease was Maram's plague. Fear was ours," she continued. "Ninian did what she did because she was afraid. As was Alyn. Even . . ."

The cup crashed to the floor, and Keely covered her face with her hands. "Even Genny. She ran away because she was afraid." The tears arrived at last, and Jack gently eased Keely back into his arms, where he held her and rocked her and let her cry.

"You never have to be afraid again," he said. "It's over. And I'm here for you . . . if you want me. I'll be here forever, unless you ask me to go."

He felt her arms tighten around him. "Ye must na make promises like that, Jack," she scolded between sobs. "I know ye can na keep them. Ye have a life o' your own, and I can na lean on ye. I must make a new life on my own."

"I want you to lean on me, at least until you are strong again, Keely. I want to help you." He raised her head and looked into the gray-green turbulence of her eyes. "Please, let me help you, Keely. I love you, and I don't want to lose you."

Her eyes widened as he lowered his head, then he saw them close as she leaned into him and parted her lips. She tasted of salty tears and tea, and it was the sweetest taste Jack had ever sampled. He wanted her to lean on him, not just for now, or until she was strong again, but forever.

Keely was not sure she'd heard correctly as she allowed herself to be surrounded by the protective strength of Jack's arms. She had heard him say he wanted to help her and he repeated again that he would be there for her. But this time, he'd used some new words. Words like "forever." And "I love you."

How she wanted to believe him. How she wanted to think he loved her and would always be there for her. But she was not sure she could ever trust again. She'd trusted Ninian above all others, as the Healer, as a mother, as a friend. She'd trusted Alyn, her own mother's brother. She'd trusted the laws of Keinadraig, and the legend of the Dragon.

And they'd all betrayed her.

Could she trust anyone ever again?

But there was something in Jack's kiss, some fierce, unnameable presence that bespoke the truth behind his promises. She wanted to believe him, with all her heart, because deep inside, she believed that she loved him, too. But love was another of those things that was very new to her, and she was not sure if she could even trust her own heart.

"Oh, Jack," she murmured, drawing away from him and leaning her forehead against his chest. "I'm still so addled."

"It's okay, Keely," he said, running his fingertips up and down her spine in a reassuring way. "You've a right to be addled. You've been through a lot. It's going to take some time. We'll just take it easy, one step at a time. Okay?"

She liked that word. Forcing a smile, she raised her head. "Okay."

Keely allowed Jack to encourage her to eat a few bites of the ample breakfast that was set before her, and she felt some of her strength returning. She took a hot shower, and afterward donned a soft knitted shirt he loaned her to sleep in. A T-shirt, he called it. How was it, she wondered in rather dazed amusement, that she never seemed to have anything to wear whenever she left the island with Jack?

He'd virtually ordered her to take a nap, and in the bedroom, she saw that he had turned down the covers of one of the two large beds. She sighed. How inviting it looked. She was weary clear to her toenails. But during the course of her bath, she'd thought about what Jack had said, what he'd told her all along, that he would be there for her. She had considered her own questions of trust. Could she trust him? Aye, she could. He'd said he'd be there for her, and he had been. He had found a way to come to her at a time when all others had forsaken her. He had risked his life for her.

And just now, Jack Knight, the stranger, had told her he loved her. That he didn't want to lose her. What did that mean? She would not be able to sleep until she spoke with him again.

She tiptoed into the sitting room where Jack sat slouched in a chair. He looked as if he were dozing, and she knew he must be as tired as she was. She hesitated, not wanting to wake him, but he heard her footsteps and turned to her. Keely's heart skipped several beats as his gaze skimmed very slowly from her head to her toes and back again.

"I thought you were asleep," he said in a hoarse voice.

"Jack, there's something . . . we need t' talk about."

He gave her a worried frown and stood up. "I'm listening."

Keely took a hesitant step toward him. " 'Tis about

what ye said just a bit ago. Ye said . . . ye said ye loved me.'' Her face grew warm at this difficult subject, but she was determined to see this through. ''Ye said ye did na want t' lose me. What . . . what did ye mean?''

The worried look melted away from Jack's face and was replaced by a slow smile that warmed his eyes and her heart. ''Come here,'' he said, opening his arms to her.

She went to him, and together they dropped into the overstuffed armchair where Jack had been sitting. She curled into his lap, inhaling his scent and exploring the texture of his stubble of a beard with her fingertips. He grasped her hand and kissed those fingertips. ''Better not do that just now,'' he murmured. ''Not if you want to talk.''

Keely wanted to talk, but the feel of Jack's body molded against hers made her want something else as well. Still, she remembered how she had felt when she had awakened after making love with Jack to find him gone. How afraid she had been that he had only obliged her curiosity toward things that happen between men and women. She no longer thought that, but she must know his true feelings for her. It would be too easy for her to become dependent on him now, only to be hurt again when he moved on with his life.

''What I meant,'' he spoke again, touching her chin lightly, ''was what I said. I love you. I think I've loved you since the first time I saw you.''

Her heartbeat quickened at his words. ''What is this thing . . . love?'' she asked, truly wanting to know. Keely had never felt like this toward anyone in her entire life. She had no reference point to describe the tenderness in her heart and the longing in her body and soul for the stranger who had come so unexpectedly into her life.

Jack looked at her long and thoughtfully, and she wondered if he was aware that he was tracing tiny circles with his finger on the bare skin of her thigh. ''Love. I'm not sure I know what love is," he said at last, and cleared his throat. "Not this kind of love. I've never been in love like this before. All I know is that when I am with you, I feel . . . filled up. I've never had anyone who gave my life so much meaning. When you left, I was devastated. If anything had happened to you . . ." He broke off and kissed her with all the fire and passion that she'd heard behind his words.

And her questions were answered.

Within his kiss, Keely let go of the betrayal and confusion and heartbreak that had torn her world apart. She allowed herself to trust her feelings, and allowed Jack to teach her about a kind of love she never knew existed. Where once she'd faced a chasm of fear and darkness, she now was consumed by light and love. Where once there had been lies, now there was truth. Truth, and love, and hope, and a whole new world, all introduced to her by a stranger.

TWENTY-FIVE

Later that afternoon, Jack's cell phone rang, awakening him from the depths of a love-sated slumber. He stirred, trying not to disturb Keely, whose body lay intimately entwined with his.

"Hello." Jack tried not to sound irritable, but his brain was still half asleep, and his body longed to return to hers.

"Sorry to waken you," Sandringham said, "but I need you both over here as soon as possible. You are not going to believe what we've found."

Although the inspector's voice was edged with excitement, Jack was uneasy. What now?

"We can be ready in twenty minutes," he said.

"I'll send a boat."

Keely rolled over and gazed up at him lazily, not bothering to cover the creamy expanse of her leg that was exposed from the hip to the toes. "Who was that?"

Fresh from sleep, her face flushed with desire, her lips rosy and beckoning, Keely had never looked more beautiful. Their lovemaking had been both tender and torrid, and neither had wanted to give it up until pure physical exhaustion temporarily forbade them more pleasure. For Jack, however, holding her in his arms as they drifted off to sleep had been a pleasure unto itself. Wrapping his body around hers, he felt at last he could protect her.

But Sandringham had just stolen away that illusion. He had ordered Keely to return to Keinadraig. God, how Jack hated to drag her back to that place. At least this time, she would not be alone.

He saw the distress in her eyes when he told her what they must do. "I'm sorry," he said. "Hopefully this will be the last of it." But he knew it would not be. Keely would be questioned now and called to testify later. God forbid if the media got hold of her . . .

She rose from their bed without a word and slipped back into her clothes, now stiff from dried salt water. Jack wished he'd had the presence of mind to ask Maggie Evans to find something else for her in a nearby store and silently promised that soon Keely would get the shopping spree of her life.

Her silence worried him, and he stopped before opening the door to their room. "You don't have to go," he told her. "I can explain to Sandringham . . ."

"I have t' go, Jack." She smiled at him. "Do na worry. I feel better now. I can do this, with ye by my side."

He took her hand and squeezed it hard. "You couldn't pry me away."

Inspector Sandringham looked tired as he greeted them on the quay, and Jack gathered he had not slept for the past day and a half. "Thank you for coming, Miss Cochrane," he said, then turned and extended his hand to Jack. "And you, Mr. Knight."

"What have you got?" Jack was anxious to get this over with. He would be glad when they could go back to London.

"Follow me."

He led them to the Council office, where he showed Keely a large, ledger-style book. "Have you ever seen this before?"

She stepped closer to where it lay on Alyn's desk and touched it lightly. "Nay," she said after a moment. She turned to the inspector. "What is it?"

"A record of some rather interesting transactions that have taken place on Keinadraig."

"Transactions?" She furrowed her brow. "What kind o' transactions?"

"Smuggling."

Jack could not have been more astounded if he'd said tourism. "Smuggling! You've got to be kidding!"

"Seems there's been an active trade here for a long, long time. Look at this." He turned to the first entry. It was written in a spidery handwriting in ink that had faded to a pale brown. It was dated 1588. "The year of the defeat of the Spanish Armada," he said, sounding awed. "Seems French brandy was the fancy of folks in those times." He pointed to a long list of goods, most of it numbered kegs of brandy. "As best we can tell, the caves of Keinadraig were used to warehouse goods coming in from the Continent until they could be moved inland and disposed of. Historically, Cornwall has been notorious for this sort of thing. But given the history of Keinadraig . . ." His voice trailed away, and he shook his head in disbelief.

Neither could Keely grasp what he was telling her. "Are ye saying th' Dragoners dealt in stolen goods in those days?"

Sandringham looked at her patiently but not unkindly. "In those days, Miss Cochrane, and these."

"What?" Keely glanced uneasily at Jack, and he took her hand.

The inspector turned to the last entry marked in the old ledger. It was dated less than two weeks before, and it recorded the transport of four crates of stolen goods from Keinadraig to Penzance, where they were entrusted to Kevin Spearman. The items were listed in detail and included jewels, antiques, artifacts, and art pieces.

"This can na be!" Keely exclaimed. And then she covered her mouth with her hands. "Ah, but, may-hap . . ."

"What is it, Miss Cochrane?" Sandringham urged her to finish her sentence.

Keely looked bewildered as she fought to understand this new information. "When I was held captive in Penzance, they took me through a large warehouse, filled with boxes and crates. The men who kidnapped me said a curious thing as they were leaving. Mr. Spearman said something about a vow o' silence, and one o' th' men told him, 'We've been doing business for years. We wouldn't want t' . . . t' bugger it up now.'" Keely twisted her nose up at the word "bugger." "What does that mean?" she asked.

Sandringham laughed. "It means to ruin things. I suspect Spearman uses those men to fence the stolen goods in London and other parts of the country. It would make sense for him to call on his underworld contacts to find you and kidnap you."

"My uncle killed Genevieve for breaking th' laws o' Keinadraig," Keely said thoughtfully, "and yet it seems t' me those laws were broken long ago when th' Dragoners became smugglers." She looked at Jack, and he saw bewilderment turn to anger. "There must have been many strangers come t' Keinadraig bringing their stolen goods. But how did th' Keepers manage t' hide what was going on from th' rest of us? This island is small."

Sandringham went to the door of a closet in the hallway. "Come. I'll show you."

Would the deception never end? Keely had passed by the door Sandringham now opened for her hundreds of times when she'd visited her uncle in the Council office. She'd fetched cleaning supplies from the closet behind it and arranged stores of dry meal and flour there.

But she'd never suspected there was another door, hidden behind a false wall.

"Our men found it from the other side," the inspector explained. "They searched the caves and discovered an extensive labyrinth of tunnels under the island. Want to take a look?''

Keely and Jack followed him down the damp stone stairway. The air was cool and dank, sharp with the smell of the ocean. The scent raised a memory of her terrifying ordeal and sent a shiver down Keely's spine. The police team had placed electric lighting on poles at intervals, but Keely was uneasy in the tomblike atmosphere.

''Most Dragoners probably don't know it,'' Sandringham said as they crept along, ''but they are actually quite wealthy, if one overlooks the fact that their wealth is in stolen goods. The owners, though, have long since passed away.''

''What are ye talking about?'' Keely asked. The Dragoners had always enjoyed sufficient income from the trade of their fish to provide food for the table and clothes on their backs. But wealth was unknown to them.

''Take a look.'' He guided them into a small chamber off the main tunnel, and Keely stared in astonishment at chests filled with gold coins that gleamed in the artificial light.

''Spanish gold, no doubt,'' said the inspector, dipping his hand into the treasure in one ancient wooden crate and letting the coins trickle through his fingers back into the stash. ''Been here for a long, long time. A little hard to fence these days, unless it's melted down and made into something else. I have sent samples to the lab to determine exactly what it is we have here.''

''Good God!'' Jack exclaimed, looking around at five more chests filled with similar treasure. ''Is this for real?''

Keely just shook her head. ''I can na believe this.''

''Oh, there's more,'' Sandringham said, almost gleefully. He led them into yet another chamber wherein were stashed hundreds of rifles and boxes of ammunition. ''Stolen from the British Army in World War II,'' he said. ''With the ammo, it'd be worth quite a bit to some third-world commando." He lifted the lid on another old chest, revealing a cache of odd antique firearms, mostly pistols.

"Your uncle was a very neat Keeper," remarked the inspector. "Everything is stored according to some kind of order and carefully recorded in that ledger upstairs. We suspect the gun he used in London came from here, as well as the pistol the girl used."

Keely leaned into Jack, who slipped his arms around her. She was overwhelmed at the depth and the duration of the lies of Keinadraig. "We never knew . . ." she muttered.

Sandringham eyed her shrewdly. "I must be certain of that, Miss Cochrane. That you never knew about any of this. We are interviewing everyone in the village."

Keely refused to be offended. The man was only doing his job. "I never knew that my uncle had been involved in killing anyone," she stated. "I never knew about th' smuggling. I never knew th' secret tunnel existed. Nor do I believe most other Dragoners knew any o' this."

"But the woman called Ninian knew?"

Moisture sprang to her eyes at the sound of Ninian's name. "Aye," Keely said, "I believe now that she knew about all o' this. And somehow, Erica found out. She probably overheard th' quarrel between Ninian and Genevieve. She was always snooping, too," she added, recalling the day she'd caught Erica administering the kiss of the Dragon to her doll.

"It must have been Erica singing in the caves that day," Jack mused. "She must have come through the tunnels."

"Aye," Keely agreed, believing it quite possible that Erica might have tried to kill Jack. Thinking back on the incident, Keely was surprised that Erica hadn't tried to drag Jack's unconscious body to the pit and dispose of him on the spot. The idea caused the hair to rise on the back of her neck.

"Who else would have known about the smuggling?" the policeman continued.

Keely gave it thorough consideration. "Nobody on the island," she answered at last. "I think 'twas a tightly held secret between Alyn and Ninian. That's why . . . they felt compelled t' kill Genevieve. Erica said they were afraid Genny would talk and give away th' secrets o' Keinadraig. I thought she meant that Genny would go t' th' police with information that people like Timothy Jenkyns had been killed for breaking th' laws o' th' Dragon. But now I think 'twas because they wanted no one t' know about . . . about all this," she finished, gesturing toward the stolen goods.

"Where does Kevin Spearman fit in the picture?"

Before answering the inspector, Keely looked up at Jack. "Can we go back up t' th' Council office? This place makes me nervous."

Sandringham offered his apologies. "I got ahead of myself," he said. "I'm eager to learn the whole picture."

Back in her uncle's office, Keely took a seat near the desk, while Jack lounged against the door frame and the inspector sat at the table, taking notes.

"Now, about Spearman . . ." he returned to his question.

"Within th' framework o' th' laws o' Keinadraig, Dragoners are allowed t' sell what we can t' outsiders in order t' sustain ourselves. Often, Genevieve and I would be sent with a boat full o' fish t' sell at th' market in Penzance. Our instructions were t' turn them over t' Mr. Spearman, wait until he off-loaded them, and t' return promptly t' th' island."

"Did you ever see him come to the island?"

"Only last night, when he brought me here t' turn me over t' my uncle."

The inspector opened the ledger again. "Have you ever heard the term 'Reave'?"

"Why, aye. Th' kidnappers used it in reference t'

Kevin Spearman. And . . ." She paused, thinking back. "So did my uncle. What is a reave?"

He found the page he'd marked and read from the historical archives of Keinadraig. "In this the yeare of our Lorde fifteen hundred and ninety-two, such dire conditions as continuing famine have caused it to become necessary to assign one amongst us to live away from us, to the ende of acting as our representative in commerce. Henceforth, there shall be added unto our Council he who shall be known as the Reave of Keinadraig. At great peril doth this Reave serve the Dragon, for he lives no longer under the protection of the island, but must appeareth as a stranger unto us. Therefore, unto him and his heirs shall fall twenty shares of every hundred of the goods and monies that passeth through his stewardship. The one who shall serve cometh from the line of Spearman of the ancient days."

Just when she could conceive of no other mysteries hidden by those who inherited control of the island of her birth, Keely was forced to learn yet another truth of her heritage. "Kevin Spearman is a Dragoner?"

"Where is he?" Jack asked.

"Unfortunately, that bird has flown," Sandringham said regretfully. "Must've seen the flotilla headed out here. But we'll get him."

The three sat in silence for a long while. Finally, Jack spoke. "So what happens now?" he asked. "Who owns the contraband? The Dragoners? The British government?"

"It will take us some time to sort it all out," Sandringham said. "At the moment, it is all in our custody. You only saw part of it. There are crates of paintings, authentic pre-Columbian artifacts, priceless china . . . you simply cannot imagine. I'm certain some insurance companies are going to be very interested in what's uncovered, not to mention the owners who lost the goods in the first place."

"The question is," Keely said, her heart heavy once again, "what is going t' happen t' th' Dragoners?"

Outside, the sun shone brightly, casting a deceptive glow against the whitewashed houses as it moved steadily toward evening. Jack took Keely's hand as they walked the short distance from what had once been her home to the vessel waiting to take them back to Penzance. She had returned to her cottage only long enough to gather a few personal items. "I could never live here again," she told him, shutting the door firmly behind her. She'd turned the building over to Inspector Sandringham to use during his stay on Keinadraig.

From the water as they departed, the village looked pristine, as charming as anything Jack had ever seen in a travel brochure. It did not look like a place that harbored thieves and murderers. But there were guards posted on every street corner as well as the island's perimeter, to keep the Dragoners in until Scotland Yard was satisfied no one else had conspired in the crimes, and to keep everyone else out.

Some things never changed.

"What will happen t' them, Jack?" Keely said, her eyes never leaving the island as it receded into the mists. "They're . . . like children. They've never had t' make any real decisions about their lives. They've never paid a bill or learned t' drive a car. They're . . . like me."

"Sandringham told me he has an excellent contact with a social worker in London. He's already asked her to come and work with the villagers to sort things out."

"What's a social worker?"

"People who specialize in helping others whose lives are disrupted for one reason or another."

"They help complete strangers?" Keely's tone was more interested than surprised.

"Yep. Total strangers. I doubt if Inspector Sandringham's friend has ever met a Dragoner, yet she's coming here to see what she might do to help them. Some of the Dragoners, probably the younger ones, will choose to leave, and they'll need help adjusting to the outside world. Others may decide to stay, and for them, life will not change so much, although they're in for a rude awakening, I'm afraid, when they learn how much was done for them that they never knew. Things they'll have to do for themselves in the future.''

Sandringham had discovered an orderly file kept by Alyn Runyon containing paid receipts for everything from the electricity that lit up their homes to the food that was purchased on the mainland and distributed co-op style. But the Dragoners knew nothing of this. The only money they knew of or thought they needed was derived from the sale of their fish. They divided the profits, which gave them pocket money to exchange for such things as the ale and sandwiches Keely sold in her little pub. But the big expenses were covered by the bounty that lay unbeknownst to them in the caverns of the Dragon's lair.

All in all, Jack thought wryly, the islanders had quite a remarkable little economy going, and if one overlooked the dark side of their activities, Alyn Runyon and Ninian Sloan had served the Dragon well in providing for and protecting the people of Keinadraig. In a way he felt sorry for the island dwellers, because no matter if they stayed or left, their simple, rustic lives would be changed forever.

Keely was silent for the rest of the short journey by water back to Penzance, and Jack chose not to interrupt her thoughts.

''Hungry?'' he asked, helping her from the boat to the dock.

She smiled at him wistfully. ''Hungry for a new life,'' she said. ''Jack, when can we leave here?''

''Sandringham said we could go anytime. He knows where to find us. I thought we'd take the first train in the morning.''

''How about th' next train out tonight?''

EPILOGUE

SIX MONTHS LATER

Fire crackled merrily in the hearth, warming the four people who nestled before its cheery glow, awaiting the arrival of their dinner guests. Outside, snow fell in large, plump flakes, and Keely heard the sound of people singing.

Carolers, Jack had called them.

This was a Christmas unlike any she had ever known, and she thrilled to the excitement of it all. She and Jack and Brad, who was recovering but still confined to a wheelchair, had decorated the tall fir tree that now stood magnificently before the large, mullion-paned window of the old town house they had leased in a London neighborhood. Brad had wanted to stay near the medical center where he was undergoing rehabilitation therapy, and it was close to both Jack's new office and the school Keely attended.

Garrison had arrived from L.A. the day before, bearing their very American-style Christmas dinner. The smell of roasting turkey wafted from the kitchen.

Keely had laid a beautiful table, studying the pictures from a book Jack had brought her from the library to know exactly where to place each plate, utensil, and piece of crystal stemware. She still had much to learn, but she was an eager and quick student, and with the encouragement and support of her newfound "family," she felt as if she could do anything.

Seated on the luxurious carpet that covered the floor, Keely tucked her ankles beneath the soft wool of her long tartan skirt and leaned against Jack's trouser-clad legs. Across from them, Garrison occupied a matching chair to the one Jack was in and sat gazing into the flames, apparently lost in thought. By his side, Brad thumbed through a book.

How different was this Christmas from last, she mused, running her hand absently over the material of Jack's trousers. In many ways, it had been a tragic year, and yet, there was so much to be thankful for.

This man, for one thing.

For Jack Knight had been true to his word. He had been there for her from the moment she'd first met him, high on a windy hill in a land that seemed long ago and far away. He had helped her break away from fear and superstition. He'd shown her loyalty and integrity and had taught her about love, and about giving and receiving.

The doorbell rang, and she jumped to her feet. "I'll get it."

Richard Sandringham and Eleanor Green stood on the stoop, their arms laden with brightly wrapped gifts, their cheeks ruddy from the cold and their coats flecked with heavy flakes of snow. "Merry Christmas," boomed the inspector, who looked merrier than Keely had ever seen him.

"Come in, oh, do hurry in from th' cold," she squeaked, so excited she could scarcely stand it. In addition to Garrison and Brad, these two had become like family in the past six months, and she was both thrilled and nervous that they had agreed to spend their Christmas Eve with them. Her pub cooking aside, it was the first time she had cooked a meal for anyone other than Jack and Brad.

"How's the social work training coming along?" Richard asked Keely as she took their wraps and handed off the gifts to Jack, who had followed her to greet their guests.

"Fine, I think," she answered, "thanks t' Eleanor."

"She's the star student," the tall, striking woman said. "She'll be out of school and on the streets in no time." She gave Keely a generous hug. "The world needs people like you. I'm glad you decided to share your experiences."

Jack returned from placing the gifts beneath the tree. He put one arm around Keely and reached out with the other to shake the inspector's hand. "I know the world needs her, but I'm not sure I want to share her." He grinned.

"Scrooge," Eleanor teased.

They joined Garrison and Brad by the fire. "Drinks anyone?" Brad said. "I'm tending bar tonight."

Keely looked across at her newfound "brother," and love and thanksgiving swelled in her heart. She was so grateful he was alive. Brad had had a tough time recovering from his wounds, but never once had he sought to lay blame on Keely or Genevieve, or even the Dragoners for what had happened. He was everything Jack had told her he was and more. He was a kind, caring man, and in spite of what had happened, Keely was glad that Genny had known Brad, if only for a short time.

Brad poured drinks and Garrison served. "Merry Christmas," he said so softly that only Keely heard as she accepted a glass of sherry from the silver tray. "Welcome to the family."

"Ah . . . thank ye," she replied. What an odd thing for him to say. She had been treated like family all along, but she wasn't and would never be a Holstedt. Although she had promised to marry Jack, that lay some time in the future. She wanted to finish her schooling and join Eleanor's practice, where her specialty would be exit counseling for people like herself who wanted to escape the clutches of whatever proverbial dragon held them down, be it a cult or an abusive family relationship.

Richard raised his glass. "Merry Christmas," he toasted. "Speaking for myself, I'd like to thank Jack and Keely for what they have brought us this year." At first Keely thought he meant the presents under the tree, but how could he know what was in them? But he continued. "Not only is Eleanor getting a prize of a professional associate, but Scotland Yard's happy to have another good man on board." He raised his glass to Jack, who reciprocated with a grin.

"I thought I was through with police work," he said. "You are a very persuasive man, Sandringham. Here's to you."

"Ah, but there's more," the inspector said mysteriously, and went to stand by Eleanor, who sat in a chair close to the fire. "El and I, well, we've been friends . . . better than friends, for a long, long time. Never tied the knot, though. Too committed to the job, you know."

Keely saw Eleanor reach up and take Richard's hand. What was this all about?

Eleanor spoke, and her voice sounded uncharacteristically strained with emotion. "But something happened during the events of the Keinadraig investigation that changed our lives forever."

Richard picked it up from there. "That night, when I ran into Jack and Garrison at the heliport, I realized that Jack was willing to risk everything for Keely, because he loved her. Later, I understood why she ran away without telling him. Because she loved him, and was willing to risk it all to save his life. And I thought, you fool, Sandringham. You love a woman, too, but you're too damned selfish to take a risk. That's why I have worked very hard this past six months to convince Eleanor to marry me. And at last, she's agreed to take a risk with me. We'll be wed the first Saturday in January."

"Oh, El, that's wonderful!" Keely rushed to give her new friend a hug. She turned to Richard and hugged him, too. "Congratulations," she said, tears of happiness about to tumble down her cheeks.

When the toasts and congratulations over this unexpected announcement subsided, Brad wheeled his chair forward slightly. "I'd like to make a presentation." He glanced toward Garrison and gave his father a broad grin. Garrison smiled back and nodded his head.

"For years, Jack has been a part of our family, although for some damned reason, reluctant kin. Now, I'm tired of having to fend off this old man all on my own, so I've decided to put a stop to it once and for all. I've had this document drawn up, and I'm giving it to you for Christmas, Jack." He paused, and his expression grew serious. "Brothers don't reject Christmas presents from each other, do they?"

Keely saw a frown cross Jack's brow, and she hoped he didn't reject whatever Brad was handing him, for she could tell it meant a lot to the younger Holstedt.

Jack read it in silence, then looked up at Brad. "You son of a bitch." And then a smile brighter than any Keely had ever seen on his face lit his eyes from somewhere deep inside.

"What is it, Jack?" she asked.

"He's adopted me," Jack said, clearing emotion from his throat. "It's a joke," he explained, holding the cartoon of a legal document up for all to see, "but you know what, brother? You're stuck with me now." He turned to Garrison. "I guess that makes me an honorary Holstedt. But don't you try to hire me again. I can't stand the strain."

Garrison laughed. "You're fired for good from Odyssey. But," he added with a rueful shake of his head, "you're still in the will."

Jack gave Garrison a long and meaningful look. "Okay, Dad," he said, his voice husky. "I'll stop fighting you. And thanks for everything you've ever done for me."

Keely thought both men might break down and cry,

but Garrison cleared his throat. "It's your turn, isn't it?" he asked Jack.

Jack looked at Keely and warmed her with that special grin. "I think it is."

He went to the stash of gaily wrapped gifts beneath the Christmas tree and rustled through the packages until he found the one he sought. It was a small box, wrapped in gold foil and topped with an elegant bow. He came to where she sat on the sofa, and placed the box in the palm of her hand. Then he knelt before her.

"I know you have promised to marry me, and I'm not pushing you for a date, but where I come from, such a promise is sealed with a token of love. Will you accept mine?"

Keely needed no token. She had Jack's love, and that was all she would ever need. But she saw that this was as important to him as the adoption papers had been to Brad. With trembling fingers, she removed the bow and tore away the paper. Inside was another, smaller box of deep blue velvet. And inside it was a golden ring bearing a stone that shone more brilliantly than the stars she'd seen overhead that night in Fowey. "Oh, Jack," she murmured. " 'Tis beautiful."

Her future husband took the ring and placed it on the third finger of her left hand.

"I love ye, Keely Cochrane. And I'll be there for ye always."

KISS OF THE DRAGON

A BALLAD

Away, hide away, on this distant shore,
Let ne'er a stranger in thy door.
Keep your secret safe, hidden in the mist,
And let no one leave who be Dragon
    kiss'd.

A sailor man from across the sea
Was found half-dead at the Dragon's feet,
They took him in, put him on a bed,
And in the morn, they did find him dead.

Then one by one, they too did fall,
Struck down by his plague that did touch
    them all,
When their poor souls did at last depart,
They were cleansed by the fires in the
    Dragon's heart.

Then up from the flames in the sacred ring
Rose the Dragon fierce and to them did
    sing:

Away, hide away, on this distant shore,
Let ne'er a stranger in thy door.
Keep your secret safe, hidden in the mist,
And let no one leave who be Dragon
    kiss'd.

'Twas many a year since the Dragon's
    song

Gave the people hope for life safe and
    long,
When a stranger dared wander through the
    mist
And loved a maid who was Dragon kiss'd.

"Come away, come away, run away with
    me,
To my fair land far across the sea
Where the warm sun shines and sweet
    birds sing,
Come away, my love, wear my wedding
    ring."

Alas, poor Bess did not heed the law
Nor did she escape the Dragon's claw.
At the Dragon's feet was her body
    drowned,
No sign of the stranger e'er was found.

Away, hide away, on this distant shore,
Let ne'er a stranger in thy door.
Keep your secret safe, hidden in the mist,
And let no one leave who be Dragon
    kiss'd.

A fisherman named Tom from atop the hill
Wandered out one day for his fish to sell,
When he returned, 'twas with a different
    catch,
With fair Aileen he desired a match.

But the Keeper to the Dragon went,
When he returned, his brow was bent,
Nay Tom, poor Tom, could ye not have
    guessed?
The fair Aileen is not Dragon kiss'd.

Late, late that night, when the wind grew
   still
Came the glow of fire from atop the hill,
Oh, Tom, poor Tom, in the fire he ween,
And who knows the fate of the fair Aileen?

Away, hide away, on this distant shore,
Let ne'er a stranger in thy door.
Keep your secret safe, hidden in the mist,
And let no one leave who be Dragon
   kiss'd.

'Twas a miller's son ran off to sea,
A privateer John longed to be.
He scorned the law and the Dragon's kiss,
And he died at the stroke of a cannon's
   fist.

Away, hide away, on this distant shore,
Let ne'er a stranger in thy door.
Keep your secret safe, hidden in the mist,
And let no one leave who be Dragon
   kiss'd.

"Oh, mother mine," cried the sweet
   Diane,
"Marry me not to that old, old man."
"But daughter dear, 'tis the Dragon's way,
'Tis the Dragon's choice, and you must
   obey."

She tried to run, she tried to hide,
By the Dragon's law, she would not abide.
They found her slain upon her bed,
By her own hand, drained of blood so red.

Away, hide away, on this distant shore,
Let ne'er a stranger in thy door.

Keep your secret safe, hidden in the mist,
And let no one leave who be Dragon
  kiss'd.

To the Dragon's back a young man came,
And Timothy Jenkyns was his name.
A chosen one for an island bride,
But his scorn for her he could not hide.

He took her coin, took the Dragon's kiss,
The wedding vow was all he missed.
He ran away, thought he'd not be found,
But the morning tide brought his body,
  drowned.

Away, hide away, on this distant shore,
Let ne'er a stranger in thy door.
Keep your secret safe, hidden in the mist,
And let no one leave who be Dragon
  kiss'd.

'Twas a fair maid who was called to serve,
But the Dragon's law she would not
  observe,
A midnight flight to another shore,
Sweet Genevieve shall return no more.

For the Dragon's reach is far and wide,
By the Dragon's claw sweet Genny died.
Oh, heed this tale, ye Dragoners all,
And fail ye not to obey his law.

Away, hide away, on this distant shore,
Let ne'er a stranger in thy door.
Keep your secret safe, hidden in the mist,
And let no one leave who be Dragon
  kiss'd.

Survey

TELL US WHAT YOU THINK AND YOU COULD WIN

A YEAR OF ROMANCE!
(That's 12 books!)

Fill out the survey below, send it back to us, and you'll be eligible to win a year's worth of romance novels. That's one book a month for a year—from St. Martin's Paperbacks.

Name _____

Street Address _____

City, State, Zip Code _____

Email address _____

1. How many romance books have you bought in the last year?
    (Check one.)
    __0-3
    __4-7
    __8-12
    __13-20
    __20 or more

2. Where do you MOST often buy books? *(limit to two choices)*
    __Independent bookstore
    __Chain stores *(Please specify)*
        __Barnes and Noble
        __B. Dalton
        __Books-a-Million
        __Borders
        __Crown
        __Lauriat's
        __Media Play
        __Waldenbooks
    __Supermarket
    __Department store *(Please specify)*
        __Caldor
        __Target
        __Kmart
        __Walmart
    __Pharmacy/Drug store
    __Warehouse Club
    __Airport

3. Which of the following promotions would MOST influence your decision to purchase a ROMANCE paperback? *(Check one.)*
        __Discount coupon

__Free preview of the first chapter
__Second book at half price
__Contribution to charity
__Sweepstakes or contest

4. Which promotions would LEAST influence your decision to purchase a ROMANCE book? (Check one.)
      __Discount coupon
      __Free preview of the first chapter
      __Second book at half price
      __Contribution to charity
      __Sweepstakes or contest

5. When a new ROMANCE paperback is released, what is MOST influential in your finding out about the book and in helping you to decide to buy the book? (Check one.)
      __TV advertisement
      __Radio advertisement
      __Print advertising in newspaper or magazine
      __Book review in newspaper or magazine
      __Author interview in newspaper or magazine
      __Author interview on radio
      __Author appearance on TV
      __Personal appearance by author at bookstore
      __In-store publicity (poster, flyer, floor display, etc.)
      __Online promotion (author feature, banner advertising, giveaway)
      __Word of Mouth
      __Other (please specify)_____

6. Have you ever purchased a book online?
      __Yes
      __No

7. Have you visited our website?
      __Yes
      __No

8. Would you visit our website in the future to find out about new releases or author interviews?
      __Yes
      __No

9. What publication do you read most?
      __Newspapers *(check one)*
        __*USA Today*
        __*New York Times*
        __Your local newspaper
      __Magazines *(check one)*

___*People*
___*Entertainment Weekly*
___Women's magazine *(Please specify:_____)*
___*Romantic Times*
___Romance newsletters

10. What type of TV program do you watch most? *(Check one.)*
    ___Morning News Programs (ie. "Today Show")
       (Please specify:_____)
    ___Afternoon Talk Shows (ie. "Oprah")
       (Please specify: _____)
    ___All news (such as CNN)
    ___Soap operas   *(Please specify: _____)*
    ___Lifetime cable station
    ___E! cable station
    ___Evening magazine programs (ie. "Entertainment Tonight")
       (Please specify: _____)
    ___Your local news

11. What radio stations do you listen to most? *(Check one.)*
    ___Talk Radio
    ___Easy Listening/Classical
    ___Top 40
    ___Country
    ___Rock
    ___Lite rock/Adult contemporary
    ___CBS radio network
    ___National Public Radio
    ___WESTWOOD ONE radio network

12. What time of day do you listen to the radio MOST?
    ___6am-10am
    ___10am-noon
    ___Noon-4pm
    ___4pm-7pm
    ___7pm-10pm
    ___10pm-midnight
    ___Midnight-6am

13. Would you like to receive email announcing new releases and special promotions?
    ___Yes
    ___No

14. Would you like to receive postcards announcing new releases and special promotions?
    ___Yes
    ___No

15. Who is your favorite romance author? _____

WIN A YEAR OF ROMANCE FROM SMP
(That's 12 Books!)
No Purchase Necessary

OFFICIAL RULES

1. To Enter: Complete the Official Entry Form and Survey and mail it to: Win a Year of Romance from SMP Sweepstakes, c/o St. Martin's Paperbacks, 175 Fifth Avenue, Suite 1615, New York, NY 10010-7848, Attention JP. For a copy of the Official Entry Form and Survey, send a self-addressed, stamped envelope to: Entry Form/Survey, c/o St. Martin's Paperbacks at the address stated above. Entries with the completed surveys must be received by February 1, 2000 (February 22, 2000 for entry forms requested by mail). Limit one entry per person. No mechanically reproduced or illegible entries accepted. Not responsible for lost, misdirected, mutilated or late entries.

2. Random Drawing. Winner will be determined in a random drawing to be held on or about March 1, 2000 from all eligible entries received. Odds of winning depend on the number of eligible entries received. Potential winner will be notified by mail on or about March 22, 2000 and will be asked to execute and return an Affidavit of Eligibility/Release/Prize Acceptance Form within fourteen (14) days of attempted notification. Non-compliance within this time may result in disqualification and the selection of an alternate winner. Return of any prize/prize notification as undeliverable will result in disqualification and an alternate winner will be selected.

3. Prize and approximate Retail Value: Winner will receive a copy of a different romance novel each month from April 2000 through March 2001. Approximate retail value $84.00 (U.S. dollars).

4. Eligibility. Open to U.S. and Canadian residents (excluding residents of the province of Quebec) who are 18 at the time of entry. Employees of St. Martin's and its parent, affiliates and subsidiaries, its and their directors, officers and agents, and their immediate families or those living in the same household, are ineligible to enter. Potential Canadian winners will be required to correctly answer a time-limited arithmetic skill question by mail. Void in Puerto Rico and wherever else prohibited by law.

5. General Conditions: Winner is responsible for all federal, state and local taxes. No substitution or cash redemption of prize permitted by winner. Prize is not transferable. Acceptance of prize constitutes permission to use the winner's name, photograph and likeness for purposes of advertising and promotion without additional compensation or permission, unless prohibited by law.

6. All entries become the property of sponsor, and will not be returned. By participating in this sweepstakes, entrants agree to be bound by these official rules and the decision of the judges, which are final in all respects.

7. For the name of the winner, available after March 22, 2000, send by May 1, 2000 a stamped, self-addressed envelope to Winner's List, Win a Year of Romance from SMP Sweepstakes, St. Martin's Paperbacks, 175 Fifth Avenue, Suite 1615, New York, NY 10010-7848, Attention JP.